AISTHESIS AND AESTHETICS

THE FOURTH LEXINGTON CONFERENCE ON PURE AND APPLIED PHENOMENOLOGY

AISTHESIS AND AESTHETICS

THE FOURTH LEXINGTON CONFERENCE ON PURE AND APPLIED PHENOMENOLOGY

edited by

Erwin W. Straus, M.D., Ph.D., (h.c.), LL.D., (h.c.)

and

Richard M. Griffith, Ph.D.

Duquesne University Press
Pittsburgh, Pa.
Editions E. Nauwelaerts, Louvain

PHENOMENOLOGY: PURE AND APPLIED. The First Lexington Conference.

PHENOMENOLOGY OF WILL AND ACTION. The Second Lexington Conference.

PHENOMENOLOGY OF MEMORY. The Third Lexington Conference.

Library of Congress Catalog Card Number 70-98553

Printed in the United States of America

IN MEMORIAM

Richard M. Griffith

The

Veterans Administration Hospital

Lexington, Kentucky

invites your participation in the

Fourth Lexington Conference on

Phenomenology: Pure and Applied

Central Theme

AISTHESIS AND AESTHETICS

April 6, 7 and 8, 1967

We are happy to express our gratitude to

THE FORD FOUNDATION

whose interest, confidence, and generosity

made this conference possible.

vii

Thursday, April 6

2:00 p.m.   Opening Session

THE FUNDAMENTALS

Chairman: HERBERT SPIEGELBERG, Ph.D.
                    Prof. Philosophy, Washington University
            Welcome: AARON S. MASON, M.D.
                    Hospital Director, VAH, Lexington

SENSORY EXPERIENCE: PHILOSOPHY'S STEPCHILD?
                    MARJORIE GRENE, Ph.D.
                    Prof. Philosophy, University of California at Davis
            Discussant: THOMAS D. LANGAN, Ph.D.
                    Chairman, Philosophy Department, Indiana University

PHENOMENON AND MODEL   HERBERT HENSEL, M.D.
                    Prof. Physiology, University of Marburg
            Discussant: RICHARD M. ZANER, Ph.D.
                    Prof. Philosophy, Trinity University, San Antonio

GOLDEN COINS AND GOLDEN CURLS: LIVED AESTHETICS
                    RICHARD M. GRIFFITH, Ph.D.
                    Psychology Service, VAH, Lexington
            Discussant: CALVIN O. SCHRAG, Ph.D.
                    Prof. Philosophy, Purdue University

8:15 p.m.   Evening Session

AISTHESIS DISTURBED

Chairman: CHARLES I. SCHWARTZ, M.D.
                    Chief of Staff, VAH, Lexington

DE-ANIMATION: THE SENSE OF BECOMING PSYCHOTIC
                    WALTRAUT STEIN, Ph.D.
                    Department of Philosophy and Religion, University
                    of Georgia
            Discussant: FRIDA G. SURAWICZ, M.D.
                    Psychiatry Department, University of Kentucky
                    College of Medicine

OPTICAL ILLUSIONS AND AESTHETIC PRINCIPLES
                    PAUL B. JOSSMANN, M.D., Ph.D.
                    Chief, Neuropsychiatric Examining Service, Boston
            Discussant: SHIRLEY SANDERS, M.A.
                    Psychology Service, VAH, Lexington

PHANTOMS AND PHANTASMATA   ERWIN W. STRAUS
                    Lexington, Kentucky
            Discussant: WILLIAM F. FISCHER, Ph.D.
                    Psychology Department, Duquesne University

viii

Friday, April 7

AESTHETIC CREATION

9:00 a.m.   Morning Session

VISION AND THE GRAPHIC ARTS

Chairman: EDMUND D. PELLEGRINO, M.D.
                    Director, Medical Center, State University of New
                    York at Stony Brook

THE FABRIC OF EXPRESSION   MAURICE NATANSON, Ph.D.
                    Prof. Philosophy, University of California at Santa
                    Cruz

AESTHETIC PERCEPTION AND ITS RELATION TO
          ORDINARY PERCEPTION
                    LOUIS DUPRÉ, Ph.D.
                    Prof. Philosophy, Georgetown University

THE SOCIAL CONDITIONS OF MODERN PAINTING
                    HELMUTH PLESSNER, Ph.D.
                    Prof. Emeritus, University of Goettingen

DISCUSSION OPENED BY ERLING W. ENG, Ph.D.
                    Psychology Service, VAH, Lexington

2:30 p.m.   Afternoon Session

SOUND AND MUSIC

Chairman: HUBERT P. HENDERSON, Ph.D.
                    Director, School of Fine Arts, University of
                    Kentucky

TOWARD A PHENOMENOLOGY OF MUSICAL AESTHETICS
                    F. JOSEPH SMITH, Ph.D.
                    Prof. Philosophy, Emory University

          Discussant: GERHARD ALBERSHEIM
                    Prof. of Musicology, Santa Monica, California

KIERKEGAARD ON MUSIC   JESSE DEBOER, Ph.D.
                    Prof. Philosophy, University of Kentucky

          Discussant: DON IHDE, Ph.D.
                    Prof. Philosophy, Southern Illinois University

ix

| 8:30 p.m. | SMOKER |
| | Fountain Room, Hotel Phoenix |

KALOSKAGATHOS　　　DR. ERNEST JOKL presenting at 9:15 p.m. the film "World Championships in Gymnastics."

Saturday, April 8

9:30 a.m.　　　　　　　　　　　　　　　　　　　　Morning Session

MADNESS IN ART

Chairman: KENNETH B. MOORE, M.D., Ph.D.
　　　　　Associate Chief of Staff, VAH, Lexington

DOSTOYEVSKI'S PRINCE MISHKIN: EPILEPSY PORTRAYED
　　　　　　　HUBERT TELLENBACH, M.D., Ph.D.
　　　　　Prof. Psychiatry, University of Heidelberg

　　　Discussant:　　ROBERT O. EVANS, Ph.D.
　　　　　　　Prof. Comparative Literature, University of Kentucky

PSYCHOTIC PAINTING AND PSYCHOTIC PAINTERS　　JAMES L. FOY, M.D.
　　　　　Psychiatry Department, Georgetown University Hospital

　　　Discussant:　　DONALD F. TWEEDIE, JR., Ph.D.
　　　　　　　Prof. Psychology, Fuller Seminary, Pasadena, California

ART THERAPY: PROS AND CONS
　　　　　　　TARMO A. PASTO, Ph.D.
　　　　　Prof. Art and Psychology, Sacramento State College, California

　　　　　　　MICHAEL WYSCHOGROD, Ph.D.
　　　　　Prof. Philosophy, City College, City University of New York

OPEN DISCUSSION

x

Table of Contents

PREFATORY NOTE

Following the tradition established with the publication of the preceding conferences, 1963, 1964, 1965, the program has been reproduced just as it had been sent out several weeks before the start of the conference. However, the reader's attention should be called to a number of last minute changes—omissions and additions.

1) Harmon Chapman, Professor of Philosophy, New York University, gave us permission to publish his paper on Aisthesis, although he had not been able to attend the conference in person. Since this essay deals with the historical and general aspects of the central theme, it is printed as the opening chapter.

2) Unfortunately, we had to forgo the participation of Professor Jonas in the morning session of April 7. This change permitted Professor Dupré, who had been invited to discuss Professor Jonas' paper, to present his own views directly. Dr. Eng, therefore, discussed in a synoptic review all three papers presented that morning.

3) We had the good luck of being able to add Gerhard Albersheim, of Santa Monica, California, to our rostrum. Dr. Albersheim, a musician and musicologist who passed Lexington on a concert tour, was willing to offer impromptu comments to Professor Joseph Smith's presentation.

Once again we want to express our sincere thanks to the Ford Foundation for its generous contribution that not only made this conference possible but enabled us to extend invitations to speakers from distant places in this country and from abroad. We are also grateful to the University of Kentucky for its continued support, providing again chairmen, speakers, and discussants.

We have to close with the truly sad news that before these pages went to press Richard M. Griffith, the initiator, co-organizer, general secretary, and contributor to these conferences suffered fatal injuries in an automobile accident. He died weeks later on February 15, 1969.

I. THE FUNDAMENTALS

WELCOMING ADDRESS

Dr. Aaron S. Mason

Ladies and Gentlemen:

Once again we find ourselves with the pleasure of welcoming you to a Phenomenology Conference at the Veterans Hospital in Lexington. As you may know, this is the fourth conference on Phenomenology "Pure and Applied." After the first, more general program, the second conference focussed on the topical theme of "Will and Action"; the third on the theme of "Memory" and now the fourth bears the title "Aisthesis and Aesthetics."

I will not try to explain this title to you or attempt to tell you why it was chosen. Quite a few people have asked the meaning of the first word "Aisthesis," pointing out that it is not to be found in the dictionary. As it may unfold during these three days of papers and discussions, the fact that this word is little known today may be a very justifiable reason for this conference and, who knows, perhaps our symposium may correct this situation and our children and grandchildren may be able to find the meaning of the word if they are not taught it in the first grade. It is significant that we received a preregistration card signed by a Dr. Webster, who may be here just from curiosity.

In due course, the proceedings of these four conferences will be available to you. The first may be ordered from the Duquesne University Press and the galley proofs of the second are now in the hands of the printer and should be out very soon. There is a long and tortuous route from the time a word is spoken into this microphone until the time it appears in print in the bookstores in your city, and the proceedings of the third conference is somewhere along this route.

As everyone knows, the presence and inspiration of Dr. Erwin W. Straus, who has been with us since 1946, accounts for these conferences in the medical setting of a Veterans Administration Hospital. Also, I wish to take this opportunity to acknowledge and commend Dr. Richard Griffith of our psychology

3

research staff for the major role he plays each year in making these conferences a success. We all are proud to have had a part in initiating and continuing this series of meetings. This hospital is grateful to the speakers who have come from distant centers of learning to present their papers and exchange their views. We appreciate the interest that you members of the audience have shown in traveling from California and Florida, from Texas and Canada, to be with us. We are grateful for the support of our past sponsors, including the University of Kentucky Medical College.

It is particularly appropriate and a pleasure for us to acknowledge the financial support of our present sponsor, The Ford Foundation. Their willingness to award the necessary grant was exceptionally gratifying, not only because it made this conference possible but because their judgment in doing so affirmed our own belief that this series is worthwhile, that the type of interdisciplinary exchanges which we hope to foster is desirable in the current state of the sciences and the arts. We are most pleased to welcome in person and to address these words directly to a representative of The Ford Foundation, Dr. Edward D'Arms, who was able to come from New York to be with us today.

Before stepping away from this podium so that the fun may begin and the fur begin to fly, let me say that the hospital staff and I are at your disposal to make your stay in Lexington and your hours in our hospital as enjoyable and as rewarding as possible. Please feel free to call upon us if we can help in any way.

AISTHESIS

Harmon Chapman*

IN THE Theaetetus (155d-157c) Socrates offers a theory of sense perception which is quite new, quite without precedent, and manifestly of Plato's own devising, as Cornford has pointed out.[1] If Socrates describes it as a doctrine taught in secret by certain wise men, eminent poets and philosophers, among them Protagorus, (no one of whom ever taught anything of the kind), it is only to facilitate that self-effacement and detachment which he is so fond of assuming in playing the role of disinterested arbiter—or midwife. Not only is the theory Plato's own; it is also Plato's belief. It is not refuted but taken as established in the ensuing discussion of sense perception; and it is repeated in substance in the Timaeus (67c).

The theory itself, as Cornfed remarks (ibid.), contains elements borrowed from Protagorus and Heraclitus. The principal thesis is Heraclitean: "everything is motion (or change)" (τὸ πᾶν κίνησις ἦν 156a), that is, what we ordinarily call objects are really processes. This thesis is supplemented by three divisions of motions into kinds: 1) change of place (φορά) and change of quality (ἀλλοίωσις), 2) fast (ταχύ) and slow (βραδύ) motions, and 3) motions which have the power (δύναμις) of acting and those which have the power of being acted on, i.e., the "power" of responding to the former as cause or stimulus. These three divisions represent a three-way cross classification of motions which permits for any given instance of motion a number of possible combinations.

Without going further into detail the gist of the theory is this. Since all things are motions (κινήσεις), both sentient bodies and the bodies they perceive are motions, motions of the "slow" variety. Now when two of these slow motions meet and the one

---

* Prof. Chapman was not able to attend the meeting in person. [Ed.]
[1] *Plato's Theory of Knowledge,* Liberal Arts Press, New York, 1957, pp. 48-49.

(the object) acts as agent on the other as patient (the sentient body), there springs from this encounter (ὁμιδία) a countless multitude of twin motions all of the fast variety capable of shifting rapidly from place to place. The twin motions thus generated are inseparable, like Siamese twins, one member of each pair being the thing perceived (αἰσθητον) and the other member the perception itself or the act of perceiving (αἰδθησις). In every instance this cognate pair, perceived and perceiving, springs up together giving rise to such things as a color seen and the seeing of the color, a sound heard and the hearing of the sound, and so on. At this point "the eye becomes filled with vision . . . , becomes a seeing eye; while the other parent of the color is saturated with whiteness and becomes, on its side, not whiteness, but a white thing" (*Theaetetus,* 156e).

Socrates concludes from all this "that nothing *is* one thing just by itself, but is always in process of becoming for someone, and being is ruled out altogether" along with every "word that brings things to a standstill" (op. cit., 157a-b). With "being" thus ruled out the claim that sense perception is knowledge is vitivated at once; for knowledge, as we already know, is of being, not of becoming.

But there is another conclusion to be drawn from this which Socrates barely notes in passing, as when he remarks in the above quotation that sensible things are "always in process of becoming *for someone.*" What this implies is that the sensible qualities of things are relative to sentient observers. This is not to say that the *existence* of sensible things is relative to sentient observers; for manifestly things exist, if only as motions, prior to and independent of sense perception. Only the sensible qualities of things are thus relative, relative to the extent that if you were to remove all sentient creatures you would also remove all sensible features; the world would cease to be a sensible world and become solely intelligible, an insensible world like that described by modern natural science, a kind of Cartesian *res extensa.*

This is not quite as radical as it sounds. For it is not sentience alone and unaided that vests the world with sensible qualities. This vesting is the joint product of sense-organ *and* object.

Only the two together, on meeting in a common medium, can produce the twin product of seeing eye and color seen, hearing ear and sound heard, and so on. The import of this is plainly that even prior to the advent of sentience the world is already such as to become sensible, that its intelligible character does not preclude, but rather includes, the imminent possibility of acquiring sensible qualities. The advent of sentience merely realizes this possiblity already inherent in the nature of things. As Aristotle put it somewhat later, prior to sense perception things are only "potentially" sensible, after sense perception they are "actually" sensible.[1]

It is this conclusion that interests me, not Socrates's first conclusion, and not the theory itself. The theory itself is of the "process" variety, not unlike that propounded recently by Whitehead. Its premisses, beginning with the thesis that all things are really processes, can be challenged, as Aristotle later did. Moreover, the argument is not clearly worked out by Plato; many details are so obscure that I despair of expounding it satisfactorily, let alone defending it. I repeat, it is solely the conclusion that interests me, and this for two reasons.

The first reason is that this conclusion, first drawn by Plato, is the same conclusion drawn by almost every successor of Plato down to the time of Descartes. These successors may advance differing theories of perception, but they arrive at essentially the same conclusion. Aristotle, for example, does not find perception cut off from being; his "substance" contains being as well as becoming inasmuch as change for him is the transition from potency to act with respect to an abiding substrate (matter). But again, I gloss over the varying details of theory in order to focus on the unvarying conclusion and to stress the fact that it is the same for the whole classical tradition prior to Descartes. Throughout this tradition there is basic agreement that perception is an event or occurrence in the world of experience, i.e., that perception is an empirical phenomenon in which two very distinct potentialities are simultaneously actualized, the sensible

---

[1] Or better "sensed," since there is the connotation of potentiality in the suffix of the word "sensible."

(active) qualities of the world and the sensing (passive) powers
of the sentient body.

The second reason is that this "classical" conclusion is sharply
opposed to the conclusion which issues from the theory of
perception that Descartes introduced into modern philosophy.
According to this theory sense perception is not empirical at all,
but wholly non-empirical, a private and subjective process taking place in a mind or consciousness cut off from the world.
This follows from the assumption that sense perception begins
with sense impressions or sensations which occur in the mind
somehow as the result of external objects acting causally on our
sense organs. These sensations are purely mental in character
and cannot possibly exist outside the mind. Inside the mind,
however, they may be variously combined (associated, synthe-
sized) so as to give us "ideas" (perceptions, representations) of
sensible things comprising a sensible world. But since this world
is "inside," not "outside," the mind, it must be distinguished.
sharply from a real world outside—if, indeed, there be such at
all. But whether or not we assume such an external world, we
retain in either event the (internal) world we directly "experienced." It is a sensible world, but it is sensible at the cost of
being subjective, a product of mind wrought out of its own sense
data. Thus perception is solely the work of the mind, an inner
and private operation, in which external things—again, if there
be such—participate only to the extent of supplying a cause for
the occurrence of impressions.

There are two distinguishing features of this theory which set
it in direct opposition to the classical theories of perception.
These features are 1) Descartes' theory of sensations, and
2) his *metaphysical* dualism of private non-empirical mind and
public empirical world (thought and extension, mind and matter, psychical and physical, soul and body, subject and object,
etc.). The first feature—sensations, impressions, and the like—
is all too familiar. So is the second feature, Descartes' dualism.
What is not familiar is how thoroughly these two features have
come to pervade modern philosophic thought, supplying it with
unthinking predilections. This is more true of dualism than of

sensations, since sensations have recently come under fire. But dualism is still exempt; we still accept without question the metaphysical abyss between things mental and material. Nowhere is this tacit acceptance more evident than in our notion of the "empirical"; things material or physical are empirical, things mental are not. Because they are not empirical, things mental have only a dubious status, so dubious, indeed, that many are impelled to rule out the mental entirely, to reduce consciousness and its operations to modes of bodily behavior.

This restriction of the empirical, together with its underlying dualism, is absent entirely in the classical approach. To be sure, soul and body are empirically distinguished throughout the tradition, but never metaphysically distinguished as substances occupying two mutually exclusive orders of being. At times Plato may talk as though they were when, as in the *Phaedo,* he argues that the soul can survive the death of the body. But then in the Phaedrus and thereafter he argues for immortality on the ground that soul is the primal source of all motion and change in sensible things. Moreover, whenever he considers soul and body in conjunction, as he does frequently, he finds them acting as one, even though differing empirically as agent and instrument (*organon*). In every instance the two are so intimately conjoined as to preclude any such metaphysical dichotomy as that implicit in modern dualism. For Plato and Aristotle and their successors soul is no less empirical than body, and their original togetherness is an empirical fact, a pretheoretical datum which no theory dare impugn. This datum may not explain how soul and body consort, or even what they are; but it does establish as an inviolable fact of experience that they do consort and that together they make up the empirical creature called man—a fact which modern dualism in effect precludes.

And so the classical tradition knows nothing either of sensations or of dualism; it lacks utterly both these distinguishing features of the Cartesian theory. For us moderns these features are literally conspicuous by their absence, so conspicuous indeed that many modern expositors of classical texts feel constrained to supply their want, thus imposing their own predilections on doctrines in which they have no place whatsoever. It is this very absence from the classical approach that I wish here to emphasize and by this emphasis to call these features into question.

Consider the consequences of their absence for Plato. Innocent of Descartes' dualism, Plato finds no difficulty in viewing perception as a process both mental and corporeal, psychical and physical, as a process moreover in which subject and object interact through a physical medium and in which there is no unbridgeable gap between private and public, inner and outer, subjective and objective. All of these are present together in the empirical phenomenon of "perception" wherein alone they are discernible and distinguishable as components. Being an empirical phenomenon, with its many aspects both private and public, perception for Plato is not the private performance of a mind operating in the solitary confinement of its own inwardness, but an empirical performance, as much public as private, in which mind is but a contributing factor along with body, medium, and object.

Innocent, too, of Descartes' theory of sensations Plato has no private impressions to synthesize and somehow to project outward so as to appear as public qualities of things. The quality sensed is already "out there" where it is actually beheld; only the sensing (the activity of seeing or hearing the quality) may be said to be "subjective." But it is subjective not in the Cartesian sense of a mental process cut off from the world. It is subjective only in the sense of pertaining to a "subject" which is both a mind and its sentient body functioning as one in company with other empirical things. The whole situation is empirical throughout; no part or aspect is cut off from the rest in response to a preconceived metaphysical dualism. Hence it is that the act of seeing or hearing, with its mental and physical (physiological) aspects, can supervene, as it were, on the causal activity of object and medium and bring to actuality (to the status of being actually seen or heard) a sensible quality which otherwise the object would possess only potentially.

The upshot of all this is evident. In the absence of sensations and dualism, perception is not the private performance of a secluded mind operating on contents (sense data) exclusively its own. It is rather an empirical phenomenon or event, in which mind, body, medium and object work in concert to actualize simultaneously two disparate potentialities, that of perceiving and that of being perceived. In this dual actualization perception reveals its dual function, that of rendering the world actually sensible (or sensed) and that of rendering the sentient creature an actual perceiver. This dual function, be it well noted, is one; it is dual only in aspects, the one aspect being cosmic, the other individual.

Implicit in the individual aspect is the notion that mind or consciousness is not "closed," but "open," to the world, that our inwardness is not a monadic privacy but a lively awareness of an outer reality encompassing us all. Perception as the primitive mode of this awareness may be likened to an open window or portal through which the world comes shining in. But this portal analogy falls short; perception is more than a placid shining in of the real. For Aristotle, at least, perception is an operation in which "the soul becomes in a way its object," shares in the being of its object and through this sharing makes the being of the object an intimate part of its own being—as the doctrine of intentionality would seem to entail. This might also be put in terms of a recent metaphor: the soul in perceiving allows the "reverberations of being" from without to resonate through its own being and to bring it to that state of being called human.

Manifestly this sharing is an involvement with the real. As perceivers we are not passive observers, but active participants immersed in an encounter wherein our very being is at stake. The issue hangs on our ability to enter into a living rapport with the real; to become microcosms, as it were, so that the world may become for us the macrocosm—recalling once again that the dual actualization is one.

But this is only the first stage. Our living rapport must extend beyond the perceptual; it must engage also our understanding of things and people and causes, our sense of values, and our power of decision. With this extension the rapport we seek becomes ever more intricate and fragile and ever more subject to the forces that divide and alienate. It is at this level that the business of becoming human is most fraught with hope—and the threat of disaster.

Returning to the level of perception, we may note once again how radically classical *aisthesis* differs from its modern counterpart. From the beginning, the classical theory finds us involved with the real, committed to the "other" just as it is, not as it is not—what else could the "openness" of mind entail? From the beginning, it is this other in its otherness that enters, in the characteristic fashion of awareness, into the constitution of our own being. This is to say that the real itself is the original content of our inwardness, the prelude to our very selfhood.

By contrast, the modern theory begins with a private manifold of sensations which it assembles into a sensory world. Whether this world be the macrocosm itself or only an inner image thereof, it is in either event but a projection of the mind itself, a thing fashioned for the mind's beholding, an "object" to be contemplated at arm's length, like the mathematical world of the scientist. Further involvement is either illlusory or dubious, for the real as other is either constituted by mind or represented by a constituted surrogate. In neither instance can the mind enter into direct contact with a genuine other, only with an other which is but a projection of the mind itself. Lacking this contact the mind can know no other and hence can know itself only as the selfless identity of a monad, the victim of an inviolable privacy.

In fine, the great difference between the two theories of perception is that the classical theory regards perception as the dual actualizing of both self (mind) and other (world), whereas the modern theory regards perception as a private process of constitution which estranges the other and reduces the self to an anonymous observer of its own fabrications. There can be little doubt which theory of *aisthesis* lies closer to the exigencies of human existence.

SENSE-PERCEPTION: PHILOSOPHY'S STEP-CHILD?

Marjorie Grene

MY TITLE was suggested by Dr. Straus—all but the question-mark, which is my addition, because when I think about his theory of sense-perception, as I have been doing lately, I am not so sure that philosophers have always mistreated its principal subject, as the phrase "philosophy's step-child" suggests that they have done. Or rather, I am not sure for which wing of his own theory of sense-perception—the 'sensing' wing or the 'perception' wing—Dr. Straus is accusing us of stepmotherly misbehavior. So I think I had better look at some of Dr. Straus's own arguments about sense-perception alongside some traditional philosophical approaches to the problem. This may help me to sort out the confusion in which I find myself about the title under which I have, rashly, it seems, consented to speak. Much of what I have to say may be, of course, to the physicians and/or the philosophers among you, a twice-told one; for this I apologize. But I hope that my exposition may also help us, together, to establish, as our opening session is intended to do, the fundamental concept of "aisthesis" from which our discussions of more specialized themes are to develop.

As a psychiatrist, Dr. Straus starts out from a critique of psychological theory, and in particular of Pavlov. In its underlying metaphysic, he has argued, C-R theory is still Cartesian, and in particular it still rests on the "time-atomism" which cuts off Cartesian thought from the original structure of experienced time. In this connection he introduces a distinction difficult for philosophers to grasp, but essential for his interpretation of sensory experience, and important also, therefore, to the theme of *aisthesis* with which we are here concerned. I refer to the distinction between *stimuli* and *objects*.

Within the tradition of empiricism it has been held that we must penetrate to the ultimate units of experience as presented: sensa, atomic facts, or whatever we call them. Everything else has been held to be superstructure upon these primary givens. Dr. Straus reverses this fundamental conception: it is *objects* that are primary, and "stimuli," the "scientific" equivalents of atomic facts, that are abstracted from them. True, the ur-empiricists, Berkeley and Hume, were looking for presented, not constructed, data. Berkeley really thought he could find a minimal visible, a minimal audible, and that it was judgment which, with the help of God, built objects out of them. Hume too, *pace* the missing shade of blue, thought he had found such minimal givens. But we can see now that this search was dictated, even for Berkeley, by an epistemological, if not a metaphysical, atomism: by the acceptance of a reduced and purely passive Cartesian *simple* which *must* be the isolable unit of knowledge, the building brick out of which an aggregate equivalent to "experience" could be constructed. With the further reduction of mind to ghost or less, however, these singulars of "experience" have become the presumably separate impacts of isolable physical events upon separate nerve endings. The physiological model of action takes over. So, says Boring (as Dr. Straus quotes him), "to understand man the doer, we must understand his nervous system, for upon it his actions depend."[1] But if no one has ever discovered Berkeleyan minimum sensibles or Wittgensteinian atomic facts, so much the less can an observer discover in his own experience their presumed physiological equivalents.

To begin with, stimuli exist only as pure physical events, "unstained by any secondary qualities": they are neither audible, tangible nor visible.[2] Indeed, they have no existence independently of the nervous system that has received them. But the objects with which we deal in our ordinary experience are not of this refined and reduced character. "The wall over there, the writing pad, the pen and ink": these are things I confront, but they are not "stimuli." True, as Dr. Straus admits, the light, once reflected from the wall or the paper, might be described as a stimulus, but only after it has reached the optical receptors, a

---

[1] Quoted in E. W. Straus, Phenomenological Psychology, New York, Basic Books, 1966, p. vi.
[2] *Ibid.,* p. viii.

process which I may postulate but have never experienced. And the experimenter, for all his alleged sophistication, is in no different situation in confronting his rats, Skinner boxes or what you will. How can he set out to work, not with rats and apparatuses, but with the hidden, hypothetical events of which, on his own theory, his own behavior consists? Indeed, he cannot —for the temporal relation between objects and the experimenter's action upon them is precisely the converse of that between stimuli and responses:

> Because stimulation precedes response, nobody can handle, nobody can manipulate stimuli; they are out of reach. I as an experiencing being may stretch out my hand toward the pen on my desk; a motor response cannot be directed to optical stimuli already received in the past.[3]

Thus "stimuli" can be neither *observed* nor *manipulated*.[4] Nor, since they are, by definition, events *in* the receiving organism, can they be shared, in a psychological experiment, between "subject" and experimenter:

> Those stimuli which provoke responses in the experimental animal never reach the eyes or ears of the observer. Stimuli cannot be shared by two organisms.[5]

On all these grounds, then, it appears that "stimulus" and "object" are by no means synonymous terms: "stimuli are constructs, never immediate objects of experience."[6]

How, then, if not in terms of S-R theory, are we to describe experience? We must reinstate the whole experiencing being in its whole experienced world. An experiencing being, Dr. Straus argues, moves, not among stimuli, a life which even Pavlov's dogs sometimes resisted, but in a surrounding field within which things approach it and it approaches things. Its basic experience

---

[3] *Loc. cit.*
[4] Cf. *ibid.*, pp. 269-70.
[5] *Ibid.*, p. viii.
[6] *Loc. cit.*

is of what Dr. Straus calls an I-Allon relation—where "allon" means not just other persons but the organized totality of objects within which the living being moves. The stimuli with which the scientific observer operates, on the contrary, are not *alla* to an experiencing being; they are not objects at all, but highly abstract constructs which split apart and render unintelligible this primary relation.

If he were consistent, therefore, the S-R theorist ought to legislate *himself* out of existence. If he too is a congeries of physical stimuli and physiological responses, he ought not to pretend that he can observe the behavior of his subjects or manipulate his apparatus. But, "spellbound by the magic of a venerated metaphysic" he neglects to notice his own inconsistency.[7] He continues, a necessary exception to his own alleged cosmology, to act as an experiencing being among objects which he can observe, manipulate and share. Thus experimental psychology, in its classical form, rests on a fundamental inconsistency.

That is not to say, however, that causal investigation in terms of S-R theory is useless; but it should be put into its due place *within* a theory of living beings and their experience. Causal analysis investigates the necessary, but not the sufficient, conditions of sensory experience. Thus "the stimulus delimits what will be seen and determines that it will be seen."[8] "Intentionality of vision and causality of seeing," Dr. Straus insists, "are fully reconcilable."[9] But causal analysis can operate consistently only *within* the all-embracing I-Allon relation; it cannot put Humpty-Dumpty together again out of senseless fragments. Indeed, Dr. Straus argues, traditional theory has never even embarked upon its proper subject, which it has eliminated before it even begins. He writes:

> The relation I-Allon is slashed. The Allon alone is left, but in a profoundly mutilated form. Perceptions are many; they follow one another in the order of objective time. They do not

[7] *Loc. cit.*
[8] *Ibid.,* p. 26.
[9] *Loc. cit.*

belong together in a meaningful context; they stick together through synaptic welding. Positivism from Hume to Skinner preaches the gospel that sense is repeated nonsense.[10]

This is step-motherly abuse with a vengeance, and on behalf of philosophy, or at any rate one major philosophical tradition, I plead guilty. Now in place of this absurd situation, Dr. Straus proposes that we abandon the myth of "sensa" or "impressions" and examine the process through which we do in fact find ourselves in contact, through sensory channels, with the world around us, a process which he calls sensing (*Empfinden*) in contrast to perception.

Sensing, as Dr. Straus interprets it, embraces both *gnostic* and *pathic* aspects—where "gnostic" denotes the primitive fore-runner of the cognitive, and "pathic" "the immediate communication we have with things on the basis of their changing mode of sensory givenness."[11] But it is primarily pathic. For sensing is a way of receiving not merely atomic cues from a prompting environment (*Umgebung*), but moods, as well as lines, from fellow actors, from the stage set, from the whole ensemble within which we discover other things and persons, through cooperation with (including rebellion against and revulsion from) whom we develop our own roles as actors in a scene. My metaphor limps, for the *Umfeld* Dr. Straus is speaking of is no artifact. It is the living nature in which every animal is immersed and through contact with which it expresses its style of living and of being. From this encompassing Allon, we, and also to some degree other higher animals, have abstracted a perceptible world of stable, manipulatable, and (for us at least) intelligible kinds of objects. But our primary, pathic sensing is the ground on which alone the chiefly gnostic achievements of perception can develop.

Now this is indeed a revolutionary conception: Strausian sensing philosophers have not in fact neglected or abused; they

---

[10] *Ibid.*, p. 272.
[11] "The Forms of Spatiality," *Phenomenological Psychology*, pp. 3-37, p. 12.

have never—well, hardly ever—noticed its existence. Like every fundamental conceptual reform, however, this one, again, is difficult to assimilate. I can elucidate it, perhaps, by making a number of comparisons with more familiar philosophical theories of experience and in particular of sensory experience.

Dr. Straus presents his theory as a reversion from Cartesianism to the open vision of an experienced world. Let us begin, however, not with the subtly ambiguous Cartesian, but with the more crudely ambivalent Lockean position, from which, through refinement and excision, traditional empiricism has developed. The real givens of sense for Locke were single separable ideas, pieces of mental content whose originals were resident in some material, but unknown, X, and which the mind could manipulate, abstract from and return to for its intuitive knowledge, such as it was, of a "real" world. But this was the real world of a good Newtonian, of a founding father of the Royal Society, for whom the "corpuscular philosophy" had proved a liberation from the dead tags of scholasticism and useless Latin learning. It seemed common-sense because of the nonsense it had abandoned and because of the prospects for natural philosophy which it appeared, at first sight, to permit. Yet, except for our primary experience of motion, solidity, and weight, the experienced surface of the world, its colors, smells, and sounds, were held to be but secondary: mere expressions of as yet unknown processes in those underlying X's. But are our apprehensions of color, smell, or sound, in fact less experienced, less substantive in their shaping of our ongoing experience than our apprehensions of motions and shapes and of the solid resistance of bodies to touch?

Travel from the Sacramento valley an hour's drive into the snow country of the Sierras: this experience is not described, in its immediate quality as experience, by substituting for one congeries of "ideas of sensation" another that includes more white bits and fewer gray and red and yellow, or more "silences"—what are they in empiricist terms?—and fewer loud noises. The traveller finds himself *in* a different medium, his very being changes. Or compare, similarly, the difference between the impact on the ear—or rather on the person, through the ear, of a grating Bob Dylan ballad with the experienced effect of a well-performed baroque concerto. The first slaps at us, the second surrounds us: it places us, auditorily, in a different *landscape*. The summative plus representative plus hedonistic account of these experiences triply falsifies them. It forces us to reduce what is comprehensive to an alleged (not an experienced) atomic base, and to this it adds, on the one hand, an invented intellectual superstructure (like Helmholtz's "unconscious inference"), and, on the other, a "merely subjective" feeling tone. But why must we insist that we infer, unconsciously or otherwise, the snow from the whiteness, the music from its discrete sounds? We have known since Ehrenfels that melodies are not experienced like that and since Wertheimer that nor are visual objects, let alone whole landscapes. Let us leave these cramped constructions and return, Dr. Straus exclaims with Husserl (though in a different spirit), to "the things themselves."

Not that that is easy or infallible. Dr. Straus performs no "reduction" and hence possesses, or can claim to possess, no stringent method. On the one hand (to be sure, I must confess with apologies to my esteemed phenomenological colleagues on the platform and in the audience), I agree with Dr. Straus in suspecting the over-intellectual, and, indeed, the presumptuous, method of phenomenological reduction. Yet, admittedly, if we stay *in* the "life-world," as Dr. Straus urges us to do, rather than bracketing its existence to seek its "pure" structure, we risk substituting what are our own personally slanted descriptions, however universally we intend them, for what is truly universal.[12] But that *is* our condition, and we do better to face it than to substitute for the rich multidimensionality of our experience, both shared and single, some skeletal surrogate, whether in an abstract Lockean reconstruction of sensation or in the Husserlian highroad to "transcendental subjectivity." What Dr. Straus is seeking is a reinstatement of the life-world as lived, of

---

[12] The concept of universal intent is derived from Michael Polanyi's *Personal Knowledge,* London: Routledge, 1958.

that comprehensive horizon of earthbound experience which Descartes had distilled to a geometer's two-halved paradise: an impoverishment which is still the starting point as much of Husserl's enterprise (whose *Cartesian Meditations* are not for nothing so entitled) as of Locke's *Essay*.

The phenomenological enterprise which, in its starting point, Dr. Straus's most resembles is Heidegger's, and it may be useful, therefore, to compare his approach briefly with the *Daseinsanalyse* of *Sein* und *Zeit*. Dr. Straus's I-Allon relation is a variant, if you like, of Heidegger's being-in-the-world. A *Dasein* is an experiencing being, and the I-Allon description, like the first part of *Sein* und *Zeit,* does genuinely turn its back on the divided world of *res cogitans* and *res extensa* to plunge directly into the inspection of human being in its entirety. The differences, however, are also significant for philosophy, as well, I should guess, as for psychiatry. Two points should be mentioned. First, despite one passing reference to a possibility of authentic *Fürsorge,*[13] *Mitsein* characterizes Heideggerian *Dasein* only on the level of forfeiture. The authentic existent who emerges in the second part of Heidegger's argument is, despite the bow to national destiny later developed in the chauvinistic vision of the *Introduction to Metaphysics,* the one, rare existential hero, utterly cut off in his true being from the contemptible *"das Man"* from whose distracting influence the rest of us never escape. In Heidegger's authentic existence there is no Allon. Not so for Dr. Straus. As a psychiatrist, and a humane psychiatrist, he looks with equal openness at the general character of all. This he accomplishes by seeing the pathology of the individual case as a rending in one way or another of the seamless whole that constitutes the norm of everyday life. Thus the I-Allon relation stands as the paradigm which becomes, in illness, split apart or deformed. For Heidegger, on the contrary, as for his hero Nietzsche, the norm is the deformity, and only the rare soul who hates and repels the norm can be said to live authentically.

---

[13] M. Heidegger, *Sein und Zeit,* Halle: Niemeyer, 1927, p. 122.

And there is a second important difference. Heidegger's *Da-sein,* like Sartre's *pour-soi,* or for that matter Jaspers' *Existenz,* is *only* human. Dr. Straus's "experiencing being" is human *or* animal. It is the structure of all sentient living, not only of our relatively self-conscious living, that he wishes to reinstate as the foundation of knowledge and of action. And this aim—to rein-state man in nature—is an essential one for any philosophy that would finally exorcise the persistent Cartesian ghost.

For both these reasons, it seems to me, Dr. Straus's approach is more fruitful than that of some other (so-called) "existen-tial" psychiatrists, notably, for example, that of Ludwig Bin-swanger. Binswanger simply takes Heideggerian being-in-the-world, the very essence of which demands arrogance and hatred as the road from me to thee, and injects into it, with sublime incompatibility, a generous dose of love. But to restore a bal-anced vision of existence we need, both in our recognition of its positive rootedness in communion and in our recognition of the kinship of men and other animals, a broader and firmer founda-tion from the start.

There is one other effort to overcome the Cartesian tradition, in particular the Cartesian-empiricist theory of perception, with which one is tempted to compare Dr. Straus's proposed reform. He rejects, as we have seen, the empiricist concept of sensation in favor of a theory of sensing (*Empfinden*) as the fundamental sense-mediated road that links object with experiencing organ-ism, and contrasts this pervasive process with the more sophisti-cated and at least primarily cognitive sensory awareness of objects in *perception.* This is obviously not the stock psychologi-cal distinction between sensation and perception,[14] but it is reminiscent, at least at first sight, of Whitehead's distinction between *presentational immediacy* and *causal efficacy.*[15] Yet, it is also, again, in some essential ways different. Whitehead is con-trasting what *is* really present, what is "enjoyed," in "sensa" or

---

[14] See for example D. Hamlyn, *Sensation and Perception,* New York: Humanities Press, 1961.
[15] A. N. Whitehead, *Symbolism: Its Meaning and Effect,* Cambridge: Cambridge University Press, 1927.

"pure" givens, with the opaque but powerful impact upon us of the processes beyond and around us in the world. The latter— causal efficacy—does in fact resemble Dr. Straus's "sensing." It is the constant interchange of experiencing being and surrounding field, the way in which an animal becomes the figure it is, expressing unity and contrast with its medium as ground, that they are both concerned to describe. And it is indeed this living dynamic of sensory awareness, a dynamic expressed in ancient thought in Aristotelian *aisthesis,* that the modern tradition has neglected and even denied. "Presentational immediacy," however, is very different from Strausian "perception." It is the illusory surface of sense experience, while for Dr. Straus "perception" is the sensory-interpretative process through which we know presented things as stable objects amenable to classification, definition, explanation, and the like.

On the other hand, if we liken Whitehead's distinction to Dr. Straus's distinction of stimuli and objects, we find that causal efficacy, which is another name for sensing, in indeed our everyday path to objects (in an ordinary, not a "scientific" sense), while stimuli are by no means the givens of presentational immediacy, but intellectual artifacts constructed by abstraction and hypostatization to suit the demands of a physicalist metaphysic. So this distinction is not quite parallel to Whitehead's either. At the same time, we should notice that the data of presentational immediacy are after all the data, detached and delusive, from which Berkeley and Hume generalized to produce their theory of ideas (or of impressions), and they are the data which experimental psychologists have first fastened on and then forgotten in order to build beneath them the apparently solider neurophysiological foundation with which they suppose themselves to work. The import of the two analyses seems to me, therefore, to be convergent, even though the distinctions used are not entirely congruent. In both cases it is the reinstatement of experience in its concrete significance that is at stake.

For the arbitrary models of empiricist psychology, then, Dr. Straus would substitute the conception of an experiencing being in its relation to a surrounding world. A host of philosophical issues are given new illumination by this change of ground. I have already touched on some of them but will mention briefly two, the concepts of time and space, and the problem of universals, which are related to our theme of sensory experience, its powers and limits.

Philosophers in the empiricist tradition, and experimental psychologists, who have depended on this tradition for their metaphysical nourishment, have taken, by and large, time and space as either objective and Newtonian or as subjective constructs equivalent to those uniform containers. But our experience of time and space is not thus uniform. Nor, in the case of time, does this assertion imply setting a Bergsonian *durée* or a literary stream of consciousness over against the uniform chronology of the "real" world. Chronology is a product of culture, which we rely on to set our alarm clocks, to meet classes, or fry chicken, or catch planes; but like clocks, classrooms, frying pans, and Boeings, it is an artifact which we use in order to move about *within* the richer framework of lived time. And lived time is neither Cartesian-atomic nor Newtonian-continuous. It exhibits all, and more than, the modalities that Rosalind enumerated. It is not a measure, but a medium.

The concept of lived time, of course, is by no means original with Dr. Straus. His exposition is paralleled in Minkowski, in Merleau-Ponty, or, in a different style, in Heidegger, and it is reminiscent again, in its metaphysical implications, of Whitehead's philosophy of process. What distinguishes his work, however, is its linkage to specific psychological themes: as in his demonstration of the difficulties that follow from the time-atomism of Pavlovian theory, in his treatment of the theory of memory-traces, or of infantile amnesia, or of time-disturbances in endogenic depression. It would be superfluous to present these topics in detail here.

Even more striking, moreover, because the topic is more habitually neglected, is Dr. Straus's treatment of space. Here again I need not specify, but just remind you of his distinction between acoustical and optical space, or, allied to this distinction, his account of the contrasting modes of lived spatiality in walking and in the dance. Thus in the essay on "Forms of Spatiality," Dr. Straus writes,

> The space in which we live is as different from the schema of empty Euclidean space as the familiar world of colors differs from the concepts of physical optics . . . As immediately experienced, space is always a filled and articulated space; It is nature or world.[16]

The contrast between dancing and walking indicates, not a contrast between lived space and Euclidean space, but between two forms of lived spatiality. Our ordinary motility is the progressive one of purposive movement, and it is this that is reversed in the abandon of the dance. But purposive movement is not Euclidean, spread out in three dimensions indifferently to time, it is *historical*. It is the space of action. In it we move ahead in preference to back, out from a stable *here* to the goal of our proposed action. This, not the infinite extension of geometry, is the ordinary lived spatiality which we forget in the self-abandonment of the dance. Thus the contrast between acoustical space, which predominates in dancing, and, the optical space in which we conduct the routine business of living, is still a contrast within the pathic aspect of sensing.

Such an exposition is not only illuminating in itself: it can serve to rouse us, as philosophers, from our dogmatic slumber. We take it for granted that non-Euclidean geometry has undermined the Kantian theory of spatial intuition. But why should we ever have thought that our everyday experience of space was that of the "infinite container" Kant envisaged? We could find, if we seek philosophical precedent, a more faithful rendering of our experience in Aristotle's concept of place, or we could find a corrosive critique of the empiricist conventions about sensation in Hegel's argument, in the *Phenomenology of Mind,* on the here and now. In the main, however, philosophers have failed to build on these insights; and here, moreover, we have an alternative approach tied, not to alternative philosophical systems, but

---

[16] E. W. Straus, *op. cit.,* p. 72.

to concrete psychological insights. Such an account may perhaps induce us to abandon the poverty of our usual school examples —the desk or the tree, the building across the quad—not, indeed, for irrational wallowing in "situation," but for the structured descriptions of phenomenal realities, which may serve as the coping stones of a sounder metaphysic.

So far I have been talking about Dr. Straus's theory of *sensing,* and just now about its implications for the philosophical problems of time and space. Finally, I want to raise briefly some questions about another venerable problem, the problem of universals. Here the other wing of Dr. Straus's position, his theory of perception as distinct from sensing, seems to me to make the situation more complicated. Which sort of sense-experience is supposed to be philosophy's step-child, and is it really so? Or is it Dr. Straus himself who here joins some earlier thinkers in turning *aisthesis* out in the cold?

Both in ancient and modern philosophy, the problem of universals has arisen from the contrast between the mere particularity of sensory givens and the generality of language or of thought. Take Plato's position in the *Theaetetus.* Knowledge, to be knowledge, Plato argued, must be both *infallible* and *real.* Sensation, as the particular, immediate, *given-to me,* is indeed infallible. But it fails the test of reality, since "existence" can be grasped, not by sense, but only, *through* the senses, by the mind alone. Sensation, therefore, cannot qualify as knowledge. It presents us with the particular, meaningless *this;* but only through the comprehension of general concepts, like existence, can we *know* that the presented datum not only presents itself, but *is.*

Dr. Straus's position seems to stand in a peculiar relation of agreement and disagreement with this classic text. On the one hand, he is convinced that philosophers, from Plato and Democritus onward, have been, in the main, unfair to sensory experience. Sensing is not a delusive blooming buzz of meaningless particulars on which we must turn our backs in order to reach an intelligible world where the mind can feed on its proper objects. It is an all-inclusive road of access to the world, our means, over the varied spectrum of the five senses, of communicating with reality. It is thought, not sense, which cuts itself off, by a negation of which men alone among animals are capable, from immediate rootedness in the real, to spin out its gnostic constructions in separation—or at least in quasi-separation—from the more immediate immersion in reality of sensing in its pathic mode. Such sensing, moreover, far from being a congeries of meaningless bits, is itself already general. Though limited to, or at least ranging out from and returning to, the *here* and *now*, it nevertheless grasps the presented world in its generality. The experience of generality is intrinsic to sensing, and also common, therefore, Dr. Straus suggests, to men and animals:

> I maintain that animals, too, experience the general—for example, sound. They have this experience not because they think in general terms, but because the relationship of an experiencing being to the world is a general relationship, whereas the singular moment is merely a constriction of this relationship. The content of each moment is determined in part by that from which it is distinct, that is, by what it no longer is, as well as by what it is to be. How, otherwise, could animals experience signals, which are midway between an undifferentiated and a differentiated situation and which announce the transition from the one to the other?[17]

This seems to me an important insight, and one which helps us to recognize a minimal continuity at least in the styles of being-in-the-world of all sentient beings. "Generality" is not a human invention which we have superadded to the merely particular data that make up, Hume-wise, the raw givens of animal experience. It is of the very fabric of sentience itself. And it is from *within* the world of an experiencing being that we extract, as it were, the more refined universals of language and of the articulate knowledge which it enables us to acquire.

So far, so good—or so it appears. But if Dr. Straus rejects the contrast between the sensed as merely particular and the

---

[17] E. W. Straus, *The Primary World of Senses,* New York: Free Press, 1963, p. 96.

known as general, and professes to find in sensory experience
the full-bodied medium of all experience, even of the most
refined cognition, he insists, at the same time, as strongly as did
Plato, that sensory experience is *not* knowledge, is not even an
"inferior" brand of knowledge, but differs radically from it, and
differs precisely in this matter of generality. Thus in contrast to
perception—*Wahr*nehmung—, which *is* cognitive, and grasps
things in their objectivity as things, of one or another kind,
sensing, *Empfinden,* after all, Dr. Straus asserts later in the
same argument, grasps only the here and now :

> In sensory seeing the thing is for me, for me here and now in
> a passing moment. But after the step to the world of percep-
> tion, this being-there-for-me is apprehended as a moment in a
> universal, general chain of events.[18]

It is "only by the use of universals," he argues "that I can
describe a thing as it is for me . . . and for every one,"[19] and
such description, he seems to feel, is entailed in the very act of
perceiving. Sensing, in contrast, permits no such generalization,
no such enlargement to logic and taxonomy, to the rational use
of "all" and "some." This contrast is surely Platonic, but a
strange transposition of Plato's dichotomy. In the *Theaetetus*
we have the contrast of *aisthesis* with knowledge ; here we have
a different dichotomy : sensing (= aisthesis?) is indeed non-
cognitive, and perception—which is not to be identified with
sensory experience—is taken as at least the primordial level of,
if not equivalent to, knowledge. "Perceiving," Dr. Straus writes,
"and not sensing, is a knowing."[20] Its theme, we are told, is the
factual, which is constituted—made (*factum*)—by means of a
breach in sensory experience, in the singling out of some*thing*
against a neutral background of objective space and time. Thus
by a fundamental negation man breaks through the sensory
horizon, in which he like all animals originally experiences the
world, to attain the geographical space of objectivity. He never

---

[18] *Ibid.,* p. 317.
[19] *Loc. cit.*
[20] *Ibid.,* p. 329.

does so totally, indeed, except in illness: the melancholic is precisely he who has lost touch with the landscape; "frozen in unmoving time, . . . he looks at the world . . . in a bird's eye view."[21] But normally we live in both spaces, that of landscape and that of geography. Routinely we sense, reflectively we perceive.

Indeed, as Dr. Straus introduces the distinction of sensing and perceiving, perception seems to be the sharpening of our sense-mediated attention that arises in response to language:

> We see a thing a thousand times and yet have not really seen it. A question forces us to look at it properly for the first time. The first seeing was a sensing, a participation in expression; the second seeing, however, is a perception. Questions force us into a new order of understanding. We are asked about "something" and wish to answer what and how that something is. We speak now of things or of a thing, we speak of its properties, its possible modifications. We speak of one thing which we see at this moment in front of us, or which we visualize in its particular place. We speak of one single thing, but we distinguish it with general words.[22]

So we have, if you like, generality in sensing, but "true" universals, let us say, in language-mediated perception. Indeed, the perception *of* speech, in which the phoneme—the *heard* unit of speech—is itself universal,[23] becomes the model for the perception also of events and objects, which are seen or heard as such only within the universe of discourse that language has already shaped. Can it be that the "generality" of sensing is that of the concrete universal, while perception, like all cognitive processes, depends upon the more abstract universals that language enables us to understand? It may be some such dialectical solution that will enable us to reconcile the seeming contradiction.

In that case, of course, however, only language users perceive, and at one place at least Dr. Straus suggests that only lan-

---

[21] *Ibid.*, p. 328.
[22] *Ibid.*, p. 317.
[23] *Ibid.*, p. 163.

guage-users learn.[24] Thus, starting out to put our sensory experiencing on a par with that of other animals, and to exhibit the continuity on the ground of which our unique achievements have arisen, he seems, in his doctrine of perception, to outdo even the Cartesians in his relegation of animals to outer darkness. Yet surely that animals learn and in some sense acquire knowledge is as well attested as that human knowledge is in some way unique.

Moreover, in his account of perception, even Dr. Straus's analysis of human experience is strangely contradicted. In his account of the dance, for example, we have seen that he contrasts both "presentic" or expressive and purposive or "historical" with the uniform, infinite space of Euclid or Newton. Here, however, he contrasts the presentic space of landscape directly with the uniform space of geography and geometry, which he identifies with that of history. Thus, he points out, a "remote valley" is, geographically, on a uniform plane with my present location in this room. But the farmer living in the remote valley, he remarks, is immersed in it as his landscape.[25] Granted; but the farmer ploughing a furrow, for example, is not moving like the dancer *in* a space, he is advancing purposefully—and historically—*through* a space to reach a goal. Both these forms of spatiality are to be contrasted—as Dr. Straus himself has contrasted them—with the geographical framework, say, of an agricultural survey. It seems, therefore, that we have here not a simple dichotomy, but a many-one relation. On the side of sensing there are diverse forms of lived spatiality; on the side of perception, there is the one geographical space accessible to objective thought. And the concept of "history" seems, if with different significance, to fall into both categories. Purposive action is historical; an expressive activity like the dance is not. But the universal framework of history entails "history" in a more refined and critical sense.

Such ambiguities need ironing out if philosophers are to work with Dr. Straus's basic concepts, and particularly, when we are

---

[24] *Ibid.,* p. 147.
[25] *Ibid.,* p. 319, p. 410.

faced with the teasing question of the distinction between men and animals. As he argues in "The Upright Posture,"[26] in agreement with the comparative studies, for example, of Adolf Portmann, men differ fundamentally from animals even in their anatomical and developmental endowments as animals. But is the division to be seen so sharply that perception and knowledge are wholly denied to other animals? There seems to be here a radical transmutation indeed, but of a common gift. Were not generality embedded in sentience itself, the power of language to mediate assertions with universal intent, and hence to aim, not at awareness only, but at truth: this power would remain, as it does for traditional empiricism, an unintelligible mystery. In this context, therefore, I must confess, I find that some contemporary philosophers at least (notably, for example, Merleau-Ponty in the *Phenomenology of Perception*), who interpret the whole of sense-experience (Strausian sensing *and* perception) as our unique gateway to the world, and as the primordial paradigm of knowing as well as living—of knowing as a form of living—: I find that such thinkers reinstate *aisthesis* more completely and more correctly in the philosophical family, and therewith man himself, as experiencing being, more completely and more correctly in the family of nature, than does Dr. Straus, with his sharp dichotomy between the utterly non-cognitive process of sensing and perception as the perquisite of language-users alone. [With this very cursory reference to Merleau-Ponty's theory of perception, it seems appropriate to turn over the discussion to Dr. Langan.]

---

[26] Phenomenological Psychology, pp. 137-165.

COMMENT ON PROFESSOR GRENE'S PAPER

Thomas Langan

As Dr. Grene shows, the theme established for this conference inevitably raises the central question: What *is* given primordially? And she underscores among others one aspect of Dr.
Straus' rich contribution to this cardinal question: I refer to his
efforts to break down the rigid separation which would place the
universal uniquely in the sphere of intellectual cognition and the
particular in the sphere of sensible experience. Before comment-
ing further on this central issue, I would like to express my
hearty agreement with Dr. Grene and Dr. Straus, when both
imply that there is no definitive methodological gimmick, proper
application of which will insure the phenomenologist that now
he has before the mind's eye the truly *given* and only what is
given. Note that even the simplest phenomenological reduction
coupled with the most elementary sort of constitutive analysis
suffices to break the hold of common sense realism at least
enough for the philosopher to realize that what is *there* in the
perception is not all here and now sensibly *given*. The form of
the Cartesian methodical doubt which Hume adapted as a reduction was able to achieve that much. But not even the most
sophisticated reduction gurantees that all presuppositions carried over from common experience have been neutralized; and,
perhaps worse yet, there is nothing in a reduction as such to
restrain the philosopher from going too far, as the empiricists
did when they assumed that only the unanalyzable can truly be
said to be given. It is doubtful that any methodological prescrip-
tion can assure the phenomenologist of victory in his counter
attack against the empiricist. His task is to try somehow to show
that our primordial experience is, as given, more structured than
the Humeans are willing to admit and that their alleged ultimate
given atoms of experience are not *givens* at all but *abstractions*
from the total primordial given structure of experience.

Baldly put, the question, then, is this: How does one settle disputes about what is primordially given? How does one show, for instance, the falsity of the assumption that everything which can be further analyzed must be a fabrication of the subject, a *mere* fabrication that is, not wholly authorized by reality, which the synthetic intention then is doubted to represent as it is in itself? Isn't the tacit assumption here one of those "metaphysical assertions" which the logical positivists have pointed out cannot be shown to be either false or true? For is not the tacit assumption that all perceived wholes are formed as a result of organizing categories structuring a sensible stuff? In that case, as what we perceive is the already structured product, there is no way experience can refute the assumption that, prior to experience, there existed a structureless stuff. Against the common sense realist, the phenomenologist can focus critical attention on actual experience and show that some aspect of the total perceptual situation, thought by the uncritical realist to be here and now given, are in fact added by the perceiving subject from past experience or are anticipated by him as he opens his perceptual horizons toward the future. But the phenomenologist cannot attack thus directly the empiricist's claim that what is actually given—the full structure of experience—is not the "ultimately real." What more can the phenomenologists do (and indeed this was a major philosophical accomplishment) than show that the empiricist's "really real" elements, sense data, are as such never given but rather are abstracted by a theoretical intelligence guided by historical presuppositions? After that the burden of justification for positing "sense data" is squarely on the empiricist.

In the absence of any possibility for direct attack on the sense data dogma, Erwin Straus has taken what is, in my opinion, the only sound course remaining: experiment and description directing our gaze again and again to many aspects of the given and back and forth between the sense given and the perceived and understood world. The gradual eroding effect on the empiricist's thesis of this attending to the full fabric of experience is at least a good beginning.

In that rich effort, to several important aspects of which

Professor Grene has alluded, nothing is more central, in my opinion, than Dr. Straus' definitive contribution to breaking down the traditional Platonic separation of the sensible (thought of as the hopelessly particular) on one side and the intelligible on the other (thought of as the stratosphere of the universals which somehow manage to reflect on to the aesthetic some structure never really possessed by the radically individual sensed things themselves).

But if one begins with the fact that things are given as structured, then the rigid separation of the particular and the universal can be broken down. All structure as such is potentially intelligible: an intelligence can grasp the *sense* of the peculiar way its parts *"belong together"* in forming the structure. The result of the intelligence's insight into the sense of the structure is a complex universal. It makes no difference whether the structure whose sense an intelligence grasps is the profile (*Abschattung*) of a particular thing; or a relationship between things perceived as belonging to the same situation; or my own relationship to a thing or things. All three sorts of structure are intelligible. Now, how is this formal insight, resulting in a universal, grounded in the given structure? It is precisely here that pay off Dr. Straus' efforts to show that neither the perceived profile, nor things perceived in relation to one another, nor the perceptual situation linking perceiver and perceived is either in itself radically particular or universal; but rather as *structured,* they are potentially universalizable while actually particular. For what is given, be it profile, things in situation, or the perceptual situation itself, is a whole analyzable into parts, which parts are not given in isolation but rather as *parts-in-relation,* which is the same as saying *as parts.*

Now, leaving aside here the very significant but still violently disputed question of whether there are any *simple* parts or whether each analysis in fact just yields sub-structures, I would point out that each structure, because it is a whole, stands in relation to its parts in something rather like the way the universal stands in relationship to its particulars. But while reminiscent of the universal-particular relation, in that the whole includes or stands over or subsumes the parts, it is none the less a different sort of relationship and one which makes possible the universal-particular one.* Husserl, Straus, the Gestaltists, Heidegger, Merleau-Ponty, and many others have explored different kinds of whole-part relationship. We recall, for example, Husserl's description of the relationship of the thing to the many perceived *Abschattungen* in which it is revealed; or of Merleau-Ponty's description of the many manifestations of the person and that *unité de style* running through and joining them and unifying them all; or of Straus' analysis of the unity of the melody uniting the many notes. All of these examples point to the same truth: our experience of the real world, yielding, as primordially given, *structures,* reveals a world in which neither things, nor aspects of things, nor moments of our experience, whether of things or of ourselves, are in fact isolated. That is why the philosopher, Hegel, could go so far toward rendering credible the idealist thesis that everything is all-in-all. But whereas Hegel comes to his task with an ontology he is determined to prove, what is rather needed now is more sober experiment and description aimed at discerning just what the given links between things, participants in situations, and moments of experience *actually are.*

Despite all of the impressive efforts already expended by phenomenological psychologists and philosophers, this task is still in its infancy. Yet, while their successes to date merit wide support of their future research, there is reason to fear the phenomenologists are not retaining the interest even of the more favorable disposed among contemporary social scientists, literary and historical critics and psychologists. [I bring up this *ängstlich* subject and dare close with a free swinging editorial remark on what I think the cause of this discredit to be, only because the title set for Professor Grene by Dr. Straus so strongly suggests our host thinks the philosophers have let the

---

* If there are also simple universals, then the insight into the simple universal must obviously be something different from that grasp of the sense of the belonging together of parts which is the insight into the structured universal.

psychologists down, that I cannot resist putting my oar in, however indelicately.] Mrs. Grene readily concedes that the philosophers in the Humean tradition have indeed let the psychologists down. Despite the fact that there is no time here to establish what I have sought elsewhere to show at some length historically, I shall nevertheless dare say that I think the great phenomenological philosophers have let you down, too, but in a different way. I shall here assume that in his evening flights above the vineyards of psychological experimentation and description seeking "the sense of it all," the philosophical owl does more than merely report the results of the day's work; rather through his interpretations he tends to determine somewhat the morrow's course of inquiry. If this is so, then, were the philosophers supporting a tradition of psychological research to encounter frustration in their efforts to solve fundamental ontological problems, the psychologists in that tradition would be left on their own. At that point the philosophers might have to look to the psychologists for traces of a new path to take them beyond their present ontological troubles.

This is what I find has happened to the phenomenological movement. The working psychologist can get away with making sense of some phenomena by employing holistic formulae which imply an idealism and then turning right around and pointing to features of experience which imply a realism, indeed at times something very close to naive realism. But the philosopher, charged with showing the sense of it all, cannot allow himself such inconsistency. He must either find the way beyond the idealism-realism opposition and in his synthesis find a place for both sorts of phenomena; or he must reinterpret everything either completely idealistically or (what is not likely to occur in the phenomenological movement) realistically.

Now, if the historical critique I have attempted elsewhere* holds up then the following is our plight: having failed to

---

* In Gilson, Langan and Maurer, *Recent Philosophy,* Chapter I-IV and XV; in *Merleau-Ponty's Critique of Reason,* esp. Chapters 1, 5, 6; and "Heidegger on the Thing," to be published in a symposium on Heidegger by Duquesne University Press.

achieve the goal of an ontology beyond idealism-realism, the philosophers of the phenomenological movement have ended up despite themselves and despite even the best efforts of the late Heidegger, in an idealism; more specifically in some form or other of historical relativism. If this accusation can be justified, then there is a great deal at stake *ontologically* in the psychologists' patient work with the primordial presentation of structure in *ice*-thesis. Unless the ontological dimensions of the present crisis in phenomenology are attended to, I do not see how the phenomenological psychologist of perception can see the extent to which he has indeed been let down. He may have to go it alone now in the work of establishing by experiment and description just what sort of potentially intelligible structure is in fact manifested in the perceptual situation. If under the pressure of the need to be consistent the phenomenological philosophers have begun à la Merleau-Ponty interpreting all givens as structured only by *a prioris* which themselves are but ancient cultural accretions, then inevitably their concern is going to be riveted on problems of internal interpretation of the cultural object, and not on analyzing the evidence for the reality in themselves of the natural structures in the world, in which, for reasons deep in the historical philosophical tradition, they do not much believe anyway. But if Dr. Straus is right when he shows psychology, free of Humean prejudices, must puruse its task of describing how it is with perception, then it is equally so that psychology must also not be misled by phenomenological idealism. "Sense perception philosophy's step child?" Rather let philosophy resume its proper place as sense perception's child!

PHENOMENON AND MODEL

Herbert Hensel

OUR RATIONAL world and its conceptual and linguistic structures are deeply rooted in a stratum which we call *sensory experience*. As Husserl rightly emphasized, sensory perception 'spielt unter den erfahrenden Akten die Rolle einer Urerfahrung, aus der alle erfahrenden Akte einen Hauptteil ihrer begründenden Kraft ziehen.' Kant expressed the same view, in regard to purely rational perception, when he said that the understanding has its *Schema* in perception, or, as he said in another place, that perception is the major basis, and conceptual thinking the minor basis, of our understanding. In any case, we can expect an examination of the structures of human perception to furnish important evidence in regard to the question of how our rational world originated.

Sensory experience is a specific, unalterable, and irreplaceable foundation of our knowledge of the real world, and even the most abstract and least 'sensory' of the empirical sciences, such as Physics, are forced to rely on sensory perception as their ultimate source of evidence. For this reason, all philosophical or scientific attempts to deny, distort, or falsify sensory phenomena will always fail, in view of the fact that phenomena as such are directly certain and beyond doubt.

But is the testimony of the senses alone sufficient to establish certain knowledge? It is easy to see that this is not the case. Although sensory experience cannot be denied or ignored, it is, at the same time, fragmentary, transitory accidental, and unconnected. The objects of perception appear only partially, and in a limited spatial and temporal aspect. Furthermore, they are strongly dependent upon the percipient subject. The perceived world is by no means a complete, unified, or final entity which we can accept without further question.

This awareness is one of the special characteristics of Man. The very incompleteness of the perceived world makes it possible for us to fill out our fragmentary perceptions with *free interpretations*. In refusing to accept data simply as such, in experiencing them rather as problems, we incite our will to transcend the state of mere sensory experience and to integrate our data into a higher system of relations.

The extent to which sensory data can be elaborated conceptually is shown by work in the experiental sciences. On the one hand, these remain bound to certain points of sensory empiricism, but on the other they go far beyond the scope of mere perception with their theoretical extrapolations. The purpose of scientific thinking is to integrate and co-ordinate apparently isolated, independent phenomena by arranging them in a conceptual system. Thus we are able to discover relations which would never occur to a person whose mind is limited to sensory perception only.

The spontaneous patterns formed by our rational thinking, which turns fragmentary sense impressions into more comprehensive structures, can be designated as *models*. On the one hand, a conceptual model is, to a certain extent, *independent* of sensory data. The model can be separated, abstracted, and applied to various perceptual structures, in the same way that any given fact can be interpreted by means of various types of models. In other words, for any particular phenomenon we do not necessarily have a definite concept or definite model; rather, the latter is created only by a spontaneous act of cognition. Human sensory perception does not involve the necessity of any particular interpretation. Whether I formulate a concept to explain something I have observed, i.e. whether I set up a model, adequate or inadequate, in connection with the phenomena perceived by my senses, is largely a matter of my free will. Some person may suddenly discover a comprehensive rational explanation of phenomena which others have paid no attention to. I can also deliberately refuse to indulge in explanations and judgments, and limit myself to observing pure data. This relative freedom and independence of our minds in regard to perception also manifests itself in a negative manner, i.e. in the possibility of error and misjudgment.

On the other hand, however, we expect a model to agree, in one way or another, with our experience, in contrast to the products of free imagination. In other words, we expect the model to be *adequate* to our experience. This means that the model, although not identical with the original, must have certain structural characteristics in common with it. In regard to these characteristics, the model and the original are isomorphic. Thus Euclidean geometry is an adequate model for many of the facts of the sensory world: for example, the fact that the sum of the angles of plane physical triangles is 180°, or that the size and form of rigid physical bodies are invariable in regard to rotation and movement in space.

Naturally, this definition exceeds by far the limits of what we ordinarily mean by a model. In this latter case, there is usually a considerable perceptual or qualitative similarity between the model and the original. In many cases this similarity is deliberate and desirable. On the other hand, models in our sense of the term are not required to show any qualitative agreement with their originals. The only requirement is that a certain step in the model clearly corresponds to a certain step in the original, in the sense of an implicative 'if—then' relation.

It is only when the phenomenon and the model are united or combined that we have what I would call full reality. This concept of reality is essentially different from the idea of perceptual data. Reality in this sense is not something that is found pre-formed, or static, but rather is a dynamic design in which the processes of human perception and cognition are constitutively involved. If our knowledge of the real world were based on sensory experience alone, then all scientific endeavours would be useless and unnecessary. We could dismiss our scientists, close down our laboratories, and save billions of dollars.

It is easy to see that natural realism is also based on this concept of reality. Not only the scientist, but also the ordinary person with an open attitude towards the world in which he lives, is familiar with the errors and illusions emanating from the sensory world. We correct these errors on the basis of new experience. In regard to practical behavior, we can easily distinguish between sensory data and reality. An object which is disappearing from the horizon of our perception may still seem to be real, depending on the circumstances. Vice versa, we identify a mirror image as being unreal, although it would seem to be a compelling sensory fact. All of this presuppose a model of the real world which is by no means congruent with our mere sensory experience. Actually, even naive realism is based on a complicated theory of reality, and the naiveté of this realism does not consist in a simple equation of data with reality, but rather in the non-reflective manner in which the models are formed.

Our ordinary perceptions cannot be taken as being purely phenomenal in the sense of uninterpreted data, since they are intermixed with conceptual definitions and categorical formations, just as our every-day thinking in turn contains many elements of sensory perception. A naive person believes that he perceives things directly, but it would be just as easy to claim that these perceptions are the result of conceptual operations. On the other hand, we often describe a common sensory experience as being 'logical' although it is really empirical.

Once we see these questions clearly, we also see that a special method is required in order to obtain pure perception, free of interpretation, and a correspondingly pure cognition. This method could be designated as 'phenomenological reduction' in a Husserlian sense, or as *'analytical reduction'* in the stricter form introduced by Reenpää and others into modern sensory theory. The leading idea here is consistent abstention from judgment, or 'epoche'. By bracketing together all conceptual interpretations, evaluations, and judgments, especially the natural postulate of being, we succeed in going from the real world of pre-formed categories into the sphere of pure phenomenality. We find a particularly striking characterization of the phenomenological attitude in the work of Peirce. He wrote: "It will be plain from what has been said that phaneroscopy has nothing at all to do with the question of how far the phanerons it studies correspond to any realities. It religiously abstains from all speculation as to any relations between its categories and physiological facts, cerebral or other. It does not undertake, but sedulously avoids, hypothetical explanations of any sort. It simply scrutinizes the direct appearances, and endeavors to combine minute accuracy with the broadest possible generalization. The student's great effort is not to be influenced by any tradition, any authority, any reasons for supposing that such and such ought to be the facts, or any fancies of any kind, and to confine himself to honest, singleminded observation of the appearances. The reader, upon his side, must repeat the author's observation for himself, and decide from his own observation whether the author's account of the appearances is correct or not."

Once we have excluded all pre-formed knowledge and predetermined concepts, what is left is *immediate data,* pure sensory experience. This is the point at which the chain of reasons or explanations comes to an end. This experience is not provided by prior experience; rather, it is self-originating. We could say of it that "nulla 're' indiget ad existendum" (Husserl). If I recall an object, the object is only mediately present in my memory, since it is connected with a prior perception. The same is true of the sentence: 'I hear a *car.*' The car is indirectly present, since it is only on the basis of a series of previous perceptions that I can relate the acoustic phenomenon to a car. If, on the other hand, I should say: 'I *hear* a car,' the statement refers to something immediate. The phenomenon of hearing as such appears here as primal; it requires no other content or perception, not even physiological or physical knowledge, in order to exist as given. In Peirce's terminology, sensory phenomena have the character of presentness or 'firstness.' Thus sensory perception is one of the basic principles of our knowledge, one on which all methods of proofs are based. Proof means: pointing out reasons, arriving at principles. However, the principles themselves cannot be proved; they can only be revealed, i.e. made clear and evident. In the last analysis, reasons are only perceptible. This is true of mathematical axioms no less than of sensory experiences, which thus could be designated as 'phenomenal axioms.'

Logically it is thus impossible to make apodictic assertions about sensory data, as has been attempted again and again by philosophers and, more recently, by natural scientists as well. These attempts reveal a lack of philosophical radicalism, a lack which consists in not accepting uninterpreted data simply as the final point of phenomenological reduction, and in trying to make something of them with the use of a priori concepts. Depending on our metaphysical point of view, a catalog of prejudices in regard to sensory experience could be drawn up.

The prerequisite for every phenomenological analysis of sensory data is our practical ability to make *distinctions,* i.e. our capacity to classify qualities according to the principle of similarity (dissimilarity) and dependence (independence). This produces a phenomenal structure which can be designated in its entirety as *sensory manifold.* This manifold can be described on the basis of its qualitative content; it can be conceptualized and examined in regard to its mutual interrelations. All this can be done without exceeding the limits of immediate data. A good example of this is the phenomenological classification of colors, the structure of which is completely invariable in regard to the 'mode of being' of the colors, especially in regard to their subjectivity or objectivity. This classification holds good regardless of whether we are dealing with surface colors, colors from light, after-images or hallucinations.

The use of analytical reduction makes it possible to arrange sensory manifold in four mutually independent, or orthogonal, basic dimensions: *time, space, quality,* and *intensity.* Everything perceived by the senses has a particular temporal aspect; it is located in space, either in the external world or in the body of the perceiver; it also has a specific, unmistakable quality which appears with a certain degree of intensity. Orthogonality is the same as phenomenal independence: for instance, color and form are orthogonal, since they can be varied independently of each other. Our experience of similar or independent relations is the foundation on which we construct our basic concepts or categories, i.e. the categories of time, space, quality, and intensity.

Time is the universal dimension of perception. Its fundamental significance consists in the fact that it differentiates between the phenomenal and the conceptual. Concepts lie beyond the scope of time; they are timeless, without any temporal reference or limitation. For instance, if we form the concept 'red,' we do so without reference to the appearance of red at a particular time or place as a sensory phenomenon. The timelessness of concepts is closely connected with what has been called the generality of concepts. In regard to the time dimension, we could express this generality by saying that concepts break through the temporal individuality of separate actual data. To continue this example: no matter when and where the color red may appear, it always occurs under the concept 'red.' Thus we can say that the concept is the possibility of appearances. To conceptualize observations thus means to derive them as possibilities from general principles.

In the sphere of phenomena we find no generality, but rather only temporal-spatial individuality and multiplicity: each sensory object exists 'here' and 'now.' Its time dimension is actuality. We perceive an object at one glance; it appears on the horizon of our perception. Then we look away, and the object disappears from view. The temporal mode of sensory data is aptly designated as a 'moment.' Since sensory experiences lack an extensive time dimension, phenomenal time can also be designated as 'zero-dimensional' in the sense that it is reduced to the experience of the present moment. What I perceived at some earlier time is no longer sensory perception, but rather recollection, and what I have not yet perceived is not sensory perception, but expectation. We have no immediate sensory perception of past or future, but only of the present. On the other hand, sensory impressions, because of their presentness, have a singular and accidental character; they are unique events, containing nothing which points to past or future.

In turn, timeless or general concepts are lacking in multiplicity and individuality. We cannot derive the sensory world from mere concepts, since it is contained in the concept only as a possibility, but not in its factual presence or reality. If I no longer perceive an object, I may have very good rational reasons for believing that it is still in a particular place at the present moment, but only direct sensory experience can verify this belief.

Thus temporality is revealed to be a natural and universal criterion for differentiating between sensory phenomena and conceptual models. The most general property of models is that they extend the limited time dimension of phenomena into a sphere in which time is unlimited. This becomes particularly clear in the very formation of the concept of time, which occupies a key position in all the empirical sciences. In this concept of time, from which physical time is also derived, we comprehend time as an extensive continuum, whereas phenomenal time is restricted to the period of the present. Thus I think we are justified in taking the concept of time as a model of phenomenal time. With the aid of this conceptual model we are in a position to assign each moment of the present a particular place in the time continuum, and thus to predict events in time. In passing, we may note that the concept of the time continuum also casts light on the origin of the concept of causality.

The *space dimension* of sensory experiences, their locality provides a demarcation between what Kant called the 'outer' and the 'inner' sense. Borrowing from Reenpää, we could define temporality alone, without reference to space, as *thought* or *conception*. Sensory perceptions exist 'here' and 'now'; they possess temporality and spatiality, whereas thoughts and conceptions appear 'now,' but not 'here'; they lack spatiality or localization. Finally, concepts are both timeless and spaceless; they exist neither 'here' nor 'now.'

Time and space thus constitute a categorical triad : *perception, conception,* and *concept.* This triadic structural theory means an important step beyond the traditional dualistic theories of knowledge, which included only the senses and the understanding, or perception and concept. In the dualistic systems, there is the conceptual on the one hand, but on the other hand, only an unclear structure including elements of both perception and conception. According to the new triadic view, only the conceptions of recollection and expectation can be assigned to the category of conception, but not sensory perceptions.

What happens if we systematically continue the method of

analytical reduction? We finally arrive at elements which cannot be further analyzed conceptually; that is, they have a purely phenomenal character. These are the so-called *one-digit* sensory experiences, for example, the experience 'red.' I think it is important to point out here that such elementary perceptions be analyzed phenomenologically from sensory manifold, but that they can also be presented directly by experimental means, as in the 'artificial,' purely phenomenal objects of sensory physiology. Here we have a case in which the postulate of a pure, non-conceptual perception is realized.

The concept of the elementary need not trouble us here, since it means only that the limit of analytical reduction has been reached, and that the phenomenal content cannot be further broken down conceptually. What 'red' is cannot be defined rationally; it can only be experienced, and thus we can speak of the logical simplicity of qualitative elements. Phenomenal elements are *one-digit* in the sense that they can exist primarily and independently of other elements or data.

Language takes this into account by exercising an indicative or *semantic* function instead of a demonstrative or *apodictic* function in regard to elementary sensory experiences. That is, language indicates that we have a corresponding experience or, in other words, the word serves as a symbol of a pure phenomenon. This form of statement corresponds roughly to what Wittgenstein called an atomic sentence. In regard to the phenomenal basic objects, conceptualization thus takes place in a very elementary manner. Here it is not a question of structural relations within our conceptual models, but rather of the basic connection between phenomenon and concept. The latter points directly to perception; the concept is adequate to the perception or, as Kant would say, it is deduced from the perception. As we have already seen, this deduction from perception is to be interpreted as a removal of the limitations of time.

In addition to the one-digit elements, sensory manifold also contains *multidigital* elements. It is these which give phenomena a connective relationship or structure. Without them, the world of the senses would be merely an accumulation of completely heterogeneous and isolated experiences. It seems to me particularly important to see clearly that the multidigital elements, which I want to turn to now, are purely phenomenal in nature and are not derived from the constructions of conceptual thought, as the theory of associations à la Mach believed. Vice versa, however, it is quite possible for phenomenal structures to be illustrated to a certain degree by conceptual models. But that is an entirely different question, which we shall come back to later.

Among the two-digit elements of sensory manifold we find phenomenal *identity* or non-identity, *similarity* or dissimilarity, and *dependence* or independence in regard to two sensory experiences. For instance, let us observe a surface color. Here we simultaneously perceive two one-digit elements: a color quality and a locality in space. The two are connected by the two-digit elements of phenomena simultaneity, which is an identity between the time dimensions of the two experiences.

The structure of phenomenal simultaneity (:) can be examined in stricter form by means of a procedure corresponding to the truth operations which Wittgenstein introduced into symbolic logic. Here we list what we call the *truth* of an assertion on the conceptual side, and the *reality* of a sensory experience on the phenomenal side. The term 'reality' is to be understood here as meaning that sensory experience is evidence of reality. If the qualitative experience (q) is real and, at the same time, a local experience (1), then simultaneity (q:1) is real (r). If we perceive the quality, but not the locality, then simultaneity is unreal (u). The same is true if the locality is experienced, but not the quality. Finally, if neither quality nor locality is experienced, the simultaneity of the two will naturally not be experienced either; thus it is unreal. As Table 1 shows, phenomenal simultaneity distributes reality values in the pattern: ruuu.

Table 1

b	1	q : 1
r	r	r
r	u	u
u	r	u
u	u	u

Now let us turn to the conceptual side. We designate the concept of quality with q', and that of locality with l'. In place of the factual presence or absence of a phenomenon, we use the truth (T) and falsity (F) of logical assertions. The distribution of values as shown in Table 2: TFFF, corresponds to the logical conjunction q' · l' (read as 'q' and l''). Thus the phenomenal simultaneity of quality and locality has the same distribution (ruuu) in regard to reality and unreality as the logical conjunction in regard to truth and falsity (TFFF). We can say that the two structures, the phenomenal and the logical, are isomorphic, or that logical conjunction is an adequate conceptual model for the phenomenon of simultaneity.

Table 2

q'	l'	q' · l'
T	T	T
T	F	F
F	T	F
F	F	F

We can also designate the multidigital element of simultaneity as a 'phenomenal axiom.' Linguistically, this could be roughly paraphrased as follows: Since in regard to time all perception is 'now,' there is always an element of simultaneity which joins the two individual elements. This element of simultaneity or association (:) is *commutative* in regard to the two partial elements of quality (q) and locality (l) in an object of perception. However, it is *associative* in regard to three elements, e.g. if we add the intensity (i) with which the object is perceived. In other words, if the simultaneity (:) of quality and intensity (q :i) is perceived together with locality (l), this is the same phenomenal object as if the quality appeared together with the simultaneity of the intensity and the locality (i :l). Thus the axiom of simultaneity is:

$$(q:1) = (1:q) \quad \text{commutative}$$
$$(q:i):1 = q:(i:1) \quad \text{associative}$$

This formulation of simultaneity corresponds to the mathematical axiom of addition, which is likewise commutative and associative:

$$a + b = b + a \qquad \text{commutative}$$
$$(a + b) + c = a + (b + c) \quad \text{associative}$$

Here again we see the isomorphism of phenomenal and conceptual structures. Logical conjunction and mathematical addition are thus adequate conceptual models for the multidigital phenomenal element of experiental simultaneity.

Now let us look at the two-digit element of *identity*. The logical relation of identity can be expressed in the well-known proposition:

$$(p' = q') ; (q' = r') \rightarrow (p' = r')$$

Here, p', q', and r' are symbols of conceptual objects, and $\rightarrow$ stands for implication. In words, the proposition would be: From the fact that $p' = q'$ and $q' = r'$, it follows that $p' = r'$.

If two-value logic were universally applicable to phenomena, the corresponding proposition would be

$$(p \equiv q) ; (q \equiv r) \rightarrow (p \equiv r),$$

where p, q, and r are objects of perception, e.g. intensities, and $\equiv$ stands for the experienced identity, or equivalence. However, this proposition can be shown to be false. Assuming that the intensities p and q differ from each other by an amount which lies below the threshold of perception, then they are phenomenally equal or identical. But assuming that the same is true of the relation between q and r, are p and r then phenomenally equal? This is by no means necessarily the case, especially when the sum of the two sub-threshold differences lies above the threshold of perception.

Thus there is no absolute structural isomorphism between logical and phenomenological identity (Hensel). When we say that two sensory experiences are perceptually equal, this obviously does not mean exactly the same thing as logical identity. The difference consists in the fact that logical identity is completely determined, whereas phenomenal identity contains a basic element of indeterminism. It is impossible to tell beforehand whether phenomenal equality will really prove to be equal in the course of further operations.

From this, decisive consequences can be drawn, especially for that particular act of model-constructing which we call *measuring*. All quantitative measurements are based ultimately on the concept of identity, or equality. We can say that measuring is an isomorphic reproduction of empirical facts by means of whole numbers, or more particularly, the assigning of numbers to objects in accordance with a conceptual rule with which the objects are chosen in regard to particular properties. The prerequisite here is that the objects can be included in one class of equalities, and that the equality covers least one property.

Thus the problem of measurement depends upon the concept of empirical equality. Since absolute identity exists only in logic, but not in the empirical world, we must always make certain postulates and idealizations in the phenomenal sphere; we must arbitrarily determine what is to be considered as equal. Depending on which properties we postulate as being equal, we will obtain scales of varying structure and accuracy. In setting up classes of equalities and assigning them numbers, we necessarily introduce an operational principle the validity of which can be proved only by its pragmatic consequences. As Wiener very aptly put it, 'things do not, in general, run around with their measures stamped on them like the capacity of a freight car; it requires a certain amount of investigation to discover what their measures are.'

The two-digit element of *qualitative similarity* seems to me particularly indicative for our topic. Let us take as an example the qualitative similarity of colors. Why are red and orange more similar than red and green? There is something in the nature of red and orange that connects them, but what is it? It cannot be a third element, since the two qualities of red and orange are each indivisible; they contain no visible common element. If I ask why red and orange resemble each other, I cannot find any logical reason; I can only say that I experience their similarity. It is precisely this non-rational relation, however, that corresponds to the nature of qualitative similarity. It cannot be reduced to a logical or rational similarity; rather, it forms a kind of connection which is sui generis. It could be characterized as an immediate dynamic relation between the two elements, as a unity in duplicity, of the type found in the concept of polarity. Here it is important to note that there is no third, connecting element, no medium, no law which can define or 'explain' the relation.

Logical similarity on the other hand means the same as partial identity, i.e. agreement in at least one common characteristic, one invariable. Thus the logical similarity between two elements is not a double, but rather a triple relation. Two comparable facts are connected by means of a third element which they have in common, the *tertium comparationis*. All logical relations, as well as all laws and explanations, belong to this category. Qualitative similarity means that we *experience that* a relation exists; logical similarity means that we can *explain why* it exists. This triadic structure of conceptual relations also reveals itself in the three-part form of the syllogism, with its major premise, minor premise, and conclusion, which are connected by a common *terminus medius*. Using again Peirce's terminology, we can ascribe qualitative similarity to the category of secondness, while logical similarity is a case of thirdness.

With the element of qualitative similarity we have touched upon an essential problem: that of *sensory qualities* in general. Qualities are logically irreducible, or, if you will, *non-rational*. This means that no conceptual model can be conceived which would make it possible to derive sensory qualities theoretically from other data. We can only accept the variety of these qualities, but cannot explain them rationally.

Thus, for instance, a color can never be the logical equivalent of a wavelength, since the color has only a color quality, but no quality of length. The color is not inwardly or necessarily connected with wavelengths. It makes sense to say that the color red has an aggressive character, but it makes no sense to say that it has a long-wave character. The implication of colors and wavelengths is an empirical fact, and purely coincidental from the point of view of a deductive physical system of concepts. This means, however, that the relation can only be approximately valid and, even more important, that the limits of its validity cannot be derived from the physical system. This of course is true not only of wavelengths, but also of all other physical or physiological dimensions which could be introduced in order to obtain a more accurate reproduction of color qualities.

Quality is a category of *content*, and is fundamentally incapable of being formalized and presented in the form of a model. Or in other words: We can experience qualities only in their original form. It is possible to present the variety of qualitative dimensions formally as orthogonality in mathematical models, but the content of the quality does not lend itself to a mathematical structure. This is precisely the reason why we can abstract the formal structure and apply it to any model. In the conceptual network of mathematical relations, quality has only the value of an x. In regard to its content, however, quality is a specific experience, which is not interchangeable with other qualitative experiences. Thus, for example, we experience the color red as something quite different from the color green. Here we could perhaps speak of the *meaningful character* of qualities: the nature of qualities consists in the fact that they mean something to the human mind, and are not simply arbitrary or optional.

Thus the analytical reduction of the rational world, to the extent that it is based on the testimony of the senses, leads us to elements which themselves are no longer rational in nature. Rather, they belong to the realm of the *emotional*. On this emotional basis of the senses, man as a free interpreter of data constructs his rational designs & models. However, in this freedom of interpretation there lurks the danger of error and misjudgment. If my models are not already necessarily present at the moment of perception then I must continually ask myself whether my model is truly the equivalent of my experience, whether its structure is isomorphic with phenomenal structures, or whether the limits of isomorphism have been exceeded, so that the experience is accompanied by contradictions. Whenever this is the case, we can do two things : either adapt our experience to fit the model by suppressing the contradictory experiences, by eliminating them from the system as 'bad facts,' to use Peirce's phrase. As Goethe wrote in his essay "Der Versuch als Vermittler von Objekt und Subjekt," 'Man wird bemerken können, daβ ein guter Kopf nur desto mehr Kunst anwendet, je weniger Data vor ihm liegen ; daβ er, gleichsam seine Herrschaft zu beigen, selbst aus den vorliegenden Datis nur wenige Günstlinge herauswählt, die ihm schmeicheln ; daβ er die übrigen so zu ordnen versteht, wie sie ihm nicht geradezu widersprechen und daβ er die feindseligen zuletzt so zu verwickeln, zu umspinnen und bei Seite zu bringen weiβ, daβ wirklich nunmehr das Ganze nicht mehr einer freiwirkenden Republik, sondern einem despotischen Hofe ähnlich wird.—Einem Manne, der so viel Verdienst hat, kann es an Verehrern und Schülern nicht fehlen. . . .'

The second possibility is to leave our experience unchanged and revise our models. This process is very common in the medical and biological sciences on account of the slight range of their models ; in such fields, this process also takes place without causing any particular commotion. The more exact sciences, however, are more demanding in this regard, and tend to look upon this process of model-revision as the collapse of a world-concept.

If we cling only to phenomena, we express an attitude which could be called *phenomenalism.* The phenomenalist believes that data are identical with reality, but here he fails to recognize the spontaneity of cognition, and the ability to create models which transcend mere data. The phenomenalist may accurately reproduce the world of perception, but he still will not attain reality, because he remains passive in the face of data.

The other extreme is *operationism.* The operationist believes that he can attain reality only by way of conceptual definitions ; he believes in the power of models. But here he overlooks the fact that all measurements and definitions are possible only because sensory experience is present in the background, unquestioned and non-thematic, and that the phenomenal world is only perceptible, but not derivable. The phenomenalist denies cognition, the operationist denies perception.

It is only by acknowledging both areas as autonomous, and by properly uniting experience and cognition, phenomenon and model, that we can achieve what we call our real world.

LITERATURE

Goethe, J. W.: Sämtliche Werke, Bd. 1-40. Stuttgart u. Tübingen: J. G. Cotta 1840.

Hensel, H.: Sinneswahrnehmung und Naturwissenschaft. Studium Generale *15,* 747-758 (1962).

Hensel, H.: Allgemeine Sinnesphysiologie.—Hautsinne, Geschmack, Geruch. Berlin, Heidelberg, New York: Springer-Verlag 1966.

Husserl, E.: Husserliana, Bd. 1-9. Haag: M. Nijhoff 1950-1962.

Kant, I.: Kritik der reinen Vernunft (1787). Philosophische Bibliothek, Bd. 37 a. Hamburg: F. Meiner 1952.

Mach, E.: Analyse der Empfindungen, 3. Aufl. Jena: G. Fischer 1902.

Peirce, C. S.: Collected Papers, Bd. 1-8, ed. C. Hartshorne and P. Weiss. Cambridge, Massachusetts: Belknap Press of Harvard University Press 1958-1960.

Reenpää, Y.: Allgemeine Sinnesphysiologie. Frankfurt am Main: V. Klostermann 1962.

Wiener, N.: A new theory of measurement: a study in the logic of mathematics. Proc.Lond.Math.Soc. *19,* 181-205 (1920).

Wittgenstein, L.: Schriften. Frankfurt am Main: Suhrkamp 1960.

A CRITICISM OF
HERBERT HENSEL'S "PHENOMENON AND
MODEL"

Richard M. Zaner

IN WHAT follows, I have decided to restrict myself to an internal criticism of Professor Hensel's paper, and to forgo the temptation to use this opportunity to present either directly or indirectly my own views on the nature and significance of *aisthesis*. An outstanding scientist in his own right, Professor Hensel has nevertheless offered what purports to be, not a scientific but a philosophical theory of phenomena, models, and their interconnection. As such, it is both possible and necessary to engage the theory in philosophical criticism. It goes without saying that his paper is well-deserving of such critical concern, and that we are all indebted for an extensive and serious effort. It will be immediately clear that I find myself in basic disagreement with much of this theory; that this is so, however, obviously does not imply disrespect: the life-blood of philosophy, after all, is precisely critical dialogue. Unhappily, time-limitations force my criticisms to be both sketchy and restricted in number.

(1) At a point which he takes to be decisive, that concerned with his "new triadic view," I find myself somewhat at a loss to know what he wishes to maintain.

On the one hand, decisive or not, "new" or not, perhaps the crucial component of this triad—i.e. "conception," which is crucial just because he *defines* temporality (which he unfortunately makes synonymous with "time") by *"thought* or *conception"* (p. 12; also pp. 9-11)—this component is not only left undefined and undiscussed in itself, but also is promptly dropped from the entire presentation (its only mention is on p. 12).

This peculiar failure is puzzling enough; the difficulties increase. Temporality is said to be the universal dimension of sensory experience, a point he spends several pages in stressing; but he also defines temporality by conception. His argument would thus seem to run: *if* all sensory data are essentially temporal, and what is temporal is in the sphere of conception, *therefore* sensory data are in the sphere of conception. Despite the necessity of this conclusion, however, just this he denies, for he asserts that sensory experience is *not* in the sphere of conception (p. 12). Hence, his argument necessitates a conclusion it also explicitly denies.

(2) Another difficulty is present in his treatment of time. He argues that the concept of time is the model of phenomenal time; the former is an extensive continuum, the latter "restricted to the period of the present" (p. 11). *All* concepts, however, are *essentially* "timeless" in themselves and have *no* "temporal reference or limitation" whatever (p. 9). But if the *concept* of time is to be isomorphic with *phenomenal* time (as it *must* be to function as a model), it cannot be essentially "timeless"—yet, to be a concept just that it must be.

Professor Hensel tries to get around this, apparently, by asserting that "the most general property of models is that they extend the limited time dimension of phenomena into a sphere in which time is unlimited" (p. 11). This, however, is either a plain *petitio principii* or a self-contradiction: the timelessness of the concept of time can no more "extend" phenomenal time unlimitedly than, say, the concept of change changes phenomenal change. A temporal *continuum,* limited or unlimited, is hardly the *timelessness* he attributes to concepts. Moreover, "purely phenomenal time" is said to be strictly a matter of the "now." The concept of time, on the other hand, is said to originate in the experience of similarity or of independent relations regarding two or more sensory data (p. 9). Such relations are themselves later asserted to be "purely phenomenal" (p. 14). Thus, the concept of time is said at once to be the *model* of phenomenal time, and to have its *origins* therein—and this, I submit, cannot be done on the terms of his own theory, which asserts the "autonomy" (p. 24) and the spontaneity (p. 4) of the sphere of models. On the other hand, as William James,

Husserl, Gurwitsch and others have definitively shown, not only is phenomenal time *not* merely a "now" or a series of "nows," but also no succession of "nows" nor comparison of "nows" can possibly yield the temporal continuum (succession) Professor Hensel equates with the concept of time: a succession of ideas is not the idea of succession, but rather presupposes it. Hence, the theory presupposes what it purports to account for.

(3) To a considerable extent, these difficulties seem to derive from a serious ambiguity in the central thesis: the isomorphism between conceptual and phenomenal structures. "Isomorphism" is a highly problematic notion: he speaks, in apparently equivalent terms, of "agreement" (p. 3), "adequacy" (pp. 4, 13), "congruence" (p. 5), "correspondence" (pp. 4, 17), of concepts as "pointing directly to" perceptions (p. 13), of "equivalence" between them (p. 23), and even of "uniting" or "combining" them "properly" (p. 24), where "properly" is left surprisingly unclarified. Additionally, he speaks of the two areas as having "certain structural characteristics in common" (p. 4), or sharing "formal" structures (p. 22)—and neither "structure" nor "formal" receive analysis or clarification. Beyond that, however, and beyond the obvious ambiguity introduced by such variation in terminology, at no point are we shown on what grounds the completely "autonomous" spheres of perception and concept (p. 24) could *in principle* have anything in "common."

It might be that, following Kant, Professor Hensel wants to say that *time* is the "common form"; and there are some reasons to suppose this. Time is the primal feature of perception; it is the "natural and universal criterion" for differentiating the two spheres (p. 11); and, it is defined as conception. Yet, even assuming this to be his intention, and leaving aside the difficulties already noted, the fact is that this will not do: inasmuch as concepts are essentially timeless, atemporal, with no connection or reference to time, the requisite isomorphism has been defined as impossible. Hence, the argument makes necessary what it explicitly denies as possible.

(4) Several final criticisms are in order, but can only be briefly noted.

(a) He claims that he has made use of phenomenological reduction, but in what he regards as a "stricter" form—viz., the so-called "analytical reduction" (p. 6). However, despite the quite excellent and correct reference to Peirce, it soon becomes quite clear that "analytic reduction" is hardly phenomenological; it is rather, I think, a form of what Kant called "abstractive isolation" (*K. d. r. V.*, A 20-22/B 34-37; B 145; A 131/B 170; and A 176/B 217-18). What Professor Hensel attempts to do is precisely to isolate each element of the whole of human knowledge, and then to study each abstractively, or separately. On the other hand, very much like Locke, Professor Hensel seems to regard any element which can be abstractively or conceptually isolated as really existent and independent in itself —a thesis most phenomenologists would rigorously deny. (Cf. pp. 8, 12) Like Kant, but quite unlike Husserl, he contends that his method leads to "pure experience" and "pure cognition" (p. 6). It becomes clear, however, that the real fruit of this analytic method is the *"immediate data,* pure sensory experience" (p. 7). "Uninterpreted data . . . [are] the final point" reached (p. 8). This "final point" he equivalently calls "phenomena," "sense data," "sensory experience," "the purely phenomenal," and the like.

But, first, "phenomenon" is most emphatically not synonymous, for Husserl or any other phenomenologist, with "sensory contents," "data," or whatever. To make this equivalence is to have missed the fundamental point. Not only are phenomenological reductions and epoché's not restricted, furthermore, to the region of sense experience, but such "data" are in no sense the "final point" of phenomenological study. Even when constitutive phenomenological explication is carried as far as possible, as Husserl showed in his "Time-lectures," what is disclosed is the richly articulated *Erlebnisström*—including not only what Husserl calls "hyletic data" (which cannot be identified with "sense data"), but also the functionally correlated kinaesthesias, and the impressional/retentional/protentional noetic components. Thus, whether or not his statements are ultimately correct (and we have tried to show some reasons for questioning this), it seems to me a serious mistake to interpret this theory as phenomenological, either in method or results (further criticism would of course be necessary to substantiate this more fully—a main thrust of which would be to show that Professor Hensel's contention that concepts are always and essentially "general and atemporal" and percepts "individual and temporal," is seriously in error; not only are some concepts historical, and others what Husserl calls "ideal individuals," but also the sphere of perception is a milieu of generality, as both Merleau-Ponty and Straus have said).

(b) A final general point. It is not clear whether we have been presented with a theory of *reality* (which is sometimes affirmed, pp. 1, 4-5, 24), or with a theory of *knowledge of* reality (which is also affirmed, pp. 1, 5, 17, 22). This ambiguity turns up in a quite significant place in his argument. Contending that "sense data" are unalterable, primal, independently existent and conceptually irreducible (pp. 3, 7, 8, 10, 12), a contention quite reminiscent of Hume, Professor Hensel *also* argues that what is primal, independent, etc., is sensory *experience of* data (pp. 1, 7, 12, 13, 22). Thus, he speaks equivalently of "qualities" and "experiencing of qualities," of "red" and the "experience of red," as primal and irreducible, and goes so far as to conclude (without substantiation, however) with the assertion that all such primal affairs are non-rational, i.e. *emotional* (p. 22).

These equivocations (sense data/sensory experience/ emotiveness, and reality/knowledge of reality) strike me as remarkably similar to those present in Locke's theory of ideas. Indeed, I would suggest, Professor Hensel's disclaimers notwithstanding, the fundamental tendency of his theory is toward traditional empiricism: his argument that the fundamental stratum is that of "one-digit" elements, and his notion of "multi-digital" elements, both run quite parallel to Locke's notions of simple and complex ideas; his understanding of time seems far closer to, say, Hume's, than to any phenomenologist's. Not only is this the case, however: despite his earlier denial that "reality" can be equated with "sense data" (p. 4), he later seems to argue, very much like Berkeley, that *precisely that equation is to be made*. Speaking of the *"reality* of a sensory experience," as distinguished from the truth of propositions (on the conceptual side), he explicitly states that by "reality" he means that "sensory experience is evidence of reality," while truth pertains solely to propositions (i.e., the relation between concepts and percepts is a truth-relation, while that between percepts and sense data is a reality-relation) (p. 15).

With his emphasis on the primal place of "immediate data," and especially of "one-digit" elements, consistently portrayed as non-general, particular, atomic and fundamental; his contention that "what is primordially given" is what is conceptually unanalyzable; his treatment of time as an extensive temporal continuum of "nows"; and the "reality" of "sense data"—not to mention the equivocations already noted—it is quite difficult to see why his theory is not, contrary to his own explicit statement, a new version of traditional empiricism. Although it is a theory deeply informed by Kant, even the conceptual elements tend to become submerged as the theory is developed.

GOLDEN COINS AND GOLDEN CURLS: LIVED AESTHETICS

Richard M. Griffith

BLIND HOMER, the first in written record to pluck the strings of language for the strains of poetry, tells us Circe, waylaying Odysseus but being won by him, loved but released him with words of tender warning of the dangers to his way:

> Square in your ship's path are Sirens, crying
> Beauty to bewitch men coasting by;
> Woe to the innocent who hears that sound!
>
> . . .
>
> The Sirens will sing his mind away
> On their sweet meadow lolling. There are bones
> Of dead men rotting in a pile beside them
> And flayed skins shrivel around the spot.

Two thousand years later, Heine set into the music of poetry the German myth:

> (. . . the sunbeam of evening on the brow of
> the mountain glows . . .)
>
> The fairest of maidens sitteth
> In wondrous radiance there,
> Her jewels of gold gleam brightly,
> She combeth her golden hair.
>
> With a golden comb she combeth it
> And sings so plaintively;
> O potent and strange are the accents
> Of that wild melody.
>
> And the boatman in yon frail vessel
> Stands spellbound by its might;
> He sees not the cliffs before him,
> He gazes alone on the heights.

Heine doesn't report the words the Lorelei sang; perhaps they were lost from the olden times from whence the tale came, perhaps the boatman was too far to catch more than the tune of the powerful melody. In which case the story is not complete: distinct from the music of an instrument, the song of a maiden's voice, however charming the mere sound, also conveys *words*, poeticized and *expres*sively articulated. But Odysseus, his oarsmen deafened, their ears plugged with honey-comb wax, himself strapped to the mast, heard the words of the Sirens, words irresistible in their import as the honeyed tones in their bewitching charm: "The song," they sing, "instructs the soul, and charms the ear . . . Approach! and learn new wisdom of the wise! . . . Oh stay, and learn new wisdom of the wise."[4] "We ken all things,"[5] they sing, and "have knowledge of all future happenings on earth."[6]

These ancient tales, alone, themselves—these tales of tantalizing tunes, which would themselves beguile us—would tell us, we suspect, "the wisdom of the wise" if we would stop to listen. But the wisdom of the wise we will have to do without in this, our present paper. We hope to get someplace and cannot afford to be diverted. The victims of the Sirens and the Rhine Lorelei were on a voyage with a definite port in mind. They were "on their way," on their life's way, but were caught—and wrecked —by that which was "by (beside) the way."[7] The sensual which was by-the-way to their serious intents and undertakings made them forget the business they were about, made them forget *themselves*, as it were, with results similar though more tragic than for the comic voyager of thought who, with his head turned up to the stars and thinking of lofty things, fell into the ditch beside his road. A goal in mind on a topic assigned to us, we have asked that we be bound to the mast, on the advice of *our* Circe who foretold the spell the sweet music of these two old tales would cast upon us; promising to reveal hidden links between innocence and sensuality, sensibility and sensuousness, sensing, knowing and being, deep secrets of mysteries of the I-World relationship and things epistemological and ontological; the sound of the sweet song of metaphysics' celestial music, our

Circe said, would seize us, and our bones would whiten on those
sands before we could be done.

Thus, our paper, concerned with everyday things, appeals not
to "the soul but to the ear." Both "greybeard and rower-boy,"
the Siren says, "goeth (away) more learned." She lies. Odysseus knows she lies. Standing knee-deep with the bones about
her (of psychologist-feign-philosopher) and the skin still flayed
upon them, she lies; her words lie, he knows that. Yet he strains
at his bonds and would gladly starve himself to death at her feet
to hear to his end the sweet tones of her melody.

Beauty can encapture us, these tales say, beauty can lure us
with forces more potent than all the facts we know; *fascination*
grips, they say, more tightly than do *facts;* before reason, and
even against all reason, through tone and in appearance, beauty
presents herself through our senses—*without Kant's judgment
interposed*. This is the first message of our myths, and the only
one with which we can concern ourselves this day.

"You go too far! and much too fast; restrain yourself," our
Circe says, "also before the face of beauty. 'Beauty is truth,
truth beauty' (Keats); 'The perception of beauty is a moral
test' (Thoreau); 'Beauty is as beauty does'; 'Where beauty is,
there will be love'; 'Beauty is the purgation of superfluities'
(Michelangelo) . . . you can't encompass beauty. Don't pre-
sume to challenge the poet and the artist any more than the
philosopher. Before you know it you will try to explain art—
come into the art gallery and the music hall from off the street
and path of the everyday which I warned you to stay on—and
move into transcendence. Leave these things to the speakers who
were imported for the event; let *them* live dangerously. Restrict
yourself to the direct experience of the sentient creature, man
and animal. Beauty can be cool. And we bide our distance from
it. Don't treat of the beauty of the Sirens' and Lorelei's voices,
but of the ineluctable charm of these sounds from out the world,
the *Allon,* which, floating to Odysseus over the waves and down
from the peaks to the boatman, ensnared them with bands as
strong as those which held Odysseus to the mast—pulled them,

enticed them, enchanted and enthralled them. What does this tell us of our lived-world experience?"

"But may we not begin," we ask, "with simple things and derive the sense of beauty from them, such as, let us say, a toenail. You know the paper on the foot, called *Anthropodology*, in which it is demonstrated that this marvelous human organ smells of the sweet fragrance of metaphysics. Why, space and time. . . ." "_____ _____ _____," our Circe breaks in. (What Circe says is censored.) "Very well," we say, "we will try to stay on the hinder side of beauty, and to write an ordinary paper."

In an uncontrolled and out-of-hand movement toward abstraction—a capacity marvelous in itself but perverse in its present application—science claims the senses feed bits of information into a computer-processing machine. From a world homogeneously neutralized, stimuli flow as bundles into a neuter brain. But these abstractions cannot touch experience; a relationship is in question and no relationship is possible between things neutral to each other. Senses belong to motile creatures who have to care for themselves. Senses are not organs of an abstract mind but of a living creature, and they serve him in his livelihood. He does not reach the world, nor the world reach him with his senses; he finds himself *in* the world *through* them. Sensory experience is not to be understood as events within a body but as opening up the world to a living creature in his bodily existence. The relationship would not be possible were he not both in op- and in in-position to the world. The hyphen in the I-World hyphenated combination symbolizes this quite well; it holds the creature and the world apart but also unites them with each other.

Everything arises within his world with implications, first of all, for his creature existence. Everything comes decorated with value: appetizing or repulsive, comforting or frightening, soothing or grating, pleasingly warm or cool or burning-hot or freezing-cold. Of all the varied "attributes" of the structures of the world their existential valences for the experiencing creature first and foremost dominate all others. They beckon or repel—as food and for mating, as friend or foe, as lullaby or thunderclap —, they stir longings or induce a shiver of foreboding. In the I-World, condition and situation blend across that hyphen; longings pre-condition belongings.

As the condition of the experiencing creature alters, the world is altered to him. The goblins don't pursue the child into his mother's arms. He finds it hard to remember the fright he had just then. At 3:00 o'clock Thanksgiving Day the turkey appears quite different than it did at 2:00, and a piece of mincemeat pie is not to be looked in the face. Relieved of a pressing business debt, Spring can come to a man, even though Winter is the season. All sensory experience revolves about a center: an ego, a creature in *his* condition. It is always personal at core. Even a brother's eating cannot sate one's hunger. No one can share a toothache.

"The world with its implications . . ."—the Latin for implications is involvements. Prior to any possible exercise of the power of abstraction the sensing creature is involved (wrapped up in), engaged (en-pledged), concerned (mixed with) and interested (*is* amongst, in midst of)—the sensing creature is *in* the game and is not yet spectator to it. (Later we will see that he will and could never be simply and entirely spectator to it.) Thus, sensory experience does not proceed from neutral abstractions onto which significations are then attached. No, the world must *first* be neutralized through active interplay. Concern precedes discern. Only when his business can be left to take care of itself is he relatively freed of tight involvements with the world about him. Only when things are no longer in-the-way is he liberated to attend to the by-the-way. Embarked on his course, his vital needs taken care of on-the-way, secured against, impedance on the path, and the dangers which might step into-the-way. Then can he devote himself to that which is by-the-way —the by-the-way which is the place of beauty.

Detachment rests in and on attachment (Detached from what?). Before the creature can be detached—a condition practically limited to man—he must first be firmly and comfortably settled through and in attachments. Securely situated, at home in his belonging, nestled around by his belongings—only in (note we don't say "from"), only in such a secured base can he disengage himself to make the movement to abstraction. This is the disengagement essential to science, mathematics and the arts. And only from such a re-instated, full-bodied sensory base can the bloom of aesthetics proper properly emerge. Without such a grounding in the rudimentary sensory experience aesthetics would be senseless.

"Stop!" our Circe cries. (We would prefer the tone to be a little sweeter.) "For a while your course was right and you were on your way more or less safely. But how could you speak of aesthetics like that?" "But," we interrupt, "you will remember the word is in our title." "Yes, but now you would only continue the rape and the travesty of such an honorable term. Your use of it goes in the face of all you've said, at least from an historical perspective. This is just what this conference is all about. Time was when the Greek 'aesthesiology' was the '-ology' of 'aisthesis,' when these words applied just to the type of full-bodied sensing (which is not a bad phrasing—by the way) as you have described it. Then sensing was stripped of all its flesh, and finally automatized. Knowing, objective knowing of logic and science, was elevated to a primary status and aesthetics was relegated to subaltern office. About 200 years ago "our Circe continues," the term 'aesthetics' was completely alienated from its original meaning. The circumstances of that alienation are characteristic of the dogmatism which has been forced upon sensory experience. The word 'aesthetics'—in the sense still given it by Kant in the *Critique of Pure Reason,* where he speaks of the 'transcendental aesthetics'—is no longer at our disposal. (Though, of course, I know that *you* will mention the 'aesthetic stage' of Kierkegaard. But then in his later work the *Critique of Judgment* Kant accepted the betrayal of the sovereignty and participated in the defamation of sensory experience. Baumgarten, in mid-eighteenth century, had made sensory experience out—in agreement with Descartes—to be a confused form of cognition. Aesthetics is then a *gnoseologia inferior;* as a theory of sensory cognition it is a logic of lower cognitive ability. Philosophical criticism, which first dealt only with the cognitive value and the validity of the sensations, has construed the content of sensory experience to suit its own needs and in so doing has estranged itself completely from everyday life experience. This is a paradoxical situation. For in all his performances —observing, testing, demonstrating, communicating—the scientist, himself, remains within the sphere of everyday experience. Science itself, to the degree that as human action it is rooted in everyday experience, presupposes the latter's validity. There are axioms of everyday life on which all intercourse of men with each other and with things is based. In them the essence of sensory experience is made known.[8]

"Going your own way you have brought in artistic production and appreciation; very well, if you must, though that introduces special problems; but please don't call these aesthetics. However I can only chart your course; you must travel it. Why don't you get on with your aesthesiology? Do be more careful with your terms. And inasmuch as you mention it, may I remind you of your title?" "Oh, the gold in our golden title!"

"Her jewels of gold gleam brightly,/ She combeth her golden hair./ With a golden comb she combeth it. . . ." To begin with, we switch here to the visual mode of presentation. Lorelei appeals visually, as well as through sound; her visual presentation fascinates as seductively as does her haunting melody. The sight grips the boatman and he cannot release his eye.

The senses engage in a corporate partnership; contributing differently in the orchestration of experience, they are in the dance together; united in the central enterprise, their donations drop into a common pot; experience is not monotonous (monotonus). We know these things if we do not close our ears to the very words we say: a sweet song, a mel-ody—but who can taste an ode?; a chilling sound—but sounds have no temperatures; a touching sight, a tasteful scene—but sights or scenes don't touch or taste; 'tis bitter cold, a harsh wind blows; a foul deed! methinks something stinks to heaven; "all the perfume of Arabia will not sweeten these little hands" (Lady Macbeth). Our senses dance a merry tune. And, more than that, our language tells us that we can never stop listening to that tune, that it is the beating heart of our corporeal existence; and that if the best of that tune stopped all else would quietly expire, including the airy inspirations of our arts and sciences.

Only a crass commercialist-scientist today, his vision blurred by dogmatic blinders, could rationalize that the gold of golden comb and golden hair of Lorelei captured the Rhine boatman because of an "associative linkage" to the greenbacks of money; his crime against fact would be as great as the crime against sensibilities by one who would mistake the golden curls of the maid in the street to suggest a price on her favors. The golden locks of Lorelei were different goods in a different coin than whatever the cargo the boatman transported in his hold. Gold is a treasure to be treasured even if it could not be spent. Its value followed late behind its primary value, its fundamental appeal in and of itself. Essentially, gold is useless, nonconsumable; yet our commerce is based upon it. The gold in our title is there as senator for our senses, to stand on the floor and speak to the point that the "commerce of our daily life" trades in the coin of sensory valences.

Golden fleece and golden apple, golden grain and golden age, golden anniversary and golden arm, the golden gates of Heaven where the streets are paved with gold . . . the metaphoric applications are so wide that in perfect good sense we could ask: "What is golden about gold?":

a) *rare*—it "stands out";

b) *pure*—it "stands alone" (resistant to tarnish, it maintains its integrity);

c) *imperishable*—it "stands," i.e., abides, lasts (placidly inert, it does not rust away nor mix with something which would absorb it);

d) *useless*—it stands nobly, bending its back to toil no more than does a king;

e) *lustrous*—gold wears a golden veil covering solid coin; lustre speaks in soft and muted voice without sibilance; [9]

---

[9] The "sound" of gold could be a topic to itself. If one recaptures from the Western movie the cheap, tinny, surface noise (it would be wrong to call it "ring") of the counterfeit coin the cowboy tests on the top of the

f) *radiant*—the sun brings out its character (Loreli: ". . . kissed by the sunbeam of even,/ the brow of the mountain glows./ The fairest maidens sitteth/ In wondrous radiance there. . . .) ;

g) *veritable*—its mark of truth upon the touchstone is more certain than signature or oath; it does not semble nor dissemble, imitations are easily caught in their lies.

But the problem of source and genesis is not central to our purpose, though we must add that something within us rejects the notion that gold charms us because it resembles feces. Our point is that the chemist's balance cannot distinguish gold from lead. Its charms which tug men around the world in perilous voyage, through the snows of the Klondike and across Californian Death Valley, the charms which sustained alchemists through futile centuries (chemistry attaining its necessary starting point when to some fatigued alchemist *Au* came to look as good as gold)—these charms are intrinsic to the relationship of sentience meeting substance across the hyphen of I-World. And the universality of that charm is the further point: when Cortez found the Aztecs he found gold already horded to be plundered. Gold is rich to humans because it is so richly human.

Gold leads us up to the borderland of artistic production and appreciation—to step inside would throw us into the mystery of a transcendental footing. Man sensed art in gold's charms, an art which could enhance and substantiate his art; he early prized it as material for his artistic creations, be they golden domes or golden bracelets, for decoration or beautification. And when gold was then poured and stamped for coin, that was done artistically. Let us approach that border of art and abstraction from another direction, returning to our few comments on the spectrum of the senses.

Touch, taste, smell and muscle sense are the most corporeal of the senses—though, again, that is a dangerous way of speaking;

---

bar, or of the dull "thunk" of lead, one appreciates the mellow secretiveness of the ring of gold, and, conversely, possesses fresh insight into the richness of silence and the silence of richness. Gold is not garrulous.

they are immediately in the business of the welfare of the body, including appetites and dangers. Hearing and seeing—the "distance" senses—subserve these functions, too; the eyes identifying and guiding, the ears directing sight and maintaining vigilance to the sides and to the back. Although the culinary "arts" and ancient body perfumes require a promissory footnote, in general it can be stated that the arts have only developed within the modes of the distance senses.

The corporeal senses are the ultimately intimate ones, witness the caress of the lover, the taste of soured milk, the prick of a thorn. The eyes and the ears may sit on the coach's bench, but the other senses are always on the field, absorbed bodily in the game. (However, for future reference; the coach is always "with" his players, is never "unconcerned.") Sound is more intimate than sight.[10] In the realm of overlap between the appetitive and appreciation, we find more latitude with sound than with sight; sight is habitually more "objective." Let us try to say what we mean. The arts are human. We know of no animal which appreciates the visual arts. In the *Merchant of Venice* (V,1) Shakespeare describes a herd of wild colts madly bounding, bellowing and neighing which is stopped short by the sound of music: "If they but hear perchance a trumpet sound,/or any air of music touch their ears,/You shall perceive them make a mutual stand,/ their savage eyes turn'd to modest gaze/By the sweet sound of music. . . ." Music (or any curious sound) can arrest the beast; perhaps with sufficient diligence the cavalry horse can be taught to keep in step to the beat of music on parade or the circus dog to conduct an orchestra with the beat of baton stuck in paw; but, though sounds may be sweet to an animal and pacifying, the one with an appreciation for music belongs in an other-worldly circus of the extra-extraordinary. Which is one way toward a few comments on music and man:

---

[10] Significantly, with both of these the greatest intimacy is reserved for the "reciprocal sensing:" to ex-press oneself in speech, to be looked *at*. And we can't go on without first noting that to be touched is more touching than to touch.

As with Shakespeare's colts music snares attention and makes pause. At the next stage music evokes participation, moves, excites, motivates. The foot taps, fingers drum, the body gently sways, leaps through space or jerks in frenetic Watusi. Some music translates powerfully into the language of the body. Sounds of music—the calling, the warning; the lullaby and the martial tune—charming, calming, stirring or "socially unifying" . . . sounds and the sounds of music set the tenor of the terms of my bodily residency. But in the same musical scene Shakespeare lets Jessica say: "I am never merry when I hear sweet music." With this listening—in pensive state, largely disembodied—the mystery of the artistic fully emerges and, with it, the problem of that which is by-the-way to bodily existence and yet which is central to the human enterprise.

Gold, the fascination being visual, vision being the most disembodied of the senses, left us close to this mystery. Art does not *attract,* is not appetitive. Distance is demanded. Alfie says, in the film of that name: "But then what does look pretty close up to it?" Appreciative viewing is a beholding, a process distinct from seeing, richer to the soul and less bodily.

Our Circe sits spellbound, or maybe turned to stone. We may as well drive on to our conclusion. "No, no . . ." Circe says distantly, "the time has come. . . ." "Just another sentence . . . and a dozen footnotes or so. . . ."

Beholding, man is held. He could never be totally embodied nor totally disembodied being always in synthesis. Kierkegaard says: ". . . when mediacy emerges it has that same instant annulled immediacy. The annulment of immediacy is therefore an immanent movement within immediacy, or it is an immanent movement in an opposite direction within mediacy." Now this means . . . that man can never be simply animal in his sex, nor totally freed of animality. Beholding is a viewing in interest of revelation and in revelation of interest. Beholding, man is never disinterested. . . .

"I fear I am," Circe says. "Why don't you finish with your paper? for you were, long ago, finished. We knew the ending to your paper before you were begun. And it is overdue. You may as well give it, the last stanza of the *Lorelei.*"

> Methinks the waves will swallow
> Both boat and boatman anon;
> And this with her sweet singing
> The Lorelei hath done.

COMMENTARY ON DR. GRIFFITH'S PAPER

Calvin O. Schrag

THE PECULIAR predicament of the messenger, Barnabas, in Franz Kafka's novel, *The Castle,* is that he is singularly uncertain about his function of helping Joseph K. arrive safely at the Castle. There is a sense in which the plight of Barnabas is also the plight of every commentator or discussant. I, too, am a bit uncertain concerning my function as a discussant of the aisthesiological odyssey of Dr. Griffith. Dr. Griffith is "on the way" toward an elucidation of lived aesthetics. My fear is that my commentary, like the Sirens of Greek mythology, may succeed only in entangling the sojourners who accompany Dr. Griffith with that which lies "beside the way," and thus puncture all possibilities of arriving safely in port. This indeed would produce an undesirable state of affairs, not only for Dr. Griffith, but for all of us. To have such a commentator would be about of the same value as having a messenger like Barnabas.

It will hardly do to summarize or paraphrase what Dr. Griffith has said with the intention of encapsuling the meaning or sense of his paper. This will hardly do for two reasons. In the first instance, it will not do for the meanings which Dr. Griffith is seeking to elucidate can never be encapsuled. The mode of expression is so interlaced with these meanings that any severance of the two could lead only to aisthesiological disappointment. In the second instance it will not do for what Dr. Griffith has said he has said very well—I would say exceedingly well— possibly in the only manner that it could be said. Had he said it differently he would have written another paper, as Flaubert would have written another *Madame Bovary,* or possibly no *Madame Bovary* at all, had he opted for another style and another grammar. So if those who are aisthesiologically disenfranchised persist in asking, "But what does it all mean?", Dr. Griffith has no other choice but to re-read his paper time and again with the hope that eventually the "penny will drop," the "ice will break," the "light will dawn."

Nor will it do to transpose what we have learned about golden coins and golden curls into a more metaphysical key. This assuredly would be to founder on a reef "beside the way" and lose the direction which would keep us "on the way." What is at issue is not metaphysical coins, nor metaphysical curls, nor metaphysical gold. Dr. Griffith's coins, like Kant's proverbial hundred dollars, have a status in sensory existence; his curls are curls that one can touch and which entice; his gold is a treasure that appeals by eliciting a visual fascination.

It is precisely this transposition of aisthesis into a metaphysical key that has shipwrecked and shattered the illfated aestheticist in his journey through the history of value theory. The modern phenomenological Circe could have fore-warned him. He would lose his cargo—the cargo of "full-bodied" aisthesis— or at best (which could turn out to be the worst), he would barter it for a mess of disembodied aesthetical pottage! That this indeed happened comes as no surprise to Dr. Griffith—for how could it have been otherwise? The bewitching beauty of the Sirens and the lustrous gold of Lorelei's hair were destined to be too much for these ill-stared wise men, and the salvage boats of existential phenomenology came too little and too late.

So let us take the advice of the modern sorceress to heart. Remain true to the earth—the earth of full-bodied corporeal senses—and be wary of those who speak to you of super-earthly beauty! (It would seem at times that our modern sorceress bespeaks the mind of Nietzsche's Zarathustra.) Remember the original gospel of aisthesis: *In the beginning was appetition!* This appetition became incarnate principally in the corporeal senses of touch, taste, and smell. Beware of the distant senses —particularly sight! Sight is a usurper. Sight objectifies. Sight is the most disembodied of the senses. Given a chance it will rise up, fraternize with the intellect, subordinate the corporeal sense, and relegate aisthesis to a lower chamber. This will all be done, mind you, in the interests of *truth*—the truth of art. But we have aisthesis so as not to die of truth. The truth of art, with its requirement for distance, disembodies the senses, loses the appetitive, and sacrifices fascination for appreciation. "Restrict yourself to the direct experience of the sentient creature," says our modern Circe. "Everything comes decorated with value: appetizing or repulsive, comforting or frightening, soothing or grating, pleasingly warm or cool or burning-hot or freezing-cold." Thus speaks the modern sorceress.

Until another Circe makes her appearance we do well to heed the advice of the current one. But this heeding must not keep us from listening for the voice of another—a voice which will warn us about the too easy separation between the appetitive and the appreciative, between the sensorial and the intellectual, between the concretely particular and the abstractly universal, between aisthesis and aesthetics itself. Maybe such a sorceress yet to come will be able to admonish us on how to appreciate the appetitive and have an appetite for appreciation. Maybe she will point out a path along which one can move with the passion of the senses and the reason of the intellect without sacrificing the one to the other—move, that is, with an impassioned reason and a rational passion. Maybe she will be less derogatory of logic and science, for they too issue forth from embodied logicians and embodied scientists. Maybe she will teach us how to find the universal in the concrete and the soul in the body. Maybe she will be able to save aesthetics from itself—its own worst enemy —and show that the blood of aisthesis still flows through its veins.

We are here of course speaking the language of wonder and waiting. But if such a sorceress should come we might do well to heed her too. She may whet our appetites for aspirations yet not aspired to. She may speak of unities undreamed of even by a Hegel. She may foretell of yet greener pastures—pastures in which the lion of aesthetics and the lamb of aisthesis lie down together and feed upon the same earth.

II. AISTHESIS DISTURBED

DE-ANIMATION: THE SENSE OF BECOMING PSYCHOTIC*

Waltraut J. Stein

One can also say, one learns what man is on the edge—the man who has reached the edge of being.

Martin Buber
Between Man and Man

Familiar diseased brain processes which are intelligible to us affect the psychic life as though someone had struck a clock-work with a hammer to disturb it chaotically. On the other hand, these processes [of schizophrenia] appear as though someone had modified the clockwork in a complicated way to make the clock run differently, unaccountably, so that we say it is running crazily.

Karl Jaspers
Strindberg und van Gogh
(my translation)

THE mystery of the schizophrenic mode of existence continues to fascinate investigators with many different orientations, hypotheses, and emphases. Even if it did not involve such deep human suffering and such waste of human resources, schizophrenia would offer a challenge to man's will to conquer the world intellectually. As a philosopher and somewhat of a psychologist, my interest is in finding a way to develop categories or concepts that will make these phenomena intellectually accessible so that we can say more than that the schizophrenic is functioning "crazily."

To do this, I propose to approach schizophrenia as a particular kind of feeling. This leaves open the question of whether it is a disturbance of the psyche or the soma, since feeling usually involves both. In fact, it may be that in attempting to determine the etiology of this disturbance, we need categories other than those of psyche and soma, since neither seems to be leading us to

* Published in *Psychiatry* 1967, 30:262-275; reprinted with permission.

fruitful insights. The psychosomatic approach, while giving
credence to both categories, nevertheless retains them. Perhaps
the following presentation will enable someone to see in what
direction such categories may lie. This paper makes no pretense
of having found them.

In this analysis the schizophrenic is considered as he who has
the sense of becoming psychotic, the feeling to be analyzed. By
"schizophrenics" I refer to people whom psychopathologists
diagnose as suffering from paranoid, hebephrenic, or catatonic
schizophrenia. Although the manic-depressive psychoses are
usually considered as a separate classification, sudden and extreme shifts of mood may appear in schizophrenia.[1] Shifts from
catatonic stupor to catatonic excitement also exhibit this kind of
change in affect. From examining detailed case studies of schizophrenics, I have come to the conclusion that the classification
into types of schizophrenia is in terms of the *predominant*
symptoms, rather than in terms of symptoms that appear *exclusively* in one form of schizophrenia or another. As long ago as
1935, Kurt Schneider said that there is not much point nowadays in dividing schizophrenia into types.[2] To give just one
example, the case of Renee which M. Sechehaye discusses in
Symbolic Realization is diagnosed as hebephrenic schizophrenia.
However, at various times in her illness Renee displayed unmis-
takeable paranoid symptoms when she talked about "the system"
and the voices. At other times she appeared as suffering from
catastupor or catatonic excitement. Furthermore, diagnosticians
are generally agreed that as schizophrenia progresses it becomes
increasingly difficult to maintain these classifications into types
and a common symptomatology appears. Arieti has described
these last stages particularly well in his *Interpretation of Schizophrenia.*

---

[1] Arthur Burton (ed.), *Psychotherapy of the Psychoses.* Donald L.
Burnham, "Autonomy and Activity-Passivity in the Psychotherapy of a
Schizophrenic Man." (New York: Basic Books, Inc., 1961), p. 216.

[2] Kurt Schneider, *Clinical Psychopathology.* Trans. by M. W. Hamil-
ton, (New York: Gurne and Stratton, Inc., 1959), p. 91. First Edition
in 1935.

If it is true that the classification of schizophrenia into types is in terms of predominant symptomatology, then it is not unjustified to suppose that we have here instances of the same disturbance whose principal form of appearance or expression varies. While it is interesting and probably useful for therapeutic purposes to note this variety in the forms of schizophrenia, we must first of all attempt to determine what is being expressed or appearing. It seems to me that this is a feeling, and I would like to describe what it is.

My thesis is that whatever the person's predominant schizophrenic symptoms, his appearance can be understood as the expression of this basic feeling. I shall cite the writings of psychopathologists working in a variety of orientations and patients themselves whose illness has been diagnosed as one of the schizophrenias in order to substantiate the analysis.

Let us begin by considering the familiar notions of "being out of contact with the world" and "living in a world of one's own" which express not only the way the schizophrenic appears to others, but also how he feels. What does it mean to feel oneself losing contact with the world and withdrawing into a world of one's own? To understand this, we must distinguish between *the* world and *my* world, while retaining the frame of reference of the life world, the world as experienced by a living person in a situation.

In the most general terms, we might define the human world as the totality of what man apprehends or of what impinges upon him in any way. To be in the world as a person who lives through his relation to it is to have a sense of being bound to the not-self, i.e., to have a sense of possession of it so that it is *my* world as well as *the* world. However, a person does not feel himself in possession of all that impinges upon him. He recognizes that some of *the* world is not *his,* and he desires to make more of it his.

Let us examine further this sense of possession I have of my world in contrast with the possession of my self. (The "I" in this discussion is, of course, to be taken as a generalized "I".) I express this sense of the possession of my world by saying that

I feel I belong to it and it belongs to me. I have a sense of intimacy with it. In ordinary language, I say I feel "close" to other people, that I "participate" in human concerns or in the world's activities. As I understand it, this is the central subjective sense of Heidegger's concept of being-in-the-world. On the basis of such a sense of possession, I use the expressions *my* family, *my* occupation, *my* home, *my* country, or *my* religion.

This possession I have of my world is a shared possession in the sense that whatever I possess of the world others can or do possess, too. While it is true that I possess some things alone, such as my clothing, and legally I must give my consent to the transfer of this possession, it is also possible for someone else to take possession of these things without my consent. He may, for instance, rob me of my clothing or take possession of it at my death. My consent is not *necessary* for someone else to possess it, too, or to take my possession from me. On the other hand, both my brother and I possess my father. This is a shared possession that does not originally depend on the consent of either of us, and only under unusual circumstances do I desire to dispossess myself of him who shares this possession. This sense of mutual possession of the world which does not depend on our consent, but which we nevertheless embrace, can be seen as what binds us together into a society. For instance, many of us participate in the sense of possession of America as *our* country. Because we share this sense of possession, we *belong* to the group of people called Americans.

Now, besides this sense of shared possession of my world, I also have the sense of possession of myself, which possession I may or may not share with others. No one else does or can possess me completely as I possess myself.[3] By self I mean here my feelings, my ideas, and my body as I experience it from the inside. Even though I communicate or share my feelings, my ideas, and my lived body with others, there is still always a sense

---

[3] No one ever knows another person entirely. We do not become completely transparent to one another. Nietzsche speaks of the unteachable core of unique individuality that remains in everyone. I can only appeal to the reader to see that this is so.

in which I retain a possession of this self that others do not have. This is the sense in which I say that another cannot "read my thoughts," for instance, though he can share them with me if I choose to communicate them to him. The same is true of my feelings. Another can only understand what I am feeling insofar as I choose to reveal this. If I find that I can no longer control the expression of my feeling and express it involuntarily (which indicates that I no longer control the feeling itself), then in a very significant sense I no longer have possession of it. It appears to have possession of me or to be possessed by him who understands my involuntary expression. In this way it is possible for my feeling to take its place among things in the world which I either do not possess at all or the possession of which I share without my consent. It no longer belongs to me as my thoughts do. It is no longer a part of myself and may or may not be a part of my world. Of course, as long as I experience it at all it is a part of *the* world.[4]

It is also true that, insofar as I experience my body as a part of myself, I have controlled possession of it. I can put it at the disposal of another (as in sexual relations), but I can also keep it to myself. It is not public originally or essentially. But, again, my possession of my body can take its place among other things in the world. For instance, a physician can take it over in an operation. At such a time I have no sense of possession of it at all. If someone forces me to do something with it that I do not consent to do, then he at least shares in the possession of it as much as I do. In this case, another can and does possess it, too, without my consent. Just as in the case of feeling, then, my body can cease to be a part of myself.

---

[4] While I do not want to deny that there may be such things as unconscious feelings, it seems to me that their epistemological status is very close to that of Kant's *Ding an sich*. An unfelt feeling is a contradiction in terms just as an unknowable thing is. Both may have causal efficacy, in fact, be required *because* of their causal efficacy, but such a requirement points to a limit of what the analysis can illuminate, rather than to the fact that there actually are such things. In any case, an unfelt feeling would be entirely foreign to the experienced self, which is what is under discussion here.

We may conclude, then, that when I have the sense of possession of myself, in contrast with the sense of possession of my
world, my consent is essential to sharing it with another. Thus it
becomes clear how *we* do not possess *my* self together as *we*
possess *our* father. It is further the case that this self always
remains mine alone in some respects and that I never share it all
with someone else.[5]

We have been making the distinction here between *my* world
and *the* world in terms of the sense of possession. Some of the
world I recognize as foreign to me and would like to make mine.
For instance, I may want to make a stranger I meet into my
friend. On the other hand, most of this world that I do not
possess belongs to another, and it quite frequently happens that
I have no particular desire to make it mine, such as the world of
the astronaut. Now, I think that it is also possible to make a
distinction between *a* self and *my* self in terms of the sense of
possession. No doubt it is I who possess myself in the particular
way we have described. This "I" that possesses can in turn be
possessed by another "I" but need not be. It can remain simply
an "I" that possesses *my* self. By this I mean that I can
recognize my thoughts, my feelings, and my body as my own
and then turn and recognize myself as the possessor of these
feelings. But I need not do so, and I do not frequently do so.
The possessing "I", like the reflecting or knowing "I", has the
possibility of an infinite turning back on itself. But it need not,
and actually *cannot completely,* realize this possibility because it
is an infinite possibility.

There exist, then, both a world not possessed by me and an
"I" that I do not possess. As we go through life, we usually feel
that we are increasing our possession of the world and "getting
a firmer grip" on ourselves. Further, we feel comfortable and
secure in our existence. But it may happen that there comes a
time when we feel that we are not making this kind of progress.
Then we say that we have "lost our grip" on things or somehow
"lost our touch." What we do no longer seems to be as effective

---

[5] Cf. footnote 3 above.

in realizing our desires and increasing our possession of the world as it used to be. As we realize this, we may perhaps stop, reflect, and, first of all, ask ourselves, "Why have I lost my touch?" and then, "Why do I want to do this at all?" It may be that we do not find a really satisfactory answer to either question.

If these questions become of increasing concern to us, we may begin to feel that, not only are we not making progress in gaining the possession we desire, but also we are actually losing the possession we thought we had. As we realize that we are no longer effectively participating in the world's activities and that these activities and this world is losing the meaning it used to have for us, we may feel that it is slipping out from under us and becoming alien or foreign to us. This is the beginning of what it means to feel that one is losing contact with the world. To lose contact is to lose the secure sense of possession of some of *the* world as *mine,* which means not to feel *close* to it any longer, to feel oneself less and less in living relation to it.

This sense of the foreignness of the world appears very clearly in Heidegger's utterance, "Why is there anything at all, rather than nothing?" This question cannot arise unless one feels that there is a gulf between himself and things. Otherwise things are always there to be used, molded, considered, taken possession of, or even to be left alone. In the ennui of Sartre we can see how this sense of the loss of possession causes dread as it spreads to include more and more of one's existence. Boredom comes over Antoine Roquentin, the hero of *Nausea.* Nothing matters in one sense, but in another sense his existence itself is at stake. For if nothing at all matters any more, life does not matter, either, and there is no reason not to commit suicide. What he still desires and must get is *things to matter* or he will kill himself. For this reason his boredom is so oppressive. The world appears strange to him because he cannot get through to it and make it matter. All his activity is ineffectual in accomplishing this. He can no longer find or put any sense in it and so feels he has lost his possession of it, any living contact with it.

This is the beginning of what it means to feel psychotic, and we can now turn to an examination of the particular way in which the schizophrenic feels. He may realize that he no longer understands the world, just as he does not understand a foreign language, though he may be able to identify some of the words. The sounds are audible enough; he can hear all right. But the sounds *no longer make sense to him*. They do not seem to fit into any intelligible context. He feels that this world that is slipping away from him is quite literally becoming more and more distant. It is no longer "close" to him. Thus the voices that speak the foreign language come to him as someone calling softly from a distance or as echoing from the older side of a canyon. In this way *my* world appears strange and foreign to me and I am no longer comfortable in it, just as I would not be in the world of the astronaut or even in the world of the ant. I use this latter analogy to show that the foreignness is more than just the foreignness of my *human* world. Renee in *The Autobiography of a Schizophrenic Girl* expresses this sense of losing contact so well that I would like to quote her here:

> One day, while I was in the principal's office, suddenly the room became enormous, illuminated by a dreadful electric light that cast false shadows. Everything was exact, smooth, artificial, extremely tense; the chairs and tables seemed models placed here and there. Pupils and teachers were puppets revolving without cause, without objective. I recognized nothing, nobody. It was as though reality, attenuated, had slipped away from all these things and these people. Profound dread overwhelmed me, and as though lost, I looked around desperately for help. I heard people talking, but I could not grasp the meaning of the words.[6]

With the sense of the loss of the world, there also arises the sense of the loss of oneself. Let us see if we can understand this latter feeling. As I who feel myself becoming psychotic lose more and more contact with the world, I also lose more and

---

[6] Quoted by Walter C. Alvarez, *Minds that Came Back*, (Philadelphia: J. P. Lippincott Company, 1961), p. 99. Original Source: M. Sechehaye, *Autobiography of a Schizophrenic Girl.* (New York: Grune and Stratton, 1951).

more of my grip on myself. I feel unable to do anything with myself, to control it, because there is a gulf between me and it. It appears as though *my* self is becoming simply *a* self, just another thing in the world as distant and as meaningless as the other things in it. Again, Sartre points to this phenomenon when he says that the self or ego is an object in the world and the subject is completely empty or negative (*The Transcendence of the Ego*). In normal experience, it seems to me, this is simply not the case. The relation between me and myself is different from the relation between me and everything else I encounter, as I have just tried to show. However, this notion of the transcendence of the ego describes beautifully, I believe, the psychotic's sense of the loss of himself and his feeling of emptiness. For instance, the sounds the schizophrenic hears are echoing in a canyon far away from him and at the same time in an ear that is also far away, that he does not *feel* as his at all. If he puts his hands over his ears to hush the sound, it may not stop, but continue to echo. This further indicates that there is something very strange going on. The sound is perhaps in the ear that is not his rather than in the canyon. It is very difficult for him to locate it at all. Nothing makes the sense it used to. Two quotations from a patient express what I have been trying to describe:

> For now I hear myself speak as if someone else were doing so. . . . The outer world is no longer self evident. I am even a stranger to myself.[7]

The schizophrenic recognizes this lack of possession of himself particularly clearly when he feels that his lived body is no longer his at all but a thing that occurs at a distance from him. It appears to him that the sensation of moving his arm *occurs*, though it is not he who feels it. Binswanger has examined this sense of the foreignness of the lived body in his articles on

---

[7] Jakob Wyrsch, "Über den Zustand des Bewusstseins bei Schizophrenen," *Weiner Zeitschrift für Nervenheilkunde*, 14 (1957), p. 132, my translation.

psychotherapy,[8] and Merleau-Ponty uses Binswanger's analyses to come to a general understanding of what it means to live in one's body.[9]

Should such a loss of possession become complete, to all intents and purposes the person is dead and only the world remains. The schizophrenic appears as a person who is suffering this loss, living through the process of losing possession of himself and of his world. From time to time he glimpses the complete loss or death toward which he is moving, but it does not actually overtake him until he at last resigns himself to it. Even this is seldom a final resignation. As long as he continues to breathe, his spirit from time to time again takes up the fight to regain possession of what he has lost, but with continually decreasing effectiveness. This means that probably every schizophrenic retains some sense of a self and world that he possesses. For this reason I shall continue to use the personal pronouns in attempting to describe the schizophrenic's experience, while I keep in mind that the possession to which they refer is a possession that is decreasing, rather than increasing, as in ordinary experience.

Now let us consider a little more closely what this sense of the loss of possession means in the realm of feeling. If my self has become a thing or person in the world that is not mine, along with other things that are not mine, then feelings will not occur as *my* feelings. Their origin, in the sense of what arouses them, can still be anything at all, but now they no longer overflow me as feeler and color the world. This structure becomes blurred so that I cannot tell whether they arise in me, in another person, or even perhaps from things. And they "color" everything indiscriminately, including me as feeler. This means that I am unable to distinguish whether the feeling arises in me or is coloring me and arising elsewhere. Feeling *occurs* and does not seem to be rooted or anchored anywhere, so that I literally feel confused

---

[8] Ludwig Binswanger, "Über Pschotherapie," *Der Nervenarzt,* 8 (1935), pp. 113 and 180 ff.

[9] Maurice Merleau-Ponty, *Phenomenology of Perception.* Trans. by Colin Smith. (New York: The Humanities Press, 1962), p. 160 ff.

because the structure itself has dissolved. This phenomenon has been referred to by Freudians as the loss of ego boundaries, and the literature on psychopathology is replete with reports of this kind of experience.[10] Patients confuse themselves with their therapists or with machines; they seem to have no sense of property even to the point of "owning" their bodies.

But there is another phenomenon here that seems at first to contradict this blurred structure of feeling, but later appears as dependent on it. This phenomenon is central to the understanding of what it means to feel psychotic and has been implicit in our discussion all along. The schizophrenic first has, we have noted, a sense of powerlessness to act effectively and then a sense of powerlessness to control the slipping away of the world. This is what it means to feel that one is losing possession. Now the sense of powerlessness before a process that is going on implies that the power or control resides elsewhere. Though his feeling involves great energy and he feels compelled to do something about it, as I shall show, he seems to have no power to control it. Someone or something else is exercising this control to the end of his destruction! He does not know who or what this other is, but he feels it as foreign, opposed to him, understanding him so well that it can control him in a fashion to destroy him. Though the power remains always invisible to the schizophrenic,[11] we may call it the power of "de-animation" that is taking from him his humanity and attempting to turn him into a thing that does not possess its world or its self at all. The schizophrenic has the sense that this power is actively engaged in dispossessing him of himself and of his world. This feeling may be called the sense of "being dispossessed." As soon as he begins to become aware that his actions are losing their effec-

---

[10] A particularly good description appears in the article by Otto Will entitled "The Schizophrenic Reaction and the Interpersonal Field" in *Chronic Schizophrenia*. ed. L. Appleby et. al. (Glencoe, Ill.: The Free Press, 1960), p. 218 ff.

[11] Jaspers quotes Strindberg in *Strindberg und van Gogh* (Bremen: Johs. Storm Verlag, 1949) as follows: "Someone or other has permitted me to get into this condition! Where is he so that I can fight him?" p. 57. my translation.

tiveness and that the meaning of the world is slipping away, he also begins to feel that his self is actively being taken from him and that someone or something is actively robbing him of his world.

This means that the sense of the loss of contact not only involves a feeling of distance, but also simultaneously a smothering sense of closeness.[12] What is dispossessing me as schizophrenic is so close to me that it is drowning me or I am drowning in it. I feel an intimacy with what is at a distance and as though I am being invaded by what is foreign. Since "it" is close to me, I must also be close to "it" ("I" now a more or less dispossessed "I"). Even though I do not understand its power, I see this power expressed in feelings directed toward me. These feelings appear in a peculiarly transparent way. I have no trouble identifying them. Just as I feel myself transparent to the other, the other becomes transparent to me. This is probably related to the loss of ego boundaries so that where the feeling arises is blurred. But however I identify the feeling, it always appears as threatening, and I feel powerless to control it and that another controls it. The stronger the feeling is, the more threatening it appears. Also positive feelings, such as love and concern, appear as more threatening than negative ones. Precisely why this is so requires a lengthy analysis that cannot be undertaken here.

Now we can see how the experience of being out of contact with the world at the same time involves a closeness to it that goes beyond the closeness of everyday existence. It is a closeness of the other's feeling, which feeling the schizophrenic identifies very properly, and often with remarkable sensitivity. But its intention is construed as threatening no matter what the feeling is. This sense of intimacy is quite different from the sense of being subject to the world or of being immersed in it that he used to have. Then he felt *cradled* in it. The world, to be sure,

---

[12] Cf. Alfred Storch, "Beitrage zum Verstandnis des schizophrenen Wahnkranken," *Der Nervenarzt,* 30 (1959), p. 50. The author notes the inability of the schizophrenic to gain a distance from what is overwhelming him.

always to some extent resisted his efforts to do what he wanted. But now it seems to have taken from him the possibility of realizing his desires at all; not only is the world resisting him, it has *abandoned* him, and he has no choice but to fight against this sense that he is losing his power to deal with it.

When this sense of being dispossessed overtakes me as schizophrenic, I do not possess this feeling or feel it as mine. Rather, I *become* it to the exclusion of being or having anything else. Dispossession is *I*, but it is not a personal "I"; rather, it is a foreign "it." I, de-animated, become an "it" that is possessed and is constituted solely by this possession or dispossession. To put it in terms of the unpossessed possessing "I" we indicated above, we can say that this "I" is now possessed by what is foreign to it and loses its possessions, i.e., its self and its world. As it was previously only the "I" possessing, it is now only the "I" possessed. (Once more we must note that this is the end state and that the sense of becoming psychotic is the sense of moving in such a direction. The schizophrenic does not feel completely dispossessed but as though he is *being* dispossessed.)

I as schizophrenic can feel that I am being dispossessed of myself when meeting the gaze of another. Again, Sartre notes this and psychopathologists have recognized his analysis of the look as significant for understanding paranoid phenomena. A case in point is the article by C. Kulenkampff entitled "Erblicken and Erblickt-werden."[13] I can also feel that others are taking over my thoughts or my feelings, that they have invaded what previously was mine to share only with my consent. John M. Shlien reports, for instance:

> He (the patient) plunged into a description of the "machine on his brain." He thought "on," and it went on, broadcasting his thoughts over radio and television; he thought "off" and the broadcast stopped, but his thoughts continued to repeat in his brain.[14]

[13] C. Kulenkampff, *Der Nervenarzt,* 27 (1956), p. 2. There is also a comment on this article by J. Zutt on p. 183 of the same volume.

[14] John M. Shlien, "A Client-Centered Approach to Schizophrenia: First Approximation." *Psychotherapy of the Psychoses,* p. 310.

These "others" are very often indefinite precisely because the schizophrenic cannot identify the force invading him. Strindberg reported:

> A calming feeling steals over my body: I realize that I am the victim of an electrical storm which is going on between the two neighboring rooms. The tension grows. . . . They are killing me.[15]

Finally, he may feel invaded or threatened when he tastes his food. It may "taste" poisoned. He may also have the experience that "others" are attempting to use him against his will in a plot to destroy the world, which world is now no longer clearly distinguishable from himself.

These are, of course, paranoid symptoms. They have always been of particular interest to observers of psychopathic phenomena because they appear to point to a para-psychic realm beyond any conceivable experience of the normal psyche. Ordinary people do not hear voices, see visions, believe that someone else is reading their thoughts, or that something is making them act against their will. Because of this, primitives have often concluded that the schizophrenic must be either a demon or a god.

It seems to me that we can gain some understanding of these phenomena in terms of the analysis we have been making. We have said that, because the schizophrenic is losing his sense of possession of himself and of the world, he can no longer make a clear distinction between them. This means that he does not clearly distinguish between himself and others, either. Ideas occur; feelings occur; sensations occur; voices occur. The schizophrenic at first asks himself, "Are they real? Are they things in the world that I share with others?" But how can this question be answered when everything is becoming strange and unreal and the world that he used to share with others is so distant![16]

---

[15] *Strinberg und van Gogh,* p. 62. my translation.

[16] "It is the public, objective character of the visible and audible that makes communication possible; whereas for the hallucinary the border separating mine-ness from other-ness has shifted, and he has lost the

Perhaps they are real; perhaps they are not. As his sense of being actively dispossessed increases and the distinction between himself and the world becomes more and more blurred, the sense of being dispossessed tends to pervade him entirely and to become the *only* reality. Everything that has any power appears to have the force of the de-animation that is invading him. This is the same kind of phenomenon that occurs in deep mourning where the mourner continues to hear the voice of his beloved and to see his face everywhere. Sometimes he "recognizes" his beloved's voice when other people are speaking, but he may hear him when he is all alone, too. Many strangers he encounters look like his beloved, though he probably does not see his beloved's face when he is alone. In other words, his beloved continues to be present. He who is overcome by grief at the loss of his beloved cannot "think" of anything else.

The same kind of thing is true in the case of schizophrenia where the person is overcome by the feeling of being threatened with the loss of his existence. Add to this the confusion over ego boundaries and it is no wonder that he sees this power everywhere and is convinced that what is occurring is *real*. He finds he cannot deny the evidence of his own strong feeling. Something or someone is indeed present as threatening, whether others acknowledge this or not.

A number of excellent studies of paranoia have now appeared in the context of phenomenology and existentialism. Some of these attempt to account for the preponderance of aural paranoid phenomena over visual ones, for instance.[17] These investigations have set paranoid phenomena in a non-naturalistic context where they do not appear nearly as utterly foreign to ordinary experience.

Commonly Visible and audible." E. W. Straus in *Congress Report,* IInd International Congress for Psychiatry, vol. IV. (Zurich: Orell Fussli Arts Graphiques S. A., 1957), p. 451.

[17] E. W. Straus, *The Primary World of Senses.* trans. by Jacob Needleman. (New York: The Free Press of Glencoe, 1963).

E. W. Straus, "Ansthesiology and Hallucinations," in *Existence,* ed. Rollo May, *et. al.* (New York: Basic Books, Inc., 1958).

J. Zutt, "Blick und Stimme," *Der Nervenarzt,* 28 (1957), p. 350.

Here, then, we gain some sense of how it feels to be drowning in the world. The schizophrenic feels that someone or something is drowning him and he struggles desperately to "catch his breath." He does not distinguish invasion by the forces of de-animation from invasion by death so that he is sure that he is dying. And in a very real sense he is indeed dying, as he feels less and less like a person. This sense of dying can come upon him slowly or suddenly. In either case, panic is possible at any time, should he catch a glimpse of complete dispossession, of death. Then he feels totally disorganized and runs "every which way." He knows that his behavior is "crazy," and he no longer doubts that he is indeed "crazy."

This panic eventually subsides, and sometimes with it the sense of being dispossessed. If it does, the schizophrenic is at least temporarily returned to greater possession of himself and of his world. Jaspers reports how this happened to Strindberg:

> With pen in hand and sitting at the table, I fell over: An attack of fever laid me out flat. Since I had not been seriously ill for fifteen years, I was frightened by this attack, which came so inconveniently. . . . The fever shook me as one shakes a feather bed, grabbed me by the throat in order to strangle me, set its knee on my chest, so heated my head that my eyes seemed to step out of their sockets. I was alone with death in my garret. . . . But I did not want to die! I resisted, and the battle was stubborn. My nerves became weak; my blood throbbed in my veins. My brain wriggled like a polyp thrown into vinegar. Suddenly, I became convinced that I was going to succumb to this dance of death. I let go, fell over backwards, and gave myself up to the horrible embrace of the monster. Immediately an unspeakable calm seized my being, a pleasant sleepiness fell over my limbs, a complete peace encompassed my soul and body. . . . With what fervour did I wish that it were death! Gradually, I lost the will to live. I stopped trying, feeling, thinking, I lost consciousness.

Jaspers says that the next day on awakening, Strindberg was entirely well and wrote:

> I felt as though I had not really slept at all for the last ten years, so rested and fresh did my over-worked head feel. My

thoughts, which had previously raged about unruled, now collected themselves like ordered, classified, powerful troops.[18]

It is also possible for the panic to subside while the sense of being dispossessed remains. The schizophrenic then may have the sense of "waking up" into a curious "world of his own" very unlike the world he used to possess. Again, Strindberg says:

> Having fallen out with humanity, I am reborn into another world into which no one can follow me. Unspeakable events attract my attention.[19]

We have already given some indication of what this might mean, but let us now see if we can indicate the new sense of possession that arises. Since this is most clear in the case of the schizophrenic's relations to others, I would like to analyze it in terms of them.

The schizophrenic's relations to others involve both a particular lucidity and a particular opaqueness. The lucidity is this: He is convinced that another can know or identify his feelings and control them better than he can himself. For instance, he may realize that another recognizes that he is in a rage before he himself does. Furthermore, the other is able to restrain him physically, i.e., to control him, when he cannot control himself. This situation makes him feel dispossessed of his feelings. He, in turn, is so sensitive to what another is feeling that he can usually detect the underlying disinterest or hostility in an apparently sincere expression of concern. Because of this sense of mutual lucidity, the schizophrenic feels that he can empathize with another and another with him to the point where they can *absorb* one another's feelings. This structure, which I believe arises out of the loss of ego boundaries, plays an important role in the symbiosis that can develop.

At the same time that the schizophrenic has this sense of mutual lucidity, he also has a sense of real opaqueness. For some

---

[18] *Strindberg und van Gogh,* pp. 34-35. my translation.
[19] *Ibid.,* p. 58. my translation.

reason he finds himself unable to "get through" to the other, even though he understands his feelings. This is parallel to what happens in the case of language. We have already noted that the schizophrenic finds the other's words clear enough, but they do not seem to fit into any intelligible context, to make any sense. He feels that this is not only true of what the other is saying to him but that the other apprehends him just as unintelligibly. He feels that the intention or sense of his own feeling is being misunderstood. While the other may appear to him to have more control of his feelings than he himself has, it also seems to the schizophrenic that the other has not the vaguest notion what they mean to him. Another does not understand at all what can be putting him into such a rage, and the schizophrenic finds himself unable to explain to the other how it is that he feels he is dying. He cannot do this because the answer to the question of how it is that he feels this way is just as opaque to himself as it is to the other. He feels confused and cannot understand his own feelings any more than the other can. Yet he does know that he feels he is dying, but finds that simply communicating this does not make it possible for the other to understand how he feels.

Neither can the schizophrenic grasp the intention of the other's feeling. No matter what the other's feeling is, its intention appears as threatening because the schizophrenic is overcome by the sense of being dispossessed. He has no idea why another should be threatening him, and he finds himself unable to "get through to him" to ask him why. This is so because the other denies he is threatening. Thus we see how communication between a schizophrenic and another does not go beyond the identification of one another's feelings.

Now we can also see why the schizophrenic has the sense that he is in a world of his own. A binding human relation requires more than empathy or the grasping of another's feeling. It requires the giving and receiving of emotional support or at least taking feelings from another that he does not want to give (hostility). The support which the schizophrenic desires would require, first of all, an understanding of the sense of dying and then help in his struggle to overcome this. The schizophrenic cannot accept such support because he is not convinced that another understands that he is dying. Furthermore, the other always appears as the instrument of what is making him feel that he is dying. All proffered support appears as threat. The schizophrenic cannot support the other in his feeling as he understands it because this would mean that he actively partici- pate in his own destruction. There is, thus, no positive sense of being bound.

There is a negative sense of being the object of aggressive hostility and the schizophrenic takes defensive action against this. But this relation, while truly felt as present, is based on the misinterpretation of the other's intention so that he who acts to ward off this threat as he would against actual hostility, finds his action ineffective and feels that there is a unilateral gulf between him and what is threatening him. He cannot make contact with it, though it is making contact with him.

Here we see, then, that the schizophrenic is unable to share his feelings so that he may feel that he *belongs* to another or to a group, except in the very oppressive sense of being smothered or drowned by another. The world in which he finds himself is *his alone,* as a world pervaded by the threat of destruction.[20] Let us consider for a moment how it feels to exist alone in this way or what kind of a structure such a "world of one's own" can have. It may best be characterized as a waking dream world with a loose, unstable structure that is hardly a structure at all. I as schizophrenic find myself existing in a strange new way very close to the power of deanimation which can invade me again at any instant. This unstable structure of my new world appears through the labile structure of my feelings. One moment I feel wildly ecstatic; the next moment in deepest despair. One mo- ment I feel I can conquer the world; the next moment I cannot even control myself. My feelings also change very rapidly in relation to a particular person or thing and move from one object to another as if they were slippery. I cannot be sure of them at all. They have run away from me. There is one thing that I now know I cannot control. This is my sense of being

---

[20] *Ibid.*

dispossessed, of existing in this strange new way that I most certainly do not desire. Because I have lost the distinction between myself and my world, everything "runs together," is mixed up, blurred, as though someone has placed a water color painting in water. The pattern of my existence is lost, and I find myself unable to make myself really at home anywhere.

It is as though I am watching the drama of a dream being played out on a stage. I do not give my consent to it, but my consent seems to be irrelevant anyhow, just as I do not consent to my dreams, but only to falling asleep.

This is the structure of the phenomenon of autism. The psychotic finds himself withdrawn from the everyday world into a very peculiar world of his own that seems to be taking possession of him. It is conceivable that this world may take on a more set structure as he continues to exist in it, and possibly may even in some ways again become a world he possesses. We can see evidence for this kind of congealing in the systematized delusions of some paranoids. But he never feels really at home or comfortable in this world of his own, and its structure is not the firm, secure structure of the world he used to know. The threat of de-animation continues to be very close.

Jaspers cites this poem by Hölderlin, which expresses the feelings of a schizophrenic whose panic has subsided:

> Mit gelben Birnen hänget
> Und voll mit wilden Rosen
> Das Land in den See
> Ihr holden Schwäne,
> Und trunken von Küssen
> Tunkt ihr das Haupt
> Ins heilignüchterne Wasser.
>
> Weh mir, wo nehm ich, wenn
> Es Winter ist, die Blumen, und wo
> Den Sonnenschein
> Und Schatten der Erde?
> Die Mauern Stehen
> Sprachlos und kalt, im Winde
> Klirren die Fahnen.[21]

---

[21] *Ibid.*, pp. 126-27.

This poem is translated as follows by David Gascoyne:

> Adorned with yellow pears
> And with wild roses filled,
> The earth hangs in the lake.
> And wondrous love-intoxicated swans
> In peaceful holy waters dip their heads.
>
> My woe! When winter comes
> Where shall I find the rose?
> Where shall I find the sunshine and
> The shadows of the earth?
> The cold unspeaking walls rise up,
> The flags flap in the wind.[22]

I have tried to show how the sense of being psychotic can arise out of the ordinary ways of being human in the human world. The schizophrenic, we may conclude, has lost the sense of participating in this world and is existing in *a* world alone that is not *the* world, the possession of which he used to share with others. It is *a* world in the sense that it seems to be disconnected from any world he used to be in. He feels powerless and passive before this feeling of losing his humanity. Like any other feeling, it can overwhelm him "out of a clear blue sky" or he can permit it to overflow him.[23] In spite of the resulting powerlessness he feels, I believe that it is usually the case that the schizophrenic actually at some point gives his initial consent to the sense of becoming psychotic. It seems to me that this is the same kind of decision as the decision to fall into sleep, to let oneself go, to give in. For that matter, the schizophrenic sometimes associates falling into sleep with giving himself over to death. Let us see if we can understand why anyone would ever give his consent to breaking contact with the world.

It may be that as he feels the world slipping away he says to

---

[22] David Gascoyne, *Holderlin's Madness.* (London: J. M. Dent and Sons, Ltd., 1938), p. 22.

[23] Cf. Paul Ricoeur, *Freedom and Nature.* trans. by Erazim Kohak. (Evanston: Northwestern University Press, 1966), p. 250 ff. His contrast of the emotions of awe with the emotions of shock is particularly relevant here.

himself, "My, this is a curious feeling! Why don't I give in to it for a moment and see what happens!" He could also give in because letting the world go appears as an escape from frustrated attempts to fulfill his desires. He may think, "After all, if the world insists on being immalleable and impervious to my action, why not just let it be!" But he quickly finds that his desires continue to be with him and that he can now fulfill them even less than he could before. The feeling turns out to be not at all what he expected it to be. Furthermore, like the decision to give into sleep, he finds that it is irreversible. He finds he has been deceived and enticed by a false security, for there is seldom any satisfaction or comfort in psychosis to compare at all favorably with the comfort he used to have.

In this way he finds that, once he decides to give in to the feeling, it takes possession of him and such confusion takes hold of him that he cannot extricate himself from it. Everything is shifting. There is nothing to hang on to. He has lost control. He is, in the final analysis, possessed by a feeling that is destroying him. He cannot get out. He is losing his life.

Now, even though he has this sense of utter powerlessness or of being a passive observer of his own destruction, he still from time to time makes abortive attempts to resist dying, just as a drowning man who cannot swim nevertheless struggles frantically. After the first panic has subsided, he may even be able to make some more or less organized attempts to escape his feeling because the world takes on some structure and he finds that he is not yet completely dispossessed. He is not yet dead. At first it seems to him that there must be some way of making a decision to get out of this world of his own, just as he made the decision to let it overflow him. But there is no such decision. In the same way that he cannot decide to awaken from sleep, he cannot decide to stop feeling that he is dying. Perhaps he will wake up; perhaps not. He has no way of knowing *now*.

How can we account for this? Other feelings can almost always eventually be controlled, even very strong ones. It seems to me that in order to extricate himself from his psychosis, the schizophrenic must deal with the power of de-animation threatening him. In order to do this, he must get very close to it. Running from it is fruitless because it continues to overtake him again and again. The only solution is to attempt to *neutralize* the force or to destroy the "things" in which it is present. But the closer he gets, the more he feels threatened and the more panicky he becomes. He is confronted by a power greater than his and he is at its mercy. As long as he feels this threat, there is nothing he can effectually do, just as there is nothing a man who cannot swim can effectually do when he gets beyond his depth and has nothing to hang on to.[24] He may have a great deal of energy, but he needs help.

Like the drowning man, the schizophrenic continues to struggle with surprising energy. He tries to "learn to swim" to come to terms with his psychosis in some way. Perhaps if he can go along with it for a time it will cease to disturb him so and he can find a way to overcome it, he thinks. But eventually he finds that it is too late and that there is no going along with it. Whatever he does, this power is always against him. Usually he finds that his efforts even increase his sense of being dispossessed. Why this is so requires an elaboration that would take us too far here.

These movements to extricate himself from his psychosis are of at least three kinds: to exorcise it by acting it out, to neutralize its power by some kind of destruction, and to neutralize its power by putting himself on its side, as one gives in to the enemy in order to avoid destruction. This is to be distinguished from resignation. Most of the schizophrenic's activity can be understood as an attempt to make all or some of these movements to extricate himself.

As he continues to find that he cannot go along with it, fight it off, or neutralize its power by destroying it, that in fact there is no peace, he finally resigns himself to his feeling. This should not be understood at once as a final resignation. Rather, we can compare it to a fish that is firmly hooked and "plays" at the end of the line. When it finally begins to become "played out," it

---

[24] This metaphor of drowning also appears in a similar context on p. 289 in the article by Shlien already cited.

seems to resign itself to death for a moment. But again and again a new energy appears and it renews its struggle. These struggles become increasingly less effective, but the fish does not cease to struggle once for all until it is very nearly actually dead.

In the same way we can understand how the schizophrenic resigns himself to his psychosis. When he becomes "played out" with resisting the sense of dying, he for a time loses the will to live and embraces living death. It is only then that he loses his desires, including the desire to return to the world he once knew. He appears literally to lie down and die. From time to time he makes continually less organized attempts to overcome this sense of dying. It appears that his desires have not disappeared once for all. Finally, though, his resignation affords him a way to come to terms with increasing emotional lability and confusion. He finds that he no longer has any feelings left and that his confusion has become so integral to his existence that it no longer disturbs him, either. Peace has returned, but he has lost his life.

This analysis is but a beginning. We need concepts for describing in greater detail the schizophrenic's mode of relating to others, his guilt, and his relation to death.[25] Finally, we eventually strike head-on the question of the relevance of this kind of analysis to questions of etiology, prognosis, and treatment. Do we have here, after all, nothing more than an intellectual exercise that satisfies some of our curiosity but is irrelevant to the prediction or control of this disturbance? Edmund Husserl, the founder of the phenomenological movement, said that the pure description of phenomena must precede any investigations by natural scientists because it prescribes what knowledge of the natural world must include. Very simply, we cannot find the cause or cure of a disturbance until we clearly understand what it is. Even though a natural scientist would probably not concede that such description is solely the task of the philosopher, he will surely acknowledge the necessity for describing what is before

---

[25] Cf. Waltraut Stein, *Intersubjectivity and Schizophrenia*, unpublished doctoral dissertation, Northwestern University, 1963.

him before he tackles questions of cause and cure. But even presuming we have such a description, its relation to these other interests is by no means clear, for one certainly cannot directly deduce cause and cure from it. At this time I am only ready to say that I hope that something in the description presented will provide those investigators who are concerned with etiology and treatment with a clue to areas for investigations or experimentation.

COMMENTARY ON DR. STEIN'S PAPER

Frida G. Surawicz

DEPERSONALIZATION has been widely described and occurs in patients with brain tumors, sometimes prior to or after an epileptic seizure, with certain drugs, such as mescaline and LSD, in patients suffering from borderline states, obsessive-compulsive neurosis, depression and schizophrenia. It is also said to occur in normals under certain circumstances, such as prior to falling asleep or after severe stress.

The origin and meaning have been explained with a multitude of explanations. Depersonalization has been compared with sleep and with complete surrender. It has been conceived as the loss of feeling of a living mental and body-ego, as a maneuver to deny its existence and therefore also to deny the forbidden impulses arising there. Dr. Peto compares it with "playing oppossum." This view is supported by the observation that occasionally an impulse breaks through and an attack of anxiety can at any time interrupt the depersonalized state. In lesser cases, secondary anxiety about the unreality develops and is expressed as a fear of insanity. Dr. Rosenfeld feels that depersonalization is a defense against guilt, depression, persecutory feelings and is related to destructive impulses within the ego, which are felt to be alien and projected onto the outside world. Melanie Klein sees in depersonalization a regression to the paranoid-schizoid position of early childhood. And the most familiar explanation holds that depersonalization is an extension of the body image with loss of ego boundaries, so that the body becomes part of the universe and dissolves into it, creating an oceanic feeling. Many people have been struck by the mask-like, bland facial expression. The person with depersonalization is also preoccupied with death, feeling more or less disembodied, like an empty shell. He does not create the impression of an anxious person at all and, for this reason, we believe that depersonalization serves to immobilize anxiety.

As to what brings on a state of depersonalization, it seems to be the general consensus that anxiety from without creates it. This can be brought on by rejection, by a serious setback, for instance. This mobilizes overwhelming anxiety within the individual. A girl in a paper by Dr. Obendorf described several stages when she underwent depersonalization. It started with uncertainty, then anxiety, next restlessness which turned into nervousness, unreality and finally a feeling of not being a person. Dr. Stein has described excellently how it feels to go through this experience, and I am only adding one quote by a patient in a paper by Dr. Peto, who states "somehow I am a melon and a slice which is neatly cut out and carefully removed from the whole. It is a desperate feeling of being in the nothingness, being meaningless and longing hopelessly to be a whole."

Many authors feel that depersonalization can occur in a normal person and some people have described it when they heard their recorded voice for the first time or when they saw their own picture on a home movie for the first time. Depersonalization must have been with us as long as humanity exists, and we are all familiar with the saying that "a person is literally beside himself," which must have been coined by a phenomenologist who went through the experience of depersonalization. Probably the most serious episodes of depersonalization occur in schizophrenia and with LSD, sometimes strikingly similar. Catatonic patients apparently can stop to feel any sensation in their body, being completely dispossessed of it, and are known to have mutilated themselves, cut off an arm or an ear. A similar feeling is said to exist with people on LSD. They describe their limbs as feeling detached or they experience a loss of body symmetry and often a feeling that they cannot separate where the body leaves off and the rest of the world begins. Other people have felt like automatons. Some people on LSD could not recognize their own voice or their image in the mirror.

With all that I have said this far, we can assume then that depersonalization means that a perception has been altered and it would be easy to explain this in people with organic disease or on drugs. We are still stuck with the schizophrenic person, and I

would like to explain why his perception of the world is at times
so different. Recently much work has been done on the childhood experiences of the schizophrenic in his family. When we
raise children we would like them to develop into mature people
and we have three criteria in mind, namely, we would like the
child to develop good interpersonal relationships, we would like
him to know what he can and cannot do or, in other words, have
him know his capabilities and his limitations. With these two
criteria, the third criterion, namely, to be able to plan for the
future and to face it without too much anxiety, comes naturally.
We follow this pattern of education by giving the child a sense
of self-value, by making him feel loved, wanted and secure. We
encourage activity and a sense of self-assertion, a pride of
accomplishment. Dr. Lidz has described many families in which
one or more children later on became schizophrenic. These
children have, in many ways, unusual childhoods. They are
placed in an unusual nuclear family setting, in which the parents
do not mutually support and reinforce each other but display a
severe breakdown in communication. In addition, the sexual
identity of one or both parents is often confused and the father
may be weak and ineffectual whereas the mother may be masculine and domineering, though all possible variations have been
noticed. A third occurrence is the lack of separation between the
generations, whereby the father may regress to the son's level,
competing with him for the mother's attention, or the mother
may try to elevate her son to the role of her husband, or may
thwart the child by never letting him develop his ego boundaries
completely, so that the child and mother continue to be part of
or extensions of each other. When the family remains a closed
unit, the patient may function in a very precarious adjustment
but when he transcends the family world, he is confronted with
a world which he perceives as alien and unfamiliar. One way of
coping with this is not to get involved with other people because
they are seemingly unpredictable, or he may look for a relationship that was just like the one he had with his mother, and we
often see a schizophrenic young man marrying a woman who is
much older than himself and relating to her in a similar fashion

as to his mother, or he may underachieve and never have any sense of accomplishment, or he may overachieve in only one limited area, which often does not involve interpersonal relationships, such as mathematics, for instance. Another possibility is to create a fantasy world because fantasies are safe and one can do anything with fantasy people without getting into trouble. But, as Dr. Laing has pointed out, if a person acts in fantasy only he ceases to be real. So we see in a schizophrenic life style a limitation and distortion of the self-world as well as a limitation and distortion of the outside world.

Now we come back to Dr. Stein's paper about the patient losing his world. I would like to emphasize here that we have only limited control or limited possession over our world and our body. There are several key situations in life where the limited possession of our bodies is even less and where, by the same token, the outside world seems to be larger. The first situation that comes to mind is the period of adolescence. Adolescents conceive that they have a limited control over their body. The sexual drives are perceived as quite alien. By the same token, the world expands and becomes different, because he is being related to as a sexually mature person. Under these circumstances even normal adolescents have severe feelings of depersonalization. Adolescence is often the time of the first episode of a schizophrenic breakdown. Another key situation is childbirth. Here again the concept of the body has changed. With the pregnancy one had limited and diminished control over one's body. After the child is born, this control is even less, because the child is still conceived of as part of or an extension of the body, but the control over it has diminished. By the same token, the world of the mother has expanded and now includes motherhood. She has to absorb the world of the newborn and it is during a situation like this that some mothers become schizophrenic.

Can it happen without a schizophrenic background? I would be inclined to agree. A person shapes his world and is also being shaped by it, and there should be congruency between his self-world and the world he adopts or possesses. If we remove him from his world, for instance, and put him in prison, we put him into an entirely different environment. This person would literally not know what to do with himself and might become psychotic. Or suppose that a person suffers from a severe disease which cripples him to such an extent that he cannot function in his world anymore. Again, before he reaches the period of adjustment, he might become psychotic. We find similar situations in psychiatry. We find a high incidence of psychosis among immigrants, who have to give up their familiar world and settle down in a new world with many discrepancies. The Peace Corps is keenly aware of this and looks for fairly healthy individuals before they put them into a different world, otherwise he might get a severe case of culture shock. The war neurosis in soldiers, who cannot adapt to the world of the battlefield, has frequently periods of depersonalization and we are all familiar with the frequent occurrence of psychotic breakdowns in people with a serious physical disability.

OPTICAL ILLUSIONS AND AESTHETIC PRINCIPLES

Paul B. Jossmann, M.D., Ph.D.

GOETHE has, in the second part of "Faust," Lynceus express his experience with the world's beauty, while watching from the tower. He is not concerned with details of his surroundings as a geographer, or agriculturist, or geologist, or highway planner, or a meteorologist, or an astronomer. He is just enjoying the world's beauty. In the language of Kant's "Critique of Judgement," he is "without interest," he is aesthetically oriented. In this respect he typifies the phenomenological problem set in the subject of this conference "Aisthesis and Aesthetics." In the multi-disciplinary approach to this problem, this presentation limits its scope to the question: what is the structure of the relation between visual perception and the appreciation of a product of art? More specifically and more simply termed: how does the spectator see a picture? This line of procedure seems to lead far off the initial experience of Lynceus who enjoys the world's beauty. But it will be shown that beauty of and in nature is only a specialized phenomenon, fundamentally not different from "beauty" in its intrinsic meaning. Both types share the common denominator of organized space, both are experienced in and by vision. One of the main differences is the fact that a product of art is created by man, but an object in nature is not. Yet products of art are related to objects in nature. They are by use of optical illusions. The roll of illusion in the fine arts has been known and discussed, practically since the beginning of artistic creativity. To quote only a few significant examples: in the contest between the two Greek painters, Zeuxis and Pharrhasios, the prize was given to the painter who had deceived his colleague who had asked to draw away the veil before the picture: but the curtain was the painting and the human being was deceived. The other painter had pictured grapes which deceived birds so that they flew close to pick at them; he had deceived only animals. (Nowadays the animal behaviorist would not agree with this deception of the jury because it needs more deceptive artistry to deceive animals than men). One of the most famous German painters, Dürer, called painting an "augenbetrug," "a trompe l'oeil," a deception of the eye. He, as well as Leonardo da Vinci and contemporaries, and later artists have written theoretical books on how to measure, modify and adjust objects for artistic purposes with the goal to arrive at Golden rules, how to accomplish beauty. None of them has ever been able to determine beauty by rules of perspective, composition, coloring, etc. But all have understood and used the illusory structure of pictorial representation. The most recent publication on this subject is E. H. Gombich's book "Art and Illusions" which gives not only a history of this interrelation but elaborates on its manifestations and impact during the history of fine arts and the individual styles. It is a truism that illusion is a prerequisite in the fine arts, but it is a problem how optical illusion accomplishes this function. Here we have to turn to the spectator of whom it was said *"he sees* the picture." The understanding of what "seeing" means appeared as a problem late in the history of physiology and psychology. Berkeley, from the standpoint of his sensualistic philosophy, pointed in his "A New Theory of Vision" to the relation between the visual and tactile senses, he stated that visual experiences resulted intrinsically from the related tactile sensations and experiences. Goethe, in his Optics, stated that "it appears strange that the eye sees forms while it is factually capable only to distinguish light and dark, and also color." He made this remarkable statement before the structure of the retina was known, and before the physiology and neurophysiology had discovered the details of the visual pathways. But the essence has remained true that the reaction to the stimulus alone does not constitute the act of seeing. In other words: sensation and perception are not identical. Simple tests can demonstrate this dichotomy. For this purpose a few optical illusions are presented here for interpretation. It is not the intent to analyze the term "illusion" itself. Merely as a working hypothesis, the following definition is offered: an illusion is a misleading image, or perhaps more elaborately: an illusion is a perception of something objectively existing in such a way as to cause misinterpretation of its actual nature. A constructive analysis of optical illusions will start by reviewing a variety of them, some different in structure.

Figure 1 shows the well known Müller-Lyer, or arrow illu-

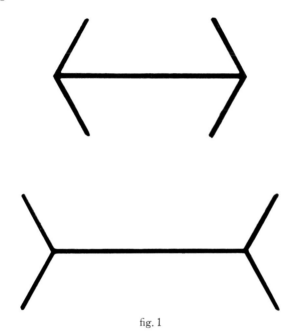

fig. 1

sions. The figure with the outgoing fins looks longer than the figure with the ingoing fins. By the way, the same illusion is produced if the lines between the arrows are omitted.

Figures 2 & 3—the Hering figure or fan illusion. The radiating lines bend the straight lines placed upon them; these straight lines are factually parallels but in the illusions they appear concave or convex, depending on the superimposed radiating lines.

Figure 4 shows long lines which are factually parallels but due to the cross short lines appear converging or diverging.

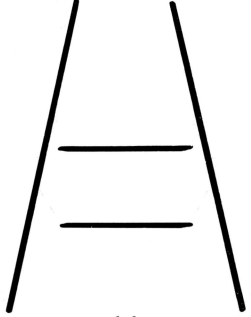

fig. 2

Figure 5 shows the Ponzo or railway line illusion. The upper horizontal line looks the longer. The same line continues to look longer in whichever orientation the figure is viewed.

The optical illusions shown so far have one factor in common : geometrical structures are perceived different from their

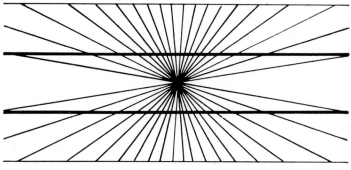

fig. 3

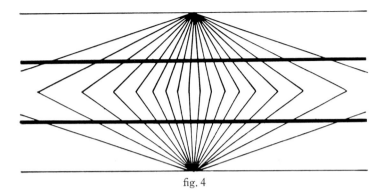

fig. 4

actual nature if exposed simultaneously with other structures. In other words, while the stimulus remains identical the perception is not commensurate with the elementary reaction *to* the stimulus. Perception *adds* something which has to be analyzed further. A first approach to explain the optical illusion as shown so far was the hypothesis that they are caused by eye movements which in following the "distracting" lines cause wrong interpretations and extensions of the basic geometrical forms. However,

fig. 5

this hypothesis was shown to be not valid because tachistoscopic
exposure of these figures had the same illusory effect when there
was not sufficient time to perform any eye movements.

Another type of optical illusion is shown in Figure 6. This

fig. 6

figure alternates, so that sometimes it is seen as a pair of black
faces in profile, sometimes as a white urn bound by meaningless
black areas. The alteration depends entirely on the spontaneous
decision of the spectator. Again the stimulus causing the sensation remains identical but in this illusion there are no interfering
additional visual structures which may account for the different
perceptions. They are entirely the viewers making. A function is
thus being demonstrated which has been instrumental already in
the previously shown optical illusion, but which is more obviously demonstrated in this type of illusory alternation, the
function of *relative independence from the stimulus*. The statement should not be misconstrued as a devaluation of the stimulus without which no visual experience is possible. However,
already Johannes Müller's law of "specific sense energies" in-

cludes a relative independence from the specific stimulus to the corresponding sense organ. Sensation, as it may again be defined as reaction to the stimulus, is not identical with perception as it is relatively independent from the stimulus.

For further illustration Figure 7 shows a cube in spatial

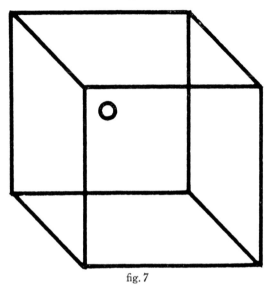

fig. 7

perspective. This figure alternates: a small circle appears sometimes in the front face, sometimes in the back face. Factually, a two-dimensional geometric stimulus is presented. However this is immediately transposed into a three-dimensional structure which then in addition can be "inverted" according to the spectator's decision. There are other similar optical illusions, e.g. the well known stairway shown in perspective which can be "inverted" into an overhanging protruding cornice or architectural ornament. Another illusory phenomena is observed in this illusion: in the act of inverting, especially when performed rapidily, an illusory *movement* is seen; while inverting the spectator sees first the front and back faces shrink until they are flattened within the plain of the paper and then the structure expands anew to assume the new inverted figure.

Figure 8 shows the imaginary illusion in a related but somehow different context. The curved lines, superimposed by quad-
rangles appear as a spiral in movement away from the spectator.
Factually there is no spiral but a number of concentric circles.
This illusion then is based on the already known interference of

fig. 8

different geometric structures superimposed, and on the imaginary movement in space, away from the spectator. Figure 9
shows the pattern similiar to the products of what is known as
op-art, done by an amateur. The alternation of dark and light
rectangles of different sizes, distributions and linear arrange-
ments produce a distinct impression of a wave-like undulating
movement throughout the whole pattern. On closer examination
and by experimentation the studies of perceptual psychology
have demonstrated that all optical illusions are caused by the
phenomenon of movement. As mentioned before, "movement"
in optical illusions is not of the type of movements of the eyes,
or the head, or the whole person, or on the other hand, of the

fig. 9

object or any of its parts in reality. Movement means in this relation not *factual* but potential movement. Under "potential" is understood the capacity of a visual structure to change its position in the three-dimensional space. Man orients himself and acts in the three-dimensional space on the basis of his capacity to move, and it is of secondary importance whether motion is actuated or intended. In the optical illusions a large variety of potential movements, and their results, are experienced. To name only a few: lengthening and shortening, enlarging and shrinking, pushing and pulling, revolving and circling, moving towards or away from each other or the spectator, moving seemingly through the illusory space dimension of foreground, middle-ground and background, etc. Regardless of the type of movement, it should be reemphasized that potentiality, which is not intrinsic in the elementary stimulus, constitutes illusion.

An unexpected confirmation of this determination of the optical illusion was found in the field of neuropathology. A group of patients presenting the syndrome of "agnosia" showed a peculiar reaction with optical illusions. It is not intended to discuss agnosia per se. For the present purpose, agnosia represents a disturbance of the so called higher visual functions. The patients have a normal sense organ, their eyes and their neurological structures back to the occipital lobes function normally. That means that visual stimuli, as light and color are received without difficulty. However, these patients are not able to identify objects by vision, which they otherwise immediately are capable of recognizing by touching them. Further: they see in a picture lines, curves, colors, they can also copy details of the pictorial subjects. But they still fail in recognition. This symptom called "mind-blindedness" is frequently associated with other manifestations as disorientation in space, for instance geographical or topographical errors, right-left disorientation, miscalculation of perspective in depth, disturbances of following the lines in reading. These patients were tested by presenting them optical illusory figures as shown here before as well as pictures ranging from primitive pictorial representation of objects and scenes to specimens of the fine arts. The paradoxical result in many of these individuals was that they were not subjected to the optical illusions, that they, for instance, found the two lines in Figure 1 of equal length, they saw the seemingly convex and concave lines as parallels, they saw also the crossed-thru lines which to the normal seem to converge and diverge as parallels. As to geometrical structures drawn in perspective, they did not see a cube but two quardrangles linked by lines: they never saw a cylinder or pyramid, drawn perspectively. They were not capable of inverting. The self-evident explanation of this paradoxical behavior is that the pathological condition of the brain causing the agnosia syndrome makes these individuals more *stimulus-bound,* to a degree that the integration of sensual data into perceptive wholes is impaired. The stimulus in optical illusions is factually an assembly of fragmented singular stimuli to which the sense organ reacts.

Further proof of the abnormal condition resulting in a forced restriction of the act of seeing to the stimulus itself, is the experience with testing these individuals by pictures. They could not identify simple pictures of objects whenever they included perspective. Scenic illustrations confused them. They could only give information on parts which they could not inter-relate. But the most impressive failures occurred in the tests with confrontation of fine art products. The faulty recognitions increased with more stylistic principles manifested. The pictorial represen-

fig. 10

tation of the three dimensional space, as it differs from reality, was one of the most confusing factors. For instance, a wooded hill in the foreground painted quite large was considered much higher than a glacier covered mountain in the background which assumed a much much smaller space in the picture. Persons painted as moving or resting could not be localized in their spatial relation or their activity. Rembrandt's (Figure 10) landscape with a cottage and large tree shows a straw cover of a house roof which was interpreted as a "forest" because of its pictorial closeness to the tree which is factually a separate entity in a different space. The patient however who is stimulus bound is not able to differentiate and integrate the pictorial illusions. A still stranger misinterpretation by a patient was given to Rembrandt's (Figure 11) "Old Man Shading His Eyes With His Hand." The patient turned the picture around several times and

fig. 11

finally identified it as "Half a Butterfly" pointing to the barret as the body and the rest of the drawing as one wing of the butterfly. This failure of recognition does not only manifest the inability of visual integration but also the futility of substituting an intellectual guessing. In all these misinterpretations the failure was evidently caused by the inability to interrelate the discrete data. The incapacity of these agnostics to act and orient themselves in space is paralleled by the inability of using the illusory properties in pictorial representations. They cannot integrate the discrete parts of a picture into a meaningful whole because they lack the capacity of potential movement in space. It is now apparent that "form" as determined by lines, contours, borders, directions, relations to other lines, absolute and relative measures, is *one* modality in pictorial representation. Theodor Lipps determined "form" as expressing possibilities of motion. Another modality is color. It is of particular interest that the painter Kandinsky in his book "The Spiritual in Art" has attributed to color the quality of potential movement. He sets up a whole scale of different movements, as linear, circular, revolving, turning towards and away from the spectator, and related these movements to specific color schemes. It is immaterial whether his individual correlations are acceptable, but it is essential that such motor components can exist in color per se. If this motor component appears combined in form *and* color, then the effect is enhanced particularly.

The relative independence from the stimulus is demonstrable also in specific aesthetic principles of individual styles, as already shown in the Rembrandt drawings. The following two Figures 12 and 13 will illustrate this function further. This figure, No. 12, shows an upside down photographic portrait. It is recognized immediately as that of a man with a mustache, necktie, jacket, etc. If shown in normal position, it is better identifiable but the pictorial presentation is not much different from the upside down presentation. By the way, it's the portrait of Helmholtz.

Figure 13, in upside down position, appears at first sight almost meaningless. Some spectator may identify a head, and possibly a female one because of the hairdo, but this is all, and the rest is a hard to recognize assembly of lines, strokes and patches. If presented in normal position the picture immediately is recognized as a sleeping relaxed woman, a most articulate work by Rembrandt. The previously seen assembly of meaningless lines assumes now a highly recognized pattern representing clearly not only the entire body but also its parts as they are integrated into the aesthetic concept of complete relaxation. The

fig. 12

fig. 13

remarkable principle in this drawing is the scarcity of technical
elements which are presented as primary stimuli to the optical
sensation. The word of the German impressionist Liebermann
should be quoted here: "Drawing is leaving-out," which means
that the artist creates by selecting the essential characteristic
intrinsic elements of his object which are as few or as many as

the aesthetic principles demand. These aesthetic elements are in most instances fewer than but at any rate they are not identical with the stimuli for sensation as offered by objects of reality. Again; what constitutes the aesthetic quality in Rembrandt's drawing is an optical illusion initiated but not formed by the primary sensation. The agnostic patient failed completely to recognize the picture as a whole and was even doubtful in regard to the meaning of parts of the body represented; for instance, she called the chin line a mustache, but did not even identify the head as such.

A silhouette, figure 14, should not necessarily put too heavy a demand on the ability to interpretation or recognize the object because the modalities of pictorial representation are reduced to a minimum consisting essentially of contours. However, the agnostic patient was evidently faced with almost insurmountable difficulties. The donkey was called a horse. The reins were considered a ladder. In addition to two persons she identified as such, she called the trees also persons. The lines indicating waves in the water were called plants. The surface of the water was not recognized. Neither was the mirror effect. Composition and meaning of the whole escaped the patient completely. It is evident that scarcity of elements in the primary stimulus, as represented in the silhouette complicates the function of recognition to such an extent that not even a partial identification is possible any more.

The agnostic patient, the more he is stimulus bound, the more he is subjected to another type of optical illusions, as alloesthesia, which means the transfer of objects from one to another spot of the visual field, or metamorphosis, which means distortion of a seen object. These anomalies are of no interest in the present study, but they are significant in their inhibitory function which restricts the relative freedom from the stimulus.

The relation between optical illusion and styles has been the main problem in Heinrich-Wölfflin's book "Basic Concepts in the History of Fine Arts" which discusses mainly the Renaissance and Baroque. He outlines five pairs of aesthetic principles which determine the basis for the differentiation of style. There are: (1) linear—picturesque, (2) plain—depth, (3) closed—

fig. 14

open from, (4) unity—multitude, (5) clearness—indistinctness. In the discussion of all these modalities the function of movement, which means potential movement, is always referred to.*

* Wölfflin characterizes this structure of aesthetic principles in the following quotation: "The fact that Dürer could become the man of destiny for German art was due primarily to his ability to conceive in three dimensions. In order to overcome the vague perception of space, an artist was required whose senses were single-mindedly directed toward

In summary of his exhausting analysis he considers the visual recognition of the spectator as the point of departure. In order to arrive at an aesthetic experience he gives the following brief formula: we see only what we seek, what we are looking for. But we are only looking for what is fit to be seen. Wölfflin points to the stimulus, as "fit" to be seen but he also postulates the capacity of relative independence from the stimulus when he refers to the function in seeing which "seeks," the integrating faculty of the aesthetic experience.

The relation between optical illusions and aesthetic principles was analyzed on the basis of observations of a neuropathological condition. The question now arises: is optical illusion aisthesis disturbed or not? The answer is not a straight Yes or No. The function of optical illusion in Fine Arts, as experienced by all normal individuals, is not commensurate with the dictionary definition of a "misleading image"; on the contrary it is one of the foundations of the aesthetic experiences. Consequently, aisthesis is *not* disturbed. On the other hand, reaction of the agnostic patient manifests no "misinterpretation of the actual nature" of an object, yet it prevents the formation of an aesthetic act. Either aisthesis, though including a correct sensation, *is* disturbed. A reflection on Goethe's verses will help to clear this somewhat paradoxical impass. It is not redundant to find in these verses the verbs "to see" and "to view." These synonyms, to which others could be added, indicate varieties of visual perception designating individual categories of aisthesis, different in their relation to the elementary stimulus. Aisthesis is the modality determined by the integration of the measurable into a transcendent experience which cannot be quantified. The eye *sees,* the sense organ which includes also the neural pathways back to the striate area in the occipital lobe *reacts.* But it is the person who has the visual experience. The relative independence

---

what could be grasped and touched; an artist who experienced objects in space as actually displacing air and who would feel their shapes and contours. Dürer was such an artist. With a kind of passion he embraced corporeal form and experienced up and down, the in and out, of surfaces as actual movements."

from the stimulus should not be misinterpreted as a degrading of the measurable external and biological entities. A stimulus is not only a stimulus-from, but always also a stimulus-for. Aisthesis then is never exhausted by the measurable stimulus and reaction, which is a phenomenon in the sense that the person experiences the sense organ as *His* eye, as part of *his* organism, the reaction to the stimulus as *his* individual function. The problem of the relation between quantity and non-measurable phenomenon, as posed in aisthesis is not within the scope of this study. Suffice to say that it should be solved on a methodological basis.

It hardly needs special emphasis to preclude a misinterpretation of the roll of optical illusion in art. The spectator as well as the artist are unaware of the mechanisms involved, although they may be cognizant of the illusory nature itself. Dürer's definition of painting as deception of the eye is not to be understood as a falsification of objects, persons, nature, etc. His and Leonardo's writings demonstrate significantly the failure to create beauty by using a code of measurable entities, intended to serve as elementary stimuli. On the other hand, his own outstanding creative work illustrates the transcendence of aesthetic principles. As stated in the beginning, beauty in nature has a common denominator with beauty in art. When Lynceus enjoys the world's beauty, his visual experience is formed by aesthetic principles. He sees the world as if he had created it. He is "without interest," he also is relatively independent from the stimuli. Restriction of this independence, as it was demonstrated in pathological conditions, puts the person under the dictatorship of stimulus and reaction. The freedom of aesthetic principles constitutes the autonomy of art.

126

COMMENTARY ON DR. JOSSMANN'S PAPER

Shirley Sanders

Dr. Jossmann's paper, so rich in diverse observations, was very exciting to me. The possibilities for comment are many; indeed I find myself bound to the immediate stimulus possibilities and hence unable to transcend them. My current agnosia, in addition to limitations of time, however, impose the restriction of discussion to but a sparse few themes which hold personal interest for me.

The experiencing of the world's beauty from afar is indeed an essential problem in the conference and Dr. Jossmann's approach to this problem, investigating the manner in which a spectator sees a picture is a fundamental step towards clarifying it. However a preliminary clarification may be needed. Does not a spectator see a picture as a picture; does he not see it differently than he sees a thing? I would like to extend the basic inquiry to include this qualification.

When an observer looks at a picture, he knows that it is a picture—a *representation* of something, and not the thing itself. In a museum, for example, I do not mistake the portrait of the Mona Lisa for a living person. Although a portrait stands for a person who may have lived or is currently living, it is clear that the picture itself is not alive. A representation of an object is both similar to and different from the object it represents in a variety of ways. It is similar in that both the picture and the object are visible, they are seen by the eye. The differences however are more essential to our inquiry and so let us begin.

Dr. Jossmann noted that both art and nature exist in an organized space. But do they share the organized space? There is a fundamental difference here between the space in which each respectively exists. Objects in nature exist in a spatial-temporal dimension which encompasses them. They are completely surrounded by the broad unlimited panorama. This space embraces the viewer too and permits him both to take action in and to make contact with the objects sharing this space with him. The picture space, however is illusory. It does not extend in 3 dimensions, encircling the observer. There is only surface, but no real depth. The observer cannot enter into the picture space and he cannot act nor interact with the objects there. There is no before, behind, or next to. If you turn a picture around, you lose sight of it.

The picture is different from the object it represents in other important ways. In addition to the difference in space, it is also different with respect to time. For a picture is timeless. Although it may represent the historical past, I see it now in the present. It will look the same tomorrow, or next week, or next year. It does not move as do the hands on a clock or change with age as do living things. Time stands still in the picture, representing one moment eternally.

Size and weight are of no consequence to a picture. An 8″ x 10″ painting may represent the empire state building in its entirety. Yet it can easily be lifted or carried about. Furthermore a picture may be enlarged or reduced in size and still be recognized as what it is. It may have no constant relationship to the object it represents, to the surroundings in which it is located, or to the viewer. A life size picture is of no advantage. Of what use would *be* a life size map of the United States?

What is the consequence of these essential differences between object and representation? What else can an illusory space *be,* lacking all essential relationships with reality, but an *abstraction.* A picture disengaged from the continuum of natural spatial and temporal relationships exists as an abstraction, to be contemplated by sight.

What is the purpose of this abstraction and how is it achieved? Dr. Jossmann pointed out that illusion is a prerequisite in the fine arts, but it was not too clear how this is the case. Could it be that the abstraction is achieved by the illusion—the illusion of space, time, movement, size, perspective. The illusion, by detaching an *idea* from the material object, expresses the idea in full relief. In this way an idea can be contemplated, at a distance from worldly things, or as Dr. Jossmann says, with disinterest.

Dr. Jossmann perceptively described the imitation aspect of art and how art can be a "deception of the eye." But art as representation is not a deception of the eye. No one for example, takes a picture of a horse as a horse. A picture, as we have said, stands for something else, but it is not an imitation of that which it represents. Finally the very abstractness of the picture separated from actual space by a frame clearly identifies it as an artifact, an artificial object which stands for something else. It is essentially different from the reality for it is a transformation of it. There is no ambiguity or illusory deception involved in the seeing of picture as picture.

Although we have said that the illusion achieves the abstraction of the picture, and that pictures may be designed as imitations of reality to deceive the eye, we can now ask from another perspective, is a picture an illusion? If an illusion is a misleading image that causes misinterpretation of its actual nature, we must say no for there is no illusory deception. Let us consider whether a microscopic picture is an illusion? Here a deception of the eye is involved for light is refracted by lenses and mirrors. The slide is magnified hundreds of times. The light waves actually are bent—is our sight deceived? Or do we see the slide as it is even though the light waves are distorted?

Another deception is involved in the familiar experience of looking out the window between two narrow slits of a venetian blind. I can see the house across the street from this narrow perspective. The image should be interpreted as a very small house because I can see its entire length and width between these two small slits. Yet the house is in actuality a very large two story house. Do I in this case, misinterpret the actual nature, or do I know the reality of it. It is an illusion, that of size constancy, which prevents me from misinterpreting the size of the house. We learn that objects at a distance look very small, and that they appear to change size if they are brought gradually closer or farther away.

Is not much of everyday perception grounded in illusion? We tend to see things as they are, even when they appear to us in different perspectives. We can even see form with just the merest hint of suggestive lines as Dr. Jossman pointed out. Indeed it is the case that sensation and perception are not necessarily identical.

My final comments will move briefly over one or two questions concerning (1) potential movement, and (2) the inability of the agnosia patient to interrelate discrete data. According to Dr. Jossman, potential movement involves the capacity to change position. However, he says little about direction. Is movement not directed to something. Does it not involve a change of position from the now to then, from the here to there, from the incomplete to the complete? Where is potential movement directed in perception, in illusions?

Secondly, Dr. Jossmann's agnosia patients, unable to interrelate discrete perceptions, were unable to see a picture as a whole. They were bound to the given. They were unable to disengage themselves from it and to transcend, to move beyond, the immediate sense datum. But is transcendence achieved by the mere interrelationship of discrete elements? If this were so, the transcendence of the aesthetic experience would require starting with the single datum and should itself be quantifiable. It is questionable whether we do start with discrete data in looking at picture as picture. Rather the case could be developed that we start with the picture as a whole and then go to the parts.

Finally, the agnosia patients were characterized as stimulus bound. For example, the chin line in one picture was interpreted as a mustache. If the patient is stimulus bound, then how did she arrive at the concept mustache—why did she not report a line or light and dark patterns? Perhaps I am not clear on exactly what is the stimulus for picture.

In conclusion, I feel Dr. Jossmann has presented a stimulating paper which presents many possibilities for further exploration.

THE PHANTOM LIMB

Erwin W. Straus, M.D.

MANY, MANY years ago I worked as a young medical student for some time in Edinger's famous neurological laboratory, which in those days was still housed within the Pathological Institute of Frankfurt's Municipal Hospital. On the way through the dissecting room one was startled by an odd Latin inscription, familiar and strange at the same time. For the familiar memento mori: *media vita in morte sumus* had been inverted into *media morte in vita sumus*. This switch reminded undergraduates and graduates, alike, that studying the dead they were acting in the service of the living. I have reasons to believe that Eugen Albrecht, the Director of the Institute and author of the inscription, also intended to call our attention to the fact that ever so often disturbances first may alert us to wonder about the norm.

In the field of "Aisthesis" it was left to neurologists to discover in this century a problem within the realm of the utterly familiar. Confronted with the perplexing facts of motor apraxia, autotopagnosia, anosognosia, Liepmann, Pick, Babinski could not avoid to raise the question: How do we experience our bodies? In order not to prejudice the answer one actually should say: How does each one of us experience his body—or, to make it still more precise,—How do I experience my body, and experience it as mine? Perhaps any formulation of this question must be biased, since it forces pre-logical, pre-reflective, pre-linguistic experience into the area of language and reflection.

Liepmann, Pick, Babinski certainly were keen observers; yet acumen and sagacity alone were not sufficient; also required was the courage to accept their patients' strange behavior on its face value and not to dismiss it as just another absurd attitude. Since Liepmann's first publication hundreds of patients with motor apraxia have been seen and reported. Likewise, Babinski's first communication was followed by a great number of papers confirming his observation. No doubt similar cases could have been noticed long before. They had been ignored because they were "off limit" in the area of theoretical understanding. In sharp contrast to all these syndromes with their long Greek names, the illusory presence of a lost limb is noticed by the patient himself. We can be pretty sure that one or the other of the warriors fighting on either side of the Trojan walls had a phantom limb, although the fact has not been reported by Homer, nor even by Schliemann.

It is, therefore, by no means surprising that the recorded history of the phantom reaches back into the 16th century. The French surgeon and court physician Ambroise Paré wrote in 1552: "Verily, it is a thing wondrous strange and prodigious, and which will scarce be credited unless by such as have seen with their eyes and heard with their ears the patients who have many months after the cutting away of the leg grievously complained that they yet feel exceeding great pain of that leg so cut off."*

In full agreement with Paré's evaluation, the phantom was presented in most of the earlier writings as an oddity, i.e., as something rare in occurrence and surprising in its manifestation. It should therefore be emphasized that the condition described by A. Paré is listed in modern terminology as just one small sub-group, viz., as the painful phantom.

Neither Paré nor Descartes, neither Haller nor any of those who referred to the fact in olden days, actually used the word "phantom." The term was coined by the American physician Weir Mitchell (1829-1914), the inventor of the "rest-cure," the first scientific explorer of mescaline. During the Civil War Mitchell was Chief of a US hospital for diseases and injuries of the nervous system, in Philadelphia. He reported his observations, 1872, in a book entitled *On Injuries of the Nerves and Their Consequences*. There he used the term "phantom limb," though not for the first time. Actually, Mitchell had already

* Kolb, L. C. *The Painful Phantom*. Springfield, Ill., Charles C. Thomas, 1954.

written about the phantom limb the previous year in Lippincott's magazine of "Popular Literature and Science." The choice of a popular journal is not so surprising in Mitchell's case. While he had limited—as we would say today—his medical practice to neurology, he had by no means limited his interest to this one area. A man of many talents, he wrote and published poetry and fiction. The term phantom limb was a distinguished offspring from a successful marriage between neurology and poetry.

Since Mitchell's days—not to mention those of A. Paré—the number of amputees has grown in geometrical progression. With the industrial development and the two World Wars the frequency of injuries burgeoned; through medical advances the legions of survivors multiplied. Studies not limited to patients complaining about pain changed one aspect of the *curiosum:* its exceptional character; yet they even reinforced the other one: the strangeness—not to say the absurdity—of the phantom experience. Ewalt* and co-workers who examined more than 2000 amputees in an American army hospital during World War II found that 98% of these men had a phantom experience. In this large group not more than 8 patients (not 8%) complained about a painful phantom. The result of this and many other studies is: 1) after the loss of a limb the experience of a phantom is a perfectly regular occurrence (today one tries to account for its absence); 2) among the amputees only a few experience a painful phantom; 3) the phantom undergoes characteristic changes, such as shortening with discontinuity and telescoping. Listening to the story of amputees, as reported by Haber, Cronholm, and many others, A. Paré may have repeated his expression of bewilderment. For in the course of years a phantom limb does not simply lose in intensity and clarity, gradually fading away, the phantom usually shrinks. Yet this process is by no means uniform. While the distal parts—heel and toes (especially the big toe), thumb and little finger—are preserved, preserved without exception, intermediary parts, as,

---

*Ewalt, J. R., Randall, G. C., and Morris, H. The phantom limb. Psychosom. Med., 9:118-123, 1947.

for instance, the forearm, may be completely erased from the phantom experience. Finally, the hand may approach the stump until, in a considerable number of cases, at the end of this process (called telescoping) hand and/or fingers appear placed next to, or even within, the stump.

A theory of the phantom therefore has to account: 1) for the regular appearance of the painless phantom limb; 2) for its rare occurrence under comparable conditions (for instance after amputation of the female breast), and 3) for the deformation of the phantom through shrinking and telescoping, together with the persistence of its distal parts. In addition, the painful phantom presents a medical problem of its own. But it is the *painless phantom* which confronts us with a central problem of AISTHESIS.

As long as the phantom was practically identified with the painful phantom the cause of the pain was held responsible for the origin of the phantom experience in general. Many physicians expected that with an improvement of the condition of the stump, removal of a neuroma, etc., phantom and pain would disappear together. When both persisted, the level of the surgical attack was elevated from the stump to the spinal roots, from the roots to the spinal tract, and eventually from the spinal cord to the sympathetic ganglia, and to the brain itself. The patients' response—the rare success and the frequent failure—permitted within obvious limits an evaluation and justification of the various procedures. There is no such touchstone available for the evaluation of theories which try to account for the appearance of the painless phantom, or simply for the phantom limb as such.

As to be expected, two factions are actually competing with each other: a psychological school opposing a physiological team. The psychological theories assume a conflict between the narcissistic desire for the integrity of the body and the fact of its mutilation. The ego, unwilling to accept the loss denies the fact, and the unconscious, cooperating with the denial produces a phantom limb as a substitute for the lost arm or leg. If this assumption were right, the phantom would be the result of some kind of neurotic reaction, an interpretation contradicted by the strictly regular occurrence of the painful phantom after amputation. One may of course claim that under certain conditions any one would react with manifest neurotic symptoms. However, if unconscious wishes were able to produce a phantom illusion, their overall workmanship must be rated as surprisingly poor. Why do these wishes not also provide for an optical illusion? Actually, with one glance at the amputated stump the illusion is unmasked and exposed as such. Indeed, the denial is not only untenable: it is malicious. For a telescoped phantom, with the fingers moved upward into the stump of the upper arm, actually mocks any attempt at a denial. The denial reaction also fails to operate under those conditions where one should expect it to act most passionately—viz., after amputation of a female breast or after castration. There are papers reporting a phantom breast or nipple. Yet the experience in these cases seems more often than not an initial sensitivity of the surgical scar and in later months an awareness of the loss and absence rather than an illusory presence of the breast. The complete absence of any pertinent reports in the case of the castrates in the Occident or of the eunuchs in the Orient may be symptomatic and well indicate the absence of phantom genitalia, especially of the testicles, in all these cases. As mentioned before, in a leg phantom the big toe is most obstinate. Could it be because of its symbolic value? But if it were a substitute, *a quid pro quo,* the *quid,* namely the big toe, would carry a higher narcissistic kathexis than the *quo,* the phallus itself. And a last point! Among the many anecdotes reported about Julius Caesar, one claims that he became bald-headed early in life. Although this defect did not chill Cleopatra, Caesar disliked it intensely and used to cover his head with a laurel twig. However this may be, never has a bald-headed man experienced a phantom Beatle tuft.

After the failure of the denial theory, we must reconsider the physiological hypotheses, in their main varieties. There is one group searching for the cause in the periphery, blaming the stump as the malfactor; the other one suspecting and accusing cortical centers. Most of the physiologists, psychologists, surgeons, are convinced—in line with the dominating doctrines of epiphenomenology—that the experience of the phantom must and can be reduced to pathological processes within the stump, where inadequate stimuli are replacing the natural and adequate ones.

Many arguments have been and must be raised against the periphery theory; too many, indeed, to enter into a discussion today.*

The partisans of a central theory, not satisfied with counter-arguments alone, advanced positive reasons speaking in their favor. They emphasized that the phenomena of a) telescoping and b) gradual fading and persistent vividness of distal parts were in agreement with the cortical representation of arms and legs.

This agreement, however, is by no means perfect; for the information about cortical representations, illustrated through the graphic allegory of the so-called homunculus, has been obtained by direct stimulation of the open brain with small electrodes, its effects referred in the experience of the patient to an integer periphery. The central theory of the phantom limb, however, demands the strange hypothesis of an auto-excitation of the postcentral gyrus. In short, it demands to dispense with some basic tenets of neurophysiology.

The idea of a body schema located as a special cerebral apparatus in the parieto-occipital lobe, or lobes, yet detached from the postcentral gyrus is not exposed to such criticism. New problems, however, arise while the old ones do not altogether disappear.

Postmortem studies in cases of anosognosia, finger agnosia, etc., have frequently demonstrated destructions in more or less circumscribed areas of either hemisphere. If the disturbance of behavior was due to cerebral destruction, then it seemed justified to assume that normal behavior was related to intact structures. Indeed, in the case of a phantom limb the anomaly did not

---

* Haber, W. B. Reactions to loss of limb: Physiological and Psychological aspects. Ann. N.Y. Acad. Sci., Vol. 74, pp. 14-24, Sept. 30, 1958.

indicate a deficiency of the cortical body schema, but just the opposite: the continuance of its function after an amputation. Therefore certain cortical areas were designated as the locale of the body schema in action, which, according to Gerstmann, supposedly "is a kind of inner diagram representing one's body as a whole, as well as its single parts . . . . (while) tactile, kinetic and optic experiences . . . . contribute in the integration of the body scheme."* How afferent impulses received through specific receptors conducted over isolated pathways to confined cortical areas could be integrated at all remains—to say the least —a physiological puzzle.

In practice it is a small accomplishment to touch something visible. Even a dog is initiated into the mysterium. He, like us, is able to smell *and* to see *and* to touch, *and* to grab, *and* to taste, let us say a sizzling steak. Even so, it remains enigmatic how all these different impressions could be united while they are also left separate.

With all this we are only at the beginning of our predicament. An amputee does not notice the mutilation of THE human body. He is not aware of the absence of *an* arm, or *a* leg; he tells us about the illusory presence of *his* arm or *his* leg, or to speak appropriately in the first person, in the phantom limb experience: MY arm appears still present to me. Contrariwise, in the case of anosognosia the patient does not recognize *his* left arm as his own. But how could a cortical area, located in the midst of others and connected with them and the periphery, be responsible for the experience: MY BODY? How could—as Gerstmann postulates—"the normal functioning of the specific central apparatus subserving the body image and . . . . every new set of afferent impulses . . . . brought into proper functional relations with the mechanism of the body image by the activity of the brain rise into consciousness (with the intimacy characteristic of all experiences which one appropriates as one's own)"?†

---

* Gerstmann, J. Problem of imperception of disease and of impaired body territories with organic lesions. Arch. Neurol. & Psychiat., 48, 1942, pp. 890-912 (p. 901).
† loc. cit., p. 902.

Gerstmann's account is in full agreement with the official doctrine that if we want to understand the experience of the body schema we must first understand "the basic physiological principle underlying the condition." The brain studied by scientists is considered as belonging to the "real world" where afferent impulses released by stimuli produce objective cerebral events, which after appearing in consciousness as subjective data, sensations and perceptions, are finally projected outward and thereby produce an "external world." Since the pretended relationship between an individual brain and its projectile, the external world, is necessarily solipsistic, there is no room for a distinction of MINE from NOT mine.

All these unsolved problems are reflected in the vague terminology, vacillating between body schema and body image. The term body schema (Koerperschema) was introduced by Paul Schilder in a booklet, published in 1923. There Schilder used—but at the same time radically modified—Head's concept of "schemata," interpreted by the British neurologist as a physiological substratum organized through past sensory experiences. In a nice simile Head explained: "Every recognizable change enters into consciousness already charged with its relation to something that happened, just as on a taxi meter the distance is represented to us already transformed into shillings and pence."

Yet, already in his first publication Schilder defined the body schema as the "spatial image (Raumbild) everybody has of himself." He changed the title accordingly in a later compendious work to the "Image and Appearance of the Human Body."* (1935) In this book Schilder made passionate, though fruitless, efforts to deal with the problematic situation he could never clearly formulate. "The image of the human body," Schilder wrote in the Introduction, "means the picture of our own body which we form in our mind, that is to say the way in which the body appears to ourselves. . . . We call it a schema of our body or bodily schema. . . . The body schema is the tri-dimensional image everybody has about himself. We may call it

---

* Kegan, Paul.; Trench, Teubner and Co., London, 1935.

body image. . . . There is a self-appearance of the body . . . Although it has come through the senses, it is not a mere perception." A few pages later Schilder said in the Introduction : "When a leg has been amputated a phantom limb appears. . . . This animated image of the leg is the expression of the body schema." And he immediately asked, "What apparatus of the brain is the basis of these phenomena? What is the physiological basis of the knowledge of our body?"

Schilder's very phraseology is revealing. He speaks about a picture of our body formed in our mind. In a casual conversation not recorded on tape we may say something like "our own body," disregarding the essential fact that this body is never OURS but EXCLUSIVELY MINE. Yet the question: How do I experience my body as mine? is not even raised. Schilder presented that tri-dimensional image (sic.) as a circumscribed area within the total realm of perceptions of the "external world" in juxtaposition with all the rest. My mind it seems plays host to both—the image of my body and to the images of other bodies. If this were so, we would have to search for some signs which distinguish the image of my body among all the others. However, I experience my body not in juxtaposition together with other bodies but in a decisive, radical—though not absolute-opposition, characterized by an unparalleled immediacy.

What then is the meaning of the word MINE in reference to my body? Once again we are struck by the contrast between the facility of prelinguistic experience and the laborious task of giving an adequate account *expressis verbis*. In everyday life we use the word MINE, each of us, ever so often. But the meaning of MINE varies with reference to my property, as e.g., my house, my gloves, compared with phrases like my family with its manifold relations to my parents, my wife, my brothers and sisters ; while my children belong to me, I belong to my country, my town, my alma mater. Furthermore, my pleasure and my pain, my hunger and my thirst, are exclusively mine, in spite of all empathy and sympathy. This list is still far from exhaustive: My gloves fit my hands exactly ; yet what difference is there in the meaning of the word MINE : my hands, my gloves, I buy

my gloves, I put them on, I take them off, I place them somewhere; I may forget or lose them, or I may present to some one
a pair of suedes. My hands I cannot buy, neither can I lose
them. Gloves and house are my possessions; *I* am the possessor.
If I sell my house it will become the property of others. Do I
possess my body in the same way? To distinguish my copy of
"Being and Time" from other copies I wrote my name on the
title page or I may affix an *Ex Libris* to it. No sign is needed to
mark my body as mine for me. There is no doubt possible, no
effort necessary. What then characterizes my body for me—the
possessor of so many other things? Obviously it is not a common property. Mr. Procter and Mr. Gamble many years ago
may have said, "This is our factory." Yet *my* body is never
ours. It is unique for me, although it is one among many for
everybody else.*

Referring to my house or my gloves, my country, or my
university, to my friends or my enemies, if any, I am referring
to a kind of partnership between house and owner, father and
son, country and citizens. It seems that there is but one exception: Only in reference to my body there is no partner—at least
so it appears. Indeed, there is a partner, nothing remote or
concealed: just the opposite. The partner is a commonplace in
the literal sense of the word. For my partner—and the partner
of each one of you—is the Earth, which may well be spelled
here with a capital E. In our primary experience, unaffected by
the teachings of Copernicus and modern astronomy, the Earth is
the permanent, timeless ground, resting in its apparently effort-
less power. This certainly is a formidable partner! No wonder
that some of our patients, the agoraphobic, actually collapse
when they are confronted through mere sight with the basic
situation of man and animal, who, no longer rooted in the

---

* My hands are parts of my body. Yet other parts—the heart, the
adrenal glands, the reticular activating system—are not mine in the
same sense, for two reasons: 1) Not immediately acquainted with them
I only know of them through anatomical studies and instruction; 2) I
do not master them; as a creature, they possess me. Since a loss of those
organs or parts—if not fatal—is not followed by a phantom experience,
I may omit a further discussion of this topic.

ground like plants, are set free, but thereby also left or made rootless, forlorn, in lonely opposition.

In a conference dedicated to Aisthesis and Aesthetics, it may not be amiss to call a poet to the witness stand. Goethe, in a poem entitled "Meeresstille," which may be translated "CALM AT SEA," described in eight lines the situation of man lonely facing the boundless expanse of the ocean:

CALM AT SEA

"Silence deep rules o'er the waters,
    Calmly slumbering lies the main
While the sailor views with trouble
    Naught but one vast level plain.

"Not a zephyr is in motion!
    Silence fearful as the grave!
In the mighty waste of ocean
    Sunk to rest is every wave."*

Since great poetry is never fully translatable, I may read for the benefit of those who understand German the original version:

Tiefe Stille herrscht im Wasser
Ohne Regung ruht das Meer,
Und bekummert sieht der Schiffer
Glatte Flache rings umher.
Keine Luft von keiner Seite!
Todesstille furchterlich!
In der ungeheuern Weite
Reget keine Welle sich.

In the line before the last, Goethe used the word "ungeheuer" which shares with "unheimlich" the meaning of the "uncanny"; but "ungeheur" signifies also the boundless; it is the enormity of tension between sailor and sea which stains the boundless with the hue of the uncanny and turns silence into "deadly silence-terrifying" (Todesstille furchterlich).

_____

* Johan Wolfgang von Goethe, *The Poems of Goethe*, trans. by E. A. Bowring (Estes and Lauriat, Boston, 1883)

Howsoever evolution may have operated, the result is that all animals have been granted some freedom against the ground, from which they have been made. This primary detachment permits us, but also demands from us, to rise against gravity and to "ex-ist" in the original meaning of this word. Neither race nor individual have made themselves. But once born, the individual has to take over and to establish himself in lonely opposition to the whole to which he belongs. Yet the conquest of gravity is never complete; therefore a characteristic ambivalence dominates our corporeal existence. As an earthly creature, my body is MINE and not completely mine at the same time.* Gravity is never fully overcome, but gravity, against which we rise, also gives us the support we need. In getting up I establish, as the center of my sensory experience, MY HERE, which is both: my transitory position, moving along with me, but also one definite locality on the globe accessible to others. Getting up, rising against gravity—I am not referring only to the upright posture of man—first makes locomotion possible. In arising, my body becomes truly mine, authentic for me alone without any mediation.

While a balloon, lighter than air, is lifted by the air, while an airplane, through its engines, wings, and forward movement forces the air to a lifting, man and animals rise by their own power. While a balloon cannot descend without reduction of the inflating gas, while a plane can neither climb nor land safely without speeding forward, man and animals are able to sit or to lie down; in short, to get up as well as to relax through their own activities.

In our days, when most biologists hope to solve all the riddles of life with the help of techniques opening access to micro- and ultra-micro-structures, it must be said with a loud voice that all the acts of rising, standing, and moving are performed on a stage of "natural size." The upright position of man and ani-

* I want to refer here to Professor Zaner's presentation of the problem in his book on the *Problem of Embodiment* (Martinus Nijhoff, The Hague, 1964), and especially to his recent paper on "The Radical Reality of the Human Body," Humanitas, 1966.

mals is accomplished through a concerted action of individual bones and muscles, as they are known by their proper names like atlas and femur, or longus capitis and quadriceps femoris. The labor of contractile elements were lost, should they not function as integrant parts of this or that particular muscle; in turn the labor of the muscles were lost, were they not attached to specific parts of the skeleton. In the final situation the organism as a whole is brought in position, not the single bones, joints, muscles, let alone fibers and fibrills, cells and nuclei, myosin and DNA.*

Biochemistry alone cannot account for the upright position, since it necessarily disregards the architectural design of the animal body and its component parts, whose functions are meaningful only with the encompassing relation: individual-world. Biochemistry cannot solve the problems of *morphology*. An organism built so that it can oppose gravity, through its own natural structure and power, is beyond the scope of problems of physics and chemistry, because this situation does not permit a complete reduction to elemental quantities. In getting up we gain, though continuously threatened by falling, our positions in the world; viz., of belonging in opposition, challenging and overpowering Nature itself—a basic attitude in radical contrast to mere adaptation.

The act of "getting up" is a unique accomplishment. It is not a locomotion, which carries us from one circumscribed topos to another one. It is not a transportation from a lower level to a higher one, comparable to being lifted by an elevator from the ground floor to the upper floor. Upright, we still remain down, on the ground. The upright position is never fully accomplished; it is never per-fect. As a state of becoming open to the future, it demands my continuous effort, counteracting the permanent forces of gravity. In this precarious equilibrium, oscillating

---

* In the human performance of rising from the horizontal to the vertical position, the skeleton of the feet is turned from the vertical to the horizontal while the skeleton of the legs are turned from the horizontal to the vertical; when the operation has been completed the arms hang down from the shoulders.

between vertical and perpendicular tendencies we never reach security, firmly established.

In getting up, we oppose—each one for himself alone—the universe in its totality. Our relation to the world is that of standing in opposition, a part facing the engulfing whole as such. This unique relation of a part to the whole creates a situation in which locomotion becomes possible.

In the history of Western philosophy, Aisthesis (if not *nous*) was given pre-eminence before motion. It is my intention to show that motility, and with it the partial conquest of gravity, actually provides the foundation also for *Aisthesis*. Accustomed since birth to an environment populated with mobile creatures of many kinds, a group which we join early and eagerly, we have forgotten to wonder about the amazing facts that there are beings freed from the absolute dominance of gravity which holds moon and earth in their orbits. We are therefore not inclined to ascribe any ontological importance to that truly fundamental situation which provides the possibility for *Aisthesis* and for all interpersonal relations. For only in opposing as a part the whole to which I belong can I meet other parts as my partners responding somehow to my intentions. Because we exist as parts, together with others, related to an encompassing whole, it is our bodily existence which on this one ground first makes interpersonal relations possible.

Aisthesis and kinesis are confined to our awake hours. Sleep and awakeness are not our own deeds. I fall asleep, overwhelmed by fatigue. I am awakened, perhaps by an alarm clock which pierces the defensive threshold barriers of sleep. We are not masters of our own bodies. In awakening, I am first returned to my egocentric position in the world. Ready to get up and to stand on my feet, I do not in my consciousness design space as a three-dimensional Euclidean manifold, I find myself situated *in* space; i.e., in a gravity dominated terrestrial environment.

The transition from being asleep to being awake affects and transforms the organism as a whole. Whatever the role of the reticular activating substance may be, to be awake is not identi-

cal with any localized function of internal organs or cells.*
Contrary to the sleeping organism, the wake animal cannot be
studied as an isolated body. Awake, the world is open to me.
Awake, I find myself in an I-Allon relation which cannot be
reduced to events within a nervous system, as afferent impulses,
stimuli, input and output. Perhaps one could say: Asleep, the
organism is located together with many other things of various
kinds within surrounding space, exposed to the mere effect of
quantitative changes. Awake, the animal is in an open relation,
in a contra-position, facing its environment, meaningfully responding to its structure and events. Through the I-Allon relationship a horizon is opened for Aisthesis. Within this fundamental structure its basic traits generate, namely: Intentionality,
Activity, Polarity, Unity and Modal involvement.

Because of the late hour, I must limit my comments to a few
remarks.

1) *Intentionality:* I see this auditorium and the audience. I,
in my corporeal existence encounter—not an external world—
but on the common ground of terrestrial space persons and
things as objects; they are accessible to me without being incorporated. This situation, accepted without any doubt in every-day
life and also in the laboratory *practice* appears offensive in
scientific reflection. Every-day life parlance, far from referring
to an illusion, reveals our actual situation. The I-Allon relation,
established in our active emancipation from the ground, prior to
all particular events, provides the key for our understanding
how causality and intentionality can be brought into accord.

----

* No doubt EEG records taken during sleep and during wakefulness
show characteristic differences. But disregarding the fact that such distinction require an observer, alert and awake, by himself, the qualification
of the records demands a preceding insight into the conditions of the subject. Because we notice that the subject was first asleep and then awake,
we are in a position afterwards to grade the EEG records accordingly.
The records per se are mute; they receive their qualification from our
prior distinction between a subject asleep and a subject awake. They do
not tell us what it means to be awake. We—awake ourselves—notice
whether or not a subject relates himself actively toward his, better to our
common, environment. Therefore the condition of wakefulness, and with
it that of aisthesis and kinesis, cannot be studied in an isolated body.

2) *Activity:* The physiological term "receptor"—Sherrington invented even the paradox expression of distance receptors—refers to the presumptive passivity of sensory experience. Yet we use, probably not without some good reason, such expressions of action as: to watch, to look for, to keep in sight, to cast an eye upon, to attend to, to listen, etc. Indeed, to see, to hear, to touch, to smell, to taste—all these words, signifying sensory experience, are used as transitive verbs with the obvious meaning of seeing, hearing, touching, tasting, smelling something.

When I look around in this auditorium, the movements of my eyeballs do not provide me with cues, instrumental for adding a third dimension to an otherwise flat "image." The fact that "I see you" implies that I see you from here. Although indispensable for the intentional act of seeing, this *Here* is by itself not an optical datum, but established as a pivotal within the all inclusive I-Allon relation.

Eyes and ears are not instruments mounted on a moveable Fisher-body but organs of a creature standing up in opposition to the ground and thereby potentially related to objects (objecta).

3) *Polarity:* In seeing, hearing, etc., I experience things in relation to me in my corporeal existence. We see the same play together. The show is one; the sights are many. Returning to this place, we see this auditorium again, i.e., our acts of seeing are repeated while the hall is encountered as the same. In walking, I experience myself in motion, but street and houses at rest.

4) *The Unity of Sense Modalities:* As mentioned before, we can see *and* hear *and* touch *and* smell *and* taste the same object —not through association of simple ideas, nor through some sort of synthesis of hyletic data. There is no melting into one. Seen, touched, tasted, an apple remains one and the same object accessible in a variety of contacts. We do not touch optical qualities but visible things. Such modification in spite of the unaltered diversity is made possible (I am sure you guessed it!) through the global I-Allon relation.

5) *The Modal Involvement:* Through each one of the var-

ious modalities we are personally involved in or committed to the actual situation. There is an abundance of examples. To give just one : think of a physician *inspecting* the tongue of a patient ; or of a gourmet *tasting* on the tip of *his* tongue the aroma of old Burgundy ; or of two lovers dedicated to a "bilingual" kiss, or of a naughty boy sticking out his tongue, as an expression of contempt.

Here we can at last after a long but indispensable detour return to the starting point : By now it has become understandable that the anosognostic cannot experience his paralyzed left side, although he sees it, while the amputee experiences the presence of his lost limb, although it is not visible to him.

Obviously, vision is not required for my experience of my body. I see with my eyes, but I don't see them—nor do I see my back, face, or tongue, although they are definitely mine. Being up and around every day, I never see the highly sensitive soles of my feet, bare or shod. Yet I am fully aware that I am standing on my own feet. Even if I close my eyes, seal my ears, the intimacy characteristic for the experience of my body is not abolished.

There is no gradient of mineness relative to vision and illumination. Darkness does not reduce, it rather intensifies my awareness of my body. No light is needed, nor desired, for the enjoyment of the marital bed.

We do not experience our bodies as objects of some special kind, in the midst of other objects not as something given, not as something "we have," let alone as an image or perception.

I experience my body as mine within the framework of the I-Allon relation ; I experience my body as mine, acting and reacting in the two, not strictly separate regions of incorporation and extraversion. I experience my body as mine in a state of becoming open to the future. I experience my body as mine in touching and being touched. In this context the skin must not be considered a surface of an isolated body, but as a border area, a field of contact with the world.

The traditional examination of tactile sensitivity is incomplete, if not misleading. It gives reliable information about the functions and viability of individual nerves, branches, etc. Yet, taken as a complete inventory it distorts the content of sensory experience. For when we ask a patient or subject to sit down or to lie down, to close his eyes, and to respond whether, where, how, he is being touched, we transform the subject from an experiencing creature into a detached observer concerned with objective accidents occurring on the surface of his own body. Thereby we separate a person from the world—or better, isolate him within the world—we separate the sensorium from the motorium. We eliminate the direction of being touched from somewhere, substituting a mere *where* locality. No doubt Head's schemata tried to account for the fact that we find ourselves touchable before being actually touched.

Indeed, if someone reports that he was touched—let us say on the right cheek or on the left thumb, or on both places simultaneously—he must have been aware of the characteristic articulation of the whole area (in head, trunk, limbs, in front and back) before the brush made contact at one or two circumscribed spots. In our basic situation facing the world we expose ourselves actively to a distinct ingress from overthere, so much so that in the absence of light darkness itself becomes visible, "palpable obscure," and silence "deadly" with the complete fading of sound.

Facing the world through the antagonistic cooperation of a gravitational and antigravitational forces I experience my body as "heft" and "puissance,"* corresponding, in part, to the difference between the trunk—where tactile receptivity is accentuated—and the limbs, with the interlacing of sensitivity and motility. The limbs, especially the arms, function—in our experience—as *extensions* to the trunk, characterized through directions, reach and boundaries. In agreement with Head's concept of "schemata" rather than with Schilder's "body-image" the

* On the search for terms widely apart from the connotation of motor response, I decided for "heft"—a rare word, related to heave and heavy—and for "puissance," synonym to the Greek *dynamis,* borrowing this French word from Merleau-Ponty.

potential reach—once firmly established—persists as phantom, even after the loss of a limb.

In order to silence the inured potentialities new boundaries must be firmly established. The shrinking and telescoping of the phantom demonstrate the competition between the old and new boundaries while hand and fingers, foot and toes, the parts of active and passive contacts, are always preserved. Actually the shrinking and telescoping indicates a slow transformation until finally a new border will be established. Haber's and Cronholm's experiments support this interpretation. Haber* has shown that the two-point discrimination and the sensitivity for light touch and for localization is improved over the area of the stump compared with symmetrical points of the intact limb. Cronholm's† experiment is still more convincing. He has shown that in a considerable number of patients the phantom disappears when the stump is covered with a large cloth, although compared with the stimulation of single points many more receptors at the stump are activated simultaneously. They disappear—if my interpretation is correct—because with this broad covering a new border, at least for the time being, has been established.

* Haber, W. B. Effects of loss of limb on sensory functions. J. Psychol. 40:115-123, 1955.

† Cronholm, B. Phantom limbs in amputees: study of changes in integration of centripetal impulses with special reference to referred sensations. Acta Psychiat. Neurol. Scand. Suppl. 72, 1951.

A DISCUSSION OF DR. STRAUS' PAPER, "PHANTOMS AND PHANTASMATA"

William F. Fischer

As has happened in each of our previous conferences, and as we have come so unquestioningly to expect, Dr. Straus has again presented us with an insightful, illuminating paper. In his concern with making explicit "the unwritten constitution of everyday life," he has turned his attention to another aspect of the human body as it is lived. Characteristically, he has chosen to focus upon a group of related pathologies, thereby making thematic the implicit, unquestioned conditions of the norm. Specifically, he has thematized the phenomenon of bodily possession, the experience and the living of my body as mine. Dr. Straus raises two questions with regard to the lived body: 1) What is it—actions, feelings, experiences, neurophysiological events, unconscious mechanisms, etc.—that enables me to experience my body as mine, and 2) What are the major dimensions of my experience of my body?

In his answer to the first question, Dr. Straus attempts to demonstrate the inadequacies of both the neurophysiological and the psychoanalytic approaches. With regard to the former, he shows that within a strictly epiphenomenal, materialistic and hence solipsistic perspective, "there is no room for the distinction of mine from not mine." With regard to the latter, he suggests that psychoanalytic theory concerns itself with the experience of bodily possession only when that experience is threatened, that it too takes for granted the everyday state of affairs. Further, he casts doubt upon the credibility of appeals to unconscious mechanisms as defenses against mutilation.

In the place of these two approaches, Dr. Straus offers a third, his own. He argues that my body is not mine in the same sense that my gloves or my house or any of my possessions are mine. My body is mine in getting up, in rising against gravity, in opposing myself to the Allon. My experience of my body and

especially my limbs, as mine, is only understandable within the
framework of I-World relations, in my potentiality for acting,
for touching and being touched, in my openness to the future.

In his answer to the second question, that is, what are the
major dimensions of my experience of my body, Dr. Straus'
answer may be stated as follows. In touching and being touched,
my skin is not the surface of my isolated body. Rather, it is my
field of possible contact, my boundary in the world. Further, I
experience my limbs not as dangling anatomical appendages, but
as organs of action, as instruments of reach and direction.

How do these formulations help us to understand the phenomenon of the phantom limb? As Dr. Straus states early in his
paper, any theory which purports to explain this phenomenon
must account for the following facts: 1) after loss of a limb, a
phantom is a perfectly regular occurrence, 2) among amputees,
only a few experience a painful phantom, 3) the phantom
undergoes characteristic changes, such as shortening with discontinuity and telescoping, and 4) only after loss of certain
parts of the body does the phantom appear; there are few, if
any, cases of phantom breasts or genitals.

Although Dr. Straus does not, in this paper, concretely apply
his formulations of the experience of bodily possession to the
phenomenon of the phantom limb, it might be possible to utilize
his insights in the following manner. It should be acknowledged
that the approach presented below, in some sense a transcendental approach, is not necessarily implied by Dr. Straus' analysis. In fact, I am reasonably sure that he himself would not
formulate his approach in this way. Nonetheless, if I experience
my body as mine insofar as it affords me the potentiality of
acting, touching and being touched, then this body which I live
can be grasped as a network or matrix of meanings. It is not
mine because I can see it as I would a tree or a car. It is not a
thing for me, a possession which I have for the moment but
could lose. Rather, its mine-ness is rooted in its potentials for
involving me in the sundry activities that are my everyday life.
These potentials constitute a matrix of interrelated meanings
whose unifying theme is the indissolubility of my relations with

the world. Thus, the amputation of the anatomical limb is not immediately the same as the amputation of the lived meanings of that limb. The loss of the anatomical limb is an event which I can immediately apprehend with my eyes, but only from the perspective of the observer. The amputation of the lived meanings of the limb is not one event, but a continuing series thereof. Gradually learned, it can be assimilated and lived only through continued experience with loss of possibility. Thus, the phantom limb is the limb of meaningful activity which has yet to be altered by subsequent experience and learning. The phenomena of shortening with discontinuity and telescoping are testimonials to that learning. I learn that the possibilities of my involvements with the world are changed, that my boundaries and reach have been altered.

But why, one may ask, are there no phantom breasts or genitals? Surely these parts of the body are "loaded" with meanings which refer to my possible relations with the world. This is certainly a problem. At present, the best answer that I can offer is to suggest that the lived meanings of breasts and genitals are so circumscribed, so confined to a limited number of activities, that they are, in fact, immediately altered with amputation.

If the mine-ness of my body, or various parts thereof, is rooted in its or their potentials for involving me in the world, and if these potentials constitute a matrix of interrelated meanings whose unifying theme is the indissolubility of my relations with the world, then other pathological phenomena, such as hysterical paralysis and depersonalization should be more intelligible. This is not the place to enter into detailed analyses of these phenomena, but such analyses are currently being attempted.

Thus we may say that we are indebted to Dr. Straus for his penetrating insights and while we may use these in approaches other than he would prefer, this should in no way diminish our gratitude.

III. AESTHETIC CREATION

THE FABRIC OF EXPRESSION*

Maurice Natanson

IN HIS *Autobiography*, R. G. Collingwood observes that "you cannot find out what a man means by simply studying his spoken or written statements, even though he has spoken or written with perfect command of language and perfectly truthful intention. In order to find out his meaning you must also know what the question was (a question in his own mind, and presumed by him to be in yours) to which the thing he has said or written was meant as an answer."[1] If we apply this notion to art, a reversal of a sort is necessary: the question to which the art work is meant as an answer is first formulated through the work and provides the viewer with an analogue which may serve to frame an isomorphic and resonant question. Corresponding to Collingwood's dialectic of questions and answers in philosophy and history there may be a situation of probing and responding in art and aesthetics, a dialectic of uncovering or "de-sedimentation" through which the observer and participant in art locate their possible and appropriate themes and concepts. The domain in which the posing of answers and the reconstruction of questions in art creation and art response arise may be termed the field of expression. Its range is extraordinary, for it encompasses not only the traditional modes of art but also the forms of mundane experience in which art is rooted even when it transcends daily life. Expression, then, stands as a formative and encompassing term having broader reference than its classic placement in the aesthetic theories of Croce and Collingwood permits and retaining its distant but relevant association with the morphological, biological, and physiognomic enterprises of Bell, Darwin, and Lavater. Art expression, human expression,

---

* This article was originally published in *The Review of Metaphysics,* Volume XXI, 1968; published with permission.
[1] R. G. Collingwood, *An Autobiography,* London: Oxford University Press, 1939, p. 31.

and creature expression may be understood to form a unity of
meaningful relationships, a fabric contrived by intention and
response, sustained by and sustaining the perceptual world.
Through a dialectic of questions we may come to explore this
fabric of expression.

I begin with mundanity. The everydayness of experience
presents us with objects and events which are at once intimately
apprehended as familiar fragments of our lives and interpreted
in their universal, rather cold typicality. Around us there is a
swarming of objects, and we pick out of the perceptual array the
small conveniences we call "things." Within the horizon of daily
life, objects have an unquestioned status; they simply *are*. To
question them is primarily to take the way in which they *are* as
an occasion for displaying their history. Consider the following
two descriptions of shoes:

"They are one of the most ordinary types of working shoe:
the blucher design, and soft in the prow, lacking the seam
across the root of the big toe: covering the ankles: looped
straps at the heels: blunt, broad, and rounded at the toe:
broad-heeled: made up of most simple roundednesses and
squarings and flats, of dark brown raw thick leathers nailed,
and sewn coarsely to one another in courses and patterns of
doubled and tripled seams, and such throughout that like
many other small objects they have great massiveness and repose and are, as the houses and overalls are, and the feet and
legs of the women, who go barefooted so much, fine pieces of
architecture.

They are softened, in the uppers, with use, and the soles are
rubbed thin enough, I estimate, that the ticklish grain of the
ground can be felt through at the center of the forward sole.
The heels are deeply biased. Clay is worked into the substance of the uppers and a loose dust of clay lies over them.
They have visibly though to the eye subtly taken the mold of
the foot, and structures of the foot are printed through them
in dark sweat at the ankles, and at the roots of the toes. They
are worn without socks, and by experience of similar shoes I
know that each man's shoe, in long enough course of wear,
takes as his clothing does the form of his own flesh and bones,
and would feel as uneasy to any other as if A, glancing into
the mirror, were met by B's eyes, and to their owner, a natural

part though enforcement of the foot, which may be used or
shed at will. There is great pleasure in a sockless and sweated
foot in the fitted leathers of a shoe."[2]

Now the second description:

"The peasant woman wears her shoes in the field. Here they
are for the first time what they are. They are such all the more
genuinely the less the peasant woman thinks about the shoes
while she is at work, or sees them at all, or even takes any
heed of them. She stands and walks in them. This is how shoes
actually serve . . . In Van Gogh's painting we cannot even
tell where the shoes stand. There is nothing surrounding this
pair of peasant shoes in or to which they might belong, only
an undefined space. There are not even clods from the soil of
the field or the path through it sticking to them, which might
at least hint at their employment. A pair of peasant shoes and
nothing more. And yet.

From the dark opening of the worn insides of the shoes the
toilsome tread of the worker stands forth. In the stiffly solid
heaviness of the shoes there is the accumulated tenacity of her
slow trudge through the far-spreading and ever-uniform fur-
rows of the field, swept by a raw wind. On the leather there
lies the dampness and saturation of the soil. Under the soles
there slides the loneliness of the field-path as the evening de-
clines. In the shoes there vibrates the silent call of the earth, its
quiet gift of the ripening corn and its enigmatic self-refusal in
the fallow desolation of the wintry field . . . This equipment
belongs to the *earth* and it is protected in the *world* of the
peasant woman . . . Van Gogh's painting is the disclosure
of what the equipment, the pair of peasant shoes, *is* in truth."[3]

The remarkable convergence of both statements points to the
irruption of history in the midst of the mundane. In the first
description the shoes were real, their owner was observed and
reported in a way which transposed objects from their public

[2] James Agee and Walker Evans, *Let Us Now Praise Famous Men,*
Boston: Houghton, Mifflin Co., 1941, pp. 269-270.
[3] Martin Heidegger, "The Origin of the Work of Art," translated
by Albert Hofstadter, in *Philosophies of Art and Beauty,* edited by
Albert Hofstadter and Richard Kuhns, New York: The Modern Library,
1964, pp. 662-664.

hiddenness to their overt privacy. In the second description, Van Gogh's pictorial presentation underwent interpretive conceal-ment. Though it seems to be the case that more and more is revealed about the peasant shoes, in reality a thickening of information develops: the object becomes darker in its significa-tion, less available to the listening glance, until finally the shoes are returned to the earth which guards them. The descriptive convergence is indeed a strange one, for different kinds of questions are appropriate to the history of the objects at issue here. Mundane objects appear both in the everyday world and in the painter's portrayal of that world; they have their history. What questions are suitable to its uncovering?

The history of objects is a history of expressiveness. The work shoes are looked at as new acquisitions when first bought. Their luster and newness in the beginning is no realized part of what they will become with use, not merely worn but used continually as routinized props or aids for work and movement. The initial seeing of the real thing savors its central quality; later glances are tangential to the object, looking at it margin-ally, somewhat in the way a customs official inspects a passport, attending not so much to the photograph as to the way it's glued to the page and the way the seal is formed. The peasant shoes, on the other hand, are rooted in the *world* of their owner, caught in a segment of the working order which dominates and determines their space in the painting. Here it is wrong to ask of the mundane object, How old is it? or Where was it bought? The object functions in quite different ways, for its "purpose" in the painting is to secure the space open to the peasant, the embedded and rooted locus of work and earth. As mundane objects, the peasant shoes link the interior of the house with the fields outside. They are neighbouring entities, bringing together the terrain of labor and the landscape of home. The questions proper to the painting now emerge: How is the mundane object a possible being in a world in which men work? How is the space of the object rooted in a source defined by what transpires outside the realm of home? To speak of a history of expression is to suggest that these questions both constitute the mundanity of the object in the painting and provide a clue to its way of meaning in the aesthetic transaction made possible by the viewer. The real object in unimagined mundanity must undergo a transcendental mode of questioning for its expressive history to appear. Actually, real mundanity presents a backdrop, a frame of sorts over and against which or within which the object in the painting may be comprehended. Mundanity corresponds here to the street scene or courtyard glimpsed through the window of a Dutch interior in which an intimate scene transpires while an unconcerned world literally goes by. Love and despair express themselves not only within but against a world which remains temporally as well as spatially indifferent.[4] But there is also a reflecting and reflected quality to the mundane object within the painting, for it bears relationships of an intramundane order to the other objects in the same frame. The objects in the painting are there for us, as viewers; they are also there for each other. The objects reflected by a mirror in a painting may be taken as backdrops for the interiority of the world presented.[5] The questions proper to the painting lead us, in turn, to the questions posed by the painter.

At this point those who have trudged reluctantly along with these remarks may refuse to go any further. It is not difficult to list the complaints: the language is complex, the claims are rather sweeping, the references are scattered, and there are no slides. And having said that, I recognize that a little more honesty may escape with the general egress: from a pair of bloody boots a metaphysical shoe factory seems to have been generated! I have no hesitation in pleading guilty to such

---

[4] Cf. W. H. Auden, "Musée des Beaux Arts," in *The Collected Poetry of W. H. Auden*, New York: Random House, 1945.

[5] Cf. Maurice Merleau-Ponty, "Eye and Mind," translated by Carleton Dallery, in *The Primacy of Perception*, Evanston, Illinois: Northwestern University Press, 1964, p. 168. Quoting Claudel, Merleau-Ponty writes: "In paintings themselves we could seek a figured philosophy of vision —its iconography, perhaps. It is no accident, for example, that frequently in Dutch paintings (as in many others) an empty interior is 'digested' by the 'round eye of the mirror.' This prehuman way of seeing things is the painter's way."

charges because they don't touch the real question of method involved in what I'm after. But it might be judicious at this moment to pause for a methodological intermission. By invoking Collingwood's idea of a dialectic of questions and answers, I have tried to suggest that art, no less than man and nature, may be interrogated as a field of expression. Instead of turning to a painting as an already classified and defined entity, we are examining it as a signal for interpretive comprehension. As an expressive phenomenon, art stands together with a vast range of equally signifying and provocative realities, including mundanity itself. Ordinary experience, the world of daily life, is coded from childhood on, and we enter swiftly into the games of terror and humiliation pre-established for us. Neither rules nor guidelines are needed or given; we respond immediately to the initial harassment of parents and strangers. "All right, I'm leaving," the mother calls to the rooted, unwilling child, "I'm going now." And as the child persists in its squat immobility, she calls over her shoulder, "Good-bye." A few steps further along, she pauses long enough to gauge the response to threatened abandonment, flutters her fingers in what would appear to be a last gesture of farewell, and recommences the departure. Were adult lips given to the child at that moment, he might cry, "Well, if you're going, for God's sake, go!" Instead, the familiar patterns appear. Either the child retreats from the brink of divorce and runs howling homeward, or the parent marches back, grabs the child firmly, and drags the screaming creature along. In a second drama, the child misbehaving in the presence of another child, a non-misbehaver, is admonished: "Look at that little boy over there watching you! Aren't you ashamed of yourself! Aren't you ashamed to have him see you like this!" And through a train of tears and slaver, the crier looks at the paradigm alter ego: his first and unforgettable enemy encamped neatly beyond the scorched cheeks and the enflamed ego of the bawler. Such signs of expression are to appear and reappear continuously in the career of the individual; their permutations are infinite and mysterious: slyness, wariness, pomposity, cunning, and guile no less than innocence, trustfulness, devotedness, adoration, beneficence, and the admixtures of uncertainty and indifference. The translation of these signs presupposes a pre-predicative comprehension of their expressive distinctiveness as well as the fringe of remoteness and surprise which attends them. Without a set of instructions, we proceed immediately and surely to put together the contents of the perceptual package we're handed. Or, more strictly, the assembled unit springs into being without the self-conscious employment of procedural rules.

The field of expression, then, is coeval with our encounter with mundane reality. The world is originarily a significative one, and we find ourselves at every moment caught up in the interpretation of its design. The interrogation of experience involves a tracing back of an ordered accumulation of meaningful signs. I have suggested that an analogous process may be seen in art, and here we rejoin the discussion of the artist's questions. Instead of objects, let us consider events. One of the most remarkable essays in the "de-sedimentation" or uncovering of meaning in art is Ben Shahn's "The Biography of a Painting." In it he describes the genesis of one of his works, entitled "Allegory," and offers a reconstructive hermeneutic of its expression. "The central image of the painting," Shahn writes, "was one which I had been developing across a span of months —a huge Chimera-like beast, its head wreathed in flames, its body arched across the figures of four recumbent children. These latter were dressed in very common-place clothes, perhaps not entirely contemporary, but rather as I could draw them and their details from my own memory."[6] The immediate occasion for the beginning of what was ultimately to be "the painting of the red beast" was a Chicago fire in which a colored man, Mr. Hickman, had lost his four children. Shahn was asked to make drawings for the story, and he gives us this account of what developed:

---

[6] Ben Shahn, *The Shape of Content*, New York: Vintage Books, 1960, p. 30 (Cf. *The Biography of a Painting*, New York: Paragraphic Books, 1966).

"I examined a great deal of factual visual material, and then I discarded all of it. It seemed to me that the implications of this event transcended the immediate story; there was a universality about man's dread of fire, and his sufferings from fire. There was a universality in the pity which such a disaster invokes. Even racial injustice, which had played its part in this event, had its overtones. And the relentless poverty which had pursued this man, and which dominated the story, had its own kind of universality.

I now began to devise symbols of an almost abstract nature, to work in terms of such symbols. Then I rejected that approach too. For in the abstracting of an idea one may lose the very intimate humanity of it, and this deep and common tragedy was above all things human. I returned then to the small family contacts, to the familiar experiences of all of us, to the furniture, the clothes, the look of ordinary people, and on that level made my bid for universality and for the compassion that I hoped and believed the narrative would arouse.

Of all the symbols which I had begun or sought to develop, I retained only one in my illustrations—a highly formalized wreath of flames with which I crowned the plain shape of the house which had burned . . .

Among my discarded symbols pertaining to the Hickman story there were a number of heads and bodies of beasts, besides several Harpies, Furies, and other symbolic, semi-classic shapes and figures. Of one of these, a lion-like head, but still not a lion, I made many drawings, each drawing approaching more nearly some inner figure of primitive terror which I was seeking to capture. I was beginning to become most familiar with this beast-head. It was, you might say, under control . . .

When I at last turned the lion-like beast into a painting, I felt able to imbue it with everything that I had ever felt about a fire. I incorporated the highly formalized flames from the Hickman story as a terrible wreath about its head, and under its body I placed the four child figures which, to me, hold the sense of all the helpless and the innocent.

The image that I sought to create was not one of *a* disaster; that somehow doesn't interest me. I wanted instead to create the emotional tone that surrounds disaster; you might call it the inner disaster."[7]

---

[7] *Ibid.*, pp. 32-37 (with omissions). Cf. Shahn's "Imagination and Intention," *Review of Existential Psychology and Psychiatry*, Vol. VII, 1967, pp. 13-17. There Shahn writes (p. 17): "I recall a preoccupation

Shahn's account traces out in some detail a history of connotative themes and memorial episodes which contributed to the creation of the painting: a fire in the Russian village he lived in as a child, the destruction of his own house, a mad-woman, the stare of an abnormal cat, the image of a wolf, leading finally to the story of Romulus and Remus. But these are the surface elements; lying below them is the restive and polymorphous awareness of a lifetime, the taste of domination and caughtness, the surge of a distant promise, and the commingling of persons in the lost arcades of remembrance. The beast's flaming head is at once the vandalism of nature, the ferocity of societal pressure, the hot center of birth, and the wild insistence of death. What questions, then, are proper to this artist?

If we start with the painting, it is not difficult to locate and describe the central motifs. The red beast is mythic, endangering, and primitive; its mane seems out of control. We can easily appreciate the flaming quality of its stance over the small victims huddled or thrown finally in a heap beneath it. Teeth and claws show forth powerfully. Now if we ask, What is Shahn trying to express in this painting? we are put in an odd position. Without having read his account of the painting, it is quite reasonable to say that the flaming beast is a primeval figure of destruction and that the children beneath its outstretched legs are victims of its action. It is not likely that the artist's memories of childhood fires or his concern with a more recent tragedy are available in the work. The Romulus and Remus theme does manifest itself, though in a discordant way, for the beast appears to be guarding

---

with fires that was with me over a period of time. I tried to realize pictorially something of the panic that had remained within my nervous system as a result of a frightful childhood experience. I achieved the emotional impact that I sought not through an image of a burning house or of people wrapped in flames, but through the image of a dark red wolf beast exuding flames and standing arched over a small knot of victims. I remember too that as I painted the insane eyes of the beast, that curious immediate recognition took place. I doubt that I have even actually encountered a wolf. But I believe that the wolf-terror must be deeply embedded—almost archetypal—in those of us who are of Russian origin. Created images are not duplicates of experience but are always vestiges and fragments known and felt in many ways."

its kill rather than preparing to nourish them. The "Allegory" includes human figures against a background of uncertitude. What we cannot honestly say is that, without his having told us, we could recover the concrete, biographical elements involved in the creation of the painting. But to look for them is a mistake. The question, What is the artist trying to express? forces his aesthetic participant into a false position, one which demands that the symbols and themes of the work be decoded in a chronological manner, as though Shahn *first* had the idea for the painting and *then* set out to give it shape. What "The Biography of a Painting" makes utterly clear is that Shahn discovered a variety of things about himself in the career of the problem he confronted in the painting. His red beast underwent many transformations: Chimera, lion, wolf, cat, Harpy, Fury, and indecipherable creatures. It was not possible for Shahn to ask at any point: What figure will embody the powers and forces I seek to express? because the expression was the agency for releasing the question. The elements of the question are given: death, innocence, poverty, injustice, terror, but the question needs shaping, and that disconnection of end and means is the essence of the artist's predicament. Interestingly enough, the repudiation of a means-end conception of art is also axial to the aesthetic theory of art as expression. Collingwood writes: "Until a man has expressed his emotion, he does not yet know what emotion it is. The act of expressing it is therefore an exploration of his own emotions. He is trying to find out what these emotions are. There is certainly here a directed process: an effort, that is, directed upon a certain end; but the end is not something foreseen and preconceived, to which appropriate means can be thought out in the light of our knowledge of its special character. Expression is an activity of which there can be no technique."[8] Let us say, then, that expression reveals the question the artist asks and that the emergent question cannot be stripped off the fabric which embodies it. Shahn's question in

---

[8] R. G. Collingwood, *The Principles of Art,* Oxford: The Clarendon Press, 1938, p. 111.

the painting "Allegory" is: What constitutes "the inner disaster?" The way in which the question arises presents its own difficulties.

A psychology of art creation would have to face the problem of articulating the individual genesis of a component of expression. It may be, as Shahn himself indicates, that childhood recollection of stories about wolves in old Russia helped to form the later Chimera image which tormented his painting. What interests me, in the present context, is a very different issue: the structural horizon through which Shahn's question appears. What are the conditions for the possibility of the question? Questions are *situated,* they demand relatedness and a ground of pre-acquaintanceship. A question without a horizon is like a matchmaker without clients. "Would you like a friend?" a rather elderly gentleman once asked me in the waiting room of a North Carolina airport some years ago. I wasn't quite sure what he had in mind. It turned out that he was distributing religious tracts. Questions have moorings, sources, and a logic of advancement. In searching out the horizon of the artist's question, it is necessary to attend to the full range of expression. In the case of Shahn's "Allegory," we were aided if not guided by the artist's own account. I propose now to try it on my own. For the sake of continuity, I'll turn to another work by Shahn, one for which, as far as I know, he has given no biographical reconstruction.

"Handball" is the title of a painting by Shahn done in 1939.[9] The scene shows four players in the midst of a game being observed by two bystanders. The court includes one massive wall marked with a number "1" and is demarcated by perpendicular foul lines. A short meshed fence stands on top of the wall; beyond, in the background, are brick buildings, probably used or once used for stores and offices. They give the impression of being deserted, with their windows boarded up. In the near distance, to the side of the court, is a billboard with pasted up

---

[9] Reproduced in *Masters of Modern Art,* edited by Alfred H. Barr, Jr., New York: The Museum of Modern Art, 1954, p. 162.

announcements of movies. An empty lot borders the court. The
players are bent in the poses of the game, the server about to
drop the ball, his partner waiting at the side line to enter as soon
as the ball is hit, the opposing team, represented chiefly by a
dark figure leaning forward from the hips, bodily anticipating
the serve. The observers have their backs to the viewer. They
remain jacketed figures (the name "Urals" is written on the
back of one) standing between the viewer and the players, as the
wall stands between the players and the deserted buildings
beyond. Each time I look at this painting, my initial response to
it is renewed. For me it created and sustains an instant recognition of my own childhood. Not only did I play handball on such
courts and observe endless games as well, I remember the slant
of the body in the posture of serving and the stance of the
onlooker, hands folded across the lower part of the chest or
thrust in the pockets of the pants. The vocabulary of association
is packed with terms which bring back the world within which
the game was played: bone bruises, purplish swellings caused by
pounding the small and very hard black rubber ball, "killers," an
unreturnable shot made when the ball hit at the exact point
where the wall and floor meet, "hops" and "hooks," services
with a sly spin which made the ball dart suddenly as you
prepared to return it. The paraphernalia of the players included
leather gloves and athletic shoes with a special thick rubber piece
surrounding the inner and front part of the shoe. But the larger
environs included the time, years of depression and the Roose-
velt thirties, the signs of Federal projects, synthetic work. Playing handball meant coming to the court from home, a world
marked by European customs and languages, carried on in what
in today's terms must be considered an antique mode. Shahn's
jacketed figure with the "Urals" sign was the envy and goal of
myself and my associates. We were forever planning a "club,"
the chief (and as far as I can recall the sole) purpose of which
was to wear such jackets. The trouble was that jackets with
appropriate lettering had to be ordered in bulk—that meant a
minimum of six—and we could never afford them. But we were
always negotiating with a small businessman who, as I now

think back on it, was gifted with infinite patience. Home itself was a place of projects and performances. When visitors came, I was expected to entertain them at the appropriate time with recitations. I specialized in dramatic evocations of such works as "The Building of the Ship":

> "Thou, too, sail on, O ship of State!
> Sail on, O Union, strong and great!
> Humanity with all its fears,
> With all its hopes of future years,
> Is hanging breathless on thy fate!"

I also did "O Captain my Captain" with considerable fervor, which left me, if not my audience, quite moved. These times and images are brought together in Shahn's painting, but the associations which lead to the question I find posed by the artist are hardly private or idiosyncratic motifs. Doubtless, Shahn's painting can be appreciated by participants whose viewing owes nothing to the New York of thirty or thirty-five years ago (let alone that aspect of New York life I have described and hinted at). No more is it the case that an appreciator of "Allegory" had to grow up in the Chicago slums or have known Mr. Hickman. The entire point of the artist's question is that it arises in and is celebrated through a horizon which can provide a multiple content, infinitely varied in character and style, by means of which expression is achieved. My question need not be and most likely cannot be identical with that of Shahn. What I can share with him is the horizon which houses the question, which guards its potential, and which permits both artist and viewer to return to the source of experiential signification. In these terms, the handball court is an answer to a question whose horizon leads back as much to Shahn's childhood as to mine. The legend "Urals" across the observer's jacket stretches from Russia to New York or from source to occasion. The game is between cross-purposed figures, dark and mixed, observed by loiterers of uncertain intent who are, in turn, seen by us, onlookers of the painting. The buildings in the background, seen over the top of the wall and through the wire screen, are pressed together in desolation. On close inspection, the blurred announcement on the poster turns out to spell "Shirley Temple." The artist's question is: How did we arrive here, participant-observers? The horizon in which the question perches is the migration of persons in the mystery of sociality, a community of beings bounded by historical distance, social disruption, and cultural misgivings. The painting is a victory of performance over vacancy and despoilment.

In exploring expression we have been moving through a history of mundanity, including objects, events, and powers. The effort has been to emphasize the interconnections of questions and answers, to locate expression neither in the subjective intent of the artist nor in the objective resultant of his creation. Instead, the stress is on the dialectic itself, the horizon of questioning which undergirds expression and releases its focused content. Personal history and biography become forms through which distinctive questions may be posed, though the questions cannot be severed from their source. Nor is it always the case that the questions can be stated. It is perfectly sensible to say that a horizon can be grasped at the same time that its question remains fugitive. And undoubtedly, expression transcends interpretation. It is possible to return again and again to the art work precisely because its identifying questions return us to our own complex and remote sources. The sedimentation of our own individual history requires transliteration into the order we call a world. The movement outward is not only toward a world but also from a world. There is no danger of the dialectic of expression subjectivizing the phenomena of art or the contents of the material sphere, the domain of nature. Although we have turned to art alone, man and nature, man *in* nature, are present, though silent witnesses to the discussion. Clearly, two facets of expression have been taken advantage of here, though I hope not done in: the expression theory of art in its aesthetic stance and the larger encampment of expression whose entourage includes the dialectic of questions and answers and the concept of structural horizon. A unity of standpoint underlies the entire investigation, which may now be terminated with a reflexive note and a final consideration.

There is in art criticism as there is in sociological and philosophical analysis a rhythm of intellectual search which gets more rapid the larger the possibilities for expansion become. If X is true of one art form, is it true of all forms? If X is true of this work, will it provide a formula for investigating all works in this genre? If X is true and fruitful, can it be expanded into a schema which will catch all or nearly everything? The search for essential knowledge might be thought of as operating in this current. If we can find and adequately describe the essence of painting, will we not then be able to scrutinize all paintings with assured and ultimately reliable, final discretion? What restrains self-made nominalists as well as their professional counterparts from engaging in this kind of procedure is simply a blunt sense of danger and a well chosen caution about quick results. Alleviating the fear, though, may require the promise of multiple descriptions, destined to knock against and upset each other. If phenomenological method be taken to be a universalizing tactic, one which announces absolute results, a tower of essences, then it appears to the reticent observer that the only protection against massive claims is bitter expectations. The conception of phenomenology which underlies my efforts must be understood on a different plane. The universalizing impulse of phenomenology commits no outrage on concrete presentations and their manifold contexts and distinctive differences. Quite to the contrary, phenomenology turns with great patience to the detailed and the minute and seeks to illuminate the specificity and the uniqueness of what gives us a world. The result is a liberation of detail, an epiphany of the familiar. In moving toward the assimilation and interpretation of the results of biological, anthropological, sociological, and artistic research and creation, the phenomenologist is trying to come to terms with nature as well as with history. The later work of Merleau-Ponty is a brilliant illustration of this tendency. His essay on "Eye and Mind" is a highly condensed vision of a phenomenological interpretation of painting to which all subsequent investigators, myself included, must be indebted. What emerges most clearly in this work, however, is the unity of nature and consciousness in what I have termed the fabric of expression. Without reducing nature to awareness or translating intentionality into an epiphenomenon, Merleau-Ponty succeeds in reconstructing the visible world. He provides a clue as well to a final consideration.

"Only the painter," Merleau-Ponty writes, "is entitled to look at everything without being obliged to appraise what he sees. For the painter, we might say, the watchwords of knowledge and action lose their meaning and force. Political regimes which denounce 'degenerate' painting rarely destroy paintings. They hide them, and one senses here an element of 'one never knows' amounting almost to a recognition. The reproach of escapism is seldom aimed at the painter . . . It is as if in the painter's calling there were some urgency above all other claims on him. Strong or frail in life, he is incontestably sovereign in his own rumination of the world. With no other technique than what his eyes and hands discover in seeing and painting, he persists in drawing from this world, with its din of history's glories and scandals, *canvases* which will hardly add to the angers or the hopes of man—and no one complains. What, then, is this secret science which he has or which he seeks? That dimension which lets Van Gogh say he must go 'further on'? What is this fundamental of painting, perhaps of all culture?"[10] It is, to take Merleau-Ponty's question and offer our own answer, the illumination of expression, not simply the visible, but the historical weight of association and source which makes the recognition of self and fellow men possible. Rather than understand the participant in art, whether creator or viewer, as a responder to phenomena, we may take the distinctive mode of expression to be action, not reaction. The search for questions and the horizon of questioning is a way of acting, a performance in the midst of mundanity which opens up to ourselves the lexicon of expression. There one finds in the language of the visible a sovereign signature.

---

[10] Maurice Merleau-Ponty, "Eye and Mind," op. cit., p. 161.

AESTHETIC PERCEPTION AND ITS RELATION TO ORDINARY PERCEPTION

Louis Dupré

EVERYONE knows that aesthetic perception differs from ordinary perception. But there is little agreement as to what precisely distinguishes one from the other. Vincent Tomas gives the following criteria: 1) "When we see things in the 'common way,' our attention is directed toward the stimulus objects that appear to us, or toward what they signify, and we do not particularly notice the ways in which these objects appear."[1] 2) "When we see things aesthetically, our attention is directed toward appearances and we do not particularly notice the thing that presents the appearance, nor do we care what, if anything, it is that appears."[2]

The difficulty with this distinction is that it takes a physicalist view of perception. As one critic shows, Tomas simply identifies the *thing* with the pigments, the physical words, the vibrations in the air, and relegates the three-dimensional picture, the fugue, the tale to the realm of appearance or illusion.[3] Instead of distinguishing two orders of perception, Tomas considers the "real" the physical and then assumes that this is the object of ordinary perception. He apparently attempts to differentiate aesthetic perception from ordinary perception by means of Kant's indifference-to-existence factor. But his physicalism precludes any adequate definition of the terms. It is true enough that in the aesthetic contemplation of a portrait I abstract from the existential status of its subject. But this has nothing to do with physical stimuli. Tomas' underlying *stimulus-reaction* the-

---

[1] "Aesthetic Vision" in *Aesthetics and the Philosophy of Criticism*, edited by Marvin Levich, New York, 1963, p. 256.

[2] Ibid, p. 256.

[3] Marshall Cohen, "Appearance and the Aesthetic Attitude" in *Aesthetics and the Philosophy of Criticism,* p. 286.

ory of perception is merely a symbolic construction of the physical sciences, totally inadequate for the explanation of ordinary perception. Also, his absolute distinction between aesthetic vision and ordinary perception is misleading, since artistic representation (for instance, a portrait) presupposes ordinary perception and refers to it. I shall return to this point later.

Aesthetic perception is neither ordinary perception nor pure reflection. It combines the detachment of the latter with the intuitive immediacy of the former. Kant attributed this transitional stage between sense experience and objectified experience to the imagination. In the image the object *appears,* that is, it is present as represented. Mikel Dufrenne has revived Kant's theory by showing how the imagination detaches the object from the live experience by means of a process of temporalization. To imagine is to place things under the concrete universality of time and to detach them from the sensory present. "To withdraw from the game is to take refuge in the past . . . To contemplate is to return to the past in order to capture the future; I only cease to be one with the present object when I detach myself from a present in which I remain immersed in things. The *re-* of *representation* expresses this interiorization, just as the *con-* of *contemplation* expresses the possibility of a survey and a simultaneity which evokes space."[4] Representation results from temporalization. That is why Kant referred to the imagination as the reproductive faculty.

But the imagination temporalizes in two different ways, empirically and transcendentally. Empirically it connects a perception with all previous experiences and thereby produces a unified picture, an image. An example of such an enriched perception is the appearance of snow which through the prism of the imagination "looks" cold even when we do not touch it. But the imagination also has another, transcendental function by which it creates a temporal-spatial field in which a perception can

---

[4] Mikel Dufrenne, *Phénoménologie de l'expérience esthétique,* Vol. II, Paris, 1953, p. 434.

appear. According to Dufrenne, only this transcendental imagination functions in the aesthetic perception. The empirical imagination which plays such an important role in ordinary perception is almost totally suppressed in aesthetic perception. The self-sufficient autonomy of the aesthetic intuition has no use for the uncontrolled vagrancies of the empirical imagination. Nor does the aesthetic experience seek to be integrated with the everyday life of ordinary perception. "It is not *in* a world; it constitutes a world and *this world is within the experience* (ce monde lui est interieur)."[5]

The only problem with this interesting theory is that it unduly deprives the aesthetic object of the fancies of the empirical imagination. Art would be very dull if it were reduced to pure form without play. Also, it is true that the aesthetic object constitutes a world of its own, but this world must never be detached from the ordinary world. The self-sufficiency of the aesthetic object does not eliminate the intentional reference of this object to the world of ordinary perception. The existence of genuine representational art sufficiently proves this connection. I would go further and argue that all art is representational in the sense that artistic forms, however abstract, always refer to the one world of ordinary perception in which they were first discovered. This is the case for temporal arts as much as for the spatial ones. Musical composition or an epic has undoubtedly a self-constituted rhythm of succession. Yet that does not warrant Dufrenne's conclusion that the past which gives meaning to the present is directly given in the work of art, without any connection with our own past experience.[6] A novel that is not based on ordinary experience is not intelligible. The same, I think, could be said of the rhythm of a musical composition: it refers to rhythmic successions of ordinary perception. No work of art, then, can claim a full aesthetic immanence: the intentional reference to the world of ordinary perception is an intrinsic part of

---

[5] Dufrenne, *op. cit.,* p. 449.
[6] *Op. cit.,* p. 457.

all aesthetic experience. But some arts are more representational than others and not every art form intends the world of ordinary perception as explicitly as the portrait.

What distinguishes the aesthetic experience is that it is never a pure perception, but a perception colored by a subjective disposition. Schleiermacher regarded the aesthetic experience as an awareness of the self *with* the object, a conscious merging of subject and object, rather than a perception *of* an object. It is this subjective disposition which gives its unique character to the aesthetic perception. The merging of the self with its object is usually referred to as a *feeling*. Johannes Volkelt has shown how certain elements are always present in feelings: an experience of pleasure or displeasure, an awareness of corporeality, explicit or implicit representations (which distinguish feelings from mere *moods*). But all those elements are coordinated by a predominant experience of the self as such.[7] This self-experience is not cognitive; it is a totality experience in which I am aware of the self as it is united with the universe as a whole. Equally distant is the aesthetic feeling from any kind of pragmatic concern; it is an *immediate* presence to oneself distinct from the reflective presence of action and cognition. Yet the immediacy of feelings does not imply that they are superficial: unlike sensations and emotions, feelings presuppose a reflective presence to the world. That is why feelings *reveal,* while emotions simply *react.*

The revealing quality of feelings consists in their ability to read appearances as *expressions* of a subject, and to do so with the immediacy of ordinary sense perception. Because they are subject-oriented, feelings do not follow a logical pattern in anticipating the course of future events. "D'un sujet je peux m'attendre à tout."[8] The ultimate ground of these noetic characteristics is the total involvement of the self. Only by a direct participation of the self can an appearance ever be viewed as the expression of another self. This self-involvement of feelings,

---

[7] "Ein unmittelbares Sichselbsterleben des Ich in seiner Ichheit," *Versuch über Fühlen und Wollen,* München, 1930, p. 12.

[8] Mikel Dufrenne, *op. cit.,* p. 479.

however, is in no way a commitment. The self never *gives* itself in feeling, nor does the "object" of feeling ever *need* any giving. For the two are one in an immediate way without the dialectical opposition between giving and wanting that we encounter in love. Through feeling the aesthetic object ceases to be an object in the strict sense: it becomes interiorized in the subject. Dufrenne therefore speaks of an affective *a priori* which constitutes an object into an aesthetic object.

This brings us to an even more fundamental question: What provokes aesthetic feelings? What makes me respond to an object in an affective rather than in an objective or pragmatic way? Something in the "object" must beckon me, a quality by which the object becomes more than a physical presence. Somehow the appearances themselves must suggest the presence of a subject, inducing the perceiver to receive them as expressions rather than as mere appearances. At least in the case of art we may say that it is the aesthetic object which produces aesthetic feeling and aesthetic perception. This implies that the object itself must have a certain interiority and convey the impression that there is more than an external presence. We might say that an aesthetic object seems to express "objective feelings" which allow me to communicate with it as if it were a subject. But how can an object communicate feelings? In the aesthetic contemplation of nature or, for that matter, in the process of artistic creation the original object is not aesthetic by itself. It is made aesthetic by the contemplating subject. Objectively, one landscape is not more beautiful than another, nor is one subject more worthy of artistic representation than another. Even here the rule holds true that beauty is not in the object alone. The aesthetic world is always an *animist* world. Even the desolate beauty of a desert or of a dead animal *speaks* to me in a subjective way. In the case of art the aesthetic object is "expressive" because it is made to express, that is, because an artist has structured his feelings in it. This does not mean that artistic feelings precede artistic expression: the expression articulates the feelings in such a way that without this articulation the feelings would never have reached their own completion. This interpretation disposes of the common idea that artists always have lofty feelings which they occasionally communicate in their work. Santayana showed long ago how untenable such a theory of expression is. "Poets can thus arouse sentiments finer than any which they have known, and in the act of composition become discoverers of new realms of delightfulness and grief. Expression is a misleading term which suggests that something previously known is rendered or imitated; whereas the expression is itself an original fact, the values of which are often referred to the thing expressed, much as the honors of a Chinese mandarin are attributed retroactively to his parents."[9] Neither the intensity nor the nature of the preceding "feeling" matters as much as the aesthetic structuring of this feeling. No feeling is fully aesthetic until it is expressed. We may say, then, that the aesthetic feeling is born in its expression.

But how can a representation ever symbolize a feeling? This question can be answered only with a total theory of the mind's relation to the world. As long as we consider this relation to be one of opposition, as was usually done before the nineteenth century, it cannot be answered at all. But even today, when more adequate theories of man's being-in-the-world have been developed, very few detailed studies exist on the artistic symbolization process. We all know Kandinsky's study on the sentimental meaning of colors. Similar work has been done by Volkelt on the emotional impact of sculptural and architectural structures, such as the feeling of heaviness conveyed by the Doric column.[10] Some of these impressions can be explained by associative processes, but ultimately one must accept an irreducible originality in the combination of feeling and form. The music of Mendelssohn creates the very feelings which it reveals. Rather than expressing previously existing feelings, it adds new tonalities to the gamut of human sentiments.

The intimate connection between feeling and form excludes any universal interpretation of artistic symbols by which a particular form would always have the same aesthetic meaning.

[9] *Interpretations of Poetry and Religion,* New York, 1957, p. 264.
[10] Johannes, Volkelt, *System der Aesthetik* I, pp. 259-63.

Such an interpretation would imply again that the form is merely a means to express previously established feelings. The fact of the matter is that art forms from a distant culture cannot be understood without proper initiation into their entire cultural context. What does the smile on the face of a sixth century Greek god express? Or the grotesque and monstrous figures in Far Eastern art? A theory according to which *b* expresses always *a* can never answer that question. For identical forms in different cultures may articulate different feelings. To understand art it may not be necessary to know a great deal about the psychology of feelings or about artistic techniques. But it is indispensable to know something about the way in which the symbolization process (that is, the articulation of feelings) takes place. And that symbolization process varies from culture to culture.

THE SOCIAL CONDITIONS OF MODERN PAINTING

Helmuth Plessner

To OUR generation the impact of social conditions on the arts has become all but too obvious. Totalitarian regimes of all kinds have persecuted innovations in the arts as something alien to the interest or beyond the understanding of the masses. To any totalitarian regime creativity in the arts is a disturbing phenomenon, because it refuses to fit smoothly into the mechanisms of its social control. When the state is ruled by ideology, when the state controls society, then art can be nothing but an instrument of propaganda.

In pluralistic societies, however, suppression of art seems to be out of the question, and, consequently, art may express itself according to its own laws. But what does it really mean to speak of "art according to its own laws?" Art may indeed be free from intervention by the state or by the taskmasters of propaganda. But it is exposed to social mechanisms of another kind, less overt than state intervention, mechanisms which develop in the economic market governed by the laws of supply and demand. In these circumstances, art must satisfy certain demands which are largely created by society itself and which are geared to its cycles of production.

In pre-industrial societies the patron was the dominant figure in the business of the arts. The church; the feudal lord, the rich merchant were the artist's partners. Today the dealers set the prices. The antique business has been complemented by a business in "modernity." Dealers no longer wait for what the artist offers them, they themselves already direct production. Thus in the development from a partly industrialized to a totally industrialized society, the products of the art market, like other products, have come to be subjected to the laws of rapid obsolescence and of accelerated consumption. In the ever mounting flood of supplies, new art objects attract attention only according to the degree of *shock* they produce. The influence of the "modernity business" on the artist is obvious; it induces him to withdraw into a region of pure aesthetics : *l'art pour l'art.* But as a consequence of this fact our society has to accept art not simply as *l'art pour l'art,* but as *le choc pour le choc.*

But when the market demands "le choc pour le choc," then the artist must—at the risk of his creativity—avoid familiar and conventional subject matters. He must make art a difficult business. This holds not only for the plastic arts ; modern music as well has reached levels of complexity and modes of innovation which seem strange indeed to all but a few. The same could be said about literature. Think of the nouveau roman or the theatre of the absurd.

Every day it becomes a bit more difficult to find criteria of artistic quality, which could be explained to a number of people big enough to form a public, not just a clique. No wonder that the public at large feels confused and sometimes even fooled by an immense racket dealing in "The Emperor's New Clothes." The autonomy of the work of art seems to many to become instead no more than the autonomy of the market. To the more informed lover of the arts the contemporary situation is not an entirely novel or revolutionary state of affairs. The new has always been difficult to comprehend, it has always entailed an invasion of hallowed conventions or taboos. People who grew up in the golden twenties still remember the shock they experienced when they were confronted with the works of Klee, Kurt Schwitters and Max Ernst, Picasso and Brancusi, with the music of Schönberg and with the great novel of James Joyce. So they are inclined to assume that what seems incomprehensible today will turn out to be a classic of tomorrow. Indeed, this is the reaction which the art dealer expects from his public today. His gambling on an unlimited willingness to consume which negates all tradition bases itself, quite characteristically, on historical experience. This ironic activity of historical consciousness has become possible only since the power of tradition has been broken by the process of industrialization.

Let us now turn to another aspect of the situation. The

manipulated market needs an escalation of avantgardism. The public grumbles at the artist's provocations, but it accepts them. Living in an industrialized society has conditioned us to accept provocation. Thus shock alone is not enough. The artist must make a more profound appeal to his public if he wants to get in on this escalation of acceptance. And what could be easier than to appeal to the readiness of the public to *protest?*

Readiness of the public to protest does not entail a formulated protest against social injustice or attacks on Capitalism. It is a more fundamental protest, more closely related to Sartre's analysis of nausea than to Brecht's demonstration of the inhuman. We have experienced the inhuman as an integral part of so-called humanity. The universal protest which comes to the fore in modern art consists in the willingness to deny and to cast off traditional norms and categories. This protest does not show us the ways and means to replace the old standards by new ones. Protest is no instrument by which you can give shape to things. Surely we may recognize in the protest of informal painting against the tradition and in the ironies of American Pop-Art an answer to human infamy and to the collapse of culture. But you do not understand a piece of art by explaining the motives of the artist. Nausea, despair, disgust, boredom make the soil in which art can grow. But where do the seeds come from?

All artists belong to a tradition, even if the lack of tradition itself has become the tradition. In painting, the tradition of subject-matter has had the strongest force for centuries. In religious painting the artist was guided by ritual and doctrine. But even after the secularization of the subject-matter—landscape, portrait, still life—the dominance of the "school" continued deep into the nineteenth century. Only where the painted subject became unimportant and lapsed into a mere occasion for the picture, was cooperation in school or atelier replaced by another form of contact: "The Isms." Continuity between generations of painters began to dissolve. And the painting began to disappear behind its artistic values. With a Rubens, you can ask: how much of this picture did he paint himself and what is the work of his disciples? With a Picasso, there is only one question left: is it an original or a fake? In the second half of the nineteenth century, when expanding industrialization coincided with the beginnings of Impressionism, the relation between generations of artists was articulated by the concept of "Avant-garde." The repeated experience that what was new and shocking yesterday will become a classic tomorrow turned into an unlimited freedom of choice in the means of expression. Contemporary Painting, Music, and Literature rely on the possibility of ever new discoveries within an inexhaustible reservoir of artistic means.

The process of industrialization in society and the development of avantgardism in art were certainly not synchronized throughout the Western World. But we can say that the discoveries of French Impressionism paved the way for avantgardism. Their acceptance by the public demonstrated how the public itself was ready for avantgarde liberties. In the late nineteenth century man had acquired a new relation to visual reality, a relation which would have been impossible without a long process of visual education, reaching back to the very beginnings of the secularization of the arts. To the discovery that worldly subjects are worth depicting corresponded—as a complementary phenomenon, so to speak—a growing indifference to the subject itself. The major problem of the Impressionists was "how to paint a picture." The form itself became the content.

Georges Mathieu, himself an avantgarde painter, makes some interesting remarks on this subject. He says—roughly translated: "For thousands of years Western art has been carrying the burden or prejudices about imitation or representation, and for half a century it has been living on fictions about "abstraction." But . . . geometrical abstraction could do nothing but transform the whole of Renaissance Aesthetics into non-figural terms . . . The abstraction of 1910 was the dissolution of the realistic object, but not the dissolution of the corresponding aesthetics. We had to wait for another epoch, which I have called "The Move from the Abstract to the Possible," and this move begins with the annulment of all former aesthetics . . . An aesthetic art of consciousness tries to replace an aesthetic consciousness of art."

Mathieu is far from being dogmatic when he says: "Never before in history has it been possible, as it is today, to read from certain aspects of modern painting a curious phenomenon: an abdication of judgment, the loss of the ability to judge."

In this context Mathieu describes a process of dissolution which marks pretty clearly our present state of intellectual and moral decay, that is: ". . . the drama that is taking place in the consciousness of Western Man, who, since Galileo and Pascal, has lost his place in the order of being, and now exposes himself in an ever more eccentric movement to the totality of being."

Ironically enough, our avantgardist painter seems to agree with the opinion of more or less reactionary critics. But the "Loss of the Center" is for Mathieu not only a nothingness after the end, but also a nothingness before the beginning. Tabula Rasa is beginning and end at once.

It is an undeniable fact that judgment—as Mathieu says—has abdicated, and that all kinds of fakes and swindles may profit from this loss of criteria. But we should not conclude that craftsmanship has disappeared for good, or that sheer dilettantism has taken over. After all, the uncertainty about aesthetic norms corresponds to a more general uncertainty about social norms. Looking backwards, you might interpret the general state of affairs as "dissolution" and "decay." But dissolution, dialectically, opens up possibility.

Seventeenth century man, who was already aware of his individuality, found a new dimension: the dimension of consciousness. The scientific revolution of the seventeenth century also prepared a change of intention in painting. Art began to calculate its effect on the consciousness of the spectator. It took some time before "the aesthetic art of consciousness" realized its possibilities. Not before French Impressionism did it find its programmatic expression. Again, as in the time of Dürer and Leonardo, art went to school to science—this time, however, with psychological optics. Since the painter wanted to remain faithful to the visible object, he had to turn his attention to what happens in the spectator's eye instead of just describing an object. By turning his attention to the perspective of the spectator, he set in motion a process of increasing abstraction. The striving after the purity of the phenomenon was accompanied by a revision in the means of painting, which, among other things, led to the abolition of central perspective. And this is the reason why Cézanne may be considered the father of all those "Isms" which followed him without sharing his intentions. The retreat to: "What we see and nothing but what we see," was the first step of alienation and abstraction. The phenomenon, the visible object, which in the process of painting has in any case to be fitted onto the surface of the picture, now coincides with mere appearance. The decisive step into subjectivity has been taken. From now on an "aesthetic art of consciousness" replaces the older form of an "aesthetic consciousness of art."

When you want the eye to comprehend the content of what it actually sees—and nothing but that—you have to develop an analytical procedure of painting, the construction of an impression out of the mere elements. With the help of physiological optics this was done exactly by Pointillism. The technical procedures of the sciences once more gained influence on the process of painting—(once more, we must say, if we think of Leonardo). But this time we have to deal with the technical discoveries of the twentieth century, furthered by photography and film making. They have set the theme for the various ways in which interpenetration between apparatus and expression is possible: a theme which has been taken up by Futurism and Cubism. Here we meet another complex of phenomena which demands further analysis.

We have already noticed how the origins of avantgardism coincide with the abolition of so-called "realistic" painting. If the abolition of mere imitation has been caused by a changed relation of man to reality, then the question arises, what factors were responsible for this change?

The mechanism of the market is not a sufficient explanation, for the market can profit only by an increasing obsolescence of artistic creations and by a public which is always hungry for the new. The market can, so to speak, only accelerate the speed of consumption. But it can not do this without the public's playing along with the laws of supply and demand in this particular field. How did it come about that the public was prepared to abolish the "normal" or "common sense" or conservative view of things? Photography, of course, has exerted a strong influence in this direction. Painters welcomed the new art and were among its first practitioners. Indeed, they created some of the most remarkable photographs. Against the opinion of some art historians, I would like to insist that the main function of photography in its very beginnings was not to satisfy the public's demand for naturalistic representation, which is supposed to have been the traditional task of painting. Photography became an independent form of art, ranging from documentation to the graphic effects of purely subjective combinations. And it is in photography that the corporeal, plastic character of things has been rediscovered—not in painting. But why not in painting?

To be sure, not all post-impressionistic painting and sculpture has been anti-objective. Max Ernst, Chagall, Beckmann, and Picasso by now belong to the classics of avantgardism. But it would be a mistake to consider them merely as forerunners of informal painting. In the works of Francis Bacon, for instance, there are heavy, three-dimensional objects. But their presence in Bacon's pictures is far from being nothing but their own presentation. There is, however, one restricting condition in the modern painting of things: The picture of a thing must say something more than: Here we have a picture of this particular thing.

The experience that you can segregate the appearance from the thing has produced two consequences: First, the purisms of informal painting, and second, the reconstruction of objects or even the invention of new ones. But the reconstruction of objects does not cancel the original alienation. If alienation is not preserved in the visible recipe for reconstruction, then it must be brought about by other means.

Beckmann, for instance, permits only slight deformities to his figures, faces or landscapes. But he adds to the picture coded messages, which can only be deciphered by knowing his allusions. The silence of their strange melancholy asks for words of explanation, yet they retain their objective, pictorial expression —much as Giorgione or Hieronymus Bosch speak to us without telling us their hidden mysteries. It is well known how deeply the Platonism of the Florentine Academy influenced Renaissance Painting. The classicism and realism of later times tended to underrate this influence. The classicists did not realize that the new discoveries of Renaissance painting—central perspective and anatomy, coincidence of visual and pictorial space— were forshadowed by a Neo-Platonic concept of reality. The imitation of things in the Renaissance is not a photographic imitation, as the nineteenth century believed, but an imitation based on the conviction that the appearances of nature simulate the reality of ideas.

Our modern concept of reality is far from being Platonic. It is dominated by the concept of reality developed in science. For Science is not troubled by the invisibility of its elementary processes, which gain formative character and shape only through their accumulation. Physicists tell us that the new reality of Quantum Mechanics sounds but a variation on the original theme of the Pythagoreans: Reality is expressible by number. But the Pythagoreans and Plato thought of the world as a Cosmos, a sensual and moral order, in which beauty was possible because this order was the prototype of beauty. After all, "Cosmos" means also beauty and ornament.

This Platonic world order is breaking up in the second half of the sixteenth century—in the philosophical speculations of Giordano Bruno, Ficino, as well as in the manierist paintings of Pontormo, Bronzino, Vasari and many others.

In the seventeenth century, the mechanical world picture begins to take shape—together with its great unresolved *aporia:* consciousness and matter, reason and sensous experience. Let us remind ourselves that the conflict between these positions, and the resulting Irrationalist reaction, were not articulated and remained suspended for a long time.

"Les Réflexions critiques sur la poesie et la peinture" by Abbé Dubos—who was profoundly influenced by Locke—is the first document of aesthetic Irrationalism.

The steady progress of Newtonian science deprived aesthetic qualities of their support in nature, and forced them to seek a new abode in the subject. Psychology and Aesthetics arose as complements of classical mechanics. Their subject matter was sensation, passion, and uncontrollable genius. Aesthetic Irrationalism saved the quality of beauty from the growing mechanization of nature, and changed it into a quality of subjective experience. Corresponding to this first step the activity *of* the artist changed into an activity *for* subjective experience, an activity which is to be judged only by the consciousness of man.

An "aesthetic art of consciousness" took the place of the "aesthetic consciousness of art." The subject of a painting has become indifferent. Its effect is its purpose. Painted stories and declamations have become unbearable for us. The exceptions, the grand frescoes of Mexico, for example, fascinate not so much by their stories as by the language of these stories, which has gone to school to Picasso and Gauguin. The new possibilities of painting could be discovered only in opposition against history and literature, by a thorough study and revision of the painter's techniques. The aesthetic art of consciousness has sensitized us to the aesthetic values of material in all possible stages of rawness or shape. *Fin de siècle* aestheticism contained but the germs of this development. Pop and other kinds of art mark its present stage. But by pointing to this development I do not mean to trace a genealogy. It is not important whether we see Rauschenberg prefigured in Dada, which was one of the first provocative answers to our industrial surroundings. By now we can take any provocation.

It is important to understand Pop as a late form of aestheticism, as a free and unhampered manipulation of the aesthetic values of objects and, dialectically, as a denial of aestheticism, as a mirror of the scurrilous face of this world, which is no longer a Cosmos.

I have been speaking of the effects produced by aesthetic

irrationalism. As far as the artist's practice is concerned, these were indirect and unintentional. He might consider himself, in his own self-consciousness, as an isolated genius. Aesthetic irrationalism would then appear to protect him from manipulation by the mechanism of the market, and this mechanism would in turn reinforce dialectically, the argument for aesthetic irrationalism.

On the other hand, we can notice an increase of historical consciousness in art. Edgar Wind—a disciple of Cassirer and Panofsky—has traced, in *Art and Anarchy,* the influence of the history of art on the development of aesthetic sensibilities. I want to mention only a few points that might be of interest : the discovery of "formal qualities" by Riegl, Wölfflin and Worringer—and the acknowledgment of specific artistic intentions for each epoch, which made concepts like "primitive" or "decadent" obsolete. The new concepts of art historians may be disputable, but they enabled us to look at the art of strange epochs or culture with new eyes. The process of liberation in criticism has aided the increase of our sensibility to aesthetic values on the one hand, and our indifference to subjects on the other. With the appreciation of any artistic idiom, our fear of the anarchic or disorganizing features of art has disappeared. In its place we have acquired a fear of understanding, of reason. Thus, simultaneously with the growing intellectualization of painting, reason, "ratio" itself, has become suspect. Paradoxical though it sounds, aesthetic irrationalism and "Peinture Conceptuelle" are twins.

This process of intellectualization and of increasing sensitivity, however, throws a shadow : *Kitsch.* I do not think that I can translate the word. "Trash" would not do it. The nearest equivalent seems to be "emotional ersatz art." Kitsch does not denote the primitive or vulgar. It is rather a kind of sentimentalism, which introduces a class distinction within the public. The masses are supposed to be incapable of satisfying the intellectual demands of real art. But their demands are satisfied—in an efficient way—by a supposedly direct appeal to emotion. This shady part of the concept, however, is very useful to highlight a prevailing suspicion of direct appeals to emotions in general.

When we remind ourselves that the new ways of perception were discovered by segregating perception from its object, we must admit that artistic creation—in spite of the bourgeois concept of the genius—seems no longer the domain of inspiration, but a rather close neighbour of engineering or other forms of technical production. When the market becomes a manipulated field, creativity can no longer appear as an elemental and uncontrollable power and the work is regarded not for itself but as evidence of a certain tendency in production. This does not mean, of course, that artists should consider themselves factory hands in the sensibility industry. I have tried to show that art can not express itself totally according to its so-called own laws. But whatever we say about the trade in the Emperor's new clothes, art has never become completely marketable. It does not quite fit into catalogues. As long as art is not chained by ideology—including its own various ideological appeals—individual expression always has a chance. It remains equally difficult, perilous, and necessary.

DISCUSSION ON VISION
AND
THE GRAPHIC ARTS

Erling Eng

Now, what I'd like to do—and I'm going to try to do this very briefly—is to make one or two comments about each one of the presentations thus far. For those persons who have arrived late and for those others who are perhaps "too close to the trees to be able to see the forest," may I say that I have difficulty myself in really following the continuities developing here; it seems to me there's always a tendency in many meetings devoted to phenomenology for a rather considerable fragmentation to occur. I believe it is Professor Plessner who has written that Husserl once remarked to him that "In phenomenology, there is room for a thousand genuises."

Marjorie Grene's presentation appeared centered around the study of certain tensions, dichotomous tensions in the thought of Erwin Straus. And it seemed to me that, by the method of triangulation, what was implied here was something which, if made explicit, would resolve certain aporias in his writings. She contrasted, for example, the gnostic and pathic modes of knowing and suggested that, somehow, there must be some kind of continuity here.

Now, what could constitute a continuity between the gnostic and the pathic? As I listened to her, I kept thinking of an idea which may appear like one more unknown for you—the "lived body," the "own body." Like Erwin Straus, she expressed a certain suspicion, shall we say, of conceptually objectivating sciences, but less sharply so. In a friendly way, she could have been chiding him for an inadequacy she also exemplified, one which has plagued us throughout this conference: a clarification of the differences and relationships between scientific and artistic modes of knowing.

Dr. Hensel, who spoke next, had a rather difficult time because he came before us as a scientist. Because our program was oriented to the arts, he tended, in a way, to be excluded. Nevertheless he did remarkably well in showing us how sensing and logic are both involved in the development of science through their "correspondences." You will recall those which he pointed out: certain parallels between the logical structures of scientific thought and characteristics of sense data. Once again, however, he chose to leave us in the dark concerning the nature of any mediation. But in phenomenology, we are familiar with the way in which awareness of an absence may point to the possibility of a hidden presence. Very gradually we begin to sense such a possibility here. What is this presence, or in Dr. Hensel's instance, what is it that could mediate, underlie, might we say, these correspondences between logic and sensing?

Our third speaker, Dr. Griffith, was the first to introduce the notion of the "lived body," and, as is befitting, he brought it in rather cautiously. He showed us the way in which the aesthetic phenomena of fascination are involved with the experiencing of "world" in the terms of the "lived body." So enthralled did he become with these phenomena revealed through the "lived body" that he left his discussant, Professor Schrag, with the impression that he had been talking solely about a private world. But the related phenomena of art are, of course, not private; otherwise we should not have an art market, as Professor Plessner later mentioned.

This evening we're going to see a film of Dr. Jokl, in which gymnasts, quite wonderful gymnasts, reveal the "lived body" in the public world, where the "lived body" actually opens the world up to us rather than, as in the phenomena of fascination, closing us off from the wide open world.

Our first speaker last evening, Professor Stein, talked about feeling. She began, basically, with feeling and then talked about the feeling of deanimation. Of course, when we talk about feeling, we are very close to the "lived body." She didn't talk about the "lived body" as such however, but discussed how, starting from feeling, one could observe certain changes in one's relationship to one's body, to one's perceptual world. Then through the pathological occasion of psychosis, the "lived body" was revealed as having previously existed unremarked, a striking case of how loss in this instance, a psychological loss, may disclose a previously unrealized mode of being.

Next, Dr. Jossman began by showing that we normally are—the German term is "Mängelwesen"—creatures of deficiency. Characteristic for the notion of man implied by phenomenology, with its emphasis on "intentionality" and "constitutions," is that fundamentally we are creatures of lack, that we live in a world of "locks," and must somehow not merely come to terms with lack, but even contribute to its continuation.

When Dr. Jossman presented his slides of optical illusions, he was showing us how, in our natural perception, we are a bit untrue. That is, our natural perception is, in a sense, both incorrect and untrue. I take it he meant to suggest that art, in particular, draws on this kind of untruth in human experience which is an essential part of our reality. Of course one can consider this untruth as human truth, in contrast to the notion of truth as correspondence with the things of creation as divinely conceived, as mentioned by Professor Plessner in connection with Renaissance Neo-Platonism.

Our final speaker for the evening, Erwin Straus, spoke fundamentally about the way in which the "lived" body is disclosed indirectly through various possible agnosias arising from lesions in the human central nervous system. Damages to the central nervous system give rise to certain psychiatric phenomena which, in order to be understood, require us to consider the "lived body," or "body subject." As many of you know, the paradigmatic metaphor of our speaker for the "lived body" emphasizes the upright posture, or establishment and maintenance of an erect position.

This morning the first speaker, Professor Natanson, introduced the past for the first time in our conference by speaking of painting as a research of the past, a re-search which reveals something that was there all along but which had remained undisclosed. And this which was not known, Professor Duprè then emphasized as something which is concerned both with the world and with itself. Professor Natanson, in his rather explicative manner, exemplified art, it seemed to me, bringing us by his own dramatic performance close to seeing how discovery resulting from research of the past actually is self-discovery. Consequently, he tended to converge with Professor Plessner's view in which the very close relationship of art in our time to self-discovery was stressed.

Professor Duprè, I thought, emphasized well the way in which the past, pastness, the repository of the pastness, so to speak, is very intimately associated with the "lived body." Research of the past actually opens us up to the real world, the world which is *not* merely of man, but which is also non-human, making it possible for us to deal with this world in a new way. It seems to me that there is a hint to be found here too of the relationship between the arts and sciences. Professor Plessner came close to touching on the way in which the artistic revolution of the Renaissance, for example, in the development of central perspective, was followed by revolutions in mathematics and the natural sciences. This clasp of science and art is very close in the Renaissance and a very nice paper on this theme might have helped to clarify some of the tensions that arose during our exploration of the dichotomies yesterday afternoon.

Finally, Professor Plessner has brought the "lived body" into play by exploring the way in which the older concept of mimesis in art has been replaced by an emphasis on fantasia. I felt that there was a bit of ambivalence in Professor Plessner's paper. He seemed caught somewhat between the generations, but his loyalty was with the avant garde (as his quotation from Mathieu indicated). If, however, one wanted to retain the notion of mimesis, one could say that modern art is a representation of what is hidden in man. Modern art reveals the hidden in man rather than showing forth God's immediate handiwork, the presupposition of a long tradition of representational art. Thus in art today the processes of destruction even may be invoked. Professor Plessner reminded us that destruction makes new creation possible, thus is an integral part of creation. Then he spoke of the art of aesthetic consciousness. Now it seems to me that in modern art, where representation has become divorced from the natural world to a considerable degree, i.e., persons, places, and things, it means that art can move around rather freely. We have an international art style for the first time in world history. I would suggest that art has come to serve man in the realization of his own nature as human and that modern art represents a developing meditative praxis outside the sphere of traditional world religions. The question of meditative praxis is today a fundamental one. Professor Plessner seems to have hinted that modern art may serve as a meditative praxis. Thus the great diversity in modern art enables each person to discover particular "hieroglyphs" which aid in realizing the character of his particular existence. To develop this would take us both beyond aesthetics and psychology.

Thus far it is striking that our consideration of "aisthesis" has tended to exclue pain or the unpleasant in perception (save for Professor Stein's paper), even as our understanding of aesthetics has omitted its traditional concern with beauty, not to mention the sublime. This latter does not however surprise us, insofar as present day art is as much concerned with the ugly as it is with the beautiful. Have we, in our conference, replaced 'beauty" with "lived body," and neglected the way in which even the ugly and the appearance of death call for phenomenological investigation?

IV. SOUND AND MUSIC

TOWARD A PHENOMENOLOGY OF
MUSICAL AESTHETICS

F. Joseph Smith

I. The Continuing Redefinition of Phenomenology

IT SEEMS necessary to continue asking what we mean by
"phenomenology," especially in America, where due to the generous efforts of a number of professors it has begun to find its
"place in the sun." The word itself has a rather interesting
history in modern philosophy all the way from the *Neues Organon* (1764) of J. H. Lambert, where it means the philosophy of
appearance, through Hegel's phenomenology of spirit, up to
Husserl and his students. It seems useful to ask once again what
phenomenology may come to mean in America, where (despite
the warnings in Husserl's *Phänomenologische Psychologie*)[1] it
is applied sometimes meaningfully and sometimes dubiously to a
wide range of studies from an examination of the transcendental ego and consciousness in W. James to an attempt to turn
Gestalt psychology into a phenomenology of music.[2] Kant, from

---

[1] E. Husserl, *Phänomenologische Psychologie* (Den Haag, 1962) ed.
W. Biemel, Abhandlung II, pp. 247-255. Here Husserl writes that
phenomenology did not come about in the interest of psychology but of
philosophy, to make is a strict science. Transcendental phenomenology and
psychology, he claims, are quite different from each other in their fundamental significance and must be sharply distinguished and kept apart
from one another. This is so even when on both sides the apparently same
phenomena are studied. Even what we call a pure psychology in a
phenomenological sense, i.e. thematically bounded in psychological-
phenomenological reduction, is still a positive science, he continues. A
clearer statement could hardly be given on the issue.

[2] In a recent article in *Philosophy and Phenomenological Research*
(vol. XXVII, no. 2, Dec. 1966) A. Pike attempts to present the work of
L. Meyer, *Meaning and Emotion in Music* (Chicago, 1956) as an important work in the phenomenology of music. Perhaps this can be done
if one dismisses the work of the founder of phenomenology, as Pike does
in his first footnote, where he puts "historical" phenomenology from him.
But it is a less than convincing attempt, especially since L. Meyer rejects
phenomenology. His presentation is a case of Gestalt psychology and

whom both Husserl and Heidegger learned much,[3] kept asking
to the very end what "transcendental philosophy" connoted.
And, as is well known, on the very vigil of his death Husserl
was ready to begin all over again in quest of a truer phenomenology. And though we do not want to remain only with an
exposition of primary sources, it may well be useful from time
to time to remind ourselves of the fundamental literature and
the main issues of phenomenology. The style and complexity of
Husserl's and Heidegger's language make their works more
often than not inaccessible or at least formidable to many intelli-
gent Americans, who may not have had the chance to learn
German either at home or abroad. And translations, while useful, can never function as an adequate substitute for the original, as Heidegger has communicated to the speaker.

1. Phenomenology was meant originally to meet the crisis of
both philosophy and science.[4] As such phenomenology was a

---

nothing more. In the musicological world Meyer's book was not exactly
welcomed as a "highly important book," judging from such reviews as
those in *The Musical Quarterly* (Oct. 1957, A. Lippmann) or allusions
in such journals as *The Juilliard Review*. Some of these reviews were
over-severe, but they did point up some essential flaws in Meyer's attempt
to apply Gestalt to music. A considerably more felicitous presentation of
his views is given by Meyer in his essay, "On Rehearing Music" in *The
Journal of the American Musicological Society* (vol. XIV, no. 2, Sept.
1961, pp. 257-267). But in no intelligible sense is this a "phenomenology
of music," unless the word, phenomenology, is meaningless. Besides the
brief essay "Zur Phänomenologie der Musik" by Eimert in *Melos,
Zeitschrift für Musik* (1926, pp. 244-5) there is little written on this
subject to the present writer's best knowledge. The only really significant
work done on the phenomenology of music is that of Roman Ingarden,
who in *Untersuchungen zur Ontologie der Kunst* deals convincingly both
with music and with phenomenology. Cf. same, pp. 3-115 "Das Musik-
werk" (Tübingen, 1962).

[3] Kern, Iso, *Husserl und Kant* (Den Haag, 1964) pass.

Heidegger, M., *Kant und das Problem der Metaphysik* (Frankfurt,
1951) ; *Die Frage nach dem Ding* (Tübingen, 1952) ; *Der Satz vom
Grund* (Pfullingen, 1952) ; "Kants These über das Sein" (1962) in a Fest-
schrift for Erik Wolf.

Husserl, E., *Erste Philosophie*, I (1923/4) (Den Haag, 1956), cf.
"Ergänzende Texte." This is but one of many references in Husserl's
works.

[4] Husserl, E., *Die Krisis der europäischen Wissenschaften und die
transzendentale Phänomenologie* (Den Haag, 1954) pass.

critique of what we may call traditional metaphysics but also of empirical and positivistic science, which was really a kind of outrunner of metaphysics. Husserl attempted to rediscover a convincing "first philosophy" and his approach was through the suspension of judgment which he called "eidetic reduction." While it is true that this may be regarded as commonplace, it is nevertheless a fact that Husserl himself kept asking to the very end what eidetic reduction connoted. In this sense it is always possible to rediscover new meaning in terms that are apparently well understood. The full implications of eidetic reduction are just now beginning to be realized, as with the steady publication of primary sources we witness a renewed interest in Husserl, even after the experience of Heidegger and Sartre.

Given that there is a whole series of eidetic reductions to be made in phenomenology—some of the more complex ones to be witnessed in the question of transcendental ego and in intersubjectivity as the basis of any objectivity in the sciences—what can "bracketing" mean when it comes to the musical phenomenon, especially as "aesthetical?" It is here that we can no longer simply expound the text of Husserl. Instead we are challenged to "apply" phenomenology; and in this very application to musical phenomena there may be an implied critique of eidetic reduction *as* eidetic. For, what can *eidos* mean when predicated of music, which is in essence not a phenomenon but an *akumenon?* For Husserl, who does us the service in advance of bracketing any metaphor including the visual, the eidos is meant simply as the "essence" (*Wesen*) of anything whatsoever. Insofar as it is a question of essence, eidos may refer indifferently to any sort of phenomenon, whether visual, haptic, or audial. And thus the "ideality" of anything whatsoever takes in the entire range of phenomena, as such, whether they "appear" as visual or audial.

It is true that after Plato the word, eidos, is used in the description of the Greater Perfect System of Greek music, as J. Lohmann has pointed out.[5] It was especially Aristoxenos, the

[5] Lohmann, J., "Der Ursprung der Musik" in *Archiv für Musikwissenschaft* (Trossingen, 1959) 1/2, p. 161.

musician pupil of Aristotle, who gave us eidos as a musical term, as an "analytical" concept which is the result of the theoretical approach introduced by the Greeks. The eidos or "form" is a subdivision of the *genos,* which is not a "genus" but rather that special complex of fundamental tones, semitones, major and minor thirds, and microtones, which went to make up the diatonic, chromatic, and enharmonic tetrachords, that were the building blocks of the Greek scale. Hence we see some historical justification for the use of a visual term to explain the inner workings of musical system. Yet, it must be noted, that Aristoxenos was the student of Aristotle, and it was especially Aristotle who put forth the theory that sight was man's keenest sense and that it stood for all the rest. By way of contrast Lajos Szekely, who has contributed a theory of the bipolarity of sensation, holds that the sense of hearing is closer to the subject, whereas the sense of sight is closer to the object.[6] Whatever the merits of this theory, it may be true that western philosophy developed into a visually oriented thinking at the expense of subjectivity and to the short-sighted advantage of objectivity. Thus it seems to me that phenomenology will not discover a truer subjectivity until it becomes more convincingly akumenal. But historically speaking, sight stands for all the senses through the entire history of philosophy. It is seen at its clearest in Augustine, in medieval philosophy, and perhaps in Husserl and Heidegger.

2. Whatever the case may be, and despite the fact that Husserl brackets the visual as metaphor, musicologists are increasingly restless with the visual, bracketed or unbracketed, in describing the live musical experience. For both as musicologists and practicing musicians they know that music is first and foremost not a phenomenal but an akumenal experience, despite the obvious influence of the visual in western music and both musical and philosophical theory. I would therefore like to suggest that bracketing the visual or visual metaphor is not

---

[6] Wellek, A., "Musikpsychologie" in *Die Musik in Geschichte und Gegenwart,* Band 9 (Kassel, 1961), p. 1148-1169 for general background; for L. Szekely, cf. H. H. Dräger, "Musikaesthetik," pp. 1000 f., esp. p. 1001.

enough. The musician feels the need for a transition to a new
key, the possibility for which is surely given in the eidos.
Husserl gives what might be called an eidetic critique of western
philosophy and by postulation of any and all philosophy. Yet he
remains pretty well within the tradition itself, though he radically reconstitutes its horizon, conceptuality, and vocabulary.
Husserl makes first philosophy viable, as it were, but at least to
this student of music and philosophy it remains quite "western,"
if by that term we may designate Greco-European thinking. It is
for this reason that making use of audial vocabulary to describe
musical experience may be regarded as a radical break-through
as also a break from western philosophy both in its Greek
origins and in its phenomenological form as first philosophy.
And yet to a musician this "break" is merely a return to the
primordial thing itself, i.e. to music as akumenal. And thus we
would not talk so much of eidos as of musical *tonos* or of a
fundamental *ēchos,* that describes things not only as seen but as
felt and heard. For echos, as sound, takes in everything from
the tumultuous roar of the ocean and the grandeur of a summer
cloudburst to the specifically musical *tonos* of Greek music, the
tonus of medieval music, and the tonal/atonal systems of modern history. In short, echos takes in what we call primordial
world, as it sounds and swells all about us and within us, as
we are borne aloft on the crest of life. A phenomenological eidos
seems far too "intellectualized" a process to render convincingly
the primordial world of raw or of musical sound. It is far too
cerebral, like certain kinds of contemporary music. In a sense
it is even philistine, in that it can be the antithesis of the work
of art. For, philosophy and belles lettres have not often courted
one another. And belles lettres are not just beautiful letters and
literature: they are also meant to be read aloud, where their
musical essence can reveal itself.

Musical sound is more than just raw sound. The roar of the
ocean is not yet music, though it is primordial sound. Raw sound
becomes musical sound only after it has been processed, as it
were, through the grid of definite categories. We may be allowed to take a specific example from music history, a history

which at this point seems inseparable from the history of philosophy. Jacques de Liège, the protagonist of the *Ars Antiqua,* i.e. of the metaphysical theories of the Middle Ages, wrote his encyclopedic *Speculum Musicae* (1330-40) during the *Ars Nova,* at a time when the Middle Ages were waning and the Renaissance beginning to dawn.[7] What began as a reactionary treatise decrying the *Ars Nova* in music ended up as a vast metaphysical and mathematical treatise, the summation of all music theory from Boethius through the Middle Ages. In this work Jacques de Liège gives one of the clearest statements in history on the difference between raw sound and musical sound. It is the difference between physical sound and what he calls "sonorous" music (*musica sonora*), i.e. music properly so called, as musical consonance. For only in differentiating musical consonance from physical sound does one discover the building blocks of musical composition, from the *tonus* through the *diapason,* or as we would put it today, from one end of an octave to the other. It is interesting to note two things: a.) that musical sound is called "sonorous," and b.) that this means not "sensuous" but rather mathematico-metaphysical. For medieval music has to do not just with "being as being" but with "numbered being." It is only in being "processed" through a metaphysics of number and proportion that raw sounds can emerge as the building blocks of music. Thus not raw sound but metaphysico-mathematical categories are responsible for what medieval theorists called music, as an art. And this harmonic modulation, this interplay of musical proportionality, carried through the history of music and philosophy all the way up to and including Kant, who in the *Kritik der Urteilskraft* writes that the essence of music, as the free play of sensations in conjunc-

[7] Smith, F. J., "Jacques de Liège, an Anti-modernist?" in *Revue belge de musicologie* (1963); "Ars Nova, a Redefinition; some Observations in the Light of Jacques de Liège's Speculum Musicae" in *Musica Disciplina* (American Institute of Musicology, Rome) (1964/65); *Iacobi Leodiensis Speculum Musicae, a Commentary,* vol. I (Institute of Mediaeval Music, N.Y. (1966-) vols. II/III forthcoming.

tion with aesthetical ideas, really lies in the pertinent mathematical proportions of the faculty of understanding.[8]

And so we arrive at the portals of phenomenology. Husserl brackets sound, as sonorous, Jacques Derrida states.[9] As far as I am informed, this means that Husserl reduces or brackets sound as physical and acoustical, and thus as "sensuous" in an ontic or physical sense. But what really needs bracketing is not just physical sound but particularly the categorial grid, i.e. the pertinent musical metaphysics, as typified in the classic example of Jacques de Liège or any such rationalist. Both physical and metaphysical sound, thus both acoustics and the categories of the intellect, need to be reduced, in order that music may emerge in its "bodily selfness." Obviously, it can easily be argued that Husserl does this. Both the real and the ideal need bracketing, in order to lay bare the truer ideality of the musical experience. And yet the "ideality" of the musical experience is not rediscovered at the expense of what I would like to call the "phenomenological sensuousness" of the akumenal experience. To retreat from the sensuous in music would be the old error of a metaphysics of music. Phenomenological sensuousness differs in kind from mere physical sensuousness, from the merely empirical, or even the sensual-erotic in Kierkegaard's interpretation of Mozart. For, sensuality like traditional ideality is an abstraction, introduced by Christian metaphysics. Kierkegaard writes how sensuality was brought into the world by Christianity.[10] For the sensualist is the child of the idealist; and Don Giovanni is indeed the natural but unacknowledged child of the ascetical monk, as pornography is the natural result of too much hagiography. And somewhere between these abstractions the human

---

[8] Kant, I., *Kritik der Urteilskraft,* ed. Vorländer, Phil. Bibl. B. 39, pp. 181, 186.
[9] Derrida, J., "La voix et le phénomène: signe linguistique et non-linguistique dans la phénomenologie de Husserl" (unpubl.).
[10] Kierkegaard, S., "Die unmittelbaren erotischen Stadien oder das Musikalisch-Erotische" in *Entweder/Oder* (Düsseldorf, 1956) tr. E. Hirsch, p. 49 f.

being is lost. Indeed, it was an ascetical monk, Tirso de Molina
(Fray Gabriel Tellez), who reintroduced the Don Juan theme
into drama and literature. And from *El Burlador de Sevilla* Don
Juan begins his trek through modern literature and music, from
Molière through Byron, Kierkegaard, Unamuno, and Richard
Strauss. A phenomenology which treats of the akumenal experience of music does not allow the innate sensuousness and richness of music, like Stravinsky's *Rite of Spring,* to fall between
the traditional abstractions of sensuality and ideality. Rather, as
in colorful poetry, the musical word is laid bare in the full surge
of its eros, in the full range of its sacral springtime primordial-
ity.

    3. In postulating a primordial echos, as possibly more con-
vincing to musicians and musicologists, we need not thereby
imply that it is a substitute for the eidos. Merleau-Ponty is of
service at this point, for it was he who wrote of a *syn-esthesis,*
which would take in both the visual and the audial.[11] And thus it
is possible to "see sound" and to "hear sight," strange as this
may sound at first flush. It is not a question of "color music," as
it is known in music history, or of the rather odd experiments of
Scriabin in his less than lucid moments. The synesthetic enhanc-
ing of sound by sight and of sight by sound might well be best
exemplified in the opera, for as musical drama it is meant to be
both seen and heard simultaneously, and the unity of the two
(by no means always achieved!) is what makes it a work of art,
however apparently hybrid. In his important work on the ontology of the arts and of music, Roman Ingarden avoids the opera,
as a work of musical art.[12] For, he seeks the more obviously
musical work in elucidating and exemplifying his original phenomenology of music. And thus he settles for Beethoven and
Chopin, for orchestra and piano. Yet the same problem would
arise in Beethoven's *Pastoral Symphony,* insofar as it is "representational." The problem returns in *Fidelio,* his only opera. As

---

[11] Merleau-Ponty, M., *La phénoménologie de la perception* (Paris,
1945) pp. 264-5.
[12] Ingarden, R., *Untersuchungen zur Ontologie der Kunst,* p. 28.

far as I am informed only Kant has dealt with the opera as a work of art, when in his third *Kritik* he writes of the conjunction of fine arts in one and the same artistic production. He also includes the oratorio.[13]

Perhaps it is only Merleau-Ponty who has seen the possibility of synesthetic perception, not as psychological but as phenomenological. This may be the key to the perplexing problem of opera or of any conjunction of the visual with the musical, be it a pastoral symphony, the fountains in Rome or anywhere else, a locomotive, or a steel foundry. Composers through Beethoven, Respighi, Honegger, and Mossolov have worked on such representational themes, to the alarm of purists who hold to the autonomy of music as opposed to heteronomy. And yet even classical sonata form is not pure. For both the concept of theme, as such, and its being built into the archetectonic of first-movement or sonata-allegro form, depends more than is realized on the visual and spatial. Perhaps in a closer analysis of the meaning of synesthetic perception we will begin to realize that we are not looking for an eidos as much as a transcendental logos, which is the fundament of philosophy, science, and the arts. Perhaps a primordial logos is the unifying basis of any eidos or echos, and thus of the visual and the audial, whether in general or specifically in the arts. But one looks in vain in Husserl for this kind of "aesthetics." One finds it, however, in Heidegger, when he deals with the origin of the work of art.[14] Yet Husserl's whole conception of time is dependent to a great extent on what he learned of musical tone. We must recall that Carl Stumpf, whose theory of *Tonverschmelzung* is known to every student of introductory musicology, was Husserl's teacher. His influence seems to show up in such treatises as Husserl's lectures on the consciousness of time. Apparently, the protensions and re-

---

[13] Kant, I., *Kritik der Urteilskraft*, § 52, n. 182 "Von der Verbindung der schönen Künste in einem und demselben Produkte."

[14] Heidegger, M., *Der Ursprung des Kunstwerkes* (Stuttgart, 1960) intro. by Gadamer, with a *Nachwort* and *Zusatz* by Heidegger. The *Zusatz* is a new addition, not to be found in *Holzwege*, where the essay originally appeared.

tensions of time are not only illustrated by allusion to musical melody, they seem to be spawned by an analysis of musical tone. (This becomes particularly clear in *Beilage* VI.) Husserl's search for the structure of consciousness could easily have been abetted by an attempt to analyse musical consciousness and time, for he would not have fallen into the psychologisms of F. Kurth or G. Anschütz any more than he would have lapsed into some of the philosophisms of N. Hartmann.[15] Yet, at least judging from available materials, Husserl never quite reached a critique of "aesthetical consciousness," particularly as musical. And yet the raw materials seem to be present in his works; they could be developed, even as "aesthetics" is bracketed.

II. Music and Musicology: The Need for New Foundations and Horizon

1. If we are to ask about a "phenomenology of music," we must inquire not only into the meaning of phenomenology but also of music and musicology, as they stand today. It is not the easiest possible task to give a clear and distinct definition of either phenomenology or musicology, and one goes limp when asked to give a short account of either, but none-the-less I shall attempt the impossible, braving the scorn of the gods. In *The Harvard Dictionary of Music* the eminent scholar, W. Apel, takes the term through its various possible meanings and connotations.[16] He settles for the idea of research in the field of music history "in which there are still so many facts to discover and clarify." In this factualist approach to musical history he seems to agree with M. Bukofzer's critique of the place of musicology in the university system.[17] The list of musicological objectives

---

15 Hartmann, N., *Asthetik* (Berlin 1953), pp. 197-210 "Schichten des Musikwerkes."

16 Apel, W. *The Harvard Dictionary of Music* (Harvard, 1953), "Musicology" p. 473 f.

17 Bukofzer, M., *The Place of Musicology in American Institutions of Higher Learning* (New York, 1956); cf. also his essay, "Historical Musicology" in *The Music Journal,* IV, 1946.

which Bukofzer drew up seems to focus more or less on research in the field of music history—the traditional "scientific-historical" approach—and thus the many excellent scholarly studies done on music from the Greeks to the present. A former tendency to be preoccupied with "old music" is now being overcome, though "old music" is not being neglected. Musicology is also beginning to discover its present and future as well as the rich heritage of the musical past. But it seems to need a new methodology, and it is here where phenomenology may be of great service, in that it does not merely analyse music but allows music to manifest itself in its inner subjectivity and being.

For Apel both acoustics and aesthetics are regarded as adjunct fields of musicological endeavor. They are probably the same for Bukofzer, though he does state that the task of the musical aesthetician is to give the inner meaning of music. I see this inner meaning, however, not in a musical aesthetics but in a "phenomenological aesthesis," as will be explained. Bukofzer tended toward stylistic criticism both in theory and practice. He mentioned this task also in his book on baroque music, a masterpiece of musical scholarship and a perfect demonstration of what he held.[18] All of this recalls the editorial on the need for aesthetic criticism, written in *The Musical Quarterly* by its editor, Prof. P. H. Lang.[19] In another editorial in *The Journal of the American Musicological Society* the late C. Sachs pleaded with musicologists to come out of an incapsulation in their individual specialties and to work on an aesthetics of music which would show it to be an essential part of a larger culture.[20] My own question is simply this: Is all this possible if one remains within the framework of traditional philosophical and aesthetical conceptuality and vocabulary? It is my personal conviction that the inner meaning of music and its place in humane

---

[18] Bukofzer, M., *Music in the Baroque Era Monteverdi to Bach* (New York, 1947).

[19] Lang, P. H., *The Musical Quarterly*, Editorial, Oct. 1949.

[20] Sachs, C., *The Journal of the American Musicological Society*, Editorial, 1949.

culture can be seen (heard!) and expressed more convincingly, if we equip ourselves with phenomenological method. This cannot be done by "ignoring historical phenomenology." For it is only thus that music can emerge in its "bodily selfness," in its primordial nudity as the *lógos mousikós.* And it is here that music is seen to be at one with primordial world and thus as an integral part of our "culture."

2. The methodological difficulty of traditional musicology is that it has approached the musical experience as an *object* of study. In thus concentrating on objectivity it has impaired the essential subjectivity of music, whether we look at the human subject or music as a subject for study. Especially after Kant aesthetics points us from the object to the subject of an art. The beautiful and the sublime are not to be found in the objective world but rather in the aesthetic judgment of the subject, which regards the form of things and has to do chiefly with the free interplay of the faculties of understanding and of transcendental imagination in the acting subject himself.[20] And even though Kant defines music as the free play of sensations, its essence is recognized as lying in the proportional play of harmony and thus within the subject judging. (This "judging" is neither logical nor juridical, and thus "evaluative," but rather aesthetical in the sense of subjectivity.) The emphasis on the subject, as transcendental, is pre-phenomenological, i.e. it is no longer a question of what Kant himself calls the empirical idealism of Descartes or the visionary idealism of Berkeley, yet it is not a truly phenomenological subjectivity in our sense. Husserl felt that the necessary reductions failed. Perhaps it is only in an analysis of a phenomenologically transcendental subjectivity, as in Husserl, that the truer subjectivity of the musical experience can be laid bare, not as aesthetical in a psychological or even in a post-Kantian sense, but as "transcendental" in a post-Husserlian sense. And thus the work of Roman Ingarden, whose ontology of the work of art is not opposed to Husserl's phenomenology but necessarily complements it.[21]

---

[21] Tymieniecka, A.-T., "Editorial: The Second Phenomenology" in *For Roman Ingarden, Nine Essays in Phenomenology* ('s-Gravenhage, 1959).

The problem of finding a new method for musical scholarship is intensified when we realize how musicology has not only tended to make an object out of music but that it has regarded itself as a "science." Musicology as the science-of-music (rather than the study of the logos of music) arose at a time when the positivistic and historical sciences were very influential and philosophy was perhaps justifiably held in disrepute.[22] Thus musicology looked away from the subjective views of philosophy toward the objectivity of both history and science. It was a situation quite the reverse of that of the *Speculum Musicae,* the classic example of a metaphysics of music or a musical metaphysics, and even of the rationalistic tendencies that perdured into the high baroque. Musicology turned to objectivity on the one hand and then became acutely aware of the contribution of post-Kantian aesthetics on the other, with its fund of subjectivity. In the objectivity of science it found its methodology; in aesthetics it found its soul, as it were, but from aesthetics it also took an additional fund of visually conceived vocabulary. But in neither science nor aesthetics has musicology been able to lay bare the inner meaning of music. Perhaps in a return to phenomenological subject, particularly to the creative consciousness of the artist (whether this be a composer or what Aaron Copland has called the "creative listener"), we can hope to recover a more fundamental meaning in musical scholarship. But then it will have ceased being the "science" of music, since we will be dealing with art and artist and thus with that artistic fundament, which seems to be at the basis of what we call being a human being. For the Muse is in everyone to the extent he or she is human, though it slumbers in many. The recovery of phenomenological subject means reawakening the Muse within us, whatever we may be.

But in the rediscovery of this Muse within the subject, it is necessary to bracket traditional musical categories and methods, which have been given us in music theory, aesthetics, and in a

<hr/>

[22] W. Wiora, "Musikwissenschaft" in *Die Musik in Geschichte und Gegenwart,* vol. 9, p. 1195 "Grundlegung als positive Wjssenschaft."

philosophy of number. Only through a phenomenological reduction can the Muse be awakened and thus emerge in artistic
consciousness. For while we may keep the distinction between
raw sound and musical sound, we will realize that the categories
that have made sound musical for us may also have kept us
from a more fundamental musical experience. The most obvious
example of this is the *Speculum Musicae,* which is a minute
examination of the proportional relations of musical metaphysics. For the *musicus* is not one who plays an instrument or
sings; rather he is the "muser," the philosopher-mathematician
who delights in speculation concerning the harmonic modula-
tions and the proportional interplay of consonances. It is true,
these consonances are the building blocks of any musical practice; but a preoccupation with them might well keep one from
any listening or musical composing. Indeed, com-position meant
not what we call musical composition today, i.e., of a vocal,
instrumental, or orchestral piece. Rather, it meant the putting-
together or com-positing of numerical proportions that went to
make up a consonance. Specifically *com-positio* meant the com-
ponibility of one number with another; and thus the *musicus* is
in reality the philosopher of number, the metaphysician, who
sees and admires first and foremost the interplay of mathematical proportions in music.[23] He sees all this; but he does not hear
the musical art work, at least not first and foremost. And thus
he is kept from a more fundamental musical experience. Hence
the need to bracket the musical categories. In this we see the
difference between a great classic philosophy of music and the
beginnings of a phenomenology of musical sound. For the latter

---

[23] *Iacobi Leodiensis Speculum Musicae,* I, ed. R. Bragard (American
Institute of Musicology), cap. 8, p. 28, "Cui parti philosophiae musica
supponatur. Cf. also II, p. 7, "Habet enim musicus dicere de quibuscumque
sonis distinctis simul collatis consonantiam facientibus quam inter se facian
harmonicam modulationem vel consonantiam . . ."; also cf. III, p, 163,
"Sed accedat ad tantum perscrutandam materiam subtiles clerici in
numeris experti, clarum et profundum habentes ingenium in talibus. Si
amatores musicae sint theoriae delectentur. Ludant hi in numerorum
proportionibus, in variis et stupendis numerorum comparationibus.
Ingrediantur et egrediantur et pascua inveniant."

considers the musical experience first and foremost (but as consciousness, not psychologically), as it attempts within the live musical experience to lay bare the intentional structures of musical consciousness and creative activity.

3. In order to discuss the act of musical composition, as understood in a modern sense, we need to take a brief look at the question of theory vs. practice. This is both a philosophical and a musical problem. Since the time of the Greeks the distinction between theory and practice has been with us, receiving its first truly significant critique in the writings of Immanuel Kant,[24] though in the Ars Nova Jacques de Liège had written of a "practical theory" and a "theoretical practice."[25] The distinction between theory and practice begins as a philosophical and seems to end as a linguistic affair. For Aristoxenos the eidos of music was not merely theoretical or abstract, although it was a kind of "analytic" concept that came about through the observation of the musical system of the Greeks. Instead it was a "regulative idea," analyzed as part of the essential substance of the musical opus itself.[26] This idea was still preserved in Athenaios, a second century B.C. theorist, in whose *Deipnisophistai* the phrase, *"kat' eîdos,"* means not "according to ideational theory" but "according to (musical) pattern." It is possible that our modern distinction between theory and practice, which has wrought so much havoc in music education as well as in philosophy, is reducible to our inability to analyze a given pattern as unity in basic complexity.

Gestalt theory is a new beginning in the recovery of complexity in unity, yet it remains pretty well imbedded in psychology. It is not yet phenomenological, as Merleau-Ponty has shown convincingly.[27] The *whole* experience, whether musical or philo-

[24] Kant, I., *Über den Gemeinspruch: das mag in der Theorie richtig sein, taugt aber nicht für die Praxis* (1793), ed. Gadamer (Frankfurt 1946).

[25] Smith, F. J., *Iacobi Leodiensis Speculum Musicae, a Commentary*, vol. I, p. 45 f.

[26] Lohmann, J., "Der Ursprung der Musik" in *Archiv für Musikwissenschaft*, 1959, 1/2, p. 151.

[27] Merleau-Ponty, M., *op. cit.*

sophical, is neither merely theoretical nor merely practical. It is a baffling combination of both, an intentional pattern or structuring which eludes the theoretical and the practical as two separate approaches. There can be no artificial distinction between thinking and doing. And thus we work out a musical praxis which is more than just the reunification of theory and practice in "theoretical practice" or "practical theory." Rather it transcends both theory and practice, as the primordial logos is laid bare. Within this logos theory is not just intellectual speculation but rather the concrete meaning which emerges in living practice. Thus there can be no musicology for its own sake, or philosophy in an ivory tower, divorced from creative activity. Similarly there can be no blind practice which only does but never thinks or knows. The interplay of both theory and practice in a living praxis is best seen in the art of keyboard improvisation, where mind leads fingers and fingers lead mind in an exhilarating musical experience. It is here that a musicologist and practicing musician that one thinks with one's body, in this case with the fingers, which Stravinsky called his "inspirers."

The classical example of all this is Stravinsky's *augures printaniers* chord, which defies mere harmonic analysis.[28] It is quite useless with only the techniques of traditional theoretical analysis to analyze this juxtaposition of a dominant seventh chord in E flat in the right hand and a chord of F flat major in the left hand. It is very simple: there is no harmonic analysis called for; it is simply a question of how the composer placed his hands on the keyboard. It was this bodily positioning of the hands which gave birth to the complex of sound, and not some theoretical idea that made it possible. Out of this nucleus of harmonically clashing chords grew the inspiration and motifs of *Le Sacre du Printemps*. Here we see how a merely intellectual analysis arrives at an impasse and even appears ridiculous. Phenomenologically speaking it is a question of body thought, not just a psychological Gestalt: in this case the composer's hands moving on the keyboard. And his movement is his orien-

---

[28] Vlad, R., *Stravinsky,* tr. F. and A. Fuller (Oxford, 1960), p. 30.

tation to musical world and primordial sound. The intentional links are not theoretical but bodily. It is not a question of "reason" or of mere body but of bodily logos. And thereafter all that remains to be done is to spell out and develop the motifs that have been posited and suggested in this bodily positioning of hands on keyboard, in this bodily evolving of world.

Composition, like temporality and eros, which are of its essence, is a whole intentional structuring of the subject and of world, in which the subject does not merely relate to world but evolves world. And here it may be useful to recall that music is an intersubjective experience, not a solipsistic one. The evoking of world in the work of art, in this case musical, is the result of the reduction of both subject and object. Therefore the composer needs his audience, his creative listeners, in order to be truly a composer. It is not just a question of playing down to or merely playing for an audience, as it were, to feed the audience into one's boundless ego. Rather the true composer plays for and with his listeners in an intersubjective dialogue which reduces mere ego and all its external concomitants, such as fortune and fame. The same ought to be able to be said of the creative philosopher.

4. An attempt to explain the creative process in music cannot succeed if we remain only at the predicative level. At least in ontological phenomenology we study the prepredicative and prestatemental levels of speech and music, i.e., that which precedes or comes before the predicated or the statemental, in that it makes them possible at all. It may be particularly in this area that philosophy and music come together rather than in a metaphysical philosophy of number, as in the classic theories of music, such as the *Speculum Musicae*. It may be that in phenomenology we draw nearer to that which makes both music and philosophy possible, however different they emerge at the statemental level. I use the word, statemental, advisedly, since there is such a thing as a musical statement, though it is not recognized as such by many a philosopher, even by R. Ingarden. The most obvious case of musical statement is what is called a theme, i.e. the positing of a musical subject, the use of melodic types in

the building of musical configurations. It was always recognized that music was derived from number. But the concept of theme was slow to develop and is essentially a modern idea, beginning perhaps in the Renaissance, when the composer posited the musical *soggetto* as distinct from the natural *numero harmonico*. The only problem is that, instead of furthering the truer subjectivity of music in a phenomenological sense, this led toward the positing of theme as objective, i.e. as a musical object for both composer and hearer to focus on. But music has no objects, as sight does. And thus a phenomenology of music would move away from such thematic objectivity toward the restoration of a truer subjectivity, and thus with musical logos rather than with musical statement, as a kind of logic or expression of natural musical number. And here we see the importance of the restoration of musical rhythm as the heart of the musical experience. The *Rite of Spring* or Messiaen's rhythmic innovations exemplify this.

If we take the era of the Viennese Classics, we have a good enough model of the statemental in a traditional sense, for it is here that we see the high point of sonata or first-movement form. The overarching AABA structure of the sonatas and symphonies of Haydn, Mozart, and Beethoven is a commonplace to students of music, as are also the places first and second themes take in this structure over against the harmonic changes from the tonic to the dominant and return. The score of Beethoven's *Eroica* reveals a number of internal and external innovations, instrumental and harmonic (as well as the wedding of sonata with fugal form), but the general structure remains pretty well the same. The phenomenologist would be interested in the intentionalities that make this overarching structure possible. In this case we have music without words.

In philosophy we believe we have words without music, but this is true only at the statemental level. And yet, as musicological research reveals, there is a primordial unity of word and music, one known e.g. by the Greeks not only at the pre-predicative but even at the predicative level. For at least classical Greek is a musical language, and it is by far not the only such language known to man. At least in Greek poetry there is no such thing as the alienation of language from musical sound. The accents in classic Greek are not just stress accents; they are quite musical. A Greek "statement," particularly as poetic, is both verbal and musical at once. This influence carries over into formal music, as may be seen in the "Skolion of Seikilos," an early second or first century (B.C.) drinking song, transcribed from an epitaph engraved on a column at Aïdin in Asia Minor, which Ramsay discovered in 1883.[29] Though this is a relatively late example, it may not be unwarranted to note that on almost every accute accent there is a raise in musical pitch, on every circumflex a lengthening and a cadential figure. A transcription of the first phrase may be used as a sufficient example:

"*ὅ—τον ζῆς   φαί— νου...*"
"As long as you live, ring clear . . ."

This is obviously only a transcription. It cannot really be given on the well tempered keyboard, since the pitch intervals are quite different. It can only be sung by a trained expert. The Greek letters above the music are the vocal notation that accompany the words. It is interesting for our research into synesthetic perception to note, that in this drinking song we are admonished to "ring clear" while we yet live. The actual word is *phaínou,* which means "to appear" or "to shine forth." Here we have the musical and the visual united in one phrase. Actually, the verb, *phaínomai,* means "to appear," either as sight or as

---

[29] Martin, E., *Trois documents de musique grecque* (Paris, 1953), p. 48 f; cf. Apel, W. *The Rise of Music in the Ancient World East and West* (New York, 1943) section five "Greece and Rome" p. 195 f.

sound, though it usually means the former. We can grasp this the better if we realize that our word, clarity, is not only a visually oriented word, though we use it much more for sight than for sound. Yet the poets tell us of the clarion call that rings out loud and clear. We speak of a clear voice. And there are not only clear and distinct ideas; but they must also be spoken clearly and distinctly. Since we are dealing with a drinking song, it is obvious that the otherwise apparently visual word, *phaínou,* is meant to be rendered not as "appear" but as "to ring clear." After all during a drinking bout there is a good bit of toasting, accompanied by much loud and clear merriment.

Examples of earlier Greek music, such as the *stásimon* sung by the chorus in Euripides' *Orestes* (fifth century B.C.), though less interesting than our drinking song, might illustrate more faithfully how Greek accents are musical. Whatever the case may be, it is obvious that at least in the Greek language, where both philosophy and music as we know them were born, there is no separation between word and music of some sort. The separation of word and music came about only gradually in the emergence of Christian metaphysics, which spawned the music theory of the Middle Ages. We have not yet really recovered from this artificial dualism, perhaps not even in phenomenology, as we know it traditionally. At this end of history it is hard for us to grasp what the Greeks may have taken for granted. Today we seek to "relate" logical statement with musical sound, or we set words to music, ignoring the fact that live word sets itself into musical expression. The Greeks knew that logic was not just "mental," and that it was inseparable from primordial musical word. Yet we need not go back to the Greeks, except in the sense that we are searching for a convincing model. We can take the spoken word as it is in use today. As I read these words aloud, for example, I cannot escape their natural musical sound, and it is only this which enables me to speak and you to hear. The musical phrases and cadences of speech are essential to live word, and only live word is the basis for intersubjective communication. The word, as read, is always secondary or after the fact.

5. In effect, music is the "bodily selfness" of word, as alive, i.e. as in-the-world. No reduction is desirable here. The eidetic reductions to be performed would have to do only with the abstractions of acoustics or of my ontic ego and yours.[30] Any "logic" as phenomenological is inseparable from the concreteness of the transcendental logos itself, as musical. Perhaps Hegel can be of help at this point, insofar as he calls form the "becoming of concrete content," or when he writes that *Dasein,* as self-concretizing, is immediately "logical." This is, of course, very Greek, as it was meant to be. However it floats in a concept of consciousness that lacks sufficient reductions and fundament. In living dialogue (*dia-logos*), i.e. in the sharing of the logos which makes any intersubjectivity of dialogue possible, live word as meaningful musical sound is what unites us. For only in it do we give ourselves "bodily." Reading them in print is at best a substitute or a post-factum. "Logic" as merely propositional or statemental is a kind of rootless and groundless word. And thus we recoup the prelogical grounding of any logic, musical or philosophical, by recovering the transcendental logos which makes any logic whatsoever possible at all. In building any new logical system we cannot ignore this prelogical level, else we literally build on sand.

The phenomenology of the prelogical (or protological) must provide the ground for any philosophical or musical logic (or onto-logic). While the phenomenologist does not deny the many branches of the philosophical tree, he is most interested in what makes such a tree stand: the roots and the ground into which the tree has sunk its roots. The prelogical is thus not some sort of mystic postulate but rather the logos itself. Heidegger has traced the gradual alienation of the *epistéme logiké* from the logos which gave it birth. When any logic becomes an ontologic (or theologic), as metaphysical, it runs the risk of spinning itself out of primordial ground, and, loosened from its roots, it may take on an alienated existence of its own in a fantasy world

---

[30] Husserl, E., *Cartesianische Meditationen und Pariser Vorträge,* ed. Strasser (Haag, 1950) pass. We deal here with the reductions of ego and *alter ego.*

with or without much relation to the original ground. Only a logic, expression, or predicate, that does not cut itself away from its primordial source can expect to retain and evolve meaning.

III. Musical "Aisthesis" and The "Aesthetical Experience" of Music

1. We are stressing the difference between "aesthesis" and "aesthetics" in our discussion of phenomenology vis-à-vis the aesthetical experience. It is only proper that we now reveal ourselves for what we are when we speak of a "phenomenology of musical aesthetics." In reality we no longer mean traditional aesthetics at all, not even in a Kantian sense, though we admit a great debt to Kant. At this point we cannot be blamed for waxing Heideggerian, since it was apparently Heidegger who made the break-through out of aesthetics into an ontological aesthesis in *Der Ursprung des Kunstwerkes*.[31] Briefly, he criticizes aesthetics as the "logic of *aisthesis*," i.e., as the metaphysics or onto-logic derived from a more fundamental aisthesis. But, as derived, aesthetics is also deficient. And thus the call for a return from philosophies of the beautiful and from traditional ontic aesthetics to the work of art itself, as the emergence of truth (*a-létheia*) in the primordial conflict of earth and world. As musical aesthesis this would mean a return out of musical aesthetics, as we presently know it; it would be a recouping of the primordial world of the *akumena*, i.e. of the akumenal logos.

It is here that sounds emerge as "phenomenologically sensuous" in the richness of a primordial eros, as best exemplified in Stravinsky's savage and primeval *Sacre du Printemps*. We want no monkish *epoché*'s here! Though there are other examples, let this more obvious one suffice for our present purposes, for in this epoch-making composition of the younger Stravinsky (before he became an ascetical dodecaphonist!) all the eros of springtime, all the intense rhythms and the white heat of the

---

[31] Smith, F. J., "The 'End' of Aesthetics" (unpubl.).

sacral puberty rites of pagan Russia are portrayed in music so lush and overwhelming, that it caused a veritable riot on its first public performance in Paris. No place here for the ascetical analyst or the mere theorist! And the key to this masterpiece is not just the exotic orchestration or the cataclysmic harmony but rather the revolutionary break-through in rhythm. And the orgiastic pulsations of this composition portray a musical eros which is perhaps the best expression of what we might call a true transcendental logos as opposed to a merely intellectualized one. It is a commonplace and yet a musical fact worth further study that Stravinsky broke through not only the theoretical categories of harmony but especially the tight metrical categories of traditional musical rhythm. In fact, rhythm takes precedence once again over musical theme and melody—perhaps for the first time in music history since the isorhythmic compositions of Guillaume de Machaut in the Ars Nova (14th century). Musical rhythm is thus the key to this creation. It is a piece impossible to "keep time to" or to conduct in the usual manner, since the concept of time is radically altered. The most one can do is cue in the instruments, for there is page after page of highly irregular and inconsequential rhythmic pulsation, which gets its meaning not from any metrical measurements of linear time but only from what I may be allowed to call the "tensor factor" of musical time, as phenomenological.

2. This tensor factor is directly related to the dynamic intentional nucleus that begets artistic creativity in the subject. In this sense musical time is no longer conceived as extended in metaphorical or linear space and thus as durational. In the *Rite of Spring* the sense of "duration" is lost. One does not "count" such music, as one does not watch a clock while reading Rilke. It is, indeed, time-less. And only in this sense can "atemporality" be understood. This is not a psychological phenomenon but rather the emergence of the "timeless" logos of phenomenon. Neither is it a metaphysical "eternity," that hypocritical concept which the concept of time makes possible, only to be denied by it. The timelessness of music is concrete and not abstract: it roots in an overcoming of objective or ontic time and the

unfolding of the subject in its fullest essence, as ekstatic. Thus musical time has little to do with the spatial or linear, despite the tradition of western philosophy and music which extends time along a line leading to infinity. And of course the west evolved a linearly conceived musical notation! It best exemplifies in concrete practice the linear conception of time, but it is at best a derived symbolization of phenomenological time, whether we understand this in the sense of Husserl, Heidegger, or Merleau-Ponty. We make a great mistake when we take these symbols literally and predicate of the phenomenon of music a linear duration which it does not have in essence, for music is fundamentally not durational but "tensile." The ontological tensility of music cannot be graphed either linearly or even in the manner of protension and retentions. "Tensility" can best be grasped if we understand phenomenological intentionality minus the spatial visualizations. For that is what they are: visual "realizations" of an akumenal phenomenon which cannot be so realized.

This notion of ontological tensility is also a closer approach to what the Greeks called musical tonos. For the "musical tone" is directly related to the Greek kithara and to the tuning of strings. But such tuning has to do with the various degrees of tenseness, as every string player knows in his fingers. And for this simple reason the tonos, which is the fundamental building block of western music since the Greeks, is actually a "tensor" first and foremost. Only then does it concern what we would now call pitch, especially as graphed visually on a scale. Greek instrumental notation, unlike our own, was a tablature, i.e. it indicated the positions of fingers and had nothing to do primarily with the visual representation of pitch levels, as conceived in our own linear notation. And thus music was liberated from the imposition of a spatially conceived temporality. It could be what it was: an interplay of strings of differing intensities, thus producing musical sound. This is phenomenological in the sense that music is allowed to present itself as it *is* in its truer subjectivity: not as something to be seen but as something to be fingered and thus as "no-ontic-thing" to be heard. Here the haptic and the musically audial go hand in hand. The visual symbols, which are but aids to the fingers, cannot become anything more than they are. They cannot begin to dictate musical conceptuality.

It is perhaps this tonos that best exemplifies a transcendental logos whether we speak of the Greeks or of ourselves. Were we to search for a suitable word to exemplify a phenomenology of music, as Husserl and Heidegger sought and found the eidos and the logos, we would have to choose the word, tonos, and this for reasons not dissimilar. J. Lohmann must receive the credit for pointing out this historic fact: that not only philosophy but also what we now call music began as something absolutely new in the world of the Greeks. And of philosophy, mathematics, and music, the latter was the oldest![32] The word that characterizes this is tonos, as intimately bound up with the logos. Neither logos nor tonos can be understood properly unless we make passage from aesthetics to aesthesis.

3. What is this transition? In the *Nachwort* to his large essay on the art work Heidegger puts it quite clearly: traditional aesthetics has regarded the work of art as an object, literally, we might add, as an *objet d'art*.[33] Art is thus an object of aesthesis, understood as sense perception in a broad sense. This has then been interpreted as "art experience" which is looked on as the source of both the production and appreciation of art. "Everything is experience," Heidegger writes. And perhaps this is the very thing which brings about the death of true art, a death that drags itself out over centuries despite all the talk about undying works of art. Art is not an object of experience but rather the emergence of the truth of being in primordial conflict of world and earth. The transition is thus from the ontic to the ontological, from the objective to the phenomenological subject. But the return to the eksistential subject is a departure from aesthetics

---

[32] Lohmann, J., in *op. cit.,* p. 149.
[33] Heidegger, M., *Der Ursprung des Kunstwerkes,* p. 91, "Die Ästhetik nimmt das Kunstwerk als einen Gegenstand und zwar als den Gegenstand der aísthesis, des sinnlichen Vernehmens im weiten Sinn. Heute nennt man dieses Vernehmen das Erleben . . . Alles ist Erlebnis. Doch vielleicht ist das Erlebnis das Element, in dem die Kunst stirbt. Das Sterben geht so langsam vor sich, daß es einige Jahrhunderte braucht."

as subjective, whether in a Kantian or psychological sense. And thus a phenomenological aesthesis is not just sense perception or any kind of either psychological or aesthetical experiencing of the work of art. Rather, it is a phenomenological perceiving, i.e. original (in the sense of Merleau-Ponty) and intentional rather than intellectual or empirical. It is a question of the intentionality of the subject which brings forth a work of art and thus creates a world.

When the Greeks used the word, *aisthánomai,* it did not mean just "sense perception" in a modern sense, as though there were really a post-Cartesian division between mind and senses which spawned the split between intellectualism and empiricism criticized by Merleau-Ponty. There was no need even for a Kantian schema to bind together the a priori forms of sense-intuition with the categories of understanding. Rather, man himself is the sensing being (*aisthētes*), i.e. the living being who is aware of being, as it unfolds itself to him in his encounter with the world he opens up. This man is no "aesthete" who looks for aesthetical pleasure or enjoyment. Art is not pastry. The essence of this phenomenological sensing of world is the emergence of ontological truth in the primordial struggle of world and earth. World opens out and earth closes in, but this is no metaphysical closure. It is a kind of dialectic between world and earth, and in this conflict of the Titans the truth of the work of art is brought forth. Pleasure may or may not be a concomitant. There is little "art experience" or "aesthetical appreciation" here. Thus, in a certain sense Heidegger's insights begin to spell the "end" of traditional aesthetics, as the completion of a historic period in philosophy.

However, there will be a good many aesthetes who will not take too kindly to such an explanation of the art work or to Heidegger's statement in *Die Frage nach der Technik* that "on account of sheer aesthetics we can no longer preserve the essence of art."[34] In this case the downfall of aesthetics goes along with the particular trend that technology has taken in modern

---

[34] Heidegger, M., *Vorträge und Aufsätze* (Pfullingen, 1954) p. 44.

times. In our technological age everything, art included, becomes
an object to be dealt with, an object that can have a value,
aesthetical or monetary, set on it. Technology is indeed one
manifestation of *technē* (which we have translated both as "art"
and as "technique"). But Heidegger returns to a primordial
techno-logy (as the logos of *techne*), i.e. to a more fundamental
bringing forth of being (*Sein*), a bringing forth which is more
evident in the work of art as a manifestation of truth (the
"un-concealment" of being) than it ever could be in technological science. Heidegger's approach is somewhat Hegelian, in that
he brings aesthetic problems back to a consideration of truth, as
phenomenological, and away from theories of the beautiful.
Truth and beauty are not just "convertible with being"; beauty
is not just an "aesthetical idea." Rather truth, as the disclosure
of being (*Sein*), *is* beauty. The Husserlian objection at this
point would be, Why being? If it is disclosure at all, it is that of
subject not of being. But the problem of being and subjectivity
we must reserve for another occasion. When we speak of the
work of art in this essay, we are obviously speaking of ontological phenomenology, one that might be in need of considerable
correction and supplement from an intersubjective phenomenology.

4. How does "truth" manifest itself as art? How does it show
itself not as "actuality" or "reality" (those bastard translations
of *en-érgeia*) but as a work (*érgon*)? How is artistic truth not
"real" but a "work" (not *wirklich* but *werkhaft*)? Truth reveals
itself in the art work because the work is what initiates the
conflict between world and earth.[35] Out of this creative opposition truth reveals itself, as being emerges. For the work of art
holds open the region of world; it makes world possible and best
exemplifies world. Yet another "principle" besides the opening
up of world is required: the bringing forth of earth. A Greek
temple is used as an example. Perhaps we may refer to the
temple at Agrigento (ancient Acragas) as a refreshing change
from the Acropolis. The "materials" of the temple, taken from

---

[35] Heidegger, M., *Der Ursprung des Kunstwerks,* p. 51.

the earth, are not just used in the erection of the sacred edifice, as today we use up so many tons of concrete, which is regarded as nothing more than so much materiel. Matter is not consumed in its being used. Rather the "materials" are brought out *as such* perhaps for the first time. And here we must recall that matter is to be interpreted mythologically as belonging to ontological earth, the mother loam.

And thus crude rock that has become a Doric column at the hands not of a technician but of an artist comes to thrust forward and rest against the capital and roof. The "artist" (*technitēs*) literally *brings* the fluted column *forth* from the mother rock, i.e. from "matter." Thus for the first time it becomes rock in the truest sense, for its strength and beauty have been brought forth into the light from out the darkness of concealing earth. And this is the task of the artist: to bring forth. One gets this idea particularly with the unfinished torsos of Michelangelo, they struggle to emerge from the rough rock, and only the hand of the artist can bring them out in all their strength and beauty as the truth which they are. Thus the rock, as a Doric column, comes to thrust against the temple roof in dynamic "rest" and becomes rock for the first time. In the same way rough ore becomes metal and receives a lustre and sheen it would never otherwise have; and now it can become a flashing blade in the hand of a warrior, or, if a precious metal, can become "brushed gold" at the hands of a Florentine artist. In like manner colors are brought out in the creation of the artist; and raw sound becomes music, not by its being filtered through an intellectual grid, but rather because in working with raw sound the artist brings out its innate musicality, so that we have music for the first time, as we know it in a Delphic Hymn, in a medieval chanson, or in a modern symphony. All of this is brought about because the work of art, as it opens world, sets itself back into earth: into the massiveness of stone, into the firmness of wood, into the lustre of bronze or gold, into the resounding of tone, into the magic power words have to name. The art work holds the earth into the openness of world and being, as it helps earth become truly earth. World and earth are different from one another and yet never separated; they are distinguished but not apart. This is a oneness of creative opposition: the opposing factors mutually complement each other and are essentially necessary to one another.

Insofar as an art work opens up world and brings forth earth, it initiates the conflict between them. It is a conflict in which the opposites become ever more opposing, so that conflict remains conflict and is not leveled out in a false peace. Yet this is not a sterile antagonism but a creative opposing; for out of the nothingness of being truth is "created," i.e., is brought forth as a work of art. Thus Heidegger can write that "the being of an art work consists in its initiating a conflict between world and earth." The initiating of the conflict is precisely a gathering-into-movement which is characteristic of any art. And this is what we mean by "rest," e.g. the pillar "rests" against the capital and the roof. For in its thrust the Doric column gathers itself wholly into the movement of "resting" against the capital. Such rest is obviously not static repose. In like manner a musical rest is not just a pause between musical phrases; rather the musical themes come to rest all their weight against the overarching roof of AABA form. Here we see that "form" is no longer visual but dynamic in the sense of an architechtonic and musical tensor factor. For, while the AABA form can be graphed visually, audially these are but focal tensor points, at which the forces of the art work are gathered together, ready to unleash themselves again as the composition further develops itself. It is this dynamic tensility which we "feel" in a musical score rather than see in an analysis or on the printed page. Musical form is meant for the ear not the eye. And this "infeeling" as "inhearing" is what we mean by aesthesis. Thus it is neither an intellectual analysis of music nor is it a psychologically aesthetical experience, as such.

Truth emerges in interplay with ontological un-truth. Untruth is not logical or moral falsity but rather the "opposite"-of-truth in the sense of the closure and disclosure of being (*Sein*). When being discloses or reveals itself to us we call it truth; when it withholds itself, even as ontological presence, we call it

untruth or closure. Being opens-out and closes-in in the emergence of the un-hiddenness (*a-létheia*) of truth. Being reveals
of itself, it tells of itself; but it does not tell all, for it conceals
as it reveals. And thus while world opens out, earth comes forth
or is brought forth, concealing. To the "open middle"[36] of the
primordial conflict between truth and untruth belong world and
earth. Yet world is not simply the Open as earth is Closure.
Rather, world is grounded only on earth and earth thrusts only
through world. The conflict of world and earth in the work of
art is not identical with the conflict of truth and untruth, but it
depends on it and issues from it, insofar as truth "sets itself into
the work (of art)." And thus truth is what works the work of
art. Truth stands in-the-work and thus we can speak of *en-érgeia,* which has little to do with "energy," and less to do with
"actuality" or "objectivity" in the sense of an object-of-art.

5. Heidegger identifies the conflict of truth/untruth as a
"Riss."[37] This means a fissure, a tear, a breach. In the conflict of
world and earth, in their opposing tendencies to open and close,
the opposites belong essentially together and not apart. This
ontological fissure is not a splitting apart; for in this tearing
there is no rending asunder. It is a *"Grund-riss,"* i.e., a fundamental breaching, a primordial distinction that does not, as it
were, extinguish the opposites but brings them together in a
fundamental unity of being, thus giving them contour or
"shape" (*Umriss*). The conflict is brought into this breach, as
world is "set back" into the earth and thus is "set fast" into its
shape. It is now evident that this shaping cannot be understood
in the sense of a psychological *Gestalt.* Heidegger employs the
word, *Ge-stell,* a rather violent neologism, which emphasizes the
"setting-up of world," the "setting forth" of earth, and the
setting of the fissure itself. Being is what *sets* things into
"shape." And thus any *"Gestalt."* It is the hand of the artist, be
he sculptor or musician, who sets truth into its shape. This
setting-fast is not a congealing or a becoming rigid and motion-

[36] Heidegger, M., *Holzwege* (Frankfurt, 1957), "Wozu Dichter?",
p. 260; *Der Ursprung des Kunstwerkes,* p. 59.
[37] Heidegger, M., *Der Ursprung des Kunstwerkes,* p. 71.

less. It means being set into movement, just as a composer sets to work with raw sound, thus "setting an idea to music"; but this musical "idea" is not just an abstract form. It is, as it were, a springtime emergence of sound in its pure sensuousness, as e.g. in "La danse des adolescentes" in Stravinsky's *Rite of Spring* (which is the antithesis of all the saccharine "Springs" one is used to hearing), or as in the sadistic voice of R. Strauss' *Salomé,* as she taunts the dripping head of St. John (one of the most gruesome scenes in music). This phenomenological sensuousness cannot be the object of musical analysis or the subject of aesthetical experience. It can only be "felt" in aesthesis. The total effect can be felt only in a syn-aesthesis.

IV. Some Provisional Conclusions for Both Phenomenolgy and Musicology

1. Perhaps any conclusions we might reach in this essay would be the result of research into the meaning of synesthesis rather than of aesthetic experience as the immediate experience of art, which takes place in the presence of the object of art itself, even be this a judgmental evaluation of art in a post-Kantian sense. And thus the transition from aesthetics to aesthesis is a passage from the "logic" of aesthesis to the logos, which makes any logic possible at all. In music we found this logos intimately connected with tonos, as tensor factor. What then is the task of the musicologist, if he is to get beyond historical and aesthetical research? It seems to me his task will be to give a phenomenological description (rather than just an analysis or stylistic criticism) of the musical logos as it unfolds itself in a musical work of art. But for this he may need to study the meaning of intentionality in Husserl and Merleau-Ponty and of logos in Heidegger. But as he studies phenomenology he may set a new task for it, in that he gives a critique of its predominantly visual conceptuality and vocabulary. Hence the task of the phenomenologist and the musicologist may well coincide in the logos. As a musician he will be aware of the essential sensuousness of his art; as a phenomenologist he will know that this

sensuous quality is no longer physical or physico-erotic. Rather, in the emergence of the musical logos the abstractions of both traditional sensuality and ideality vanish, as the musical work of art reveals truth and essence in their original selfness, i.e. in the full primeval force of a springtime, or even in the savage pulsations of the rites of eros.

2. In a phenomenology of musical aesthesis the original unity of music and philosophy (both creations of the Greeks) is recovered. The critique a musician will make of the visual orientation of philosophy will be balanced by a return to a fundamental syn-aesthesis, in which both sight and hearing are grounded. It is only in a "synesthetic perception" that we can appreciate not only the art of sound but all the arts together as one integral art work. For in synesthesis one not only hears sound but hears world, for hearing is a basic openness for world. And thus since one hears world one also sees it, and thus one "hears sight" and "sees sound." It is only thus that one can appreciate opera, for example. It is only thus that following the score of e.g. Benjamin Britten's *Serenade for Tenor, Horn, and Strings* we can appreciate how he "set" words to music, in this case the words of Tennyson, Keats, and Blake. Here we both see and hear the words, as poetry and music : as *one*.

Ernst Kurth has written that "Music is the emergence of powerful primal forces, whose energies originate in the unheard. What one usually designates as music is actually but its echo."[38] We might say at this point that musical tonos is the echo of a primal *ēchos*, which is accessible in phenomenology, as the study of logos, but only if it becomes an akumenal phenomenology, i.e. one of primordial sound.

---

[38] Kurth, E., *Musikpsychologie* (Bern, 1947) ; cf. also "Musik-psychologie" in *Die Musik in Geschichte und Gegenwart,* vol. 9, p. 1148 f.

COMMENTS ON DR. SMITH'S PAPER

Gerhard Albersheim

I have to apologize for not doing my "homework"! Since I received some of today's papers very late I was in a quandary as to whether I should familiarize myself with them or attend these interesting meetings. As the Conference won I shall have to speak without a prepared text.

As far as this session's papers are concerned, I do not have to go into many details because they have been discussed already and I find myself mostly in agreement with them. However, feeling that we heard enough about what a phenomenology of music *should* be, I shall move from theory to practice by discussing some of the problems in whose research I am engaged.

I doubt whether I could maintain the statement that aesthetics is the interpretation of aisthesis, but I am quite sure that music is based on the aesthetic interpretation of sound. Let us clarify the musical attitude towards sounds by contrasting it with other ways of responding! In our everyday lives we interpret auditory stimulae as natural signs for what is going on around us: we "hear" (perceive) not sounds with particular auditory properties, but rather someone walking overhead, typing in the room to our right, coming down the staircase, dropping and breaking a dish; or we "hear" water dripping in the kitchen, the wind rustling in the trees, a car stopping in front of the house, etc. The biological importance of such practical interpretation of sounds can hardly be exaggerated.

At least as important is the role of sounds in the communication into larger units. In language, too,—at least in everyday completely different attitude which is based on several sets of hearing- and understanding-conventions. We focus 1) on the selective system of speechsounds (phonemes), 2) on the semantic meaning of the words, and 3) on their syntactical organization into larger units. In language, too,—at least in everyday language—we do not listen to the sounds for their own sake, but for the meaning they signify, the information they convey.

The third important auditory sphere is music, of course, which presents a different case: here we listen to the sounds for their own sake because the musical tone systems—which are also based on conventions of hearing—are organized on auditory properties. Until the middle of this century, the raw material of all musical systems was tones which are classified by the same general categories which Dr. Hensel mentioned for the classification of colors, i.e., specific (sensuous) quality, spatial localization, intensity, and duration. In the case of tones, these categories are represented by timbre, pitch, loudness, and duration which is intermodal by definition. Of these, pitch is the most important property for music, being the building stone for musical scale systems; but pitch is also that tone attribute which has caused the greatest difficulties for phenomenological definition. I agree with Dr. Smith and Dr. Ihde that we should not use any other than auditory concepts in talking about musical properties. This is what I am doing when I call pitch the location of tones in space because I am speaking strictly of auditory space. For thirty years I have been maintaining that the widely held notion that the term "space" refers to our three-dimensional physical space or to visual space, is unjustified. In my opinion, we may speak of space whenever we are confronted with a class of moveable phenomena which can be ordered in certain dimensions in which their mutual distances can be measured and compared. It is always our selves who form the concept of space, who are contained in the space continuum and within have the experience of movement in time.

All of these criteria apply to tones: they are moveable in melody and can be ordered in the dimension of pitch in which their mutual distances, the tone intervals, can be measured and compared. In music, not our physical bodies, of course, but our psychic selves are transferred into the aesthetic realm of tonal space where we experience melody as movement of sounds from pitch to pitch. Naturally, the dimension of pitch between "high" and "low" has no relation whatever to the directions of high and low in our physical and visual spaces. However, not only successions of different, but also of identical tones occur frequently in music and are also heard as melodic movement. Therefore, the outline of a melody can be thought of, and visually symbolized in notation, only in two dimensions which means that we have to add time as a second space dimension to pitch in order to define tonal space. It is interesting that in music both these dimensions are organized in quanta, the "vertical" quanta of scale steps and the "horizontal" quanta of rhythmic pulses, which satisfactorily represent phenomenal continuity. Therefore, there is no need of filling in the pitch intervals between neighboring scale steps by "glissando", or the time intervals between successive tones by sustaining the sound, in order to achieve the effect of continuous motion.

In all musical scale systems the selection of the steps is determined by certain hearing conventions of a cultural group. The individual steps are not semantically defined, but syntactically, i.e., through their mutual relationships, and thereby acquire a conceptual distinctiveness which enables us to think and reproduce them. In music, our thinking operates exclusively in terms of this vocabulary of scale steps which is the prerequisite for the "inter-subjectivity," the communicability, the intelligibility of the musical "language."

Pitch, then, is never heard for its own sake in music, but always understood as intonation of a scale step. This intonation can vary considerably without impairing the identification of the meant step. Thus, we encounter in music a similar difference between phenomenal (pitch-) and logical (step-)identity as was mentioned by Dr. Hensel in regard to colors. The aesthetically acceptable (and usually not noticed) variation range of intonation is far greater than we would expect and far above the threshold of pitch discrimination; its usual range is from approximately a quarter tone above to a quarter tone below the "just" intonation of the intended scale step. Hence, in music, we can intone the same scale step "C" on very many different pitches without any disturbing effect, just as vowels and other phonemes are being pronounced in many different ways and still clearly recognized. Conversely, a single pitch (e.g. the piano key between C and D), will be unequivocally interpreted as one or the other of two different scale steps according to the musical context (in one example either as C sharp, i.e. a raised C, or as D flat, i.e. a lowered D). Consequently, "just intonation" is a theoretical concept, but cannot be realized in practice. Therefore, the introduction of a tempered tuning and intonation system in Western music proved eminently practical, whereas recent attempts to increase the step number of the tempered scale in order to be able to produce just intonation with it, is impractical and musically undesirable.

After dealing with musical space, I should like to discuss the relationship of the aesthetic sphere to the actual world outside which was underlined by all speakers on art. In music, this relationship is formed through our experiencing, our hearing of melodic movement as a direct (not a symbolic, as is often claimed!) human expression. Tone configurations, then, are understood as human utterances, ranging from short calls or gestures ("motifs") over longer and more articulated statements ("themes" or "subjects," mentioned also by Dr. Smith) to the extended forms of richly structurized musical "discourse." Evidently, man can express himself and communicate not only physiognomically (by facial expressions, gestures, movements etc.), or through actions, through play—Dr. Dupré mentioned the play function of art today!—, through speech, through the aesthetic media of architectural and sculptural forms, pictorial designs and colors, and words in the literary arts, but also, and not the least, through the musical medium of tones!

Earlier in this session, the question was asked why we are so taken-in by music. Why does all art mean so much to us? Because it literally takes us into spiritual worlds or spaces, completely separated from our three-dimensional world of everyday life in which all experiences overlap and are interfered with through coincidences, where we never attain the deep satisfaction of all-round completion and perfection before we die. In the aesthetic worlds, however, we live through experiences of a single kind, with deep human significance and intellectual interest, which are carried through without interference to their fulfillment and which are cast into a well balanced and clearly designed lasting form so that we can renew the experience at will. Therefore, I think, is the aesthetic experience so deeply satisfactory, enjoyable, exhilarating, and uplifting.

Finally, I should like to comment on Dr. Smith's remark that vocal music is a coming together of vision and sound. I believe, it is rather a combination of words and tones, of language and music even though in opera, of course, there is the visual component of the stage action. The aesthetic problems of vocal music are best understood if we distinguish between the integration of the elements and the integration of the larger syntactical units of the two media. As far as the elements are concerned, I agree with Dr. Smith's statement that words (or syllables) and tones combine easily, as, e.g., in classic Greek language, because they have the criteria of pitch and rhythm in common. However, the larger syntactical and semantic units of language are organized on quite different principles than are the larger syntactical units of music. Therefore the two media cannot be integrated on equal terms: structurally, either language is leading while music is the "servant" of verbal expression, or music is leading, while the words serve as a vehicle for tonal (musical) expression. Hence, I have defined vocal music as either "sung language" or "sung music." Examples for the first would be Gregorian Chant and operatic Secco Recitatives in which the music enhances the words by imbuing them with an added expression and emphasis. The leading role of language in these forms is borne out by the fact that their formal structure and their rhythm is determined by the words, not the music. A chorus, an operatic aria, or an art song, however, are "sung music" because music is the leading part and completely governs their formal structure and rhythm. This explains why we are not disturbed if the text of an aria or chorus consists only in one or two over and over repeated sentences. In "sung music" the words add to the intensity and expressive power of music by giving it a concrete (semantic) significance which absolute instrumental music never has. Thus, both words and music take on a new dimension and are transformed into a special art form. In spite of Kierkegaard, music alone would never be able to represent Don Giovanni. The genius of Mozart could create this figure only through the simultaneous use of tones and words.

Even the signification of (the purely instrumental) program music originates from words, given either in an added story (the "program") or by the title, as e.g. in Richard Strauss' "Don Juan." This is also true for Beethoven's "Pastoral Symphony" which in my opinion is not an embodiment of visual impressions, as was said earlier, but rather of ideas, instilled in us linguistically by Beethoven's titles—except, perhaps, for such a directly depictive instance as the musical imitation of lightning in the tempest section.

However, I would deny that either vocal music or program music are synaesthetic phenomena; they are rather integrations of two spheres on an intellectual level. But I do agree with Dr. Smith's statement that it is impossible to translate music into words and would complement it by the opposite assertion that it is just as impossible to translate words into music. For music is not a semantic medium, but—and here I quote again—"always remains the feeling response of a human being."

SOREN KIERKEGAARD'S (S. K.'s) AFFINITY FOR DON JUAN

Jesse De Boer

The scene is Seville.
The characters are:
  Don Giovanni
  Leporello, his servant
  Don Pedro, Commandant of the Knights of Malta
  Donna Anna, his daughter
  Don Ottavio, her betrothed
  Donna Elvira
  Zerlina, a peasant girl
  Masetto, her betrothed.
The story in brief is as follows.

ACT I

BEFORE the palace of the Commendatore, Leporello reflects on his role as servant of the dissolute Don Giovanni. The Don is in the palace, attempting to have his way with Donna Anna. The two emerge, she trying to discover who he is. After she cries for help her father rushes out to defend her honor, and she leaves the scene. Though Giovanni wishes to avoid fighting an old man, the Commendatore insists, and Giovanni easily wounds him mortally. Leporello and he escape. Donna Anna now returns with her betrothed, Don Ottavio. She discovers her dead father and gives vent to a powerful expression of her sorrow. Though Ottavio seeks to console her with his love, and speaks of their marriage, she spurns the consolation and induces him to aid her in pursuit of her father's murderer—and this is her dominant purpose throughout the play.

Don Giovanni and Leporello are on the hunt for other victims. Donna Elvira appears, seeking Don Giovanni who was her former lover, perhaps her husband, and abandoned her in Bur-

gos. She does not recognize the Don, while he begins by expressing his interest in helping her. When recognition is imminent,
Giovanni escapes, and Leporello explains, with the List Song
(*"Madamina! il catalogo . . ."*), the character and exploits of
the Don. At this point a troop of peasants appear, celebrating
the impending marriage of Zerlina and Masetto. The Don and
Leporello join them, and in a moment Giovanni has Zerlina in
his power and is leading her to his house (*"Là ci darem la
mano"*), while Leporello keeps Masetto and the peasants occupied. Elvira interrupts them and promises to protect Zerlina.
Now Donna Anna and Don Ottavio enter. Elvira reveals Giovanni's identity; Anna realizes that he is her father's murderer;
the Don tries to persuade Anna that Elvira is mad, and he leads
Elvira off as if to protect her. Anna tells Ottavio of the events
of the previous night and gets him to swear revenge.

Giovanni has disposed of Elvira and he sets about inviting the
peasants to a feast and dance, hoping to make a conquest of
Zerlina and no doubt others among the young ladies. Masetto
and Zerlina go through a bit of pique and reconciliation. Giovanni invites them both to the party. Anna, Ottavio, and Elvira
come in masks; the Don invites them too. In the ballroom three
orchestras are playing, one for each social rank. Giovanni leads
Zerlina into an adjoining room, while Leporello dances with
Masetto; Zerlina screams. In the flurry to help her, Don Giovanni accuses Leporello; the three masked figures reveal themselves; the Don escapes in the confusion, and the Act ends with
an ensemble accusing the Don of his crimes.

ACT II

Leporello reproves the Don and talks as if he would like to
leave; but the Don's personal eminence is too great; besides,
Giovanni gives him money. Leporello is prevailed upon to im-
personate the Don in making love to Elvira so that the Don will
be free to try it on with Elvira's maid. Elvira answers the Don's
serenade, rendered in a comic situation, by coming down to meet
him. Leaving her in Leporello's care, the Don meets Masetto

with a band of villagers who are seeking him with weapons. In his disguise he confuses the peasants, who scatter until Masetto is alone with the Don. Giovanni disarms the young man, beats him up, and leaves; Zerlina now comforts her betrothed.

Meanwhile, Leporello has led Elvira hither and yon, until they come to a courtyard of Donna Anna's house, where he seeks to escape. Anna and Ottavio enter with lights; Leporello has to discard Giovanni's cloak and reveal himself; and he escapes in the confusion, and no doubt to the complete chagrin of Elvira. Ottavio leaves to report the Don's misdeeds to the police: a queer move for a nobleman.

Now Don Giovanni meets Leporello in the cemetery. The Don laughs at the tale of Leporello's adventure with Elvira. The two are startled to hear a voice warning the Don of his end. The Don is bold enough to converse with the speaker, the statue of the Commendatore, and invites him to dinner at his house; the statue accepts by nodding his head. After a short scene between Ottavio and Anna, in which Anna refuses to marry him soon, we see Giovanni at supper in his house. The Don is full of life, enjoying his meal and chaffing Leporello. Donna Elvira breaks in to appeal to him to repent and to return to her. She is mockingly repulsed and begins to leave; at the door she screams. Leporello is too frightened to open the door and hides beneath a table. The Don goes to the door himself and welcomes the statue of the Commendatore, who enters accompanied by trombones. Spurning the statue's pleas for his repentance, defying every law, Giovanni seals a promise to be the statue's guest by shaking his hand; at this point he is drawn down into Hell. After the statue departs the absent characters gather to hear Leporello's report on the end of the Don, and to construct their futures. Leporello will seek another master; Elvira will return to the convent; Anna and Ottavio will be married after a year; the peasant couple will celebrate their wedding promptly. The opera closes with a standard ensemble, welcoming Heaven's judgment on a flagrant sinner.

The sketch above does no justice at all to the skill of Lorenzo da Ponte, the librettist, who wrote the librettos for *Le Nozze di*

Figaro and *Ti fan Tutte* also. Professor Dent writes:
". . . Although da Ponte owes his immortality to the fortunate
chance that brought him into contact with Mozart, there can be
no doubt that Mozart's three masterpieces of Italian comic opera
owed as much to their librettist as the last operas of Verdi did to
the literary skill of Boito." (*Mozart's Operas,* 2nd ed., Oxford
University Press, London, paperback, 1960, p. 119.) While this
judgment concedes that the music of Mozart was predominant
in the mix, it invites notice of the old Don Juan legend and of
its use in earlier operas and plays. The legend arose before the
modern period, and the hero (or villain) is a combination of
profligate and blasphemer. The moral and religious point is
obvious: Repent before it is too late! (See G. B. Shaw's *Man
and Superman,* the "Epistle Dedicatory," Brentano's, New
York, 1916, p. ix.) Its first use for the stage was in a play by
Tirso de Molina (i.e. Gabriel Tellez, 1571-1641), *El Burlador
de Sevilla.* Several of the main characters and situations of
Tirso's play reappear in da Ponte's version. Molière's prose-
play, *Le Festin de Pierre* (1665), introduced Donna Elvira as a
former nun whom Don Juan had seduced and abducted from the
convent, to desert her soon after, abandoning her to a boiling
mixture of love and hate. Moliere also presented Masetto and
Zerlina as realistic though comical peasants. His purpose, however, was to display the nobility as corrupt and mostly artificial;
the play was regarded as a satire on contemporary society, and
someone has said that it was the first blow in the French Revolution. In 1676 Don Juan appeared in an English play, *The Liber-
tine,* by Thomas Shadwell, with incidental music by Purcell.
Shadwell, apparently wanted to present a thrilling, even shocking
entertainment. In 1736 Goldoni produced a verse-play called
Don Giovanni Tenorio o sia Il Dissoluto; its purpose, besides
entertaining, was to get revenge on an actress who had made the
writer look foolish. Many situations in this play resemble those
in da Ponte's, and as usual the Don ends in Hell. Last, there is a
play written early in 1787 by Giovanni Bertati, with music by
Guiseppe Gazzaniga, called *Don Giovanni Tenorio o sia Il Con-
vitato Di Pietra.* This had large success in Italy, and the libretto

and music reached Vienna early in 1787, in time for both da Ponte and Mozart to study them. Their opera is superior, yet it contains most of Bertati's libretto. Da Ponte made better drama of the material on hand, and he improved the language, and the situations. He did not create the character of Don Juan: that honor belongs to Tirso, who had behind him a legend. It is Mozart's music that has made da Ponte's tale immortal; but the music fits his tale as it would fit no other version.

We need to look at Kierkegaard's comments on the Don Juan legend and on earlier plays in order to appreciate his comments on Mozart's music. He notes that the origin of the legend is unknown; it is, however, a medieval tale, so that its background is Christianity. Don Juan defies the Christian outlook; thus he is the flesh in defiance of the spirit; and he is medieval in that he is a representative individual; he concentrates in himself the whole of the idea of the opposition to the Christian spirit. This opposite idea is sensuousness; and in Don Juan this idea is given full expression, in all its exuberance, joy, and power. This idea is so abstract. says S.K.—so hard to individualize, to present in a particular person with a story of his own, with a personal career and a history—that we could not expect to come upon a definite legend, full of concrete detail, with interesting exploits and particular conquests over obstacles. The idea, in short, is not a fit subject for story-telling. S.K. surmises or suspects that the number 1,003 may be the only, or one of a few, details occurring in the earliest tales; it is a fitting detail because it is an odd number, and as being odd is arbitrary or "accidental." It belongs to a representative, not to a concrete individual. Now, the earliest version of the story for public presentation may have been a farce, and the farce would of course be intended as a comedy. As for later interpretations, S.K. comments at length only on Molière's play and on Byron's epic poem, *Don Juan*. He treats the former as the pattern for all interpretations except Mozart's, and the defects he finds in both make clear for him the classic power of the opera. Byron's poem tries to make the Don into an actual person with a history; he is made into a reflective person. Byron sets his hero in the midst of obstacles; interest is turned toward his cunning in mastering them. Thus the Don turns into an ingenious contriver, a sleight-of-hand performer, who enjoys his own cleverness more perhaps than his sensuous mastery. This makes him interesting, but it hides his real significance; it hides his immediate power as seducer, desiring and at once gaining and enjoying his conquests. In short, Byron's treatment turns us away from the ideal figure of the sensuous genius to the means whereby he gains his ends. Molière's treatment also weakens the traditional idea. In various ways it is merely comical. For example, Molière's Don Juan is perfectly ordinary in being in debt and harassed by creditors; as S.K. remarks, this is like wanting to depict a man as a gambler and then giving him $5.00 to gamble with. Another example is Don Juan and Sganarelle pursuing a girl in a boat and then almost drowning when their boat capsizes. Yet this man is understood to have abducted Elvira from a convent and to have murdered the Commandant: Molière presents these facts as what ought to be known about his hero; he does not present the events themselves. His juxtaposition of events is confusing; the force of Don Juan as seducer is dissipated; indeed, even the seductive situations are feeble. The Don is described as having seduced Elvira by a promise of marriage; and his ploy with a pretty peasant girl, Charlotte, is pretty thin—he inspects her figure as though he were a horse-buyer at market. All this may be amusing, and it no doubt had satirical purpose and effect; but it is an injustice to the Don Juan figure. As S.K. says, "On the whole we can say that in Molière's Don Juan we get to know only historically that he is a seducer; dramatically we do not see it." (*Either/Or,* Vol. I, Anchor paperback, Doubleday and Co., Inc., Garden City, 1959, p. 114. All page references to *Either/ Or* will be to this edition.)

S.K. is going to argue that the ideal figure of Don Juan can be presented only in music. Mozart showed him this, and having seen it, S.K. knows what is weak about Molière and Byron. We must then look at S.K.'s picture of Don Juan. Who is this fascinating person? We may go back to the earlier remark of S.K. that the Don is medieval, a representative individual, and that he is the idea of sensuousness as opposed to the Christian spirit; he is the sensuous-erotic genius, the principle of sensuousness as a principle excluded by the Christian spirit.

George Bernard Shaw, who as an outstanding music critic, has useful comments on Don Juan in the "Epistle Dedicatory" to *Man and Superman.* "Philosophically, Don Juan is a man who, though gifted enough to be exceptionally capable of distinguishing between good and evil, follows his own instincts without regard to the common, statute, or canon law; and therefore, whilst gaining the ardent sympathy of our rebellious instincts (which are flattered by the brilliancies with which Don Juan associates them) finds himself in mortal conflict with existing institutions, and defends himself by fraud and force as unscrupulously as a farmer defends his crops by the same means against vermin. The prototypic Don Juan . . . was presented . . . as the enemy of God, the approach of whose vengeance is felt throughout the drama, growing in menace from minute to minute. No anxiety is caused on Don Juan's account by any minor antagonists: he easily eludes the police . . . ; and when an indignant father seeks private redress with the sword, Don Juan kills him without an effort. Not until the slain father returns from heaven as the agent of God, in the form of his own statue, does he prevail against his slayer and cast him into hell. . . . What attracts and impresses us in *El Burlador de Sevilla* is not the immediate urgency of repentance, but the heroism of daring to be the enemy of God. . . . Molière's Don Juan casts back to the original in point of impenitence; but in piety he falls off greatly. . . . After Molière comes the artist-enchanter, the master of masters, Mozart, who reveals the hero's spirit in magical harmonies, elfin tones, and elate darting rhythms as of summer lightning made audible. Here you have freedom in love and in morality mocking exquisitely at slavery to them, and interesting you, attracting you, tempting you, inexplicably forcing you to range the hero with his enemy the statue on a transcendant plane, leaving the prudish daughter and her priggish lover on a crockery shelf below to live piously ever after." (pp. ix-x.)

These words of Shaw are notably to the point; and S.K.'s comments on the Don help us to see why this is so. Christianity, says S.K., brought sensuousness into the world as a principle, i.e., as a rival and excluded life-policy in conflict with the Christian principle. Though S.K. does not work this out in *Either/Or,* the Christian principle, which he calls "spirit," consists for him, I think, in the free choice by an individual person of obedience, trust, and love toward the God revealed in the history of Israel and in Jesus Christ. The stress is on the personal choice: freedom is self-making, it is the self as decision to be so-and-so. Christianity taught that being human consists in choosing oneself, in making oneself to be the self he is. This spirit was introduced into Western life by Christianity: the Greeks did not have it. Of course, the Greeks and other pagans could be sensuous—as who cannot?—but the sensuous, in their view, was regarded as a natural component in man's psychic constitution; further the good man did not choose to be a person, his task was to realize himself, to harmonise the sensuous into a beautiful personality; and again, the sensuous was regarded as a power acting on a person from the outside—thus Eros, symbol of the power of love, was not in love himself. I paraphrase this to say that while the Greeks (viz., such eminent moral thinkers as Plato, Aristotle, the Stoics, and Plotinus) knew about the sensuous power in their lives and sought to order it within a beautiful totality, they did not identify themselves with it, nor did they seek to repudiate or exclude it. They lacked a concept of the unity of the person. When Christianity taught obedience and love to God as the principle of a life to be chosen by the self, it opened the door to the opposite choice, the choice for rebellion out of sensuousness. Thus Christianity posited the principle of sensuousness: a man is now conceivable who makes sensuousness his policy, his rule, his program and principle. This man comes to life in Don Juan. He is the representative individual, the person who concentrates in himself the whole of the anti-Christian principle. Representation and incarnation are Christian ideas; hence the Middle Ages actualize the contrasting representative individual figures, one of whom is Don Juan, another being Faust, the man of intellectual doubt, who helps himself out by appeal to the devil, the "Father of lies."

For S.K. Don Juan is the anti-Christian, the sensuous genius. He lives for enjoyment, for satisfaction of desire. He is desire, the flesh incarnate as contrary to spirit. He is a storm, impatience, passion: desire raging, conquering all; he is motion in the moment, unreflecting, immediate. To picture this man, S.K. distinguishes three stages of the sensuous-erotic person, found respectively in Cherubino, the Page in *Figaro*, Papageno in *The Magic Flute*, and Don Juan in *Don Giovanni*. Mozart has supplied all these figures, and the supremacy of Don Giovanni is seen in the way in which Don Juan is the other and lesser figures brought to the level of the complete sensuous genius. In erotic self-expression Cherubino is a child—or a dreamer who has just wakened. He cannot separate the dream from its object. So he desires but does not know what or whom: the object is not distinct from the desire, the desire does not know itself as desire for something. So the desire is close to a gloomy foreboding, frightened of what may come. Mozart's music presents this mood perfectly: there is no definite movement, the self is "gently rocked by an unclarified inner emotion." (*Either/Or,* I, 75.) The music presenting Cherubino is intoxicated, "drunk with love," and so is ambiguous as to its issue in joy or in gloom. Papageno is a figure for desire which has become awake: the dream is over, the object of desire is distinct. There is a trembling as the object comes to be separated, and the self becomes a seeker or discoverer: he hunts about in the manifold for what he desires. Thus it is with the music for Papageno: "it is cheerfully chirping, vigorous, bubbling with love." (*Either/Or,* I, 80.) These features are most obvious in the first aria with flutes and in the chime of bells. The life of Papageno is presented as an "incessant twittering." These remarks, says S.K., are offered with special reference to the mythical figures, the "essential" Page and Papageno; they do not apply to the whole presentation of these persons in the operas. Hence, says S.K., these operas fall somewhat short of the perfection of *Don Giovanni.* Here everything conforms to the ideal, except for one or two numbers (and S.K. picks out two which, I gather from modern commentators, may have been added to the original plan for incidental reasons, such as to satisfy a soloist). Don Juan is desire in full force: it is absolutely aimed at its target, it is "absolutely sound, victorious, triumphant, irresistible and daemonic." (*Ibid.*, 83.) The sensuous, in erotic form, is now fully actual. The 1,003 conquests in Spain alone picture the perfection of the Don's energy; he is the essence or idea of the sensuous genius. He is not an individual person, nor is he reflective; one is not curious about how, with what devices and cunning, he gained each victory, nor about his age or appearance; he floats or hovers between the individual and the ideal—he is a power, a force, an energy of nature, a storm or torrent. He is the incarnation, the representation of the sensuous-erotic. The principle of sensuousness as embodied in him is seduction. He is not a seducer: he seduces, or he is seduction itself. It is not by cleverness or stratagem that he seduces women; "he does not seduce. He desires, and this desire acts seductively. To that extent he seduces." (*Ibid.*, 97.) All types are eligible for him, whether a peasant girl or a sixty-year old coquette—"if only she wears a skirt, you know what he will do—*pur chè porti la gonella, voi sapete quel chè fa.*" Because he conquers one after another, and in haste, rushing from one victory to the next, he is faithless; he does not care for continuance in time, his passion is for the moment, and so for ending one occasion and going on to a new one. His moments do not cohere, he constantly finishes and starts over again. This is faithlessness; it is life without a covenant; it is life which has not accepted and made use of time. Yet the Don does not merely seduce: the women are captivated, his desire makes them happy; though they become unhappy later, they are not unhappy in such a way that they did not want this unhappiness. His energy acts seductively, i.e., the victims want to submit, they circle round him by the power of his passion—it is this power that seduces them; it is not he as an individual person that does so.

Listening to my words, I note that they have begun to falter.

Perhaps S.K. can explain why. The idea of Don Juan, he says, is expressible only by music. "But this energy, this power, cannot be expressed in words, only music can give us a conception of it. It is inexpressible for reflection and thought. . . . This force in Don Juan, this omnipotence, this animation, only music can express, and I know no other predicate to describe it than this: it is exuberant joy of life. . . . Don Juan is absolutely musical. He desires sensuously, he seduces with the daemonic power of sensuousness, he seduces everyone. Speech, dialogue, are not for him, for then he would be at once a reflective individual. Thus he does not have stable existence at all, but he hurries in a perpetual vanishing, precisely like music, about which it is true that it is over as soon as it has ceased to sound, and only comes into being again, when it again sounds." (*Ibid.*, 100-101.)

From this comment by S.K. about the magical fitness of music for expression of Don Juan's life policy, we may move on to his view of the peculiar work, or the essential idea, of music. Music expresses what language cannot express. Professor Dent says, ". . . it is perfectly impossible to translate music into words . . ." (*Mozart's Operas,* 136.) In *The Magic Flute* he writes, "Humanity has required the services of music to express, not those ideas which other arts can express equally well, but precisely those ideas of which the expression in other media is utterly impossible." (p. 92; taken from T. H. Croxall, *Kierkegaard Commentary,* Harper Bros., N.Y. 1956, p. 51.) In a lecture on ethics Wittgenstein said that on occasion he had the experience of wondering why anything existed at all (*"I wonder at the existence of the world"*)—not why the sky is blue instead of pink, not why there is a tree here instead of a horse, but why the world itself exists. Again, he had the experience of *"feeling absolutely safe,"* no matter what happens. These experiences, he says, are personal to himself: he is not claiming that they are or should be shared. (*Philosophical Review,* Jan. 1965, esp. pp. 8-10.) The point he stresses is that we have no idea of how to justify such feelings, no idea of how to defend asking the questions they give rise to, and no idea of how to test

whether an answer to these questions is the right one. By
ordinary "rational" criteria, an assertion addressed to such feelings and questions is nonsense. Our notions of rational procedures do not give us clues or directions. I can imagine that S.K.
is thinking something like this, and that he is saying that here
music plays its role. It is the perfect instrument for expressing
the feeling-response of man, as language is not. The peculiar
work of language is to express concepts: there is a gap between
the immediate (and the immediate response), and saying what
something is or is like. One cannot construct a sentence without
using a general word; doing this involves hesitation, the distance
or pause required for identifying and saying what something is.
Language is the instrument for reflection; for this work it is
perfect. In certain respects music and language are alike. Both
address themselves to the ear, and S.K. claims that hearing is
the most spiritually determined of our senses. Also, both occur
in time, whereas the other arts occur in space—painting, sculpture, architecture. Both, moreover, depress the sensible material
they use. It is a failure of speech when the movements of one's
tongue are heard, and so it is a failure in music when the
mechanism for making sound gets itself attended to. What
distinguishes them is their work; language to say something, to
minister to thought and reflection; music to express feeling—its
work, its essence is in the sphere of the immediate, of sensuousness. S.K. elaborates this somewhat by contrasting the types of
idea suited to language and to music. A concrete idea is per-
meated with the historical; he means by this, I think, that a
concrete idea presents self-commitment, free choice of a program, making a covenant, taking a vow—the self that does this
turns time into history. This commitment excludes other possibilities. An abstract idea is devoid of the historical. The most
abstract idea is sensuousness; this is most abstract since it is the
opposite of commitment, of living under a vocation; and Don
Juan is the exemplar, in the erotic-sensuous sphere, of this
policy which is absence of policy. We can say he chooses sensuousness, but he has not excluded anything and so he has no
coherence or program to be faithful to. Only music can express

his power, this lust for immediate enjoyment, this storm or passion for ever new erotic experience. This is pure succession, time without history; basically, it is melancholy. Don Juan's life, being devoid of covenant or coherence, is a flitting from moment to moment. It is time without a thread of continuity; there is no vow by which he orders and directs his moments. Music is succession, a perpetual vanishing—it exists only moment by moment, as it sounds. It is the most abstract medium, and of all arts the one best fitted to express the most abstract idea, sensuousness.

This is how S.K. expresses the point. "The most abstract idea conceivable is sensuous genius. But in what medium is the idea expressible? Solely in music. It cannot be expressed in sculpture, for it is a sort of inner qualification of inwardness; nor in painting, for it cannot be apprehended in precise outlines; it is an energy, a storm, impatience, passion, and so on, in all their lyrical quality, yet so that it does not exist in one moment but in a succession of moments, for if it existed in a single moment, it could be modeled or painted. The fact that it exists in a succession of moments expresses its epic character, but still it is not epic in the stricter sense, for it has not yet advanced to words, but moves always in an immediacy. Hence it cannot be represented in poetry. The only medium which can express it is music. Music has, namely, an element of time in itself, but it does not take place in time except in an unessential sense. The historical process in time it cannot express." (*Either/Or,* I, 55.)

S.K. expends much energy to plead that Don Giovanni is an absolute classic. I want to notice only a few items in his discussion and then bring this paper to an end. The subject of the opera, he says, is absolutely musical: only music can give voice to the sensuous-erotic as a possible life-policy. Further, it is an abstract medium: the abstractness of the medium matches that of the idea. The union of these factors in *Don Giovanni* makes of it a *conjunctio rarissima*. It was Mozart's fortune to preside over this conjunction, in fact to bring it off, to seize on the occasion and to produce music perfectly adapted to giving immortal expression to what was potential in it, and so to create something that cannot be improved on or superseded. This conjunction of abstract idea and abstract medium is a better key to what makes a classic really classic than conformity with Hegel's dictum about the union of form and content. S.K. accepts the dictum but offers the former criterion as more decisive. He proceeds to comment in some detail on a number of features of the opera which bear out his judgment of its supremacy. The presentation of Don Juan is unparalleled for consistency, thoroughness, and purity. The other characters revolve about him as planets about the sun; as he puts this, the other characters come into the light only on the side turned toward him. S.K. notes that though Leporello wants to leave his master, he is at once overborne; in fact, in the famous Catalogue Aria one hears Don Juan in the voice of the servant. Again, in Elvira's first aria the voice of Don Juan is heard in mockery; the music brings it about that we hear him in her song. The power of Don Juan as the sensuous genius is indicated by the fact that there is nothing to stop him except the supernatural. The music fits such features perfectly: Mozart uses trombones only when the statue enters; up to that time the Don is exultant, triumphant, unrestrained. As S.K. puts it, he dances over the abyss of life, dancing in dread in such wise as to express "the daemonic joy of life," (*Ibid.*, p. 129) then suddenly he sinks out of sight, like a stone that skips over water until it loses momentum and then sinks at once. The overture, finally, is a masterpiece. It is not an assortment of snatches from the opera itself; it is an independent masterpiece. S.K. calls it a prophecy, and calls attention to how we can hear the Don in it and at the end hear a premonition of the Don's end. Shaw says, "you cannot listen to the overture to Don Giovanni without being thrown into a complicated mood which prepares you for a tragedy of some terrible doom overshadowing an exquisite but Satanic gaiety." (*Shaw on Music,* ed. by Eric Bentley, Anchor paperback, Doubleday and Co., Inc., Garden City, 1955, p. 87.)

Now let us hear S.K. praise Mozart and Don Giovanni. At the opening of the long essay I have been looking at, the young man A exclaims, "Immortal Mozart! Thou to whom I owe everything; to whom I owe the loss of my reason, thou, to whom I owe it that I did not pass through life without having been stirred by something. Thou, to whom I offer thanks that I did not die without having loved, even though my love became unhappy." (*Either/Or,* I, 47.) *Either/Or* was published in 1843. In an entry in the *Journals* for 1839 (no. 296), we read, "In a sense I can say of *Don Juan* what Donna Elvira says to him: 'Thou murderer of my happiness.' For in truth: that is the play that so diabolically enraptured me that I can nevermore forget it; that was the piece that drove me, like Elvira, out of the calm night of the cloister." (*The Journals,* ed. and tr. by Alexander Dru, Oxford University Press, London, 1938, p. 76.) We may note that Don Giovanni was produced in Copenhagen each season from 1836 to 1839, so that S.K. had ample opportunity to hear it repeatedly. At this time he left his father's house and indulged in what he spoke of later as a wild mode of life. Also, he went through the experience of gaining the love of Regine Olsen and then breaking off the engagement. What then does he owe to Mozart? First, that he came to know love. And second, what it is like to live as Don Juan did. As he says over and over, it was Mozart who enabled him to understand the sensuous man as actualising one great and attractive possibility for human existence. His debts then are both personal and general. This can be confirmed by a glance at what Victor Eremita is made to say at the Banquet in Part I of *Stages* when he hears the minuet from Don Giovanni, and by looking in the *Journals* for entries that comment on Mozart and Don Juan. There is no music to which S.K. responded as he did to this opera. I quote now from *Either/Or* again. "With his Don Juan Mozart enters the little immortal circle of those whose names, whose works, time will not forget, because eternity remembers them. . . . I am like a young girl in love with Mozart, and I must have him in first place, cost what it may. And I will appeal to the parish clerk and to the priest and to the dean and to the bishop and to the whole consistory, and I will implore and adjure them to hear my prayer, and I will invoke the whole congregation on this matter, and if they refuse to hear me, if they refuse to grant my childish wish, I excommunicate myself, and renounce all fellowship with their modes of thought . . ." (p. 46.) This is again the voice of A, but the *Journals* show that it is S.K.'s own voice too. I note that Shaw testifies that his partiality for *Don Giovanni* is so great that he cannot think of himself as qualified to criticise that work. I was myself surprised recently to run into a "confession of faith" in Mozart by Karl Barth. (*Bekenntnis zu Mozart.*) "How am I to declare my 'faith in Mozart' in a few words? A 'declaration of faith' in a person and in his work is a personal matter. . . . Though I am not a musician nor a musicologist, I truly can and must express that faith. . . . I have already been asked whether or not on the basis of my theological thinking I have discovered any other masters in the field of music. I must confess: there is he and nobody else. . . . I must further confess: If I ever go to heaven I would first of all inquire about Mozart, and only then about Augustine, Thomas, Luther, Calvin, and Schleiermacher." (From *Wolfgang Amadeus Mozart,* tr. by W. M. Mosse, publ. in *Religion and Culture: Essays in Honor of Paul Tillich,* ed. by W. Leibrecht, Harper and Bros., N.Y., 1959, p. 61.)

Looking back over the praise of Mozart I have sampled, I permit myself just one critical remark on S.K.'s musical essay. I do not protest about his not being a musician, or a technically qualified commentator, a connoisseur. Karl Barth is not a musician either. The test, I suppose, is whether the listener, given that he pays attention and keeps his wits about him, is aided by the comment to hear better, to feel and understand more fruitfully. I certainly am less qualified in all senses than S.K. was, but I can testify that his work on *Don Giovanni* has helped me to hear the opera. It has helped me to appreciate the character of the Don and to appreciate the magic of Mozart's music. I have come to think I can feel led by him to the general view of music as expression of immediacy, and as especially fitted for expressing how we experience time, i.e., our temporal existence. He says himself that the ear is the most spiritually determined of our senses. This means, I take it, that hearing is especially suited for impressing upon us the temporality of human existing: what we hear comes and goes in a succession of moments, and we must decide how to order the transition, what we are to be as human. Both speech and music minister to us in this situation: music the more directly, on the level of the emotional or feeling response; speech the more reflectively. But the two arts converge or cooperate; in measure as speech develops, or as we grow in self-reflectiveness, so will emotion grow in complexity and intensity. I incline to say that S.K. has not paid attention to many of the roles and values and types of music, his comments are addressed almost entirely to a single creation: and that creation is a specimen of the mixture, or marriage, of music with words. Hence I am not attracted toward finding in him a definition of music or a general theory of its uses and significance. Rather, I feel, there should be no covering definition— just as one couldn't say what is the single purpose or essence of the total institution of law or government. Music arises out of several impulses, it provides various satisfactions and delights; it is performed on very different occasions and plays many roles. My hesitation over a general theory is not without basis in what S.K. himself says. ". . . I never had any sympathy . . . with that sublime music which believes it can dispense with words. As a rule it thinks itself higher than words, although it is inferior." (*Either/Or,* I, 68.) Let us drop the job of grading language and music: let us boldly say that each art is suited to its several roles and uses. Further, let us note and weigh the point that S.K. refuses to discuss the music that does dispense with words—and Mozart wrote a great deal of it. So we may try to learn from S.K. first and foremost about *Don Giovanni,* and secondly about works in the same family. Perhaps he has little to teach us about other types. Perhaps we may apply with all types, in fact with each experience of a performance, the test he proposes for what he says about *Don Giovanni:* over and over he says, that what he offers on this opera cannot be understood except by the man who hears and hears and hears. This is always good advice.

252

DISCUSSION OF SOUND AND MUSIC

Don Ihde

I. Detour

From the papers just presented we moved from early Greek drinking songs through the operatic seductiveness of Don Giovanni to Stravinsky's "Le Sacre du Printemps." Permit me a brief detour into some suggestions concerning the world of sound before returning to more immediate comments upon Professors DeBoer's and Smith's papers. Note that my detour is indirectly a criticism for what was not said. This section is directed towards *sound* and music and while Professor Smith called for a phenomenology of music and Professor DeBoer explicated Kierkegaard's insights into music and language via Don Giovanni neither paper went far in the direction of doing a phenomenology of *sound*. Nor can I, given my role as discussant —but I propose to suggest several facets of sound presence in my detour.

As I prepare this paper from across my yard through the open window of my neighbor's house comes the disconcerting "Mersey beat" of a set of drums and an electronically amplified guitar which characteristically approaches the 90 decible level presumably harmful to human ears. I wonder briefly if the description Professor Smith gives of "Le Sacre du Printemps" applies:

> The key to this masterpiece is not just the exotic orchestration or the cataclysmic harmony but rather the revolutionary break-through in rhythm. And the orgiastic pulsations of this composition portray a musical eros which is perhaps the best expressing of what we might call a true transcendental logos as opposed to a merely intellectualized one.

For I find the attempt to respond intellectually to the subject at hand gets blurred out by the transcendental, orgiastic pulsations of the sound and I scream, "Mercy! I can't hear myself think."

Certainly one of the phenomenal characteristics of the world of sound is its almost constant omnipresence over which I have little objective control. Ordinarily I am almost constantly immersed in a world of sound which in today's urban, industrial era can be said to have the texture of a predominant electronic or technologically created hum. If I but pay attention to my listening I find that the hum of the refrigerator, or the furnace, or the air conditioner, or the electric fan, or the motor traffic on the street is almost always there. Indeed, in this age of the hum there actually seems to exist on the fringes of our consciousness a need for its steady reassurance. In Cambridge, Massachusetts, for example, there was a church in which a particularly silent air conditioning unit was installed. Despite the fact that the thermometer and the humidity gauge indicated it was working well the parishoners complained that the building was still warm and stuffy. The problem was solved after an acoustical engineer installed an electronically generated hum which could be heard thus reassuring the parishoners that the air conditioning was on.

Not only am I immersed in a world of sound which surrounds me, but I have little control over sound. With sight, in contrast, I may change the panorama by turning my head or shut it out by closing my eyes—but much greater effort is called for with sound. I may plug my ears with my fingers with only partial success or I may physically remove myself to another room. It is perhaps no wonder that sound is closer to the subject as both papers pointed out. The shattering sonic boom or the loud arguments of the children can easily disrupt the most profound philosophic meditation. Sound surrounds me and invades my being.

Interestingly enough my control of the world of sound is not so much centered in the positions of my eyes or my head as it is in the control I have over my consciousness. My control of the sounds that compete for my attention rests in my ability to "turn off" my attention. Recently the teacher of my oldest child remarked that children today seem to be able to "turn off" much more easily than those of even a few years ago. I suspect that in a world which now bombards us with "media," in which a seer can speak in the ambiguities of an oracle for $100,000, it becomes more important to learn the skill of "turning off" the noise. The paradigm case is perhaps the teen-ager who does his algebra to the blare of folk-rock which attempts to overcome him by echo chambers and more loudly amplified sound.

I "turn off" the world of sound to "hear myself think." This notion points to a quite unnoticed dimension of the world of sound. I have been speaking of the perceived world of sound, but as I turn to my thinking self I do not turn from the world of sound, I merely turn from *perceived sound* to *imagined sound*. For just as I may present myself with a visual imagination which is the free variation of my visual perception, so can I present myself with an auditory imagination which is the free variation of my auditory perception.

If I now pay attention to my thinking self I find that for the most part my uppermost thinking is in the form of an inner speech which is basically similar to spoken English. This linguistic thinking, so well displayed in writers like James Joyce, is part of the whole range of what I call auditory imagination. I am present to myself in the inner language of an auditory imagination.

I recognize that at this point my suggestion is open to much misunderstanding because my inner directed consciousness is not synonymous with auditory imagination in the form of inner speech. However I cannot take the time to defend my suggestion but can propagandize and say that for a slightly expanded treatment you might look at the winter issue of *Philosophy Today* and at the proceedings of the Society for Phenomenology and Existential Philosophy from last fall.

What I would claim here is that this auditory imagination in the form of inner speech is seldom absent from consciousness even though it may be on the fringes of consciousness when one is engaged in certain kinds of tasks or activities—just as the almost constant hum may be present only on the fringes of my consciousness in the case of perceived sound. I suggest, for example, that you try to turn off your thinking if you wish to test the hypothesis.

There are cases, however, when my thinking presence to myself is disrupted and even times when it is almost overcome. I have already suggested that when one is engaged in certain difficult tasks that consciousness tends to be displaced into the task—I become my work. But more to the point here is the fact that it is the interruption of sound which may disrupt my self-presence such as in the cases of the drum-guitar combo or the sonic boom. A special case of both disruption and being absorbed in occurs in the case of music.

It is true that even linguistically I may become "absorbed in what he is saying" when I listen intently to a lecture or a conversation—but in equal or greater degree I may become absorbed in the march, the aria, the frenzied rhythm, the inspiring chorale. It is here that one can begin to appreciate Kierkegaard's notion that music is the demonic. Music, as part of the world of sound, intrudes into my self-presence and may seduce or captivate me. Certainly in the history of religions this has been well known. The orgiastic beat of certain ecstatic rituals, the orphic musical ecstacy, even the silent contemplation of the mystic all relate to the world of sound.

Again Kierkegaard has some justification for saying that language and music in being addressed to the ear have time for their element and that in some ways language and music are opposed. Language as both spoken and inner language can be reflective and is a predominant mode of self-presence. Music may seduce one from this reflective self-presence and thus be considered a form of ecstatic sensuousness. Yet Kierkegaard is limited by his obvious polemic in which he seeks to justify and evaluate the various stages of life in a hegelian fashion. For what he forgets is that language can also be sensuous in poetry or in the case of certain chants which are both musical and linguistic.

II. Return

But it is time that I returned to more direct comment upon the presented papers. The problem which both DeBoer and Smith face in the question of sound and music is that the phenomena of the sound world are so very complicated and multi-faceted. When Smith calls for a phenomenological investigation of music in order to get to the bodily selfhood of musical sound he perhaps points us in a promising direction. When he insists that some version of "bracketing" which removes both the concerns with physical and acoustical properties of sound and goes on to bracket out the intellectual grid of music theory which I suspect is more an impedance for him than for me I further agree. I would but point out that the whole purpose of bracketing is to remove the theoretical overlays upon experience, i.e., bracketing reduces presuppositions not experience. It is a technique which seeks to get to the pre-theoretical basis of theory. But this does not mean that phenomenology stops there or never returns to the development of theory. I suspect that at points Smith may have mixed a certain romanticism with the need for bracketing. The elevation of "Le Sacre du Printemps" over what he derides as western "intellectualized" music may hide the grandeur of that mathematized music. I for one do not wish to get rid of the bodily selfhood of a Bach piece merely because even his notation is visually and mathematically arranged.

Both Smith and DeBoer raise interesting questions about the range of phenomena within the world of sound. Smith distinguishes between "raw sound" and music; DeBoer re-raises Kierkegaard's distinctions between music and language. The question I wish to raise is how phenomenologically one deals with these distinctions, particularly if all theoretical grids are to be removed? What bodily selfhood presents itself within sound which allows us to distinguish what occurs upon the sound continuum?

For example, Smith points out that Greek poetry does not separate music from language. Poetry, particularly in its presentation in verbal form is the embodiment of linguistic music or musical language. Parenthetically I would note that not only does the Greek drinking song fill an interstice between music and language, but the Hebrew, too, in echoing his theology of word present a musical tongue. The marks added to the Hebrew letters reflect the earlier tradition of the synagogue in which the "Hear, O Israel . . ." was correctly and clearly canted. Perhaps more than the Greek from whom we have gained an emphasis upon the eternal present, we have gotten from the Hebrew an emphasis upon the living presence of word as activity.

If music and language are not to be separated in the concrete but also sensuous chant of the cantor then at the other interstice between "raw sound" and music I wonder whether the "song" of the bird or the rhythm of the babbling brook is raw sound or music. I would also add that often one can hear a tongue unfamiliar to himself as a kind of music—for example, we can hear the tinkling musical sounds of Vietnamese even though the unknown words are proclaiming us villians and murderers.

Thus I am in sympathy with DeBoer's criticism of Kierkegaard in objecting against S.K.'s "reduction" of music when it is actual multifaceted and has multiple sources. I would add the famous dictum of Hamann who argued that *poetry* was the mother tongue of the language.

But where DeBoer rightly criticizes Kierkegaard for his narrow but insightful view of music and correctly informs us that we can derive no general theory of music from Kierkegaard, he succumbs to Kierkegaard on the question of music and temporality. When he accepts the notion that hearing is suited for impressing upon us the temporality of human existence he goes on to interpret this in the Kierkegaardian emphasis upon the moment, the Now. I would suggest that this is perhaps a too narrow view of temporality which negates both the ecstatic structures of time, a la Heidegger, and more particularly the deep immersion we have in a history which comes at us from the future with urgency and relates to a past which situates us. Here the musical and passing present must yield to the wider horizons of the spoken and even more particularly the written word which opens past and future to us.

Finally, I would agree with and underline Smith's criticism of traditional aesthetics which would often reduce art to a "work" or over-value the enduring, eternal objectness of a classic. I would, however, note that in reaction against this tendency there are also theories of art which subjectify art in a kind of emotivism which denies any logos to art at all. I suspect in both cases aesthetics has been to art what classical metaphysics has been to the world, i.e., an attempt to reduce the richness and complexity of experience to the single criterion of manageable intelligibility defined by a rather narrow idea of rationality.

V. MADNESS IN ART

DOSTOYEVSKY'S PRINCE MYSHKIN:
EPILEPSY PORTRAYED

Hubertus Tellenbach

THE following analysis rests on several presuppositions, and its scientific validity depends on the acceptance of these. It proceeds on the assumption that in the great novels of Dostoyevsky the phenomenon of the human is so fundamentally open to contemplation that the differences of race, religion, nationality and language move into the realms of chance. In such a fundamental view man shows himself as a complex being: complex in the formation of his basic features like the personal and metapersonal contexts of "belonging-with" the forms of relationships with the self and the relationship to the transcendant. We furthermore presuppose, that even where Dostoyevsky lets these human conditions appear in the form of the abnormal and the diseased their essentials become transparent. Under these conditions the reader needs a suitable attitude to experience and to appreciate these essentials, a certain perception to be able to discover those notions which constitute the essential and the typical features of the disease. Thus we demand much from the work of Dostoyevsky. We presuppose nothing less than the following: that the essence of the epileptic (or at least of one type of epilepsy) appears in these novels as a vessel, the fragments of which can be met in the clinical every-day life in numerous epileptics. Of course, for the time being, contemplation of the typical of the complete personality (of the unbroken "vessel") has for the clinician only the dignity of a prejudice. Whether we can acknowledge it as the standard for a clinically reliable proof depends solely upon confirmation by clinical experience.

Among the numerous guises of the abnormal and the diseased which we meet in the novels of Dostoyevsky, the epileptic states have an unmistakable preeminence. In several of the great novels epileptics are the central figures: Prince Myshkin in *The Idiot*, Kiriloff in *The Deamons*, Smerdyakoff in *The Brothers*

Karamazov. Whether Dostoyevsky lets epilepsy appear not
as the "falling sickness" but as a psychosis in the paranoid
"Doppelganger"—experiences of Goliakin would need investigation. The repeated use of the multiformness phenomenology
of epilepsy is not surprising because these are reflections of the
conditions which the epileptic Dostoyevsky experienced in
himself. He shows in his epileptics basically his own pre-sci-
entific history of his illness. This can only reinforce our confidence in the genuineness of his nosography. Thus we can start
our venture from an anamnese which is accessible to every
reader. That we deal here solely with the one he has attributed
to Prince Myshkin is of course restricting, all the more so if one
considers that the picture of Smerdyakoff fits much better into
the picture of the epileptic which early clinicians have described
as typical. However Prince Myshkin is undoubtedly an epileptic
in his essence. If we divide epileptics into "sleep-and-waking
types" in the sense of Hopkins, Griffiths and Fox, Le Camus
and Janz, Myshkin's type of epilepsy is definitely more akin
to the waking type. If we suppose that Dostoyevsky only endowed his epileptic characters with what he himself experienced, the writer must have been both. As Myshkin, he resembles the waking type of epileptic and as Smerdyakoff the
sleeping type. This fact already indicates to the clinicians a
very central thought: the thought, that there is a possibility
that one type of epilepsy can change into another in time. According to the fact established by D. Janz, waking types of
epilepsy can indeed change to sleeping types, but of course
not the other way round. It can be seen from this fact what
cardinal clinical questions are already touched on by one simple
aspect of Dostoyevsky's epileptics. But now we have to perform a phenomenological epoché for the time being our knowledge of the clinical epilepsy. Otherwise there is the danger
that we carry clinical facts into an investigation which is to
be carried out in an phenomenological attitude. This attitude
we aspire to in so far as we phenomenologically try to reduce
the scenic richness in which Myshkin meets us as an empiric
figure, and try to uncover some decisive characteristics which

can be found in everything that concerns Myshkin—in that which emanates from him, as well as in that which comes back to him.

There is no other trait in the essence of the Prince which confronts us with such ubiguity as his childishness. His doctor confirms that he came to the conclusion that he

> was a complete child, a real child; in fact I only appear a grown-up by reason of my age and my appearance. In every mental aspect on the other hand, in the whole psychic develop-ment, in character and soul, and probably even including my intellect—I was no grown-up and I should stay like that even if I lived to be sixty years old.

When this childishness is explained more closely, it could be said that it is also found in a grown-up. Myshkin is a child in a grown-up body or better still a grown up child. This evaluation must be explained in more detail. Were we to say that Myshkin remained a child "at heart," this childlike trait could not really be sufficiently explained. Such a grown-up would be child above all in so far as he preserves his relationship to the transcendent (e.g. to the artistic, spiritual and religious sphere) as a surprise, a trust and a thankfulness, an attitude which applies in its spontaneity substantially to the intimate personal sphere. In Myshkin on the contrary all concepts (of world) are wholly formed by this childishness. But Myshkin is a grown-up as well, e.g. in his highly developed intelligence or in the penetrating ability of psychological understanding of the essence, values and tendencies of others. He is also grown-up in the consistency and even penetration of this strange gentle force with which he tries to steer others towards goals which he values.

On the other hand he is not grown up in the important relationship of the internal and external spheres of his personal-ity, [in the internal and external spheres of his personality,] in the pervasiveness of the foreground and the insignificance of the organ towards the world of the self. This is also the reason why he appears so immature in his manners, inexperienced in the knowledge of what is expected and what concerns common sense and the feeling of descretion. Immature also in his timid, shy, as well as guileless approaches to others; immature finally also in an obstinacy which is not disposed to an understanding of mutual consideration and tact. In all these his contemporaries felt him to be indiscrete, pushing and lacking in tact. He is not a person in whose "live-world" the teaching of discretion could have been lacking; rather, he appears so because the "grown-up child" has proved to exist in him. Since he does not experience this contradiction in him he does not seek a solution: in this fact lies the strangeness of the involvement between the childishness and grown-upness in Myshkin, the idios kosmos of this "Idiot." Whether this also applies to the form of his sexuality, that is whether we deal here with a conglomeration of grown-up and immature eros, ought to be analysed separately. I should not like to infer that eroticism is a determining motive of existence in everyone. Looking at a fool—think of Don Quichotte—and his serious playacting, one could not assert this to be the case. On the other hand, for the saint it could be, because here the erotic is destined to be received by what Goethe calls "spiritual copulation" and Nietzsche refers to as "Genius of Heart." It appears clear to me that the metamorphosis in the relationship of Myshkin with Nastasya is intentional; but that it is governed by the status of the "grown-up child" is not without importance for the failure of this relationship.

The childishness of Myshkin is still more clearly silhouetted when we compare it with being grown up. The aspect of trusting becomes completely overwhelming in a way in which only complete innocence can confront the world. It is as if frontiers which derive from painful experiences in others could not exist. No frontiers which are put up by a classconscious society, no frontiers which guarantee to the individual a right to distance —as if there were not the manifold markings of what Martin Buber calls "das Zwischen" (the interpersonal). Thus Myshkin knows no intercourse in the sphere of "Man" (Oneself), but only the rapport of the immediate and personal meeting. Regarding Myshkin's disarming frankness, his candidness, which is not only, not even foremost, a problem of the perviousness of boundaries, but much more likely a question of keeping-it-to-yourself of things which are destined for filing in the unconscious in the way of all things forgotten. Everything that motivates Myshkin presses towards others in an overwhelming readiness and with undisguised utterances, even the externalizing of the inner-self. It is this trust which always speaks to the other person, and which cannot be disappointed and discouraged when distrust is encountered, as e.g. from Rogoshin; that trait which will not be turned into skepticism even after a great experience of sorrow.

How much Myshkin's relationship with reality is governed by a plain spontaneity is perhaps nowhere more easily demonstrated than in his relationship with humour. Right at the beginning, he says in a conversation with Rogoshin and Lebedev, that the wife of Gernal Yepatshin was "the last of her kin" (i.e. sex). The Prince does not understand the double meaning of the remark, and the laughter at it. He was obviously quite surprised by the fact that he was thought to have made a joke—even though a very feeble one. Now a joke reflects on reality but in such a way that reality is momentarily changed. The reflection here is a force which conquers reality and converts it, which can disarm the harmful or at least mitigate it. This adaptability is denied to Myshkin. This makes it more difficult for him to confront the forces which emerge from the depth of his personality; for Myshkin is also without adaptability towards his own self. He is what the Sermon on the Mount calls the "Poor in Spirit": he has a childishness which is not aware of its riches. Feeling this, Rogoshin says: "Then you are, Prince, a regular holy fool and God loves such as you." It is this directness which looks at a man only from the point of view of his humanity, in glances which are unmistakable, astonished, searching and holding—turned towards his personality but bypassing the world of convention and the grown up world. This childishness, which is governed so much by trust as a preverbal, prereflexive attitude, now shows itself also in a differentiated sensibility for the impressionistic environmental force which comes from the world. It is this sensitivity which makes him so susceptible to the physiognomy of the extraordinary. Myshkin is overwhelmed, even fascinated—so much so that he cannot tear himself away and is therefore rejected by the mundane world. "I know myself that I have lived less than other people and that I know less of life than any one else." This stands in complete contrast to the attraction of the terrible, e.g. the terrible of the execution: "I did not like it at all and I was nearly sick afterwards, but I must confess that I had to watch rooted to the spot, I could not look away." There seems to exist a special sensitiveness for all those subjects which happen on the fringes of humanity. Time and again we see Myshkin abandoned to the refractions of the impressionistic, in such a way that he can barely free himself. The following quotation is characteristic: "For hours on end he was busy ruminating in a tormented way about what he had seen." Or after the scene outside the casino: "It seemed that he had forgotten the whole world around him and was quite willing to sit there for two years."

All this which is presented in the phenomenon of the "grown-up child," in his inner contradiction is nevertheless something thoroughly formed and typical, an expression of ordered layers in the sense of a structure. It makes little sense to present this "typical" in the horizon of a psychology of development and to speak of maturity-lag. Myshkin can never develop to maturity in the vague everyday sense, because of the resistance of the inner order of this structure. Myshkin could only mature into a grown-up, in the usually accepted term, if his formula of structure, his state as grown-up child, could be changed; that is, if he could be reconstructed.

We now go a step further and open the question, whether we can still discover a much more common phenomenon in the type of Myshkin—a phenomenon which can at the very least be met in its basic application. Such a phenomenon exists in the drastic dialectic of height and depth. If we can experience a set-back out of the turbulent and at times tumultuous happenings around the person of the Prince, it helps us see these movements in their inner formulation, as an attempt to uncover the phenomena of space and time in the existence of Myshkin. That space is shown here in the form of height and depth, and this alteration is marked by a preponderance in the direction of descent; in other words in this existence descent predominates. This is shown already in the first descriptive passage in Myshkin's autobiographical story: the picture of a water-fall. What type of depth can be seen here? Not that clear depth which lets us see the bottom, nor that clear depth which carries everything living, which life can face without pain. The kind of depth which Minkovsky already could show in the personality of Mysh-kin is an unfathomable abyss, the ragged core of the world, which Schelling calls "the home of madness" and Nietzsche refers to as the "symbol of Dionysos Zagreus." It is this mys-terious depth which permeates beauty itself and in it too frightens man. Why else does the beauty of the lake so depress the Prince: "I always feel perturbed and depressed when I look at such a beautiful site for the first time. It is beautiful and perturbing." That also is the reason why he finds Aglaya so beautiful: "that you are almost afraid to look at her." And how much more must the presence of Nastasya frighten the Prince when Aglaya "is almost as beautiful as Nastasya." Here beauty surfaces from the depths, and the poet hints at this when he says, "For beauty is nothing but the beginning of the terror which we can just bear" (Rilke in the first Duineser Elegy).

The temporality of Myshkin's existence can best be under-stood from this attitude towards the terrible. We see here quite a different description of height than, for example, Binswanger's analysis of a manic state. Remember Myshkin's stay on the top of a sunny mountain and also Nietzsche's midday poem about the moment of the appearance of Zarathustra; i.e. the creative moment where time and eternity meet (in Nachgesang von "Jenseits von Gut und Bose"). Myshkin on the other hand loses this moment in a dream of infinity.

It seemed to me that I had a mysterious call to go somewhere and I could not but feel that if I went straight on and kept straight on for a long time I should reach the line where sky meets earth and there find the key to the whole mystery and at once discover a new life, a life a thousand times more splendid and more tumultuous than ours.

Such a fixed moment is not commensurable with eternity, is not moment in Kierkegaard's sense, in which eternity reaches into the present; for Myshkin's moment of dreamt eternity is destined to turn into the timelessness of the nothing, as it is in the terrible moment of the execution before the fall of the axe. This moment of times before the execution, in which being (reality) moves on the background of nothing, can hardly be explained without the aid of paradoxes. "If life be given back to you what an eternity: and all that would belong to me every minute I shall turn into a whole century." The more time is stretched into a dream of eternity which is lived as a never ending time, the closer it comes to the point where it breaks. Just like when spanning an arrow, the spanning gets slower and slower, but the force which will propel the arrow gets stronger and suddenly dies. Nothing makes the rising moment of the terrible so clear as the mode of the temporality of sight and vision. When Myshkin asks Adelaide to paint the face of the condemned man, "about a minute before the fall of the axe," this corresponds in a Leonardo-like unconcealed manner to the expression on the face representing the past as seen at that moment, for the face also represents "that which has gone before everything," as if it cuts right across the stream of life. Such a stay on the edge of the knife before the moment stretches into infinity uncovers everything to the beholder. "I saw his face and understood all." It is the same phenomenon of time which we come across in the occurrence of the fit. The moment of the aura—the dream of eternity, the height of bliss at departure from the world, and also the moment which overwhelms through the terror of depth. We shall meet again and again these extremes which give birth to the ecstatic moments of time, even if not in such frankness as before the impending execution or in the fit. Myshkin's existence is polarized by diametrical directions of meaning. In this are also contained

Minkowsky's worlds of good and bad, which quickly alternate in moments, as in that of the farmer who prays and stabs another at the same moment. It is this conjunction of the diametrically opposed which W. Brautigam picks out as the light and dark aspects, as the salient features of the epileptic. These space-time definitions also appear in Myshkin's relationships with Nastasya and Rogoshin. At the side of Rogoshin Myshkin comes on the scene, "a whim of fate," and at the side of Rogoshin he will leave it. The relationship between them has its roots in a thread spun in depths. "I do not know Prince why I have grown to like you"—so Rogoshin proves this cohesion after the first conversation; this cohesion never breaks; only its outward appearances change. It starts with the rivalry for Nastasya, via the exchange of crucifixes, to Rogoshin's readiness to stab, and to the end where Myshkin's tears wet the cheeks of Rogoshin. Right from the beginning this relationship is directed towards Nastasya. On Rogoshin's part there is a jealous desire to possess; on the part of the Prince there is an aprioric compulsion which becomes more and more apparent.

When he sees Nastasya, he is taken back in speechless bewilderment. From depths of the unconscious Myshkin calls out: "I too feel I have seen you somewhere before," and a little later after the face-slapping scene she too says: "Indeed I have seen this face somewhere before." And shortly after that Myshkin again: "When I saw your picture today, it seemed to me that I had seen again a familiar face and at the same time it seemed as if you were calling me." We can only hint in passing at this pre-personal union which crops up again and again. What makes the Prince go to Nastasya's birthday party even though he has to ask himself, "What he intends to do there and why he went at all." And from where comes the knowledge of that compelling force in Nastasya's personal composition? "In you everything is perfect, even the fact that you are pale and skinny is beautiful . . . one just could not imagine you in any other way." What predestining forces must be at work that Nastasya leaves the decision about marriage or non-marriage to him when they hardly know one another? Yet they know each other so well that

Nastasya knows without doubt what Myshkin's decision will be. Right away he understands in her the conjunction of self-doubt and gaiety and of boundless disdain and childishness. All this is constituted in him in the extremes of up and down. And consequently, by appealing to the heights in Nastasya, he awakens in her the mighty forces of depth which drive her to Rogoshin. Here as well as in his relationship with Rogoshin, Myshkin proves in people an alternating of height and depth and releases in them movements of rising and falling. This seems to create a pernicious circle, in so far as people in his environment are attracted by him and then repelled, and this fosters in him those depressions which force him into the proximity of a seizure when he tries to govern them. While he is moved as a man by Nastasya's erotic fascination, the childishness in him suffers agonies of pity for her masochism, a destructive alternative which he understands. "Why did he always have the feeling that this woman would come in the very last moments of his life and tear his whole fate like a rotten thread?" Myshkin can only exist if the threat which binds them together in the abyss can be reconciled on a sound realistic basis with the height into which he tries to lift Nastasya—and this only if he permits Rogoshin to take a middle path between destructive, jealous possessiveness and an uptopic brother-love. This is how things stand: the prince has to learn to reconcile these heights and depths and find the compensation in a synthesis. This also is Hegel's imperative forced on this personality, a need to achieve this constant synthesis, the synthesis as compensation between height and depth. But he can achieve this synthesis to a lesser degree the more definite the alternations between heights and depths are, and many times he must steer a mediocre compromise of compensation. Indeed this movement into mediocrity can be confirmed in Myshkin time and again; e.g. in the dream about the mountain which reminds him of the landscape around Naples. While he leaves reality in the most beautiful narrative, he suddenly stops to utter this ephemeral sentence: "But then who can tell all that one thinks?"—he tries to change the mundane reality a little towards the other extreme; "I could even imagine that you could have an immensly rich life in jail." Instantly the penetrating Aglaya unmasks this tendency to find a compensation as "cheapness." "And I think you have won nevertheless, although in small coins only." She hits still sharper at the turnabout which he tries on his way into the depths, in the course of the narrative of the execution which he suddenly breaks off to the astonishment of his listeners. When the Prince is startled out of his momentary reverie and afterwards says, "Occasionally I do tend to talk in a very strange way," Aglaya remarks ironically, that his wisdoms did not quite give the impression of superiority. "With your quietism one might live happily for a hundred years. Whether one shows you an execution or a little finger, you'd be quite sure to draw highly laudable conclusions from either and remain happy and contented too." To live like that is easy! In the so central face-slapping scene the tendency to catch oneself in time is also well marked, and it brings the extremes to a compensation, but here in a much happier and more successful way. With the slap in the face before Nastasya, the Prince is very deeply hurt by the hatred of Ganya. He is pale; his lips tremble, and his face shows that convulsive strange smile which always appears when he begins to lose control. Now begins the movement towards the compromise. He starts to recover himself from the humiliation by taking on himself the insult to Ganya's sister. "Oh well I do not mind your striking me, but I shall not let you touch her," and he blunts the hatred of his adversary by, so to speak, taking it into himself. "Oh how you will be ashamed of what you have done." Immediately there follows a contradictory movement in him. Thus the expressions of sympathy by all those present lift him to such heights that the Prince faces them and alarms them with a mysterious smile.

Scenes like these, in which energetic movements towards a compromise are made to prevent the development of a critical situation, are frequent like a catalogue of crises averted. But what happens if the synthesis or the compensation to the mediocre does not succeed? Where does the development progress?

We select a constellation, which Myshkin cannot solve by

compromise. In the famous conversation in Rogoshin's house the situation is as follows: Nastasya reproduces time and again with Rogoshin the situation she experienced through Totsky, infamy and desertion. She inflames in him the wish to possess her and draws him to a fall, and in order to revenge herself she leaves him. Myshkin knows that Rogoshin will kill her out of jealousy or torment. On the other hand, even though she loves the Prince, Nastasya has to flee from him because she fears she will pull him down. What does the Prince do to solve the situation? He tries desperately to draw Nastasya to himself to free her from the "madness," that is, her demoniacal fear of the good. Without success! Then he tries to send Nastasya abroad to neutralise the situation; that too is in vain. He tries to blunt the situation by appealing to Rogoshin's inner self and brotherliness. In vain! He finally decides to renounce both of them and retire; but again in vain, because neither of them can let go of him. Myshkin fails in all these attempts. Because of his readiness to see himself as the guilty party, the guilt of this failure lies heavily on him. In the end everything converges into this certainty: that as long as Rogoshin lives Nastasya can only choose between murder and suicide. The feelings stirring in Myshkin at the realization of these alternatives are pointed out to him bluntly by Rogoshin: "If you wish, I will tell you what you are thinking at this very moment: Now, how can she yet marry him? How can one still permit this? I do know what you are thinking!" At this moment Myshkin touches his knife twice without realising it himself. The possibility cannot be excluded here that murderous impulses begin to stir in Myshkin although this phenomenon cannot be proved unequivocally. What is clear, however, is Myshkin's fear that Rogoshin is planning to eliminate him, the person who is trying to avert the death of Nastasya by any and all means. Rogoshin also sees this when he explains to the Prince: "Because of a watch I am not going to stab you." And now also guilt weighs heavily on Myshkin's soul, because he let his confidence in Rogoshin be shaken by suspecting him of wishing to kill him. He deeply feels how unjustly he has been handled, and feels ashamed when this man, as they were parting, in a last surge of emotions offered to renounce Nastasya. For an instant he had lost this unqualified implying confidence of childishness which distinguishes him in every sense. Now he says, "Is everything my fault then?" And now the ability to compromise begins to wane. When he wishes to drive to Pavlovsk, his soul is in a complete muddle. An unusual desire for complete solitude is followed by need for company. A restlessness caused by something unfathomable is followed by the consolation that he is seeking something definite. The clear sequence of events begins to resolve into single disjointed fragments of experiences which scarcely show a mnestic coherence. Absolute concentration is needed if he is not to lose the ability to differentiate between matter and man. Is it the glance of Rogoshin that he feels on himself, or the reflection of the knife in the shop window? He rushes forward and then aimlessly back again. Moments of confusion are alternating with over-bright moments, where the facts of the case are as clear as glass to him. More and more does the alternating consciousness become like the movement of a swing. A sorting out and remixing of unrelated facts starts. He contaminates Lebedev's nephew with the murder of which Lebedev spoke. "I think I am mixing everything up . . . how strange is this." While making for his hotel, he reaches Nastasya's house. He contaminates Rogoshin with the "slaughter of six people." Even though he is mortally ashamed about it, he is irresistibly drawn to search for the knife in the shop window. Once again Myshkin tries for a compensation. Should he meet Rogoshin now, he would take him by the hand and go with him to Nastasya, but the brightness of this thought is already born of the light of the approaching aura; for now he says: "Now the darkness is dispersed, the demons driven out, all doubts are dispersed, and in my heart is joy." But the reversal into depth is all the more terrible. It brings into the present the disastrous heap of rubble which he was not able to prevent for the good of all. He was not able to let the spirit of freedom enter into Nastasya and Rogoshin—even he himself was tempted to understand his relationship to Nastasya in a sexual way, and he had the much more serious temptation to suspect Rogoshin of murderous intentions. "Oh I have lost my honour . . . how will I ever be able to look this man in the face again." Arriving at his hotel while these painful thoughts are going through his mind, he sees the figure of Rogoshin. "Now the decision will come." Myshkin knows it with certainty. Did he do Rogoshin an injustice by suspecting him of murderous intentions? Will he be proved right in the most terrible way? He rushes up the stairs, rushing into the decision. He pulls Rogoshin towards the light on the stairs, and now the absurd thing happens. Rogoshin pulls out the knife and thus confirms what the Prince had felt in his own depths. Even though the Prince calls out, "I do not believe it Parfen," Rogoshin's dagger forces the Prince to believe in the right and the might of his own depth, which now overwhelms him in the attack. That the world of childishness in him, the sane world of trust—in whose spell he becomes all the more enmeshed the more he feels it threatened —that this world will protest in him in so far as Rogoshin's conduct confirms his budding distrust, this fact floods into Myshkin's consciousness to such an extent that he cannot neutralise it any more.

If in the end we move from the contemplative attitude of Myshkin's personality to the realm of clinical empiricism, we have to try and make an attempt to understand the so called epileptic personality changes from the point of view of Myshkin's change of personality. In the so called heterogenous spectrum of personality changes of the epileptic we find traits we usually call lack of distance, lack of tact, and curiosity. In so far as the clinical experience would lead us to the conclusion that the structure of the "grown-up child" has universal application to the grand mal epileptic, these traits can be immediately understood from the structure which we have presented in detail. The question is whether other traits of the change of personality which give evidence of the strangely pronounced mediocrity can be understood, on the one hand from the attitude of the epileptic to height and depth while at the same time retaining a childish impressionism through the physiognomy of these extremes— and still further from the ubiquitous and constantly active tendency to compromise into the mediocre into "cheapness" and "quietism." Thus we could understand the persistence, the sticking to, the perseverance of the Prince; e.g. when he watched the execution feeling spellbound, not being able to disentangle himself from the physiognomy of the utmost, from which he can only get away after repeated efforts at compromise. Thus piety would be a bad Mesotes to strive for religious heights, which are intended for the sake of depth. Also the pathos of justice, the pedantic, the optimistic and above all devotion—all these traits would be the results of a bad mesotes of extremes. Is the change of personality, therefore, to be understood as a well defined mediocrity of the psychic household instead of a harmonious and confident synthesis, as a tendency of the body to get away from having its presence crushed by threatening alternatives, to prevent those alternations which lead into critical situations and from these into the fit? In this case a certain antithesis could exist between the epilepsy manifested in fits and the epilepsy as a change of personality. The turning into cheapness, into the mediocre indicates then the change of personality; the failure of the synthesis on the other hand indicates the fits. It could be expected that fits at certain events could bring about a dementing but restrain the change of personality; that is, that an increasing change of personality would gradually limit the liability for crisis, that it would restrict the fits more and more. Above all one would expect that drug-controlled prevention of fits could encourage the development of the change of personality. Last of all, as to the genesis of fits: will the clinical experience confirm what can be shown in the epilepsy of Myshkin? It ought to be like this: the pre-epileptic fit situation is a critical situation only as far as the structure of the epileptic is concerned. But this situation can force the organism to modify or change this situation within the fit. Thus the fit would not be the immediate product of a cerebral malfunction, but rather the answer of the epileptic type via the central organism to a situation which has experienced its decisive determination through the type itself.

276

COMMENTARY ON PROFESSOR
TELLENBACH'S PAPER

Robert O. Evans

It is a privilege to comment on Professor Tellenbach's analysis of Dostoyevsky's Prince Myshkin. I speak, however, as a literary scholar to whom the details of psychological analysis are mysteries. These remarks, then, are from the point of view of literature.

With that qualification, first of all some small points of difference I find exist between my own reading of Prince Myshkin and Professor Tellenbach's. Omitting minor matters of interpretation, some of which may depend on translation, I find that I do not read Prince Myshkin's descent into the depths quite so deeply as does Professor Tellenbach. I do not see the Prince moved towards the possible murder of Rogozhin, even when he fingers the knife on Parfon's desk or when he returns to examine a knife in a shop window. It seems to me that Dostoyevsky is presenting several aspects of personality change on a number of levels. The knife stands symbolically for violent temptation. It is quite true that in the triangular relationship amongst the Prince, Rogozhin, and Nastasya Filipovna one possible solution might be violence by the Prince, a murder in defense of Nastasya. But here the temptation is on moral rather than psychological grounds. We must not forget that Dostoyevsky created the Prince to be a perfectly good character, and insofar as he succeeded the Prince has certain Christ-like attributes (though he is not in my opinion—which varies from that of some critics—really a Christ figure). A moral temptation, the passing through his mind of the idea of committing an evil action, is part of the manyfold characterization. In short the Prince is forced to face alternatives. But he does not really for an instant entertain this particular one. He does not seek out Parfon Rogozhin with the intention, however vague, of settling the problem by killing him. Richard Curle in a recent book on

Dostoyevsky's characters believes the Prince to be spiritually untouched amidst the passions raging around him. Part of his education in society amounts to the realization of certain alternatives in the real world, and this is an item in point.

More important is my own reading of Prince Myshkin's disease. It is not necessary for us to examine the symptoms of the disease to ascertain that the Prince suffered from epilepsy, for Dostoyevsky clearly says that he does. He distinctly avoids presenting the reader with too accurate a picture of how the disease seizes the Prince. It is enough that he tells us about it generally. On the two occasions in the novel when the Prince suffers an attack, we are given few details, other than the sensations experienced by the Prince during the extremely long aura. The author makes much of Myshkin's sharpened consciousness and his disassociation from ordinary reality. Occasionally he experiences short periods of asphasia similar to Mesmer's description of hysteria after hypnosis. But there is no description of the tonic or clonic phases of the Prince's seizures, which might provide excellent literary material for a realist. The Prince does not fall and injure himself. No one places a pencil between his teeth to protect his tongue. The duration of unconsciousness is not related, and indeed it appears that the Prince is seldom unconscious for very long periods, though regarding the seizure that the Prince experiences at the Epanchin's house on the night of his betrothal to Aglaya the author says that the fit was a light one.

On this score my interpretation of the novel differs from that of Prof. Tellenbach, but with respect to the meaning of the seizures in terms of character delineation, I accept Prof. Tellenbach's judgment with certain reservations.

His analysis is, of course, incomplete. It would take a textbook to describe fully such a complex character as Prince Myshkin. That is part of the glory of Dostoyevsky's creation. The author, as I have said, concentrates on the Prince's mental state in the hours of the aura preceding the seizures. His perceptions are at first heightened, but eventually he grows further and further away from reality until finally the fit overcomes him. On awakening, he returns to reality, or whatever portion of reality he was capable of understanding. Throughout the work, not only during the aura, the Prince is gifted with a kind of second sight, an insight into reality that is beyond the ken of ordinary people. That is not, however, a symptom of his epilepsy, except that in the period in which the epileptic aura is described this second sight is heightened. The description of Prince Myshkin's state of mind immediately before the seizures reminds one first of a mystic with reinforced insight, then of a patient under LSD, wherein ordinary reality becomes so heightened that it is finally distorted out of recognizeable shape.

The supposed characteristics of the epileptic personality are still debated. The textbooks I studied were ambiguous. One psychologist, perhaps now thoroughly out of date, recognized four traits of personality as typical of the epileptic: eccentricity, supersentitiveness, emotional poverty, and rigidity. In childhood histories he found also irritability, distractability, insistence on having one's own way, quarrelsomeness, stubbornness, restlessness, etc. (I refer to L. P. Clark.) A few of these characteristics are exploited in the portrait of Prince Myshkin. Certainly he is a great eccentric. Other characters in the book are always remarking on this facet of his personality, and it is made eminently clear near the end when Aglaya cautions the Prince about his behavior at the planned betrothal party. He is, if possible, to say absolutely nothing at the party, and to sit as far as he can from Lizaveta Prokofyevna's precious china vase, which Myshkin eventually shatters. Supersensitiveness I hardly find. It is quite true that the Prince is sensitive, but he is not supersensitive. If one examines incidents in which his sensitivness is related, such as the monumental occasion when Nastasya slaps his face, it seems that the Prince's reactions are really almost ordinary insofar as he has been highly provoked into the emotions he displays. Emotional poverty is also not a characteristic of the Prince, though he is certainly emotionally disoriented. He is capable of deep and abiding love, as his feeling for Aglaya proves. He is also capable of other, more noble or spiritual feelings, as a highly Christian character might well be. Forgiveness may be a weakness, as it surely sometimes is in terms of the society he frequents, but it is also a very refined emotional reaction to most unpleasant circumstances. And the characteristics of childhood epilepsy are almost entirely lacking in the Prince, excepting perhaps restlessness. He is certainly neither quarrelsome nor irritable.

We have, then, no exact case history of epilepsy in the novel, not at least in the sense that Myshkin demonstrates classic symptoms. There is, however, another more symbolic sense in which we do have a sort of literary case history of the disease. I mean, as a disease that only very good and superior people may contact. Epilepsy, as Dostoyevsky portrays it, is almost a saint's disease, a symptom of noble character struggling against the vicissitudes of the world of society. It reminds one of the stigmata or perhaps of the open sores that come upon the face of Manolios in Kazantzakis' novel, *The Greek Passion,* when the hero, a simple shepherd, attempts to imitate Christ. Certainly what we do not find in the novel is an exact description of the author's own ailment, as some writers believe. [See T. Alajouanine, "Dostoyevsky's Epilepsy," *Brain,* Vol. 86, Part 2 (June, 1963), 209-218.]

Dostoyevsky makes a great deal of the heightened perceptions that precede seizures as he describes Prince Myshkin. All of reality is brought sharply into focus until finally it fades away into illusory patterns, as I have said, as in an LSD induced experience. In a literary sense the structure of the whole book, though it has hardly been noticed, resembles the sensations in the Prince's mind before his fits. *The Idiot* is a very long work. It takes forever to get anywhere, until the very end when the strands are finally drawn together rather quickly. But for all its leisurely appearance, it is really a very heightened glimpse of reality. The total time covered by the novel is first 24 hours, then after a lapse of six months a period of about five weeks. The final action, which really occurs after the story is over, cannot be more than a few months later. The incidents are crowded together. We spend a great many pages following the Prince from his introduction on the train to St. Petersburg to the climactic birthday party of Nastasya Filipovna that same night. There is then a period of six months—perhaps about the interval between seizures in certain phases of epilepsy—and then another crowded series of scenes at the resort outside of St. Petersburg, ending with a shift to the city itself where the final tragic scene is played. There is close attention paid to the unities of time and place in the novel. The time is almost as compressed as it might be in a drama, and the place is carefully controlled so that while we move from house to house, or scene to scene, we are always very close to the capital. There are no scenes in Moscow or the provinces, though there are references to both and many opportunities for the author to wander away from the centralized settings. *The Idiot,* with its tightness of structure, does not resemble *Dead Souls.* It is structurally the antithesis of Gogol's picaresque novel. In a different way it is also the antithesis of Turgenev—not structurally but in terms of the philosophy expounded. Turgenev, Dostoyevsky says, when he is relating what society thinks of the Prince after he has jilted Aglaya, is a representative of modern nihilism. The Prince, on the other hand, is a hero pitted against the world, even when the world as he finds it is halfway, or more than halfway, willing to accept and absorb him.

The role of the Prince in relation to literature is easily recognizable. Dostoyevsky frequently reminds us that he is the poor virginal knight jousting against windmills. He is both Christlike and mad, but he is also a true hero. He is Don Quixote. This aspect of his character, I think, goes a long ways towards explaining his relationship with Nastasya Filipovna. Like Cervantes' knight he must devote himself to a lady. Don Quixote chose a country wench, the Dulcinea del Toboso. A fitting choice, Sancho Panza says, for not only was she able to do the chores, because she was healthy and muscular, but her morals were no better than they should be. She was ready for a romp in the hay any old time. Nastasya, who is much more clearly described than Don Quixote's lady, shares some of these characteristics. She is a woman of questionable reputation. She has been kept from her girlhood by Totsky as an extraordinary sort of mistress, though Dostoyevsky is deliberately ambiguous about what her exact relations with her protector were. Certainly in the period described in the novel she was never sexually engaged with him, nor for that matter anyone else unless perhaps Rogozhin. But she is already a fallen woman in the eyes of society. The men may gather at her soirees, but the women must not recognize her. The two occasions when they do meet her are almost fatal. First, when she is considering Gavril Ardalionovitch's offer of marriage, which would free Totsky to marry into the Epanchin family, she confronts Varvara Ardalionovna, setting in motion a quarrel which is only climaxed when Prince Myshkin attends her birthday party and offers himself to her in marriage. Second, when Aglaya confronts her as a rival, she faints, causing Myshkin to hesitate instead of running after the woman he truly loves. The engagement to Aglaya is broken forever, and the tragic series of events begins, ending only with Nastasya's murder.

Myshkin himself, as Prof. Tellenbach says, is rather childish, but perhaps there is literary reason to believe that his childishness arises not so much because of his epilepsy as because of his Quixotic nature. The old knight was at once old and childish. Prince Myshkin sees the world, especially the world of social relations, both as a man and as a child, in much the same way. Both characters can be cruel as children are cruel. The old knight in Cervantes mistakes innocent travellers on the road for enemy knights and flays them soundly. To the travellers such treatment is harsh and undeserved. Myshkin stays to assist Nastasya Filipovna and cruelly breaks the heart of the Aglaya.

But neither Myshkin nor Don Quixote are entirely childish. Both have another side to their characters. With the old knight that side often contributes to the comic situation, but with Myshkin it seems more likely to contribute to the unfolding tragedy. It would be a mistake, I think, to view Myshkin as quite childlike. He grows throughout the novel, and his growth is primarily emotional, though Dostoyevsky takes pains to point out that it is also intellectual. For example, while he was in Moscow with Rogozhin they read all of Pushkin. His knowledge of the details of Russian history may be faulty, as Aglaya complains, but his knowledge of what motivates men in society grows throughout the novel. The trouble is he cannot help forgiving them even when he understands the baseness of their motives. Rogozhin is moved by lust and jealousy, but Myshkin loves him all the more. One is reminded of Christ's predilection for sinners.

But Myshkin also occupies a unique position in literature, despite similarities to other figures. He is a hero without a past and, as it turns out, without a future. He arises out of literal idiocy which Dostoyevsky suggests was a state of childhood epilepsy. That he was well connected, is true; that is how Dostoyevsky accounts for his fortune. Money was a necessary consideration in the 19th century novel with its service to French realism. We should not forget that Myshkin put Nastasya's copy of *Madame Bovary* in his pocket, even though it was a library book. But he comes from the Swiss mountain-top with neither explanation nor precedent. He bursts on the Russian scene, as it were. And in the end he retreats into idiocy and is sent again to the Swiss mountain-top, where he no longer recognizes the society he shared for a brief moment.

His relation with Nastasya Filipovna is the key pin in the story. It causes him immense frustration, but it is not a sexual frustration, no more than is Don Quixote's relation with the Dulcinea del Toboso sexual. Myshkin is not sexually attracted to Nastasya. It takes us most of the novel to find that out. But eventually Myshkin tells us that from the instant he saw her portrait he hated her. What he recognized in her eyes, I suggest, was his own madness. It was the demon in her that attracted him. He did not desire her otherwise. He wanted her that way in order to save her but also in order to understand himself. It is as if the text of the sermon was "Whom the gods wish to destroy, they first make mad," and as if the story of Prince Myshkin were the story of a very good man trying by the practice of a superior kind of virtue to escape that fate.

The question the author leaves inexplicit is whether or not Myshkin has a measure of success. *The Idiot* is after all tragic in nature. Myshkin does not, it is true, die in the end, but he might as well have done. He effectively ceases to exist as a man. He has been effectively destroyed. But has his life, that brief 24 hours we watched and then the five weeks it took his friend Ippolit, the tubercular patient, to die, been in vain? It is not so easy a question to answer. Myshkin gave up Aglaya, jilted her in the world's eyes, even though he believed that he could not have done otherwise. *In extremis,* as Nastasya Filipovna's faint —after all a very feminine sort of trick—must have appeared to his naive conceptions of how people should behave, he did what he thought was right. It did not save Nastasya. It cruelly hurt Aglaya and alienated the poor knight from society. But it was Nastasya's own demon that drove her once more away from Myshkin as he waited at the altar, into the arms of Rogozhin whom she feared. Aglaya herself, after the story is ended, we are told, married a bogus Polish count and suffered immensely. But people still admired and loved the Prince. The Epanchins got over the mortal slight to their daughter and visited him in his sub-human state in Switzerland. Aglaya herself seems to have forgiven him. What drove the Prince finally back to the state from which he had so recently emerged was not his childishness, nor his naive goodness, nor the emotional heights and depths which he probed, nor even his epilepsy. It was instead the horror of his night with Rogozhin in the presence of Nastasya Filipovna's corpse. The incomparable horror of the depths of the human mind that Myshkin recognized and lived with during that awful night reminds me of a key phrase in Conrad's story, *The Heart of Darkness,* of Kurtz summing up what he found in the depths of his own depravity, "The terror, the terror!"

No doubt all this was brought about in part by Myshkin's epilepsy, not clinical manifestations, but morally and religiously. We have a tragic hero, so badly flawed that he is almost incapable of intercourse with the world. Yet he tried magnificently to enter human society and improve it. He failed only under the most terrible of pressures. We pity him, and we also fear his fate, for what the epileptic character was to Myshkin our own weaknesses seem to us. Dostoyevsky, for example, never fails to remind us that the characteristics he describes in the Prince can exist in other people as well. Aglaya's mother, for instance, also partakes of second sight. Aglaya herself is noble if maddeningly female. People are always forgiving someone for something or other, usually Myshkin himself for acting an ass, in the novel. Even the worst characters somehow manage to find a good side in his presence. Kolya and Ganya's father, the lying old general, to whom truth was utterly distasteful, though he is far from sane, finally takes on characteristics of a penitent and dies. Even Keller, the meanest character in the book, shows a few traces of nobility at the end. Only Nastasya Filipovna herself exhibits no good side after the initial portion of the book, and that may be partly because Dostoyevsky keeps her hidden from us, partly because she is driven by such a demon. Thus, while values of society are not exactly upheld, they are also not destroyed. Other values, moral and religious values, are somehow cryptically affirmed. Contemporary nihilism, French atheism, Roman Catholicism (in a famous passage)—a number of things—are attacked. But the goodness of the human heart is at least partly affirmed, if only in a negative fashion. Yevgeny Pavlovitch reminds Prince Myshkin that in the temple the woman, just such a woman as Nastasya, was forgiven—"but she wasn't told she had done well." Myshkin, the poor knight, the noble prince, may be forgiven for trying to save Nastasya, the fallen woman, but in this world it would be hard to forgive him, Yevgeny Pavlovitch reminds him with the voice of reason, for injuring innocent Aglaya—or for loving both women at once. Perhaps that is clue to Dostoyevsky's difficult ending. If the Prince truly loved both women at once and if he permitted Nastasya Filipovna to win out over Aglaya, then the book would end, as some critics believe, on a cynical note. The whole great novel would prove a magnificent failure. It would end as nihilistically as the Turgenev Dostoyevsky earlier attacked. But that is not what the Prince tells us. He did not love Nastasya; he was repelled and attracted by her at one and the same time. Life is a mystery. But literature is an imitation of life in which heroes often end tragically and nobly. The ending of *The Idiot* presents a paradox. But with Dostoyevsky in this his favorite novel, as with Cervantes in the great prototype, it is better to try nobly and fail than not to have tried at all.

PSYCHOTIC PAINTING AND PSYCHOTIC PAINTERS

James L. Foy, M.D.

INTRODUCTION

IF WE ARE to look at paintings from the past as well as the present, after selecting and assembling a number of color slide reproductions of them, we are embarked upon another excursion into the museum without walls. M. Malraux has advised us that upon entering this imaginary museum we shall find ourselves confronting the objects there, within an inevitably special situation. The style of the objects is there for us to see, however the objects appear extirpated from their everyday context, removed from the place of their usual daily life. We ourselves come upon them in a profoundly new historical moment. So there is this now-moment of immediate apprehension, and in this moment only a minimal historicism is a requirement, that which would be a necessary consequence of a normal capacity for seeing (21). The requirement may encompass my human reality and my personal history. The painting, the art object, may itself appear unencumbered. Then it is an apparition, erupting out of nowhere, a sudden invasion of my world. I meet it for the first time like I meet a person and during the encounter a certain disclosure is made possible. I am in its presence, and the painting does not point to any meaning beyond its own presence. Sartre writes: "Pictures have no positive force, they are no more than suggestions; indeed, their existence depends on me, I am free as I confront them" (22, p. 77).

The painting, however, may also appear under extraordinary circumstances very encumbered, burdened with its own complex historical past, and perhaps the personal history and point of view of its maker. The initial now-moment of immediate apprehension is suspended and in place a structured cognitive, perspective and backward regard will prevail. A sense of historical past, supported by various accumulations of historical data and investigative research, modifies apprehension of the painting. With this mode of perception I look into and behind the painting, rather than let the painting look at me.

Madness Portrayed In Painting

The distinction elaborated above becomes useful in the approach to works of art which have as their content the human face of madness. Looking at a sequence of such paintings from different epochs of European art poses many problems. The older paintings will have accumulated a greater reservoir of historical considerations and reconsiderations, and they will carry a set of historical allusions not readily grasped by a contemporary viewer. Madness has meant different things to different men down through the centuries of our own past. One can turn to Michel Foucault's brilliant descriptions of the changing structure of unreason in his book, *Madness and Civilization,* as a guide to the examination of three paintings depicting the madwoman (6).

Bruegel's *Dulle Griet* or *Mad Meg* strides across a Boschian landscape filled with conflagration, disorder and torture. The madness of the lady is matched by the madness of the place, which has an infernal quality. There is an old Flemish proverb which says, "When you go to Hell, go sword in hand." In the painting the artist might also be referring to the legend of St. Margaret vanquishing the devil, who seems to appear, open-mouthed and menacing at the left of the picture. The painter has surrounded the madwoman as virago with an elaborate clutter of central and peripheral elements, all enmeshed in a fabric of historical, political and religious allusion. The craziness of the scene engulfs Meg and an entire society.

Gericault's *Madwoman* is carefully isolated in a meticulously rendered realistic portrait. Historical interests are quickly confined to the costume of the sitter and the artist's graphic technique. The early nineteenth century painting of the madwoman as asylum inmate takes on the function of a documentary record, a pre-photography image of a case, and an illustration from a text on the physiognomy of the insane.

In his painting, *Marilyn Monroe* (executed in 1954 nine years before the actress's suicide) Willem de Kooning assaults our preconceptions and expectations with an image of the mad-woman as celebrity, and in showing this work the artist extinguishes our pursuit of gossip and/or history, while promoting a ruthless interrogation of the spectator. Foucault writes:

> . . . through madness, a work that seems to drown in the world, to reveal there its non-sense, and to transfigure itself with the features of pathology alone, actually engages within itself the world's time, masters it, and leads it; by the madness which interrupts it, a work of art opens a void, a moment of silence, a question without answer, provokes a breach without reconciliation where the world is forced to question itself. What is necessarily a profanation in the work of art returns to that point, and, in the time of that work swamped in madness, the world is made aware of its guilt. Henceforth, and through the mediation of madness, it is the world that becomes culpable in relation to the work of art; it is now arraigned by the work of art, obliged to order itself by its language, compelled by it to a task of recognition, of reparation to the task of restoring reason *from* that unreason *to* that unreason (6, p. 288).

If these works demonstrate the shifting meanings of madness in Western society over a period of four centuries, the changing structure of the place of and for mad unreasonableness in the midst of society and world, these same works of art remind us insistently that the points of view of painters on all subjects evolve and change from epoch to epoch. Looking at these pictures: Bruegel's from the sixteenth century, Gericault's from the nineteenth and de Kooning's from the twentieth underscores the theory of the retracting gaze of the painter in the history of art, a theory proposed by Ortega y Gasset in his essay, "On Point of View in the Arts." The philosopher wrote:

> Throughout the history of the arts in Europe, the painter's point of view has been changing from distant to proximate vision . . . This means there has been nothing capricious in

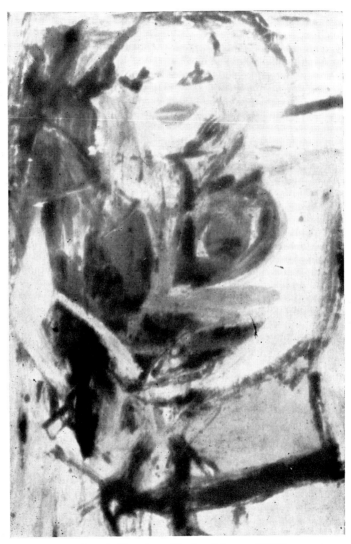

Willem de Kooning: *Marilyn Monroe* (1954).
Collection Mr. & Mrs. Roy R. Neuberger, New York.

the itinerary followed by the painter's shift of attention. First it is fixed upon the body or volume of an object, then upon what lies between the body of the object and the eye, that is, the hollow space. And since the latter is in front of the object, it follows that the journey of the pictorial gaze is a retrogression from the distant—although close by—toward what is contiguous to the eye. According to this, the evolution of Western painting would consist in a retraction from the object toward the subject, the painter. . . . The guiding law of the great variations in painting is one of disturbing simplicity. First things are painted; then, sensatons; finally ideas. This means that in the beginning the artist's attention was fixed on external reality; then on the intrasubjective (19, pp. 104 ff.).

The dynamics of the artistic portrayal of madness are revealed as contingent upon two variables, the artist's intentions in his act of painting and the societal image of psychosis. This is meant in no way to dismiss the possibility that significant artistic endeavor may, by itself, transform the societal image of psychosis or, at least, assist in such a transformation. This possibility is suggested in the paintings of de Kooning, Francis Bacon and Jean Dubuffet, artists whose imaging of madness is paralleled by the clinical reconsiderations of schizophrenia proposed by the psychiatrists, Harry Stack Sullivan, Ronald Laing, and Harold Searles.

Some Aesthetic Problems

When one considers the spontaneous paintings and drawings of non-artists working under the influence of psychosis, a disconcerting clutter and distortion can be detected because the painter mixes points of view and sometimes assembles in one composition a tangle of objects, sensations and ideas. Such practice should not, however, be too quickly identified with psychotic art, since it could be argued that synthetic cubism and especially Picasso's work in that style also partake of multiple viewpoints and collections, brought together in a complex but harmonious structure.

Before concentrating on the paintings of patients, it would be helpful to return once more to the distinction made at the outset of this paper. So much psychological writing on art and interpretations of art works fails to appreciate the ambiguous life of the painting, existing as it does with both a present and a past, the object of both immediate apprehension and historical apprehension. Freudian and Jungian explainers are driven by the urge to read the symbolic language of a visual work of art, often treating it like a Rosetta stone bearing hieroglyphics and in their enthusiasm they overlook the primary aspect of the artistic enterprise. Gombrich, in writing of this overlooking of the object, observes that it is not the individual work of art which is examined by the explainer, rather the language in which it is formulated is treated *as if* it were itself a work of art (8). The modern viewer comes to look at art with excess baggage, crammed with several psychologies and mythologies, not to speak of a laziness and even a partial blindness, when approaching perceptual tasks. His first impulse is to take a hurried look and start abstracting away from that which he sees. The modern painter wishes to combat and put down the symbol-hunting, explanation-hungry spectator. In a number of styles: action painting, figurative painting, hard-edge abstraction, and Pop art, painters have insisted upon the primacy of their made image, the thing that appears.

There are two ways in which the reality of creative performance appears to the spectator of visual art: (1) as presentation, the presence of the art object directly in perception; (2) as representation, the image perceived and analyzed by the viewer with specialized knowledge, e.g. symbology or iconology. Encountering the painting as a presentation requires it to appear as a non-discursive whole, which articulates and formulates experience through intuitive recognition. Looking at the painting as a representation requires it to appear as an assemblage of reformulations and significations, which refer to something else, that is, its historical precedents. This distinction is based upon ideas elaborated by Merleau-Ponty (13) but quite similar ideas are to be found in the earlier aesthetics of Croce and also in writings by Susanne K. Langer.[1]

Additional understanding of painting as presentation is to be found in Arturo Fallico's comments on the object of aesthetic awareness. The art object is described by this philosopher as a simple, direct presentation of possibility without practical or theoretical injunctions attached; it poses neither for what is, nor for what ought to be. The writer goes on to say:

> The peculiar composure and independence of the art-object come into clearer view when we see it is in the order of a *presentation,* rather than *re*-presentation. A representation, as the very word seems to say, presupposes another thing, somehow made to reappear under the guise of the art-object. A representation is unoriginal by definition. The essential characteristic of the art-object is precisely that it is an original—a *first* presentation of a possibility truly felt and imagined. It can remind us, really, only of itself, even if, in the process, we may remind ourselves of nonaesthetic things and events extraneous to it (5, pp. 20 & 21).

Van Gogh's *Shoes* do not copy or duplicate any pair of ordinary shoes, and in important ways they are unlike the shoes we find in the everyday world around us. More than an effigy or an emblem, these *Shoes* are an apparition. They stand neutral and apart from the ordinary spatio-temporal world. Their unex-

---

[1] In her essay, "The Art Symbol and the Symbol in Art" Langer distinguishes between her own notions of presentation and representation. She discusses the former in the following passage. ". . . it (the Art Symbol) does not stand for something else, nor refer to anything that exists apart from it. According to the usual definition of 'symbol,' a work of art should not be classed as a symbol at all. But that usual definition overlooks the greatest intellectual value and, I think, the prime office of symbols—their power of formulating experience, and *presenting* it objectively for contemplation, logical intuition, recognition, understanding. That is articulation, or logical expression. And this function every good work of art does perform. . . . The actual felt process of life, the tensions interwoven and shifting from moment to moment, the flowing and slowing, the drive and directedness of desires, and above all the rhythmic continuity of our selfhood, defies the expressive power of discursive symbolism." (17, pp. 132 & 133, italics added.)

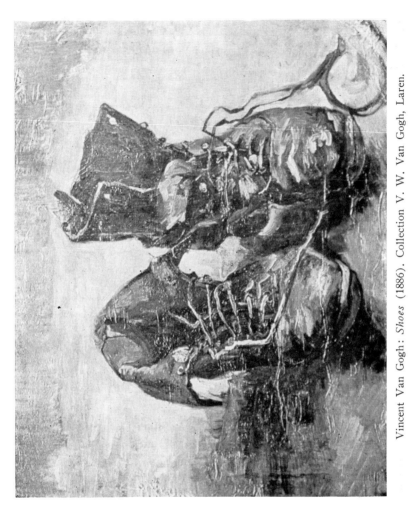

Vincent Van Gogh: *Shoes* (1886). Collection V. W. Van Gogh, Laren.

Vincent Van Gogh: *Shoes* (1887). Cone Collection, Museum of Art, Baltimore.

pected *presence* enables me to see shoes for the first time and the usually hidden physiognomy of all shoes is now revealed to me. My encounter with Van Gogh's *Shoes* allows me to erect a primary world of shoes and earth and walking on the earth, in which the essential meaning of shoes is driven home to me. After I contemplate these *Shoes* my own taken-for-granted shoes are revealed for what they are: those mundane, durable yet impermanent companions, those dependable and serviceable intermediaries between my body and the earth I tread everyday (12). Van Gogh's *Shoes*, with all their originality, innocence and ingenuousness announce a possibility for a revision of my everyday world, and they oppose the thoughtlessness with which I put on my shoes each morning without even looking at them or acknowledging them.

A very different viewing of the painting is elaborated by H. R. Graetz in his book, The Symbolic Language of Vincent Van Gogh (9). Starting from historical materials and speculative phychodynamic considerations of Vincent's symbiotic bond to his brother Theo, the writer then turns to the painting of the Shoes:

It was when Vincent lived with Theo in Paris that he first chose shoes as a subject and painted the *Two Shoes*. One shoe is a little slimmer and stands erect; its lace, ending in the form of a sickle, is conspicuous in the foreground. The upper part of the other shoe is bent down and touches the upright one. A light stroke goes from the interior of the taller shoe toward the other. Inside the shoe on the left a piece of light lace shoots upward; the other end moves to the fore. The darkness within both shoes is deepened by the contrast of the light ground behind . . . In the common expression, 'to be in someone's shoes,' the shoe stands for the wearer and, as in other still lifes, we have a portrait here, this time in the form of shoes. They seem to be a pair, though their shape could also suggest two left shoes. Time, wear, and weather have left their mark equally on them as on twin brothers, worn in *toil and sweat*. The lace on the left hand shoe changes direction and suddenly turns to the upright shoe, again almost touching it—as if Vincent's thoughts were going from him to his brother. In such close touch with each other, the two shoes are like a sym-

bolic expression of the two brothers together on their road
(9, pp. 47 & 48).

In this viewing, or rather reading, of the *Shoes* by Van Gogh
one detects a strained overreaching for explanation and motiva-
tion, which pushes the beholder drastically behind the surface of
the painting toward a secret message it presumably contains.
This reading of the painting must finally be rejected because the
commentator does not fully acknowledge the privileges of presentation in the work, while unable to set any limits on the
representation.

In an essay entitled, "Art and Phenomenology," Fritz Kaufmann wrote: "A work of art does not substitute, but institutes
an original awareness of existence on the whole; it does not so
much reproduce and represent as produce and present a total
experience (14, p. 147)."

Poverty of Presentation In Schizophrenic "ART"

A colorful icon by the contemporary Dutch painter, Karl
Appel, produces and presents a total experience. The image
intrudes upon the beholder with an undisguised, unconstrained
and freely given presence. In contrast to this an icon of cryptic
self portrayal by a twenty year old male college student introduces the closed realm of schizophrenic expression. This intelli-
gent, but artistically untalented, young man provided, in replica,
his "glorious, huge self-portrait" which he had previously
painted upon the largest clear wall of his family's dining room,
while in a state of great excitement, delusion and ecstasy. This
work and others, which will follow, demonstrate aspects of
spontaneous painting and drawing by untutored psychotic persons with scattered but limited artistic abilities. In these works
the boundaries of presentation are quickly reached and the
viewer finds himself asking questions: What does this represent? What does the painter mean by this touch and by that
symbol? To obtain answers to these questions one must go
beyond the painting, the painter himself would have to be

interrogated for the answers, or perhaps the clinical record of the painter.

Another young psychotic man, who had never used the medium before, created two fine compositions in colored chalk and called them *Angel* and *Devil*. They are models of representational drawing and even the symbolic value of the work is attenuated by the concrete, and even asymbolic manner in which the two figures stand in for the intense ambivalence of the schizophrenic in acute turmoil. A somewhat related example is offered by a schizophrenic woman who painted a strange two-sided composition with fragmentation and agglutination of dark forms on the left half and a bright, sunny, intact landscape on the right half.

A schizophrenic patient experiencing overwhelming and disfiguring anxiety may spontaneously adopt a doodle or cartoon expression, if given the tools and opportunity. This type of expression seems to demand extensive captioning and labeling. Often enough the patient himself will supply the writing-in which is designed to coax further meaning from the material for the puzzled viewer. Such written commentary is inevitably a wordy development of delusional ideas or hallucinatory experiences.

Chronic forms of paranoid psychosis may lead the patient to a rigid, stereotyped, reiterated mode of expression, at times overly ornamental. A hospitalized man in his forties suppressed his persecutory beliefs but was found to be covering every scrap of paper he could find with drawings of the human eye, filling the entire page with the same motif. He would then mail these sheets to his family, government officials, and the President, explaining later that everyone had better 'keep an eye out' for danger and conspiracy. When given art materials he reproduced the composition in painting against a striking green background. The final product was a picture with a curious but tiresome presence, which quickly impressed the viewer with its overpowering representationalism.

Of the many psychotic persons who spontaneously indulge in drawing and painting, most are endowed with very meager

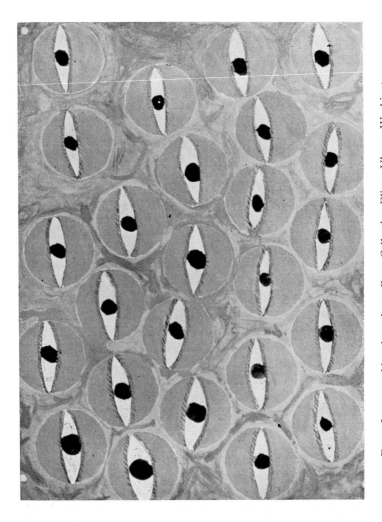

Forty-five year old male patient: *Eyes*. Collection Elinor Ulman, Washington.

artistic ability, and in this they are not unlike the non-psychotic population. Expressive, decorative and, less often, graphic production of unsuspected power may be unleashed in psychotic persons during the course of illness. This may take place in adults who have not drawn or painted since early childhood.

A long, complex series of works was executed by a twenty-four year old, single girl who was hospitalized over a period of many months during a relapsing schizophrenic psychosis with continuous paranoid features illustrates another point. She was talented and had received art school training during her early twenties. She had acquired skill in handling oil paints. The patient had an older brother, a commercial artist and illustrator, who also was schizophrenic. Several months before hospitalization the patient made a self-portrait in oils. During that time she was continuously and painfully aware of brain waves influencing her behavior, especially her sexual behavior toward both men and women. The formal and technical features of the self-portrait are well done, however, the wavy background configuration or partial halo in red links perseveration in the design to the delusional thinking. A sketch sheet by the same patient from a period of more profound psychosis and hallucination shows conventional adolescent drawings of glamour girl heads, arrayed around a sexually provocative female figure. On the left of the sheet is one full-length figure of decidedly ambiguous sex, indicating the artist's extreme confusion of sexual identity through the representational manner. During the months of hospital treatment, restitution and convalescence the patient painted for a period of time each day. She executed over twenty female portrait heads, her sitters being fellow patients, nurses and staff members. She valued her work and kept it prominently exhibited on the wall of a visiting lounge. During her illness she did not attempt any self-portraiture with the mirror, however, elements of self portrayal could be detected in many of her female portraits.

This brief review with examples of paintings by psychotic patients demonstrates that talent and previous training in the use of materials have a decisive influence on artistic expression,

Twenty-four year old female patient: *Self-Portrait.* Collection James L. Foy, Washington.

and that severe psychotic decompensation does not always result in the fragmentation and deterioration of form. There are no special formal characteristics that are unique to psychotic painting. Linear contours emphasized over color, overly decorated surfaces, repeated patterns, simplification, distortion, marked stylization, agglutination, condensation and extreme symbolism are procedures which might be found in schizophrenic painting

(11, 20) but these are attributes found singly or in combination in much of contemporary art. The psychotic patient, untutored and of meager talent, will produce works that are only slightly accessible to immediate, primary and synthetic perception by the viewer. These works have drastic limitations, and even poverty, as presentation. They do not appeal directly and openly to the spiritual needs and interests of their beholders, they do not invite participation or convergence at a particular situation in time through the medium of their mere presence. The significance of these works, and it may be striking and powerful, is their insistent appeal for interpretation. The viewer is led quickly to the personal history of the painter, and as far as the painting is concerned an over-distancing takes place with the emergent task of deciphering what is represented there. The art historian, George Schmidt, has written: "The fact that our generation has learned to recognize artistic merit in the drawings and paintings of psychotics does not mean that their work is a genuine artistic expression of our time. It is not the untutored artists in our mental hospitals who pillory the insanities of our modern epoch, but the professional artist in his studio, who for his pains is rewarded by being himself accused of insanity . . . but that is quite another issue, with novel and far-reaching implications (11, p. 19)."

Vicissitudes of Presentation In Works by Psychotic Artists

If one turns now to the artist of professional training and experience, who has identifiable gifts and vocation, and to the painting which he executes after the onset of a proven psychosis, the investigator is struck by the variety of results, the lack of system in effects and the frequent independence of creative processes and integrative process in artists of genius. Ernst Kris in a paper originally published thirty years ago (15) discussed the changes which psychotic processes produce in creative artists. He outlined four possible types of outcome: (a) artistic ability remains unimpaired and no relevant changes occur, creative activity escapes the psychotic process;

(b) artistic activity is interrupted and resumed without noticeable change after recovery from psychosis; (c) psychosis manifests itself in a change of style, but the connections with the artistic development of the person and reality contact are preserved, viewing the total work creativity remains intact; (d) psychosis manifests itself in a change of style that can only be explained in terms of a psychotic process with either disorganization or restitution.

The cat paintings of Louis Wain are the outstanding example of the last named outcome of psychosis occurring in artists. These cats will be familiar to those who have examined any of the popular documents on psychopathological expression (1). Wain was an early 20th century London painter and illustrator. Cats were his life. He lived as a recluse in a house with seventeen cats and three spinster sisters. His drawings and paintings of cats were enormously popular in the London of his time. They appeared on calendars, in the Illustrated London News, and in a special Cat Album he issued every Christmas. His portrayal of cats was sentimental but there was some tendency for the cat portraits to comment on the absurdities of the human condition. The artist would render them in clothes, with hats, pipes, and spectacles. In mid life Wain, always an eccentric, became totally preoccupied with the belief that he was being persecuted and influenced by electrical impulses. He spent the last fifteen years of his life in mental hospitals and over the years his painting continued but his cats underwent a fantastic transformation as can be seen in any selection. The cat becomes a Byzantine ornament, the staring eyes remain intact until finally they too dissolve into the kaleidoscopic symmetry of the design.

Vincent Van Gogh's late painting demonstrates a change in style after psychosis becomes manifest, but with an extraordinary linkage of this style to the artistic development of the artist and his intentions as a painter. All of us have been held by his *Crows Over a Wheat Field*. Meyer Schapiro (23) writes of this landscape as if it were a booby-trap set for the spectator. The diverging paths actually converge at the viewer, the inversion of a familiar perspective network of the open field causes space to lose its focus and all things are now turned aggressively upon the beholder. There is a violence at the horizon that cannot be reached and the black crows which advance from the horizon toward the foreground, reverse in their approach the spectator's normal passage to the distance. The pushing and pulling effects upon our perception create tension within us and a desire to flee this crossroads for the distance which is blocked to us. Michel Foucault's comments are again quite appropriate:

> Nietzsche's last cry proclaiming himself both Christ and Dionysus . . . is the very annihilation of the work of art, the point where it becomes impossible and where it must fall silent . . . And Van Gogh, who did not want to ask permission from doctors to paint pictures knew quite well that his work and his madness were incompatible. Madness is the absolute break with the work of art (6, p. 287).

"Madness is the absolute break with the work of art." Or is it? In 1888, at the age of twenty-eight Van Gogh's Belgian contemporary, James Ensor, painted his masterpiece, *The Entry of Christ into Brussels*. This must be the largest example of schizophrenic art in existence, the painting is over eight and a half feet by fourteen feet in dimensions. Ensor's psychotic view of his bourgeois, "Ostende" world became evident in his work around 1883, although he may have exhibited schizophrenic tendencies from his early youth.

If "The Entry of Christ into Brussels" creates an environment where things and faces are trying to conceal something behind sham-like outward appearances, and if this gigantic tableau induces an attitude of suspicion, defiance and hate where a familiar world is replaced by an uncanny, threatening wall of madness—the painting is also successful as a staggering Rabelaisian farce, a carnival masterpiece of scorn, ridicule, banter and waggish humor—an extravagant "Praise of Folly."

Werner Haftmann has written of Ensor: "It would be superficial to dismiss Ensor's art as a product of mental illness on the ground of its similarity to works of schizophrenics. From an

James Ensor: *Self-Portrait with Mask* (1899). Private Collection, Antwerp.

historical point of view, we should say, rather, that Ensor was normal. He shared the spiritual tensions of his time. . . . He faced and endured the tensions, he lived them; he did not escape from them, but, rather, exalted them, and identified himself with them. Because of this identification, the images he produced as personal symbols assumed the character of symbols of his epoch. In this way, he entered into the stream of history . . . Ensor experienced the tragic conception of the world characteristic of the art of this critical [nineteenth century] period so completely that dream and reality, morbid hallucination and ultra-lucid perception, satanic hatred and loving affection for the world of things became hopelessly confused. The self and the world kept changing their relative positions, but always they remained alien and hostile to one another" (10, pp. 63 & 64).

These conflicts reside in his Self-Portrait of 1899, however, the artist's madness has an unsettling, playful Pirandellan quality. All wear the mask of folly except Ensor (and in the large painting, Christ). The artist in his silly hat and Rubenesque pose mocks us with his cool gaze. After 1900 it is true that Ensor's work fell off in quantity and that a certain sterile quality frequently prevailed in his painting. But this was not the absolute break with art, nor was the uncompromising artistic expression of the 1880's and 1890's.

Psychosis and Creativity, The Example of Munch

The Norwegian master of modern art and co-founder of European expressionism, Edvard Munch (1863-1944), is another artist, whose long lifetime of creativity and extraordinary achievement in the presence of incipient then enduring psychosis, causes us to question the incompatability of madness and art. In this final part of the paper I wish to examine a wide selection of Munch's works from all periods of his artistic activity and at the same time to consider his biography as background to the production of painting. Munch was a painter of problems, essentially his own personal, psychological problems. G. W. Digby has written of him:

Caught in the almost unendurable tension of his conflicting emotions, impulses and attitudes, he strove to objectify them and express them in his art. He painted primarily his own problems striving to define them, or rather to work upon them and so release them . . . The pictorial statements of Munch's problems are always charged with acute emotion, sometimes melancholic, sometimes savage and strident. One senses above all the release of emotion which has poured into his work; the individual, personal flavor is nearly always strongly felt. And indeed, it is not surprising to find him confessing the following indication of the psychological nature of his work: 'Painting is for me like being ill or intoxicated. An illness of which I do not want to be cured; an intoxicant which I cannot forego' (4, p. 29).

The method of this part of the paper will be historical and analytic. The bold and overwhelming presence of many of the paintings will be sidestepped, as it were, while applying psychoanalytic and existential points of view to their content. I would also leave formal analysis to the art critic. It should be clearly understood that it is not my intention to apply any reductive psychoanalysis to the creative process, the making of paintings or the appreciation of paintings. Indeed I am certain that these activities cannot be reduced to something we feebly call a psychodynamic formulation. At each step of the way Munch's work surpasses his sickness and any explanation of his sickness. At first a change in style seems to be signaled by conflict, crisis or social breakdown, but later in his career a consistent mastery and a marvelous ripening of style into old age are paralleled by an unmistakable and profound, paranoid distortion of personality. Digby once more:

In his art he was able to face up to reality and make statements about his own, and human, problems to a degree, and with an integrity, which he was very far from approaching in the external circumstances and conduct of his life. Witness, for instance, his numerous sef-portraits and compare them with so much of his conduct towards friends and foes; they are frank, revealing, confessional, full of insight where his conduct was so often blind and inconsiderate. True, his vision in his art was necessarily conditioned and clouded by the same causes which disturbed his outward life, for the one side of life cannot exist uninfluenced by the other. Yet as in dreams, fantasies, visions, so in his art Munch achieved intuitive realizations which transcend the actual; in this realm of inner realization he knew and saw what he was otherwise blind to, and what in other spheres of his life he was so little able to actualize (4, p. 30).

It is not surprising to learn of Munch's prodigious production during the creative work of his long life. Like many artists of genius he had a fantastic work identity and, although he had some indolent periods, he literally devoted his entire life to uncompromising, lonely artistic endeavor. He left over one thousand oil paintings, forty-five hundred drawings, and more than seven hundred different engravings or graphic works to the city of Oslo at his death. They are now kept in a special new Munch Museum, where only a fraction of these works can be exhibited at any one time. Munch's own work was precious to him and often he could not bring himself to part with pictures. When he was forced to sell a picture, as in his early days of poverty, he usually painted a replica for himself.

An art dealer visiting Munch in 1927 wrote: "If one calls a room in Munch's house a living room and others dining room or bedroom, they are all actually work rooms, and when paintings are hung up or standing around, when drawings and watercolors are put up on the walls and doors with thumbtacks, this is because Munch's mind is continuously preoccupied with his pictorial creations. Munch said to me once: 'You see, there are painters who collect the works of other painters, I know one who has a whole gallery of French Impressionists. He needs them for his work. I can understand this very well. In the same way, I need my own paintings. I must have them around me if I want to continue with my work.' . . . He needs his old paintings because they are fuel for his imagination, because *the world he has created for himself is his actual world*. But he also needs them because he has the need to continue to paint on old paintings, because many paintings which seem finished to others are still unfinished to him, and because he can only part with a painting when it has become completely detached from him . . .

There are paintings on which Munch works for many years."
(7, pp. 45 ff., translated, italics added)

It was habitual for the artist to return to an old subject,
working upon the self-same theme again and again, sometimes
many years between separate versions of a subject. This was
true particularly in his graphic work, where he would take a
subject or motif which he had painted and reduce it and crystal-
lize it to the simplest possible terms of lithography or woodcut.

All this is indicative of the highly personal quality of Munch's
work, its persistent meaningfulness for him, and its unrelenting
hold on his creative imagination. If there is power and a terrible
beauty in Munch's work, there is also an autobiography. Stenersen his biographer observed: "Everything which Munch painted
is a mirror of his own being (25)."

Edvard Munch was born in a small town in Southern Norway, however, he was reared in Christiana, that is modern Oslo.
His father a former Army surgeon, had a general practice of
medicine in a poor district of the capital. Munch's mother died
of tuberculosis when he was five. She left five children, Edvard
was the second oldest, so all were born quite close together in
time. The father was greatly affected by the death of the mother
and this tragedy altered his relationship to his children in an
unfavorable way. He fell into a deep religious melancholia with
a great deal of morbid grief feelings and anguish. His stern and
fear-ridden religious attitude was a forbidding experience for
his son. One is reminded of Kierkegaard and his father. The
doctor was severe and in punishments even brutal toward his
five children.

The oldest child, a girl Sophie, died of tuberculosis when
Munch was fourteen. His father died in 1889, when the artist
was twenty-six. Much later the sister Laura, a favorite model
for the young painter, died in a sanitarium, where she had been
admitted because of severe mental disorder.

Munch wrote: "Disease and insanity were the black angels or
guard at my cradle. In my childhood I always felt that I was
treated in an unjust way, without a mother, sick, and with

threatened punishment in Hell hanging over my head." (3, op. cit., p. 10)

At nineteen after some University studies in art history, Munch was launched on a career as an artist with his own studio. He was encouraged by his Aunt Karen, who had been the family's mother substitute. However, he was in rebellion against his devout father since Munch quickly aligned himself with Christiana's bohemians: writers, painters, and hangers-on. In 1886 he had his first exhibition of paintings. His work was in a realistic manner, with many portraits of his family members. Some initial success in Norway, travels in Germany and France, and support from German collectors, led the artist to live a good part of the year in Germany with frequent visits to Paris. His work continued in a realistic manner but certain major preoccupations began to appear over and over again in his painting, particularly illness and a group of erotic themes. *Puberty* is a shadowy painting of the beginnings of the consciousness of sex and with it the artist announces his interest in the power of sexuality as subject matter for a great deal of work that was to continue for several decades.

After 1891 Parisian intellectuals and Gaugin's art were to have a prominent influence upon Munch. Symbolism and its color effects were now transforming his earlier, almost Impressionist realism. He entered a decade of concentrated creativity, preparing an extensive group of paintings which he was to call later, "The Frieze of Life" (*Lebensfries*), works presenting the vicissitudes of human feeling from birth to death, an ambitious, spiritual odyssey of man. In spite of the overreaching project of this gradually conceived plan, Munch was clearly successful and these are the most admired of his paintings. Basic feeling states, personal memories, symbolically elaborated portraits, and some landscapes are in these paintings. Their titles, provided by Munch, read like a modern Stations of the Cross: *The Sick Child, Death Room, The Scream, Angst, Melancholy, The Kiss, Dance of Life, Madonna.*

The Scream is probably the most widely known image made

Edvard Munch: *The Scream:* (1893). Collection National Gallery, Oslo.

by Munch. It was executed in lithograph and in oils, and has the
curious distinction of having been reproduced on the cover of
Time magazine. There has been more written about this work
than any other of Munch's always intriguing and revealing
pictures. A few facts about the picture. Munch wrote a poem
entitled *The Scream,* whose first lines appear beneath the lithograph of the same title: "I felt the great scream through nature"
(2). The artist was afflicted all his life with agoraphobia. The

central foreground figure on the bridge with men, harbor, mountains and sky in the background seems to be bombarded with sound it wants to shut out and perhaps it is turning away from sights it refuses to look upon. A shocking effect is achieved by the technique of repeating in the background the lines of the frightful head and the wavy torso, suggesting that the person is bound to his environment.

A Freudian interpretation (24) offers a castrated figure of undifferentiated sex under the threatening spell of a dying, hemorrhaging mother, and a doubled father forbidding access to a secure haven by obstructing the bridge which leads to this gratifying, womb-like body of water. A Jungian interpretation (4) offers a similar regressive longing in conflict with the resistant and horrifying figure of the 'Terrible Mother' and also with the wrathful Father indicated in the super-egoish eye of heaven, which keeps guard over the circle of attainment.

An existential interpretation must begin with what is absent, that is, the absence of the piercing sound of the scream itself, which nevertheless fills and disturbs all segments of the image and assaults the viewer through synesthesia effects. The world of the painting *The Scream* resounds with a cry and it is exceedingly difficult to tell where this cry originates. Is it from open mouth of the foreground figure, the other "mouths" which open in the unnatural features of the background, or does the cry emanate from my own mouth as I stand before the painting —an image mirroring, echoing some inarticulate scream? Whatever boundaries I may erect in viewing the painting—between me and it, between foreground and background, between figure and nature, between earth and water, between water and sky— all boundaries are immediately penetrated by the unuttered, unheard scream of panic. The painting thrusts me into a world of panic, where everything in it panics. Panic used to describe *The Scream* also suggests this world's literal and Greek derivation—the sudden, extreme and groundless fear, such as the god Pan was said to inflict on his archaic pastoral world. Panic also brings us back to the line from Munch's poem: "I felt the great scream through nature."

During the years around the turn of the century the life of the artist became more and more chaotic. He drank too much, began to suffer from a persistent insomnia and became habituated to sleeping draughts, possibly bromides. He had several stormy affairs with women but always avoided marriage. He was derogatory when speaking of women, describing them as vampires, and as having nutcracker muscles in their thighs. He believed that only the strongest man could survive marriage. About a friend who had married, he said: "After a few months he was only soup. It was as if she had pulled out all his teeth. The whole man was only mush. One had to pull him out of her arms as he lay on her bosom. She was terrible, and he was ashen and empty-eyed." (24, op. cit., p. 413.)

In the year 1902, when he was thirty-nine, Munch was deeply involved with the daughter of a wealthy Oslo wine merchant. This love affair and its outcome had a profound influence upon his development as a man and as an artist. He wanted to break off the relationship but the woman entreated him to leave his work and remain constantly at her side. When the artist went to the seashore to work, she sent a mutual friend with the message that she had shot herself in desperation and lay dying. The story was a ruse but Munch believed it and rushed to what he thought was her death chamber. When she sprang up to greet him he was enraged. In an ensuing quarrel she produced a gun and threatened suicide. "I did not believe her, but of course I had to be chivalrous and put my hand over the revolver. And don't think the bitch failed to press the trigger! Do you know what she said when she saw I was bleeding? 'I didn't mean it Edvard, I hope it doesn't hurt.' " He was never to forget this absurd melodrama. He lost the terminal phalanx of the index finger on his left hand and always wore a kind of thimble over the stump and kept his hand covered most of the time with a glove.

After this episode Munch became increasingly argumentative with and suspicious of his male friends. Between 1902 and 1905 he had a series of barroom brawls. During one assault he almost killed a man, shooting at him in fury but missing him. That time Munch fled from Norway to Germany, where friends urged him to enter a sanatorium. His drinking increased, there were periods of hallucination and paranoid delusion, and exacerbation of his old agoraphobia with severe anxiety. At the end of 1908 after a long drinking bout and mental disturbance, the artist entered the private clinic of the psychiatrist, Dr. Daniel Jacobsen, in Copenhagen, where he remained for eight months.

While at the clinic Munch wrote a prose poem, entitled *Alpha and Omega,* which he illustrated with eighteen lithographs. This is his most sharply misogynous creation and in the writing of it he expressed with dreadful clarity the preoccupations of his psychotic state. The story concerns a man, Alpha, and a woman, Omega, who live alone on an island, a sort of paradise. After first happiness the woman directs her unsatisfied passion to the beasts, snakes and flowers of the island. Omega embraces the beasts, yielding to their soft fur and their hypnotic, glittering eyes. Irony and pathos lie in Alpha's efforts to recapture her affections. His attempts are bound to fail but he cannot understand why. Omega obeys nature, and when she embraces the animals and kisses the flowers she is more a part of the forces of life than man can ever be. In a jealous rage, Alpha fights the animals for Omega's love, but is defeated by them. Finally when Alpha sees the offspring of Omega and the beasts, he despairs. The sky and the sea change to blood and he turns away in terror from the scene, covering his ears to keep out the 'cries of nature' (see the remarks on *The Scream* above). He murders the faithless Omega and he, in turn, is torn to pieces by her children, begotten by the beasts (3).

Munch left Jacobsen's clinic much improved. He abstained from alcohol for ten years, then resumed drinking but stopped periodically when he felt it interfered with his creative powers. Back in Norway the artist was honored with a commission to decorate the Assembly Hall at Oslo University. For two years he toiled at sketches and multiple versions of a group of monumental, wall-sized paintings. He is said to have done twenty different versions for one of these called *Alma Mater*. The paintings from this project signal a change in Munch's style which became more naturalistic and less symbolic.

Munch seldom left his mother country after 1909. During the last twenty-five years of his life he lived as a recluse on a farm at Ekely that he bought in 1916. He was exceedingly suspicious of visitors, critics and young artists and shut his home to all but a few. Despite strong family ties and a devotion to his sister, Inger, he invited her to his home only twice during the last sixteen years of his life. He said that he could not bear to be with her because the slightest difference between them would upset him. He could not abide flowers or women's laughter, both of which reminded him of his mother's death. Anyone who did manage to visit the artist was required to say little and listen attentively, looking down at the floor while Munch spoke. He could not bear to talk to more than one person at a time.

He continued to make copies of his old paintings throughout his life. If he sold a canvas, which he rarely did, he would paint a replica for himself before he would let the work leave his possession. He discouraged all dealers and buyers in spite of the fact that he had attained an international reputation. His attitude toward his paintings was quite strange and his homes became crowded museums filled with literally thousands of his works. He said: "I have no children save my pictures. In order to be able to work I must have them around me. Often while working on a picture I come to a complete halt. Only by looking at my earlier pictures can I begin again." (25)

He fretted impatiently during those few occasions when paintings temporarily left his possession on loan for an exhibition. At these times he read everything he could lay his eyes on which was written about his "children." Stenersen, his biographer and rare friend, claims that when Munch was disatisfied with a painting he would beat it with a whip. Perhaps echoing his father he would claim that this "horse treatment" improved its character (24).

A magnificent series of fifteen self-portraits is Munch's finest achievement in painting during his late life. The force of the visible, of the seeing seen, can be clearly felt standing before these self images and self confrontations. The secular *ecce homo,* facing a thousand threats, is plausible in Munch's series of self-portraits as it is also in the series of Rembrandt, Van Gogh, and Cezanne. There is the increasing personal statement, even a confessional coming-across, as the painter grows older. He has less and less to hide. These paintings have remarkably evocative titles: *Outward Bound; The Alchemist* (with a frieze of wine bottles) ; *Night Wanderer; Cod Lunch; Between the Clock and the Bed; By the Window Pane* (16).

The growing forlornness of modern man is *presented* in Munch's self-portraits, increasing from decade to decade and becoming more alarming. Nevertheless, they do not appear hopeless, morbid or nihilistic, since his "starting with a clean slate" is decisive for the courage to meet oneself, and assert oneself on the narrowest ground. Here is a way of projecting one's health, as Munch proved while transforming the mundane subject of his aging body and its look into an obligatory iconography of his presence-to-a-world (7).

The relation of Edvard Munch's psychotic personality to his continuous, high level, creative accomplishments, raises a host of difficult questions. Do the paintings contain the psychosis, in a kind of holding action? Does the artist create for himself a veritable universe of transitional objects, his paintings, which shield him from devastation and decompensation? Does his genius, or his towering work-identity keep his artistic form from psychotic derailment. Probably with Cezanne in mind, Merleau-Ponty wrote about the order of events (which can include psychosis) and the order of expression (painting) :

When one goes from the order of events to the order of expression, one does not change the world; the same circumstances which were previously submitted to now become a signifying system. Hollowed out, worked from within, and finally freed from that weight upon us which makes them painful and wounding, they become transparent or even luminous, and capable of clarifying not only the aspects of the world which resembles them, but the others too ; yet transformed as

Edvard Munch: *Night Wanderer,* Self-portrait (1939). Collection Munch
Museum, Oslo.

they may be, they still do not cease to exist. The knowledge of
them we may gain will never replace our experience of the
work itself. But it helps measure the creation and it teaches us
about that immediate surpassing of one's situation which is
the only irrevocable surpassing. If we take a painter's point of

view in order to be present at that decisive moment when what has been given to him as corporeal destiny, personal adventures, or historical events crystallizes into "the motive," we will recognize that his work, which is *never an effect* is always a *response* to these data, and that the body, the life, the landscapes, the schools, the mistresses, the creditors, the police, and the revolutions which might suffocate painting are also the bread his work consecrates. To live in painting is still to breathe the air of this world—above all for the man who sees something in the world to paint (18, p. 64, italics added).

The problem is how to contain a certain madness, while at the same time creatively working and inventing at a high level of efficiency. There would seem to be a set of conditions in the lives of some mad painters which result in the phasing together of integrative processes and creative processes. Madness becomes degenerative in ego and art. However, Munch is a disquieting example of another kind of mad genius and visionary, not unlike the poet, William Blake. Undoubtedly their extreme devotion to creative work, identity as artists, prolific production, and attitudes toward the objects of that production demonstrate ego strength, narrow as that strength may appear to the outsider. In Munch's case painting itself is not motivated by his madness. The lasting, even debilitating, paranoid distortion of his personality enables the artist to move closer into the realm of his own creations. One feels that if madness had truly motivated Munch's work, the results would have been disturbing: horror pictures, an empty canvas, suicide. His painting remained a response to his madness and his performance and presentation consistently surpassed his own madness. Living his madness was an accommodation he made after the act of painting, and this adaptation made it possible for the artist to construct a world of paintings possessed, an awesome world of creator and the created.

Summary

The paper is divided into five parts and with each section there were color slides illustrating the problems of description

and analysis undertaken in the text. The first part of the paper
is a brief survey and historical-structural analysis of madness
portrayed by painters. A comparative viewing of three works is
presented, each work from a different epoch of Western art.
The paintings are: *Dulle Griet* by Bruegel (16th Cent.) ; *Mad-
woman* by Gericault (early 19th Cent.) ; and *Marilyn Monroe*
by Willem de Kooning (contemporary). This procedure enables
the viewer to confront the intrasubjective content of a painting
in our own time, whether it is executed by artists or patients. It
also provides a radical perspective upon the changing structure
of madness and its changing meaning in society.

The second part of the paper deals with the aesthetic problem
of painting as perceived object. An existential-phenomenological
description of the painting as object is put forward and following Merleau-Ponty a distinction is elaborated between the painting as presentation and the painting as representation. This
difference is illustrated by two quite different viewings of Van
Gogh's *Shoes*, first in primary, synthetic perception, and second
in derivative, analytic perception. The third part of the paper
offers a critique of attempts to define the formal characteristics
of schizophrenic art, the spontaneous paintings and other
graphic productions of untutored psychotic persons. The question of normative standards is cast in terms of presentation and
representation in these works. An argument is made emphasiz-
ing the limits and even poverty of presentation in schizophrenic
painting. The artistically talented psychotic painter is discussed.
The privileges of representation in schizophrenic painting are
upheld.

The fourth part of the paper continues with a discussion of
painters of extraordinary talent and creative capacity who become psychotic. An earlier paper of Ernst Kris on this subject is
reviewed. The configurations of creativity and psychosis are
described with examples from the work of Wain, Van Gogh and
Ensor. The final part of the paper takes up the phenomenon of
the painter in whom profound and lasting psychotic disorder
does not impair outstanding artistic performance over a lifetime.
In regard to this condition, the biography and pathography of

the Norwegian master, Edvard Munch, are examined in some detail and selected paintings from all periods of his career are viewed.

References

1. Carstairs, G. M. Art and Psychotic Illness, Abbottempo 3:15-21, 1963.
2. Crockett, C. Psychoanalysis in Art Criticism, Journal of Aesthetics and Art Criticism 17:34-44, Spring 1958.
3. Deknatel, F. B. *Edvard Munch:* Chanticleer Press, New York, 1950.
4. Digby, G. W. *Meaning and Symbol:* Faber & Faber, London, 1955.
5. Fallico, A. B. *Art and Existentialism:* Prentice-Hall, Englewood Cliffs, 1962.
6. Foucault, M. *Madness and Civilization,* trans. by R. Howard: Pantheon Books, New York, 1965.
7. Goepel, E. *Edvard Munch,* Selbstbildnisse und Dokumente: Albert Langen & Georg Mueller, Muenchen, 1955.
8. Gombrich, E. H. *Meditations on a Hobby Horse:* Phaidon Press, London, 1963.
9. Graetz, H. R. *The Symbolic Language of Vincent Van Gogh:* McGraw-Hill, New York, 1963.
10. Haftmann, W. *Painting in the Twentieth Century,* Vol. I: Praeger, New York, 1960.
11. *Insania Pingens:* Ciba, Basel, 1961.
12. Jaeger, H. Heidegger and the Work of Art in *Aesthetics Today,* ed. by M. Philipson: Meridian Books, Cleveland, 1961.
13. Kaelin, E. F. *An Existentialist Aesthetic:* University of Wisconsin, Madison, 1962.
14. Kaufmann, F. Art and Phenomenology in *Essays in Phenomenology,* ed. by M. Natanson: Nijhoff, The Hague, 1966.
15. Kris, E. *Psychoanalytic Explorations in Art:* International Universities, New York, 1952.
16. Langaard, J. H. *Edvard Munchs Selvportretter:* Gyldendal Norsk, Oslo, 1947.
17. Langer, S. K. *Problems of Art:* Scribners, New York, 1957.
18. Merleau-Ponty, M. *Signs,* trans. by R. C. McCleary: Northwestern University, 1964.
19. Ortega, J. *The Dehumanization of Art:* Anchor-Doubleday, New York, 1956.

20. Plokker, J. H. *Art from the Mentally Disturbed:* Little, Brown, Boston, 1965.
21. Righter, W. *The Rhetorical Hero:* Routledge & Kegan Paul, London, 1964.
22. Sartre, J. P. *The Age of Reason:* Bantam Books, New York, 1959.
23. Schapiro, M. *Vincent Van Gogh:* Abrams, New York, 1950.
24. Steinberg, S. and Weiss, J. The Art of Edvard Munch and Its Function in His Mental Life, Psychoanalytic Quarterly 23:409-423, 1954.
25. Stenersen, R. Edvard Munch, The Norseman 1:416-428, 1943.

COMMENTS ON PSYCHOTIC PAINTING
AND PSYCHOTIC PAINTERS

Donald F. Tweedie, Jr.

THE discussant of a paper at a phenomenology conference has a peculiar and ironic mission. He is called upon to perform what is at best a task of impure phenomenology; to represent, to reinforce, to revise, or to repudiate the verbal art form of the previous speaker. This irony is compounded in the present instance inasmuch as the primary theoretical point of Dr. Foy's paper was to discriminate representation and presentation of art objects. He mentions that these two modes, in which the reality inherent in a procreative performance appears to the spectator of visual art, determine whether the artistic image will be revealed per se in perception, phenomenologically; or merely as a symbol suggesting something behind and beyond itself. In discussing his paper, of necessity representationally, I am acting out a violation of his first principle.

Opting for emphasis upon the presentational relationship of spectator and art object, Dr. Foy then presents and discusses a series of paintings, via projected slides, created by psychotic painters. There is a possible logical quibble at the outset inasmuch as none of the works of art in question were actually at the conference; merely 'representations' of them. However, I did find myself existentially engaged with the presentation in a way not possible with other conference papers *about* music and visual art. Thus, whether or not his point was well taken, at least it was well communicated.

Before I make a few brief comments, a caveat seems in order. While I feel comfortable under the ambiguous caption of existentialism, phenomenology gives me no such security. If Husserl could terminate his fruitful life as a phenomenological beginner who could not himself set foot on the 'promised land'; I am at best a pre-beginner. The possibility of my misunderstanding Dr. Foy's phenomenological considerations is significant. In antici-

patory anxiety of missing the point, prior to receipt of the
paper, my fantasies were occupied with phenomenological de-
light, the pure possibility of discussing an unwritten paper! But
such is not the lot of a conference discussant.

My reaction to the paper will be devoted to two headings:
Presentation vs. Representation; and Psychosis and Art. First,
however, a mild protest to the implications of absolute, or
objective, criteria of art assumed in the paper. There is a denial
of artistic ability to certain patients even though they felt creative and valued their work highly. I have a felt competence
neither as an art critic nor performer, but have a strong conviction that the appreciation of art is *really* relative and that
imputation of an object as an art object is basically an ego
function.

I. Presentation vs. Representation

Presentation of an art object is a primary, synthetic perception; while representation is derivative and analytic. Presentation is an immediacy as opposed to representational mediacy.
Dr. Foy encourages the acceptance of the art object as *itself*
rather than to defer to Jungian and/or Freudian symbols to
explain the significance of the artistic production. Presentation
is the direct presence of the art object; representation is an
indirect perceiving and pursuing of an image by the viewer in
the light of his private and, perhaps, specialized knowledge.

This distinction is set in a clear context by Fallico. "The
peculiar composure and independence of the art-object come
into clearer view when we see that it is in the order of a
presentation, rather than a *re*-presentation. A representation, as
the very word seems to say, presupposes another thing, somehow made to reappear under the guise of the art-object. A
representation is unoriginal by definition. The essential characteristic of the art-object is precisely that it is an original—a *first*
presentation of a possibility truly felt and imagined. It can
remind us, really, only of itself, even if, in the process, we may

remind ourselves of non-aesthetic things and events extraneous to it."[1]

Dr. Foy indicates in another paper that his theme is reflected in the contemporary world of art and aesthetics. "Whereas the aesthetics of the recent past showed an excessive interest in the motivational origins of a particular creative thrust or creative accomplishment, the major concern of the aesthetician today is with the action of creation and the unique product of that action. Where once there was concentration on the inspirational roots in the artist's personal unconscious, the pendulum has swung to the elaborated structure of the art object and the meaning this configuration gives an immediate experience."[2]

I am not able to evaluate the accuracy of the above statement, though it seems rightly to depict the direction, at least, of art criticism and artistic performance. However, the dichotomy seems too simplistic to account for the complexity and variability of the aesthetic vision.

An important mode of the object-viewer dialectic is neither immediate nor mediate, but rather inter-mediate. The existential aesthetic ecstasy of an intermediate experience of the art form is for many the most significant artistic vision. This is a mode of co-presentation, with the artist, of the art object. One perceives neither simply 'on the surface,' nor through the tangled thicket of psychic symbology, but in a mode of *Mit-sein, Gemein-schafts-gefühl* with the artist, aesthetic *koinonia*. In my judgment this identification with the artist in the presentation is the most fruitful direction for the art therapy of 'madness.' When the therapist is in a co-presentational aesthetic mode, in communion and communication with the artist; then artistic expression may become a therapeutic medium rather than an artifact in the schedule or a bored patient, or a retreat to a safer world.

At least two other modes of artistic revelation have contem-

---

[1] Fallico, Arturo B. *Art and Existentialism,* Prentice-Hall, Englewood Cliffs, N.J., 1962, pp. 20-21.

[2] Foy, James L. "The World of Vincent Van Gogh: Representation and Presentation," unpublished paper.

poraneity and, perhaps, ought to be mentioned. I present them with tongue in cheek although they are significant aesthetic modes in our present culture. They are relatively low on my axiological-aesthetical hierarchy and, hopefully, will go the way of all fads.

The first is the aesthetic mode of *sentation.* This is an artistic 'happening,' an emphasis upon the action of artistic performance and a radical de-emphasis of the art object. This is the carrying out to the extreme the contemporary aesthetic concern "with the action of creation" mentioned by Dr. Foy. So little is the art object regarded that it is sometimes destroyed as the conclusion of the artistic performance! Perhaps this is the only means of separating aisthesis from its dialectical union with aesthetics.

The second is the aesthetic mode of *-ation,* in which neither the action of the artist, nor his unique creation are regarded in themselves. In this mode of relationship the aesthetic spectator may not even perceive the art object per se, but rather relates to it as a tax shelter, an important economic investment! This seems to be an increasingly significant factor in the world of art.

In sum, the dichotomy which Dr. Foy details as the theoretic structure of his presentation, seems to me to be rather more truncating than helpfully bifurcating the modes of aesthetic relationship with reference to the spectator and his perception of the art object. Most importantly I think that this dualism obviates a significant *tertium quid,* co-presentation, that is the prime resource of any hopeful art therapy.

II. Psychosis and Art

I am not sure about the continuity between Dr. Foy's presentation of presentation as the adequate phenomenological aesthetic consideration and the slides that were projected. They depicted the art objects created by various persons, from relatively unknown neuropsychiatric patients to such famous artists as Van Gogh and Munch, all who suffered from some severe psychopathological personality disorder.

The ready inference, and the apparent implication, of the

presentation was that art objects that are created by such persons have characteristics that are correlated with their psychic states. The *explanation* of the art objects significantly involved the emotional disorder of the artists and were presented as discriminating one mode of personality maladaptation from another, i.e., manic depressive psychosis, schizophrenia, paranoid process, etc. Though it was subsequently stated that there is no specific formal characteristic in psychotic painting, and that creativity in psychosis has many possible configurations, the impression was made upon me of the use of the slides as novel 'Rorschach Plates,' useful in the psychodiagnosis of their authors. 'Psychotic' art is not presented as presentation but as TAT pictures projecting the personality of the artists.

In any case, the 'meanings' of the art objects were somehow mediated by the 'underlying' psychotic state of the artists. This seems to be in direct discontinuity of the theoretical presentation of presentation over representation, an application of the representational mode which was earlier discounted, if not repudiated.

There is lurking here, if I am not mistaken (a not unlikely event), at best an attempt to fudge on phenomenologically adequate presentation as an aesthetic mode and to bring something significating and significant from the psyche of the artist. This is, no doubt, important for psychodiagnosis and psychotherapy, but not necessarily for aesthetics. Such an approach would begin to formulate a dangerous hermeneutical principle that might drift toward the kind of psychologizing that I disparage in literary art forms of such men of personal problems as Kierkegaard and Nietzsche.

The presentation of *psychotic* painting as *presentation* of art objects seems to belie the very valuable phenomenological distinctions that Dr. Foy made in his paper. *Psychotic* painting has categorical significance, however, only as *representational* perception of art images in psychodiagnosis of as *co-presentational* in psychotherapy. Presentation as a mode of aesthetic presence of an art object to the viewer is orthogonal to psychotic painting. Presentational revelation of art objects attains synthetic purity only to the degree that the artist is anonymous; psychotic art is to the point insofar as the artist has a name and is in the process of discovering who he is. Otherwise, that an artist is mad is as accidental and artifactual as is the information that he also has a secondary occupation, e.g., is a hatter.

ART THERAPY: PSYCHO-BIOLOGICAL BASES

Tarmo Pasto

THE human being lives in a vertical-horizontal space-frame, his own creation, in which his actions are defined, limited and extended by his perceptual (motor) relationship to the object world of reality. This reality, in some form or another, is always a part of his psychic life. Inert physical objects are first reacted to in terms of felt but un-defined physiognomic perceptual qualities, where perception functions on two levels: 1) as an extension of chemo-neural activity that leads to space orientation, a form of body-image extension, 2) as an affective motor-configuration that accommodates the primitive need for identification in terms of the mythical meaning of the self in intimate contact with objective reality, the better to function in an environment. There are thus two major fields of artistic expression that need exploring: the symbolic and the sensori-motor.

That much, if not most of this activity is below the threshold of consciousness, goes without saying. In order to conserve the energy necessary to survive countless encounters with perceptual affect-arousing figures the individual has to resort to symbol formation. These may be preserved by means of primitive motor gestalts, man's native organizing tendency.

Countless past racial experiences of the same order (Jung) are re-inforced by individual experiences which activate the archetype, previously formed and preserved in some chemo-neural-electrical field as a predisposition to forming, to clarifying, to identifying.

An inefficient organism cannot survive the demands of reality adjustment and control, preparation for which self-organization and self-confrontation are essential. It is wasteful of psychic energy when it is necessary to direct the total motor organism by conscious rational effort at anticipation, prediction and evaluation of movement. This is a form of one-way communication with an environment. The efficient organism turns over much of this vast effort to sub-liminal, automatic but total, biologically primitive functioning, the better to permit concentration on rational every-day reality contacts. "It is only when we have begun to orient ourselves somatically to the object that the object is explicitly perceived."[1]

That this type of perception is not limited to the child is convincingly demonstrated repeatedly on the professional basketball courts. The player who dribbles down the court dodging opposition and shoots for the basket has made such a somatic adjustment by being totally involved in motion toward a goal that his chances of making a basket are better than if he shot for the basket from a standing position where he receives the ball from another player. Spatial orientation is more fluid and more efficient where the total body is involved in movement. This body activity must, therefore, reach some deeper source of organization, perhaps the "primitive gestalt" dealt with by Ehrenzweig.[2]

In cases of emotional stress, the primitive archetype is also aroused and affective energy organized to make meaningful this confrontation. Thus it is that man utilizes his object world primarily to organize and mold his psychic inner world into meaningful symbolic constructs by means of chemo-neural changes, precipitations and fixations.

Since this important psychic activity is so largely conditioned and carried on by total bodily processes the deduction necessarily follows that body activity must be induced in order to produce some communication in symbolic form, both inter as well as intra psychic. It therefore follows that art activity is the best medium for the production of such meaningful communication. The fact that such expression requires understanding and translation should not prohibit its use.

Art instruction or therapy which ignores these deeper meanings may be harmful when the teacher or therapist attempts to make sure that unknown emotional meanings do not interfere with the imitative following of instructions for the formation of a purely visual pre-determined construct or concept. When the student has difficulty in approximating the model he is merely urged to greater efforts at "correcting" his eye-hand co-ordination. This forced falsification of "personal reality" can be emotionally harmful in that psychic energies are dammed up, prevented an expression which is seeking clarification and confrontation. This adds enormous difficulties to fluid, effective, and pleasant learning.

Rational man feels he must ignore his long phylogenetic past, deny that he has a vast neuro-muscular organization which is seemingly in violent opposition to the "will" or the "mind." Yet it is only in those rare instances when the phylogenetic past combines with individual chemo-neural activities aroused by resistance and affect that man has made his most original and creative contributions for the benefit of society. Einstein, Poincare and Newton, were, as are most creative mathematicians, on intimate terms with their total body tendencies to organization and could respond effectively to those feelings in terms of mathematical formulae. Painters and sculptors often state that they feel body "tensions" which can best be reduced by production of an art object previously "formed" in the psyche. This inner form is vague but intense in affect. But mere discharge of tension is not enough.

These inner sensations, to become affectively meaningful, require archetypal imagery as a final and closing form for proper expression. Jung and Pauli, speaking of Kepler, stated, ". . . the symbolic picture precedes the conscious formulation of a natural law. The symbolic images and archetypal conceptions are what cause him to seek natural laws."[3] The problem is in translation.

Mental illness is spoken of as being "irrational," yet a schizophrenic follows a well defined pattern of behavior according to "natural" laws. He cannot partake of "rational" communication, for he is responding to inner chemo-neural activity and symbolic gestalt forming of a complex sensory nature. Proof that some of these chemo-neural combinations once established are quite stable and resist destruction is furnished by the experiments of James McConnell.[4] Planaria learn by cannibalism. If this is true cannot learning and transmission also take place at the time of zygote? It is a constant source of amazement that these inherited gestalts can be so complex that a Robin will automatically build a Robin's nest rather than a Sparrow's!

My colleague, Dr. Donald Uhlin, in his investigations of the neurologically handicapped has noted startling distortions of the body-image as expressed in their view of reality. "Dramatic evidence of this postural appreciation is experienced when an individual is forced into a new physical orientation after being in a fixed postural status for an extended time. A patient, for example, who is forced to lay on his back in bed for several months will, upon first sitting again, experience consciously a 'new' reality . . . This dramatic conscious awareness of postural status is seldom, if ever, experienced by most people short of falling down a flight of stairs. As a result of this lack of conscious appreciation of physiological functioning we fail to recognize the deeper basis of our meaningful experience. Creative individuals may often be viewed as people whose dramatic physical experiencing has led their psychical forces to evoke greater meaning in their reality. Once they have tasted life, like Melville or Crane, they cannot rest."

"While psychical forces do act as a fulcrum or center for accepted reality the structuring of that reality must be seen as an inter-relationship of the physical and psychical counterparts."[5]

Psychoanalysis has postulated but seems to have difficulty in stating clearly the nature of these gestalt formations in depth. This problem is insightfully and creatively investigated by Anton Ehrenzweig.[2] He speaks of the unconscious "depth" gestalt as being largely overlooked by the psychologists in favor of the more readily recognizable "surface" gestalt. It is not yet clear whether the one does not in fact support the other and whether the "surface" gestalt is really only a rational mechanical balancing of visual shapes. He has, however, convincingly demonstrated that unconscious forces in perception play a great part in emotional expression. Depth psychology here leads to appreciation of "inarticulate symbolic forms."[2] (p. 5) He paraphrases Freud, observing that "inarticulate form experiences are the

messengers from the unconscious mind and that our unwilling-
ness to give them due attention may be connected to our general
reluctance ('resistence') to acknowledge the role which the unconscious appreciation of physiological functioning we fail to
conscious mind plays in our mental life."² (p. 4) "Hence we
shall describe it as the artist's primary task to disintegrate the
articulate and rational surface perception and to call up secondary processes in the public which will restore the articulate
structure and rational content of surface perception."² (p. 14)

Henri Bergson speaks of perceptions, inner personal memories and motor habits as being intimately related. Perceptions
from the material world are "clear, distinct, juxtaposed or
juxtaposable" and "tend to group themselves into objects to
which memories adhere." These memories are detached from
the depth of the personality and "drawn to the surface by the
perceptions which resemble them." He speaks of feeling the stir
of tendencies and motor-habits, a crowd of virtual actions," more
or less firmly bound to these perceptions and actions."⁶ (p. 11)

A famous neuro-surgeon, Sir. Henry Head, postulated a body
"schema," later elaborated by Paul Schilder, which acts to make
all sorts of bodily adjustments on an unconscious level and
which is affected by the sensory cortex, or changes or injuries to
it. "But in addition to its function as an organ of local attention,
the 'sensory' cortex registers and retains the physiological dispo-
sitions produced by past events. These profoundly modify all
subsequent actions. They may be manifest in the form assumed
by sensations or images, but most often, as in the case of spacial
impressions, remain outside of consciousness."⁷ (p. 434)

One of the foremost pioneering art therapists in America,
Margaret Haumburg, has produced an insightful body of writing in support of the dynamic nature of art. She emphasizes that
art is a form of symbolic speech which is a direct expression of
the psyche. The value of art as therapy is in the free expression
of these inner images and in recognizing their emotional meanings. "When a forbidden impulse has found such form outside
the patient's psyche, he gains a detachment from his conflict
which often enables him to examine his problems with growing

objectivity. Thus a patient is gradually assisted to recognize that his artistic productions can be treated as a mirror in which he can begin to find his own motives revealed."[8] (p. 3)

That mental activity can take place best in a continuum requiring total action in which one state prepares for the next was noted by Bergson. "There is a succession of states, each of which announces that which follows and contains that which precedes it. They can, properly speaking, only be said to form multiple states when I have already passed them and turn back to observe their track. Whilst I was experiencing them they were so solidly organized, so profoundly organized with a common life, that I could not have said where any of them begins or ends, but all extend into each other."[6] (p. 11)

"Take the simplest sensation, suppose it constant, absorb in it the entire personality: the consciousness which will accompany this sensation cannot remain identical with itself for two consecutive moments, because the second moment always contains, over and above the first, the memory that the first has bequeathed to it. A consciousness which could experience two identical moments would be a consciousness without memory. It would die and be born again continually."[6] (p. 12)

The philosopher Bergson receives support for his observations from the neuro-surgeon, Head.

"Memory and intention are developed out of that march or sequence of momentary happenings would have no continuity; a series of perishing 'nows' would be useless, even at the lowest level of neural activity. Finally, the power of spacial projection enables us to endow external objects in the world around with these qualitative attributes which are developed out of selective responses to physical stimulation."[7] (p. 495)

"Mind and body habitually respond together to external or internal events. The aim of the evolutionary development of the central nervous system is to integrate its diverse and contradictory reactions, so as to produce a coherent result, adapted to the welfare of the organism as a whole."[7] (p. 496)

One is led to wonder if the educators and psychologists responsible for primers and the robot "programming" of "logi-

cal" and "rational" approaches to learning have given this problem much thought. Are they not dealing with "perishable nows"
which require constant "drill" for fixing in "rational" memory?

All the above observations imply that some physio-neural
organization or substance, rather than an abstract "mind," filled
with concepts derived but removed from percepts, is the medium
most involved in human activities in the field of expression,
learning, and self-evaluation. It is to this that we should apply
ourselves.

It is necessary also to postulate that the archetype represents
the collective experience and as such has common recognizable
conscious attributes. But the individual variations introduced by
means of distortions, emphases or context relate specifically to
the personal unconscious, those strictly private lacerations un-
dergone, and what attempts have been made to control and
alleviate the distress from such a confrontation.

That visual perception involves more than merely "seeing
rationally and objectively with the eyes" is readily demonstrated
by figure 1. We "see" a flat, black-on-white, linear design which
can be designated as a picture of chicken wire or a honeycomb.
We leap to a conclusion on the briefest of visual inspection that
what is presented is a "representation" of a describable object.
By "classifying" it we try to disentangle ourselves from it as if
to shake off a motor involvement.

But if we fix it visually for some few seconds this uninvolved
monotonous flat design "becomes" animated. Some of the penta-
gon-shaped areas become lighter than the original surface,
others become darker. These configurations or "gestalts" are
highly unstable, one following another with uncontrollable succession. Yet each succeeding gestalt seems to arise out of the
previous one as perhaps a series of mutations. These gestalts are
not "perishing nows" but variations of a life-preserving function of perceptually structuring our environment. This is beyond
our rational control, as if body demands for spatial adjustment
and object orientation are over-riding all other mental activities.

Nor can this activity be written off as due to eye fatigue or to
positive and negative after-images. There is too much selection

fig. 1

going on for the patterns are always complete compositionally and are somehow mysteriously related to our body and its vertical-horizontal field of "created" or realized space. Another startling and largely unexplainable characteristic of these gestalts is that they are three-dimensional motor excursions into sensory space. Some of the light-dark areas are felt to be located in space in front of the plane supporting the design, others are behind it, penetrating its surface. Were the design purely visual, a result of a retinal image, the gestalt would be flat. That it is not flat may be a response to our need to live in three-dimensional sensory space, that our body and its electrical-neural field is three-dimensional, or that the electrical field of space is the vital stream of consciousness of which our body is the locus or gravitational center. Perhaps we can even postulate that nothing is flat!

Figure 2 illustrates a very faulty attempt to paint one of these chicken wire gestalts. Now the instability noted in figure 1 erupts into seeming violence as the body struggles to free itself from the mechanical restraint to freedom in gestalt formation. In color the result is still more violent. Attempts to create a "meaningful" space frame related to a real object world are defeated repeatedly.

Further proof we do not need to demonstrate that our body is strongly involved, and perhaps even directing, our perceptions.

It also becomes axiomatic that Rembrandt and Van Gogh created spatial paintings which fit hand and glove with our own space-frame gestalts, our native tendency to spatial orientation.

This contrast between sensory space and conceptual space was investigated by Erwin Straus.[9] He postulated that man's walking is actually a series of arrested forward fallings, where sensory awareness of space becomes important, and vastly different from the conceptual space of geometry.

It becomes intriguing to speculate, as was done in my book, *The Space-Frame Experience in Art*,[10] that only those artists who are capable of activating a controlled sensory three-dimensionally experienced "re-presentations" of known objects. When a native tendency to forming three-dimensional gestalts, a bio-

fig. 2

logical space-frame, meets hand in glove with a created work of art that is an outgrowth and an accommodation of our gestalt forming tendency, then a work of art is being experienced. This can be on a flat canvas, or in any three-dimensional media.

This does not mean that any three-dimensional art work, i.e., sculpture, architecture, is good—for it, too, can violate or accommodate our native tendency to gestalt forming in sensory space. Art instruction and art therapy which ignore this vital aspect are very apt to be shallow and to deal mainly with conceptual knowledge long removed from dynamic percepts.

The curious thing about most art, and particularly the art of neurotics and psychotics, is that it is devoid of these dynamics of sensory space. Such art appears meaningful only as dream images whose derivations are lost to physiologic memory. It is in search of this lost meaning that "abstract expressionism" was born. But since most of such "art" was visually conceived and executed, no amount of flailing of the "body-brush" could awaken the deeper gestalts. The new visual object was the paint itself or the pattern in which it was cast. Occasionally some felt movement would occur but it was in the main unrecognized and unexploited as the language of expression. Artists soon tired of it and returned to the "pop" object with a vengeance, still seeking what made Rembrandt and Cezanne so meaningful, but remained satisfied with making literary "statements" about the unfortunate nature of our culture. This was done by de-basing the "made" object by enshrining it in an "art" gallery.

A meaningful scientific attempt to investigate body participation in perception (Werner and Wapner) led to the postulation of the sensori-tonic field theory in perception. This theory is supported by experiments where electrical stimulation of the subject alters his perceptual orientation to an illuminated vertical rod. They conclude that, "For perception of the objects in the outside world, as well as the perception of one's own body, we hold the view that the reciprocal relationship between organism and environment must be taken into account."[11] (p. 9)

Since speech, even the every day variety, is a form of allegory, substituting cerebral rational equivalents for affective bio-

logical gestalts, it follows that the normal as well as the Schizophrenic lives in a world of symbolic meaning. These meanings
can never be entirely cut off.

Jung speaks of a mental patient looking at the sun through a
hollow tube of paper and later reading about the same experience in an ancient Egyptian manuscript. Figure 3, is a colored
drawing by an 8 year old boy. This shows a tube swinging from
the sun as if in illustration of the Egyptian manuscript. The
child was the recipient of unconscious hatreds of the masculine
on the part of the mother whose alcoholic husband had run
away. The child was facing foster home placement. The other
symbols, as well as the colors, expressed in the same picture
portray his masculine dilemma. Is this not an expression of an
archetype?

Other symbols now accepted as part of emotional projective
expressions are the sun, the moon, the tree, the house, the
crucifix, etc. In other words today's society is as primitive in
many ways as were its predecessors. Our disguises only are
more effective, as they need be in the face of ever more "scientific" inquiry.

It becomes self-evident that art therapy can be the most direct
and the most meaningful approach to the mental patient and the
normal. Art provides a pre-historic, pre-verbal, pre-conceptual
approach. Thorough knowledge of psycho-biological symbolism
while very helpful, is not an absolute necessity. The patient
generally has an intuitive feeling as to the meaning of his art
productions. He needs merely a supporting hand and an opportunity to associate freely to his own productions. He needs help
in formulating an understanding of the dynamics behind his
productions, the why and how of their appearance. This, any
trained therapist should be able to provide.

Hence art reaches at once the dynamic roots of all behavior.

No civilization, however primitive, has been without its art.
That it has fallen into such disrepute and has been neglected for
so long, is perhaps merely a reflection on modern man's resistance to the unconscious. This very denial has led to a damming
up of emotion as a vital social source for good.

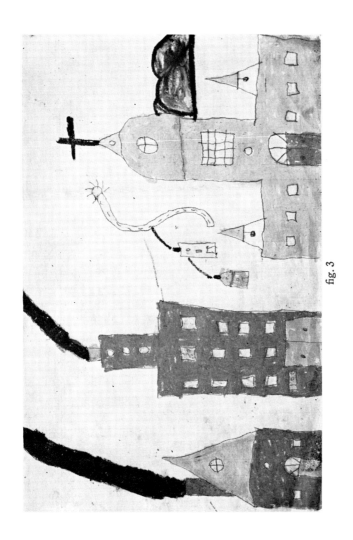

fig. 3

It is now time to face a new renaissance in emotional well-being through universal free expressions and inter-personal communications.

So now, in summary, we can postulate that man is a dynamic central force whose strength comes not from the intellect or the rational but from a chemo-electro-neural source. Man is a constellation of events acting through perceptual-motor processes in which his perceptions of the outer world are heavily colored by inner demands for meaningful organization. Perception functions to assist the organism to adjust to gravity and gravitational objects in terms of inner satisfactions.

He can be likened to an oversized atom, with central nucleus and sub-satellite systems.

The brain has developed as a sorting and storing mechanism, so that so-called rational scientific anger can push his habitat even further into his rational control. But in doing so, he has lost his place in the biological scheme of things and must be eradicated. He, like the saber-toothed tiger, has already set in motion the means to effect just that. He has become too cerebral, and the terrible mother, represented by the undifferentiated unconscious, is about to call back its own.

This return to mother earth through atomic destruction is rapidly being provided for by "programming" man's perceptual-motor input from a selected body of inert things which are overtly concrete and objective, thus destroying the central dynamic force that has activated man since time began. Or, as Jung would put it, our "abnormal learning capacity" is replacing our faith in the sureness and infallibility of instinctive behavior.

So the "aesthetic" world is basically very biological, not "spiritual," with that term's implication that basic man is somehow "uplifted" to "pure" realms of non-existence.

References

1. Joseph Church. *Language and the Discovery of Reality* (New York: Random House, 1961)
2. Anton Ehrenzweig. *The Psycho-analysis of Artistic Vision and Hearing.* (New York: The Julian Press, Inc., 1953)

3. C. G. Jung and W. Pauli. *The Interpretation of Nature and the Psyche*. (London: Routledge and Kegan Paul, 1955)
4. James McConnell. "Memory Transfer Through Cannibalism in Planariums." *Journal of Neuropsychiatry*, Vol. 3, Supplement No. 1, August, 1962.
5. Donald Uhlin. "Body-Image Projection in Drawing," *Ars Gratia Hominis*, Vol. 1, No. 3, Dec. 1963.
6. Henri Bergson. *An Introduction to Metaphysics*. (New York: G. P. Putnam's Sons, 1912)
7. Sir Henry Head. *Aphasia and Kindred Disorders of Speech*. (Cambridge: University Press, MCMXXVI)
8. Margaret Naumburg, *Dynamically Oriented Art Therapy*. (New York: Grune and Stratton, 1966)
9. Erwin Straus. "The Upright Posture." *The Psychiatric Quarterly*, XXVI (1952), 529-561.
10. Tarmo Pasto. *The Space-Frame Experience in Art*. (New York: A. S. Barnes and Co., 1965)
11. Heinz Werner and Seymour Wapner. *The Body Percept*, (New York: Random House, 1965)

Additional References dealing with the problem of meaningful form organization in the arts:

1907. Adolph Hildebrand. *The Problem of Form in Painting and Sculpture*. (New York: G. E. Steinchert and Co., 1907, Trans. 1945)
1924. Roger Fry. *Vision and Design*. (New York: Peter Smith, 1924)
1934. John Dewey. *Art as Experience*. (New York: Minton Balch and Company, 1934)
1937. Albert C. Barnes. *The Art in Painting*. (New York: Harcourt, Brace and Company, 3rd Ed., 1937)
1938. Robin G. Collingwood. *The Principles of Art*. (London: Oxford University Press, 1938)
1948. Bernard Berenson. *Aesthetics and History in the Visual Arts*. (New York: Pantheon, 1948)
1953. Susanne Langer. *Feeling and Form*. (New York, Scribner, 1953)
1955. Floyd H. Allport. *Theories of Perception and the Concept of Structure*. (New York: John Wiley and Sons, Inc. 1955)
1965. Tarmo Pasto. *The Space-Frame Experience in Art*. (New York: A. S. Barnes and Co. 1965)

ART AND LIFE IN ART THERAPY

Michael Wyschogrod

ART THERAPY exists. In many psychiatric hospitals work in painting or sculpture is an integral part of the treatment procedure, quite apart from whatever function these activities may have in a purely diagnostic context. The question I wish to pose is this: why is there no science therapy? Why are there no laboratories in psychiatric hospitals in which patients spend an hour or two daily attempting to measure the speed of light or the relationship between the volume and pressure of gasses or the laws that govern the inclined plane? Why is there no therapy connected with the history of ideas or the methodology of the social sciences, the problems connected with the theology of the synoptic gospels or the influence of Hegel on Marx? Art is after all only one of the fruits of the human spirit side by side with science and theology, philosophy and history. Why is creative work in painting and sculpture considered appropriate for the psychiatric patient whereas so far, as best as I can determine, no one has thought it appropriate to encourage the psychiatric patient to contribute to the advancement of science and scholarship as part of his therapy? What is there about art that enables it to be coupled with therapy while the same is not done with science?

The obvious answer is too crude to be true but it must nevertheless be pronounced, if only to clear the air. Science is serious business where you must know what you are doing; otherwise one is a charlatan who is making a fool of himself. Put a novice in an optics laboratory and he will succeed only in damaging the equipment; a psychiatric patient with a microscope will soon discover that not all who have eyes can see. But what harm can there be in putting the same patient before a canvas and supplying him with paint and brush? The worst that can happen is that he will cover the canvas with paint, an activity which might temporarily take his mind off his troubles. At best, he will project on the canvas his anxieties and tensions, slowly to be healed by the vitality of the creative act. In fact, it is sometimes thought, though rarely articulated, that there is an artist hidden in all of us and if only he can be released, a creative and healthy life can hardly be far behind. Art therapy is therefore training for creativity in which the activity is more important than the quality of the product. In the realm of the ethical, Kant had argued that it is intentions and not results that count. In art therapy, we transpose this contention into the realm of the esthetic.

It is clear that such an answer does justice neither to art nor to therapy. Just as it is possible to fail in the laboratory, so one can fail on canvas. To permit the psychiatric patient access to canvas and plaster and keep him from the spectroscope and voltmeter because the latter require knowledge and ability while the former do not, is to preach a philosophy of art that is objectionable on all possible counts. Just as creative work in the sciences is the prerogative of a relatively small elite who are endowed by training and ability for this exacting task, so the artist belongs to that small minority of humans whose gift it is to bring into being the form that is significant, the shape that can be called art. To pretend that a disturbed person who applies paint to canvas for an hour or two a day is creating art is just as illusory as if we pretended that free association were poetry or uninformed pronouncements about the past history. The question that demands an answer is this : why does the quality of the patient's efforts appear of so little significance to so many in the field of art therapy?

There are those for whom art therapy is mainly therapy and only very secondarily art. In the psychiatric context, it is argued, we are interested not in esthetic values but in gaining insight into the dynamics of the patient's psychic life. If we gain such insight and if, furthermore, art helps the patient to come to terms with his aggressions and anxieties, then to raise issues of an esthetic sort is to miss the point quite thoroughly. The reason for the existence of art therapy and the non-existence of science therapy is simply that in art a patient can project his inner conflicts while in science he cannot. The exponent of this point of view might agree fully that genuine artistic activity is the prerogative of the few and is to be judged by standards as rigorous, even if not as easily formulated, as those of science. His contention is that therapeutic art, however, is an activity of a totally different nature, having only the most nominal connection with art in the more usual sense.

It would be markedly pedantic to criticize this point of view simply on the ground that it misused the word "art." This would not be the first instance where a word is attached to another with the new meaning remote from the original. The problem, as I see it, touches on the question of interpretation. The psychologist interprets the patient's painting. He sees human figures that have no faces: the patient has an identity problem. Female figures look masculine: he has sexual problems, and so on. The work that is before us is psychologized. Everything on the canvas is perceived and interpreted from a psychological point of view as if the patient were expounding his psychological problems on the canvas instead of doing a painting. But the fact remains that the work before us is not a recital of psychic suffering but a painting. And while it is true that some paintings, up to a certain extent, lend themselves to psychological interpretation, it is also true that works such as paintings have a life of their own in which the medium and its being dictates the decisions made quite independently of any subjective psychological need. My point then is that however much we try to emphasize the therapy in art therapy and to deemphasize the art, even if the patient is esthetically quite untalented, we cannot completely remove the esthetic element from any activity that deals with lines and shapes, colors and textures. When we overlook this and read the resulting product purely for its psychological cues, we run the serious risk of doing bad psychology because we misjudge esthetic for psychological motivations. And I must repeat that this can happen even when the work is of poor esthetic quality. Wrong esthetic choices are still esthetic choices and not to be reduced to the psychological.

Until now we have been talking about those who think of art therapy first as therapy and very little as art. My impression is that the alternative view is perhaps more popular. The notion that meets us here is that esthetic values in the final analysis are psychological. In its extreme form this view develops into absolute psychologism, with all human activities seen as projections of man's psychic needs, whether it be in art, religion, science or philosophy. The psychological imperialist translates all issues into psychological terms. Euclid's interest in the circle and Aristotle's in the syllogism are understood only when it is determined what meanings these structures had symbolically and unconsciously to their inventors. Freud in his interest in the work of Leonardo displays such a totally psychologically reductive attitude. From this point of view, while all human activity has its roots in the psychic reservoir of energy, this is particularly the case with art. Art is here thought of as a form of daydreaming in which the projective nature of the task permits the repressed to rise to the surface and to communicate meanings otherwise forbidden to waking consciousness. Because this is so, all art is therapy because it permits a discharge of tension not otherwise possible. The expression "art therapy" is therefore a redundancy though perhaps a useful one in the psychiatric context.

The virtue of this view is that it does not sharply split therapeutic art from art in general. The question we must ask is whether it is an adequate interpretation of the phenomenon that is art. This question is particularly cogent for our purposes because this is the interpretation of art that underlies much of art therapy. It was possible for art to enter the ranks of therapeutically effective agents only after psychology had extended its hegemony over art so as to make it a viable tool in the struggle against mental illness. In fact, the psychoanalytic interpretation of art long ante-dates the birth of art therapy. Norman Brown has gone so far as to argue that whatever the value of psychoanalysis may be clinically, its real significance for the twentieth century lies in its hermeneutics of art, giving us a key to the understanding of these works just as the seventeenth

century discovered mathematics to be the key to the understanding of nature. The phenomenological critique of our time has, I
believe, shown that the nature whose key has been found to be
mathematics is an abstracted or theoretical nature determined by
the key used for understanding it. It now remains for us to see
whether there is any corresponding restriction of the phenomenon in the psychologization of art.

"Poetry," writes T. S. Eliot, "is not a turning loose of
emotion, but an escape from emotion; it is not the expression of
personality, but an escape from personality." And this is no less
true of painting or sculpture, music and the dance. All of these
are art forms and art is very different from real life. Once
again, T. S. Eliot:

> It is not in his personal emotions, the emotions provoked by
> particular events in his life, that the poet is in any way re-
> markable or interesting. His particular emotions may be sim-
> ple, or crude, or flat. The emotion in his poetry will be a very
> complex thing, but not with the complexity of the emotions
> of people who have very complex or unusual emotions in life.
> One error, in fact, of eccentricity in poetry is to seek for new
> human emotions to express; and in this search for novelty in
> the wrong place it discovers the perverse. The business of the
> poet is not to find new emotions, but to use the ordinary ones
> and, in working them up into poetry, to express feelings which
> are not in actual emotions at all. And emotions which he has
> never experienced will serve his turn as well as those familiar
> to him.

This is the crux of the error committed by the psychologization
of art. Working in real life with real human emotions, with
people who hate their fathers or who have homosexual inclina-
tions, they assume that in poetry or painting the artist simply
transfers to paper or canvas the very same emotions he is
troubled with in life. Literary and art criticism thus find themselves looking ever more closely into the biography of the artist,
with the work serving as a set of clues by means of which the
dynamics of the creator can be discovered. In the process, the
painting or the poem soon recedes into the background and no

one remembers to ask why the neurosis in question produced a work of art instead of the more usual manifestations familiar to the psychoanalyst from his daily practice. Again and again, as one reads Freud's interpretation of Michelangelo, one is struck by Freud's inability to distinguish the psychological problems of the artist from the process of artistic creation which results in the appearance of a work that has a being of its own phenomenologically quite distinct from even the most interesting neurosis.

My contention then has been that behind art therapy lurks the psychologization of art initiated by Freud and developed by a school of writers who are attuned to the psychological instead of the esthetic. Nevertheless, I do not wish to confuse a theory of art interpretation with a therapeutic tool used for the benefit of the mentally ill, however much kinship the two may have. As a therapeutic tool one difficulty with art, as I have already said, is that however poor the attempted art may be, it always retains some aspect of the esthetic and to that extent the therapist is in danger of reading psychologically what is not psychological. When Freud lit his cigar and remarked to his friends: "Gentlemen, this may be the symbol of a penis but let us remember that it is also a cigar," he adopted a phenomenological attitude prominent for its absence elsewhere in his work. In our context, we must remember that a painting is not only the wish to kill the father but also a painting and that unless this is remembered, the hypothesized meaning will totally eclipse the manifest meaning to the detriment of both. This is so because the psychologist is involved in the interpretation of a painting or a piece of sculpture and therefore he cannot be just psychologist but must also become art critic.

Finally, it seems to me, art therapy is also an aspect of what I recently called "the cult of creativity": "For some, the absence of creativity is not only a symptom of neurosis but the very essence of it. The release of creative forces, conversely, comes close to being identical with mental health. What better evidence could there be that Jane's analysis is succeeding than the fact that she now paints twice a week, sculpts or has joined a creative dance group. . . . Creativity . . . is one of the fruits, perhaps even the most important one, of mental health and therefore let us honor it, in whatever form it appears, be it the Divine Comedy of Dante or Aunt Jane's gardenias she has been culti-vating since she began analysis." I was here expressing my observation that frequently the newly won patient for psychoan-alysis is firmly guided toward one or another of the arts, with the conviction clearly conveyed that the ability to paint or dance is a sign of the newly won freedom previously obscured by the neurosis. The art that is prescribed for the ambulatory neurotic is not thought of technically as art therapy, though it is clearly a version of the same tendency. Since very often the crux of the problem is a certain emptiness in life, a lack of fulfillment in the midst of economic plenty, dabbling in the arts is thought to provide a value which can evoke involvement of individuals for whom the more traditional sources of value are inaccessible.

Some of this thinking is reflected in the more formal art therapy as practiced in the hospital setting. The mentally ill person is thought to lack the ability to involve himself in activi-ties and preoccupations which are truly meaningful and which offer happiness in a more serene key. In art, it is believed, the tensions and turmoils of the mentally ill are thought to be transmuted into the peace and repose of art, conferring on the creator some of the serenity of the work. There is no question whatsoever that true art does transmute into serenity the flux and turmoil of everyday life. The only problem is that most men are not endowed with the ability to create such works. Even for the true artist the serenity of his creation is not necessarily reflected in his life. Nevertheless, contact with the great works of Western civilization is a great source for spiritual renewal without which life would be much more difficult to live. In view of this, is it not time to shift the emphasis in art therapy from creation to appreciation, from demanding of the patient that he create to helping him profit from the accumulated resources of Western art. It would seem to me that this is a more realistic approach to the problem.